Confessions of Zeno

ITALO SVEVO

Confessions of Z*eno*

TRANSLATED FROM THE ITALIAN BY BERYL DE ZOETE

VINTAGE BOOKS
A DIVISION OF RANDOM HOUSE
New York

Preface

I am the doctor who is sometimes spoken of in rather unflattering terms in this novel. Anyone familiar with psychoanalysis will know to what he should attribute my patient's hostility.

About psychoanalysis I shall here say nothing, for there is quite enough about it elsewhere in this book. I must apologize for having persuaded my patient to write his autobiography. Students of psychoanalysis will turn up their noses at such an unorthodox proceeding. But he was old and I hoped that in the effort of recalling his past he would bring it to life again, and that the writing of his autobiography would be a good preparation for the treatment. And I still think my idea was a good one, for it gave me some quite unexpected results, which would have been better still if the patient had not suddenly thrown up his cure just at the most interesting point, thus cheating me of the fruits of my long and patient analysis of these memoirs.

I take my revenge by publishing them, and I hope he will be duly annoyed. I am quite ready, however, to share the financial spoils with him on condition that he resumes his treatment. He seemed to feel intense curiosity about himself. But he little knows what surprises lie in wait for him, if someone were to set about analyzing the mass of truths and falsehoods which he has collected here.

DR. S.

Contents

Confessions of Zeno

Introduction

See my childhood? Now that I am separated from it
by over fifty years, my presbyopic eyes might perhaps reach
to it if the light were not obscured by so many obstacles.
The years like impassable mountains rise between me and
it, my past years and a few brief hours in my life.

The doctor advised me not to insist too much on looking so far back. Recent events, he says, are equally valuable
for him, and above all my fancies and dreams of the night
before. But I like to do things in their order, so directly I
left the doctor (who was going to be away from Trieste for
some time) I bought and read a book on psychoanalysis, so
that I might begin from the very beginning, and make the
doctor's task easier. It is not difficult to understand, but
very boring. I have stretched myself out after lunch in an
easy chair, pencil and paper in hand. All the lines have
disappeared from my forehead as I sit here with mind completely relaxed. I seem to be able to see my thoughts as
something quite apart from myself. I can watch them rising, falling, their only form of activity. I seize my pencil
in order to remind them that it is the duty of thought to
manifest itself. At once the wrinkles collect on my brow as
I think of the letters that make up every word. The present surges up and dominates me, the past is blotted out.

Yesterday I tried to let myself go completely. The result was that I fell into a deep sleep and experienced nothing except a great sense of refreshment, and the curious

*sensation of having seen something important while I was
asleep. But what it was I could not remember; it had gone
forever.*

But today this pencil will prevent my going to sleep. I
dimly see certain strange images that seem to have no connection with my past; an engine puffing up a steep incline
dragging endless coaches after it. Where can it all come
from? Where is it going? How did it get there at all?

In my half-waking state I remember it is stated in my
textbook that this system will enable one to recall one's
earliest childhood, even when one was in long clothes. I at
once see an infant in long clothes, but why should I suppose that it is me? It does not bear the faintest resemblance
to me, and I think it is probably my sister-in-law's baby,
which was born a few weeks ago and displayed to us as
such a miracle because of its tiny hands and enormous eyes.
Poor child!

Remember my own infancy, indeed! Why it is not
even in my power to warn you, while you are still an infant,
how important it is for your health and your intelligence
that you should forget nothing. When, I wonder, will you
learn that one ought to be able to call to mind every event
of one's life, even those one would rather forget? Meanwhile, poor innocent, you continue to explore your tiny
body in search of pleasure; and the exquisite discoveries you
make will bring you in the end disease and suffering, to
which those who least wish it will contribute. What can
one do? It is impossible to watch over your cradle. Mys-
terious forces are at work within you, child, strange elements combine. Each passing moment contributes its reagent.

Not all those moments can be pure, with such mani-
fold chances of infection. And then—you are of the same
blood as some that I know well. Perhaps the passing moments may be pure; not so the long centuries that went
into your making.

But I have come a long way from the images that
herald sleep. I must try again tomorrow.

The Last Cigarette

WHEN I spoke to the doctor about my weakness for smoking he told me to begin my analysis by tracing the growth of that habit from the beginning.

"Write away!" he said, "and you will see how soon you begin to get a clear picture of yourself."

I think I can write about smoking here at my table without sitting down to dream in that armchair. I don't know how to begin. I must invoke the aid of all those many cigarettes I have smoked, identical with the one I have in my hand now.

I have just made a discovery. I had quite forgotten that the first cigarettes I ever smoked are no longer on the market. They were made first in 1870 in Austria and were sold in little cardboard boxes stamped with the double-headed eagle. Wait a minute! Suddenly several people begin to collect round one of those boxes; I can distinguish their features and vaguely remember their names, but this unexpected meeting does not move me in any way. I must try and look into it more closely. I will see what the arm-chair can do. No, now they have faded away and change into ugly, mocking caricatures.

I come back discouraged to the table.

One of the figures was Giuseppe, a youth of about my own age with rather a hoarse voice, and the other was a brother of mine, a year younger than me, who died some years ago. Giuseppe must have been given quite a lot of

money by his father, and treated us to some of those cigarettes. But I am positive that he gave my brother more
than me, and that I was therefore obliged to try and get
hold of some for myself. And that was how I came to
steal. In the summer my father used to leave his waistcoat
on a chair in the lobby, and in the pocket there was always
some change to be found; I took out the coin I needed for
buying one of those precious little boxes, and smoked the
ten cigarettes it contained one after the other, lest I might
be betrayed if I carried about with me such a compromising booty.

All this was lying dormant in my mind and so close at
hand. It had never come to life before, because it is only
now that I realize its possible significance. So now I
traced my bad habits back to the very beginning and (who
knows?) I may be cured already. I will light one last
cigarette, just to try, and probably I shall throw it away in
disgust.

Now I remember that my father surprised me one day
while I was holding his waistcoat in my hand. With a
brazenness which I should never have now and which hor-
rifies me even so long after (perhaps this feeling of disgust
is going to be very important in my cure), I told him that I
had suddenly felt a great curiosity to count the buttons.
My father laughed at my mathematical or sartorial bent
and never noticed that I had my fingers in his waistcoat
pocket. To my credit be it said, his laughing at me like
that for being so innocent when I knew I was guilty was
quite enough to prevent me ever stealing again. At least,
I did steal afterwards, but without realizing it. My father
used to leave half-smoked Virginia cigars lying about on the
edge of a table or a chest of drawers. I thought it was his
way of getting rid of them and I really believe that our old
servant Catina used to throw them away. I began smoking
them in secret. The very fact of hiding them sent a kind
of shudder through me, for I knew how sick they would
make me. Then I would smoke them till cold drops of perspiration stood on my forehead and I felt horribly bad inside. No one could say that as a child I lacked determination.

I remember perfectly how my father cured me of that
habit too. I had come back one summer's day from a
school excursion, tired and very hot. My mother helped me
to undress and then made me lie down in a dressing-gown

and try and go to sleep on the sofa where she was sitting sewing. I was very nearly asleep, but my eyes were still full of sunlight and I couldn't quite get off. The delicious sensation one has at that age, when one is able to rest after being very tired, is so real to me even now that I almost feel as if I were still lying there close to her dear body.

I remember the large airy room where we children used to play and which now, in these days when space is so precious, is divided in two. My brother plays no part in the scene, which surprises me because he must have been on that excursion too and would surely have been resting with me. Was he asleep, perhaps, at the other end of the great sofa? I picture the place, but it seems to be empty. All I see is myself resting there so happily, my mother, and then my father, whose words still echo in my ears. He had come in without noticing I was there, for he called out aloud:

"Maria!"

My mother made a soft hushing sound and pointed to me, lying as she thought drowned in sleep, but in reality wide awake, and merely afloat upon the ocean of sleep. I was so pleased at my father having to treat me with such consideration that I kept perfectly still.

My father began complaining in a low voice:

"I really think I must be going mad. I am almost sure I left half a cigar lying on that chest half an hour ago, and now I can't find it. I must be ill. I can't remember anything."

Only my mother's fear of waking me prevented her from laughing. She answered in the same low voice:

"But no one has been into this room since luncheon."

My father muttered:

"I know that. And that is just why I think I am going mad."

He turned on his heel and went out.

I half opened my eyes and looked at my mother. She had settled down again to her work, and she still had a smile on her face. She would surely not have smiled like that at my father's fears if she believed he was really going mad. Her smile made such a deep impression on me that I immediately recognized it when I saw it one day long afterwards on my wife's lips.

Later on, lack of money was no obstacle to my satisfying my craving, but any prohibition sufficed to excite it.

I smoked continually, hidden in all sorts of secret places. I particularly remember one half-hour spent in a dark cellar, because I was so terribly unwell afterwards. I was with two other boys, but the only thing I remember about them is the childish clothes they wore: two pairs of short knickers which I see standing up quite solidly as if the limbs that once filled them had not been dissolved by time. We had a great many cigarettes and we wanted to see who could smoke most in the shortest time. I won, and stoically hid the physical distress this strange experiment caused me. Afterwards we went out into the sunshine again. I had to shut my eyes or I should have fainted on the spot. By degrees I recovered and boasted of my victory. Then one of the boys said:

"I don't care about losing. I only smoke so long as I enjoy it."

I remember his sensible words, but have quite forgotten the boy's face, though it was probably turned toward me while he spoke them.

But at that time I didn't know whether I liked or hated the taste of cigarettes and the condition produced by nicotine. When I discovered that I really hated it all, it was much worse. That was when I was about twenty. For several weeks I suffered from a violent sore throat accompanied by fever. The doctor ordered me to stay in bed and to give up smoking entirely. I remember being struck by that word *entirely*, which the fever made more vivid. I saw a great void and no means of resisting the fearful oppression which emptiness always produces.

When the doctor had left, my father, who was smoking a cigar, stayed on a little while to keep me company (my mother had already been dead some years). As he was going away he passed his hand gently over my feverish brow and said:

"No more smoking, mind!"

I was in a state of fearful agitation. I thought: "As it's so bad for me I won't smoke any more, but I must first have just one last smoke." I lit a cigarette and at once all my excitement died down, though the fever seemed to get worse, and with every puff at the cigarette my tonsils burned as if a firebrand had touched them. I smoked my cigarette solemnly to the end as if I were fulfilling a vow.

And though it caused me agony I smoked many more during that illness. My father would come and go, always with a cigar in his mouth, and say from time to time:

"Bravo! A few days more of no smoking and you will be cured!"

It only needed that phrase to make me long for him to get out of the room instantly so that I might begin smoking again at once. I would pretend to be asleep in order to get rid of him quicker.

This illness was the direct cause of my second trouble: the trouble I took trying to rid myself of the first. My days became filled with cigarettes and resolutions to give up smoking, and, to make a clean sweep of it, that is more or less what they are still. The dance of the last cigarette which began when I was twenty has not reached its last figure yet. My resolutions are less drastic and, as I grow older, I become more indulgent to my weaknesses. When one is old one can afford to smile at life and all it contains. I may as well say that for some time past I have been smoking a great many cigarettes and have given up calling them the last.

I find the following entry on the front page of a dictionary, beautifully written and adorned with a good many flourishes:

2 February, 1886. Today I finish my law studies and take up chemistry. Last cigarette!!

That was a very important last cigarette. I remember by what hopes it was attended. I was irritated by canon law, which seemed to me so remote from life, and I fled to science in the hope of finding life itself, though imprisoned in a retort. That last cigarette was the emblem of my desire for activity (even manual) and for calm, clear, sober thought.

But when I could no longer accept all the endless combinations of carbonic acid gas I went back to law. That was a mistake, alas, and that too had to be celebrated by a last cigarette. I have come across the date on the cover of a book. That was an important one too, and I applied myself, with the utmost ardor, to the intricate problems of "mine" and "thine," and shook off forever the series of carbon combinations. I had proved myself unsuited to chemistry because of my lack of manual skill. How was it possible for me to have any when I went on smoking like a Turk?

While I sit here analyzing myself a sudden doubt assails me: did I really love cigarettes so much because I was able to throw all the responsibility for my own incompetence on them? Who knows whether, if I had given up smoking, I should really have become the strong perfect man I imagined? Perhaps it was this very doubt that bound me to my vice, because life is so much pleasanter if one is able to believe in one's own latent greatness. I only put this forward as a possible explanation of my youthful weakness, but without any very great conviction.

Now that I am old and no one expects anything of me, I continue to pass from cigarette to resolution and back again. What is the point of such resolutions today? Perhaps I am like that aged dyspeptic in Goldoni, who wanted to die healthy after having been ill all his life!

Once when I was a student I changed my lodgings, and had to have the walls of my room repapered at my own expense because I had covered them with dates. Probably I left that room just because it had become the tomb of my good resolutions, and I felt it impossible to form any fresh ones there.

I am sure a cigarette has a more poignant flavor when it is the last. The others have their own special taste too, peculiar to them, but it is less poignant. The last has an aroma all its own, bestowed by a sense of victory over oneself and the sure hope of health and strength in the immediate future. The others are important too, as an assertion of one's own freedom, and when one lights them one still has a vision of that future of health and beauty, though it has moved a little further off.

The dates on my walls displayed every variety of color and I had painted some of them in oils. The latest resolution, renewed in the most ingenuous good faith, found appropriate expression in the violence of its colors, which aimed at making those of the preceding one pale before it. I had a partiality for certain dates because their figures went well together. I remember one of last century which seemed as if it must be the final monument to my vice: "Ninth day of the ninth month, in the year 1899." Surely a most significant date! The new century furnished me with other dates equally harmonious, though in a different way.

"First day of the first month in the year 1901." Even today I feel that if only that date could repeat itself I should be able to begin a new life.

But there is no lack of dates in the calendar, and with a little imagination each of them might be adapted to a good resolution. I remember the following, for instance, because it seemed to me to contain an undeniable categorical imperative: "Third day of the sixth month, in the year 1912, at 24 o'clock." It sounds as if each number doubled the one before.

The year 1913 gave me a moment's pause. The thirteenth month, which ought to have matched the year, was missing. But of course such exact mathematical correspondence is hardly necessary to set off a last cigarette. Some dates that I have put down in books or on the backs of favorite pictures arrest one's attention by their very inconsequence. For example, the third day of the second month of the year 1905 at six o'clock! It has its own rhythm, if you come to think of it, for each figure in turn contradicts the one that went before. Many events too, in fact all from the death of Pius IX to the birth of my son, I thought deserved to be celebrated by the customary iron resolution. All my family marvel at my memory for anniversaries, grave or gay, and they attribute it to my nice sympathetic nature!

In order to make it seem a little less foolish I tried to give a philosophic content to the malady of "the last cigarette." You strike a noble attitude, and say: "Never again!" But what becomes of the attitude if you keep your word? You can only preserve it if you keep on renewing your resolution. And then Time, for me, is not that unimaginable thing that never-stops. For me, but only for me, it comes again.

Ill-health is a conviction, and I was born with that conviction. I should not remember much about the illness I had when I was twenty if I had not described it to a doctor at the time. It is curious how much easier it is to remember what one has put into words than feelings that never vibrated on the air.

I went to that doctor because I had been told that he cured nervous diseases by electricity. I thought I might derive from electricity the strength necessary to give up smoking.

The doctor was a stout man and his asthmatic breathing accompanied the clicking of the electrical machine that he set in motion at my very first visit. This was rather a disappointment, for I thought the doctor would make an examination of me and discover what poison it was which was polluting my blood. But he only said that my constitution was sound, and that since I complained of bad digestion and sleeplessness he supposed my stomach lacked acids and that the peristaltic action was weak; he repeated that word so many times that I have never forgotten it. He prescribed me an acid that ruined my inside, for I have suffered ever since from overacidity.

When I saw that he would never discover the nicotine in my blood himself, I thought I would help him, and suggested that my ill-health was probably due to that. He shrugged his great shoulders wearily:

"Peristaltic action—acid. It has nothing to do with nicotine!"

He gave me seventy electric treatments, and I should be having them still if I had not decided I had had enough. I did not hasten to my appointments so much because I expected miraculous results, as because I hoped to persuade the doctor to order me to give up smoking. Things might have turned out very differently if I had had a command like that with which to fortify my resolutions.

This is the description I gave the doctor of my illness:

"I am incapable of studying, and on the few occasions when I go to bed early I lie awake till the first bells begin to ring. And that is why I continue to waver between law and chemistry, because both those sciences oblige one to begin work at a stated time, whereas I never know at what time I shall be able to get up."

"Electricity cures every form of insomnia," announced Æsculapius, his eyes fixed as usual on his quadrant instead of on his patient.

I began talking to him about psychoanalysis as if I expected him to understand it; for I was one of the first, though timidly, to dabble in it.

I told him of my troubles with women. I was not satisfied with one or even with many; I desired them all! My excitement as I walked along the streets was intense; whenever I passed a woman, I wanted to possess her. I stared at them insolently, because I wanted to feel as brutal as pos-

sible. I undressed them in imagination down to their shoes.
I held them in my arms and only let them go when I was
sure that I knew every part of them.

I might have spared my breath. All my sincerity was
wasted. The doctor snorted:

"I hope the electrical treatment won't cure you of
that disease. A fine state of things that would be! I would
never touch a high frequency again if I thought that it was
going to have that effect."

He told me what he thought to be a very spicy anec-
dote. Someone who was suffering from my complaint went
to a famous doctor hoping to be cured; but the doctor
having treated him with complete success was obliged to
leave the town, otherwise the patient would have torn
him limb from limb.

"My excitement is not normal," I yelled. "It comes
from the poison burning in my veins!"

The doctor muttered sympathetically:

"No one is ever satisfied with his lot."

And it was in order to convince him that I did what
he had neglected to do, and studied all the symptoms of
my disease in detail.

My absent-mindedness! That was another obstacle to
my studies. When I was at Graz preparing for my first
examination I carefully made a note of all the texts I
should need up to the very last exam. The result was that
a few days before my examination I discovered I had been
studying things that I should only need several years later.
So I was obliged to put off taking it. It is true that I had
not studied anything very closely, but that was the fault
of a girl who lived over the way, and who flirted out-
rageously with me, though it went no further.

If she appeared at the window I had no eyes for my
books. What a fool, to waste one's time over such things!
I remember her small, pale face at the window, its oval
framed in gay auburn curls. I used to sit and gaze at her
and dream of crushing her whiteness and ruddy gold on
my pillow.

Æsculapius murmured:

"Nevertheless flirting has something to be said for it.
At my age you won't want to flirt any more."

Today I am convinced he knew nothing whatever
about flirting. I have reached fifty-seven and I can guaran-

tee that if I don't give up smoking, and if psychoanalysis does not cure me, my dying eyes will be lifted in desire to the nurse by my death-bed, supposing she does not happen to be my wife, and that my wife allows me to have a pretty one!

I was as frank as if I were making my confession. I was not in love with women as a whole, but only with parts of them. I was always attracted by small feet, especially if well shod, by a slender and well-rounded neck, and by very small breasts. I was proceeding to enumerate all the other parts of the female anatomy when the doctor interrupted with:

"All those parts make up the woman as a whole."

Then I said something that seemed to me of great importance:

"Sane, normal love embraces the whole woman with every quality of mind and character."

Up to that time I had never experienced such a love, and when I did, even that did not restore me to health, but it is worth recording that I detected symptoms of disease in what the specialist regarded as healthy, and that my diagnosis turned out to be right.

I found more understanding of my complaint in a friend of mine who was not a doctor. It is true he could not cure me, but he struck a new note in my life which still echoes there.

My friend was a rich man who employed his leisure in reading and writing. He talked much better than he wrote, so that few suspected how profoundly learned he really was. He was a great fat man, and when I knew him he was very energetically undergoing treatment for getting thin. In a very short time his success was such that people made a point of walking beside him in the street, in order to enjoy the contrast between their own robustness and his emaciation. I envied him his strength of will, and so long as his cure lasted I was always going to see him. He invited me to feel how his stomach was getting smaller day by day, and out of pure envy I said to him one day, maliciously hoping to weaken his purpose:

"But what will you do with all that loose skin when your cure is finished?"

He replied with the utmost calm, which gave quite a comic expression to his emaciated face:

"In two days' time I shall begin my massage treatment."

He had arranged every detail of his cure beforehand, and one felt sure he would keep to it with the utmost regularity.

It gave me a great feeling of confidence, and I described my malady to him. I remember the description quite well. I explained to him that giving up three meals a day seemed to me nothing compared with the task of making a fresh resolution every moment not to smoke another cigarette. If you use up all your energy in making resolutions you have no time for anything else, for it takes a Julius Cæsar to be able to do two things at once. It is true there is no need for me to do any work so long as my agent Olivi is alive, but didn't he think it a disgrace for somebody like me to spend his whole time dreaming, or strumming on the violin, for which I have really no aptitude?

My fat friend, now so much reduced, was silent for a while. He was a man of method and first he had to think it all out. Then with a magisterial air, very becoming to one with his reasoning powers, he explained that I was really suffering from my resolutions much more than from the cigarettes. I ought to try and cure myself without making any resolutions. According to him my personality in the course of years had become divided in two, one of which gave orders while the other was only a slave which, directly the supervision was relaxed, disobeyed its master's orders out of sheer love of liberty. So that what I ought to do was to give it absolute freedom and at the same time look my vice in the face as if it was something new and I were meeting it for the first time. I must not fight it, I must first forget it and treat it with complete indifference, turning my back on it as if it were not worthy to keep me company. Simple, wasn't it?

In fact it did seem to me quite a simple matter. And it is true that having with much difficulty banished every resolution from my mind I managed to refrain from smoking for several hours. But when my mouth was cleansed from the taste of smoke it had an innocent feeling like that of a new-born baby, and I felt a longing for a cigarette. Directly I had smoked it I felt remorse and again began making the very resolution I had tried to suppress. The way was longer, but the end was the same.

That wretch Olivi suggested one day that we should have a bet together in order to strengthen my resolution.

I think that Olivi must always have looked exactly the same as he does now. I always see him like this—rather bent, but solidly built; and to me he has always looked just as old as he does today, when he is eighty. He has always worked for me, and he still does; but I don't really like him, for I always think he has prevented my doing the work he does himself.

We made a bet: the first who smoked was to pay and then we should both be released from all obligation. In this way my agent, who was appointed to see that I did not waste my father's fortune, was doing his best to diminish my mother's, over which I had complete control!

That bet proved excessively damaging to me. I was no longer alternately master and slave, but only a slave, and to Olivi, whom I hated. I immediately began to smoke. Then I thought I would cheat him by going on smoking in secret. But in that case why have made a bet at all? So I set about hunting for a date that should match the date of the bet, in order to smoke one last cigarette to which I should somehow feel that Olivi had given his consent. But I continued to rebel, and smoked so much that I got into a state of acute mental agony. In order to shake off the burden I went to Olivi and confessed.

The old man smiled as he pocketed his money, then immediately drew from his pocket a huge cigar which he lit and smoked with immense enjoyment. It never occurred to me for an instant that he might possibly have been cheating too. Evidently I am made quite differently from other people.

My son was just three years old when my wife had a bright idea. She advised me to cure myself by going for a while into a sanatorium. I at once agreed, first because I wanted my son when he grew old enough to form judgments of his own, to find me calm and balanced, and secondly because Olivi was ailing and spoke of leaving; in which case I might be obliged to take his post at a moment's notice, and felt quite unequal to such an exertion with all that nicotine in my body.

We thought first of going to Switzerland, the traditional home of sanatoriums, till we heard of a Doctor Muli, who had opened a place of the sort in Trieste itself. I got my wife to go and see him, and he offered to put a small suite at my disposal with a special attendant to supervise me, and several others to assist her. My wife smiled as she described it to me and occasionally burst out laughing. She was so amused at the idea of my being shut up, and I laughed quite as heartily myself. It was the first time she had ever joined in my efforts to cure myself. Up till then she had refused to take my disease seriously and only said that smoking was one way of living, and not such a bad one either. I think that after our marriage she was relieved to find I never regretted my liberty; I was much too occupied in regretting other things.

We went to the sanatorium the very day on which Olivi had told me he could on no account stay on after the following month. We packed some fresh linen in a trunk and went off that evening to Dr. Muli's. He let us in himself. In those days Dr. Muli was a good-looking young man. It was midsummer, and he looked the picture of elegance dressed in white from top to toe, with his small nervous figure and sunburnt face which set off his piercing black eyes. He at once roused my admiration, and evidently the feeling was mutual.

I guessed the cause of *his* admiration and felt slightly embarrassed. I said:

"I suppose you don't believe I need a cure and can't understand why I take it so seriously."

With an almost imperceptible smile that I found rather insulting, the doctor replied:

"But why not? It may very well be that cigarettes do you personally more harm than we doctors generally admit. I only can't understand why, instead of giving up smoking suddenly altogether, you did not make up your mind to cut down the number of your cigarettes. There is no harm in smoking, but of course it is bad for one to smoke to excess."

I must confess that in my anxiety to give up smoking altogether the possibility of smoking less had never occurred to me. I said with decision:

"In any case, now that I am here let me try your cure."

"Try?" The doctor smiled condescendingly. "Once

you have submitted to it the cure is bound to succeed. It will be impossible for you to escape unless you use physical force on poor Giovanna. The formalities which would have to be gone through before you were free would last so long that in the interval you would quite have forgotten your vice."

We had arrived at the suite of rooms destined to me, which could only be reached by going up to the second floor and then coming down to the ground floor.

"Do you see? That door, which is locked, is the only means of communication with the rest of the ground floor, where the exit is. Even Giovanna hasn't got the key to it. If she wants to get out she is obliged to go up to the second floor, and she keeps the key of that door we came through on the small landing. Besides, there is always someone in charge on the second floor. Not so bad, is it, for a maternity home, which is what this was meant for?"

And he laughed, perhaps at the idea of shutting me up with babies.

He called Giovanna and introduced her to me. She was a little woman of uncertain age, which one might put somewhere between forty and sixty. She had small, very bright eyes and her hair was quite gray. The doctor said to her:

"This is the gentleman whom you have got to be prepared to box with."

She looked me up and down, blushed and said in a shrill voice:

"I shall do my duty, but I am certainly not going to fight with you. If you threaten me I shall call the male attendant, who is very strong, and if he doesn't come at once I shall just let you go wherever you like. I'm not going to risk being killed by you."

I heard afterwards that the doctor had promised her a considerable bonus for looking after me, and this had made her thoroughly nervous. But at the moment her words made me very angry. A nice position I had put myself in of my own accord.

"Go to blazes!" I shouted. "Who's going to touch you, I should like to know?" Then, turning to the doctor, I said: "Please see that I am not annoyed by this woman! I have brought some books with me and I wish to be left in peace."

The doctor said a few soothing words to Giovanna. She tried to excuse herself by a fresh attack upon me.

"I have my children to live for, two sweet little girls."

"I shouldn't stoop to kill you," I replied, in a tone hardly calculated to reassure the poor woman.

The doctor sent her away on pretense of fetching something from the floor above, and to pacify me he proposed replacing her by someone else, adding:

"She is not a bad sort, and if I tell her to behave more tactfully I don't think she will give you any cause for complaint."

As I did not want to seem to attach so much importance to the person who would have to look after me, I said at once that I would put up with her. I was in an excited state and felt the need of controlling myself, so I took out my last cigarette but one and began smoking it greedily. I explained to the doctor that I had only brought two and that I was going to stop smoking on the stroke of midnight.

My wife said good-by and went away at the same time as the doctor. She smiled and said:

"Be strong and carry it through."

I suddenly felt that her smile, which I loved so much, was mocking me. Immediately a new suspicion awoke in my mind, which was to be responsible for the swift failure of an undertaking on which I had entered with such serious purpose. I felt suddenly unwell, but it was only when I was left alone that I realized the nature of my disorder. I was frantically, madly jealous of the young doctor. He was handsome, he was free! His colleagues called him "The Venus de Medici." What was there to prevent my wife falling in love with him? As he went out after her I saw him looking at her elegantly shod feet. It was the first time I had been jealous since we were married. How miserable I felt! No doubt my abject state as a captive had something to do with it. I fought against the idea. That smile was just my wife's usual smile and not one of mockery because she had succeeded in getting rid of me. Yet it was she who suggested my being shut up, though she attached no importance to my vice. But surely she had only done it to humor me. Surely I had not forgotten that one did not so very readily fall in love with my wife? It is true the doctor eyed her feet, but of course he had only been planning what shoes he should buy for his mistress. Suddenly I discovered I had smoked my last cigarette; and it was not yet midnight but eleven o'clock, an impossible hour for a last cigarette.

I opened a book. I read it without understanding a word. I saw visions. The page I was looking at suddenly turned into a photograph of Dr. Muli in the full glory of his beauty and elegance. I could bear it no longer! I called Giovanna. Perhaps if I talked a little I should feel calmer.

She appeared, and at once eyed me suspiciously. She cried in her shrill voice: "Don't imagine that you will be able to make me neglect my duty."

For the moment I invented some lies to set her mind at rest. I said I had never dreamt of such a thing, but that I was tired of reading and should prefer to have a chat with her. I made her sit down facing me. I was completely put off by her elderly appearance, contrasting strangely with her eyes which were still young and restless like those of a timid animal. I felt very sorry for myself, having to put up with such a companion! It is true that even when I am at liberty I am not very good at choosing the companions who would be most congenial to me. On the contrary it is generally they who choose me, as in the case of my wife.

I begged Giovanna to entertain me a little, and when she said she couldn't think of anything that would interest me I asked her to tell me about her family, adding that almost everyone living had at least one.

She readily obeyed and told me that she had been obliged to put her two little girls into a home.

Her story entertained me and I could not help laughing at the thought of how easily she had dismissed the result of her two pregnancies. But she was of a very argumentative disposition, and when she wanted to prove to me that it was impossible for her to do otherwise, seeing how badly she was paid, and that it was very unfair of the doctor to say that two kronen a day were quite enough for her, since the home looked after her children. I soon began to have enough. But it was impossible to stop her.

"What about all the extras?" she shouted. "They only give them food and clothing, but there are heaps of other things they need." And out she came with a whole list of things she was obliged to get for her children, which I have forgotten now, for I tried to concentrate on other things so as to escape from her piercing voice. But my ears were already too full of it, and I felt as if I deserved some recompense.

"Don't you think I might have just one cigarette? I would willingly pay you ten kronen for it, but you will have to wait till tomorrow for I haven't a penny here."

Giovanna was terribly shocked at my suggestion. She literally screamed, and said she should call the attendant at once. In fact she got up and went to the door.

To pacify her I had at once to withdraw my suggestion, and more with a view to keeping myself in countenance than because I really wanted it, I said casually:

"I suppose one can at least get something to drink in this prison?"

To my surprise Giovanna replied at once in quite a natural conversational voice:

"Yes, of course! The doctor gave me this bottle of brandy before he went away. Look! it is still unopened. It was quite a fresh bottle."

I was in such a state that my only hope seemed to lie in getting drunk. So this was the result of having trusted my wife so implicitly.

At that moment it seemed to me that the vice of smoking was really not worth all the trouble I was taking about it. I had not been smoking for the last half-hour and I had already forgotten all about it, so occupied was I in thinking of my wife and Dr. Muli. So I was already completely cured, but I had made a hopeless fool of myself.

I drew the cork and poured out a small glass of the yellow liquid. Giovanna stood watching me with her mouth wide open, but I did not venture to offer her any.

"Can I have some more when I have finished this?"

Giovanna politely assured me that I could have as much as I liked and that the housekeeper had orders to get up at midnight even, if I expressed a wish for anything.

Meanness has never been a fault of mine and I had soon filled Giovanna's glass to the brim. She emptied it almost before she had finished thanking me, and her eyes were already fixed eagerly on the bottle. So it was really she who put into my head the idea of making her drunk. It was none too easy!

I can't remember exactly what it was she said, in the

pure Triestian dialect, after swallowing several more glasses, but I had quite the feeling that I was sitting by someone to whom I could have listened with considerable pleasure had I not been occupied with quite other thoughts.

First of all she confided to me that this was just the kind of work she really enjoyed. She thought everyone ought to have the right to pass an hour or two every day in a comfortable armchair, with a bottle of really good brandy in front of them.

I tried to converse a little too. I asked her if that was how her work had been arranged while her husband was alive.

She burst out laughing. In her husband's lifetime she had had kisses and blows alternately and, compared with all she had had to do for him, what she did now was child's play, even before I had arrived with my cure.

Then Giovanna grew thoughtful and asked me if I thought the dead could see what the living were doing. Yes, I thought so. But then she wanted to know whether, when people were dead, they would discover everything that had happened while they were alive.

For a moment this question actually succeeded in distracting me from my own troubles. It was pronounced in a very soft voice as if Giovanna had purposely lowered it so that the dead should not hear it.

"Were you unfaithful to your husband, then?" I asked.

She begged me not to talk so loud and then confessed that she had been unfaithful, but only during the first few months of their marriage. Then she had got used to blows and had loved her husband.

To keep the conversation going, I said: "Did you have your first child then by the other man?"

Still in low voice she said yes, she thought so, on account of certain resemblances. She regretted very much having betrayed her husband. She laughed as she said this, because for some reason one always does laugh at it, however much one may mind. But she had only minded since his death, for it was of no importance before that, as he knew nothing about it.

Moved by a certain brotherly sympathy, I tried to diminish her grief by saying that I thought the dead probably did know everything, but that there were certain things they would not bother their heads about.

"It is only the living who care!" I cried, banging my fist on the table.

I bruised my hand, and there is nothing like physical pain for awakening new ideas. It suddenly occurred to me that while I was torturing myself with the thought that my wife was taking advantage of my being shut up to betray me with the doctor, he might possibly be in the house all the time, in which case I could set my mind at rest. I asked Giovanna to go and see, telling her I had something urgent to say to the doctor and promising her another bottle as a reward. She protested that she didn't care to drink so much, but at once agreed to go, and I could hear her staggering up the wooden staircase which led to the second floor where our *clausura* ended. She slipped as she was coming down again, making a great deal of noise, and screaming.

"Curse you!" I muttered fervently. If only she had broken her neck my position would have been simplified a good deal.

However, she came back wreathed in smiles, for she had reached a stage when bodily pain makes very little impression. She said she had spoken to the attendant who was just going to bed, but that she could always call for him in case I gave any trouble. She shook her finger at me threateningly as she said this, but with a sly smile. Then she added more dryly that the doctor had not returned since he went away with my wife. Quite a long time! In fact the attendant had been hoping he would come back because there was a patient he wanted him to see. But he had given up all hope of his coming now.

I watched her carefully to see whether the smile on her face was a habitual one or whether it was quite new and occasioned by the fact that she knew the doctor was with my wife instead of with me, his patient, as he ought to have been. I was in such a rage that my brain positively reeled. I must confess that even at such a moment two personalities seemed to be at war within me; the more reasonable of which said: "Idiot! Why should you imagine your wife is unfaithful to you just now? There is no need for her to shut you up. She gets plenty of other oppor-

tunities." The other, the one that insists on smoking, called
me an idiot too, but in quite a different sense: "Don't you
see how easy it becomes with her husband away? And with
the doctor too, who is paid by you!"

Giovanna, who went on drinking steadily, said: "I
forgot to shut the door on to the second floor. But I don't
want to have to go up those two flights again. There is
always someone about up there, and you would cut a fine
figure if you made any attempt to escape."

"Rather!" said I, with the very small degree of hypocrisy now necessary to take in the poor little woman.
I swallowed some more brandy myself, and said that now I
was allowed so much drink I didn't care two straws about
the cigarettes. She believed me at once and then I said it
was not really I who wanted to give up smoking. It was
my wife who insisted on it. I ought to tell her, I added,
that after I had smoked about ten cigarettes I became a
perfect terror. No woman would be safe who happened to
meet me at such a moment.

Giovanna threw herself back in her chair and burst
out laughing noisily.

"So it is your wife who prevents you smoking the
necessary ten cigarettes?"

"Yes, that's it. At least she *used* to prevent me."

With all that brandy inside her poor Giovanna was
by no means such a fool. She was suddenly overcome by
such a fit of laughing that she almost fell off her chair.
When she recovered her breath she sketched, in broken
words, a wonderful little picture suggested by my disease:
"Ten cigarettes . . . half an hour . . . set the alarm
. . . and then. . . ."

I corrected her. "Ten cigarettes take me about an
hour to smoke. It takes about another hour to produce
the full effect—sometimes a few minutes more, sometimes
less."

Giovanna suddenly became quite serious and got up
from her chair without too great difficulty. She said she
must go to bed as she had rather a headache. I invited
her to take the bottle with her, because I had had quite
enough. I hypocritically said that next day I should ask
them to order me in some good wine.

But it was of something else than wine she was thinking. As she left the room with the bottle under her arm

she gave me a look which made my blood run cold.

She had left the door open and a few moments later a packet of cigarettes fell in the middle of the floor. I at once picked it up. It contained eleven cigarettes. To be on the safe side, poor Giovanna had put in one extra. They were common Hungarian cigarettes; but the first I smoked was delicious. I experienced a great sensation of relief. At first I only thought what fun it was to have scored off that house which might be good to shut babies up in, but not me. Then came the thought that I had scored off my wife too and paid her back in her own coin. Otherwise why should my jealousy have suddenly changed to a quite harmless curiosity? I sat quietly in my chair smoking those vile cigarettes.

After about half an hour I remembered that I must escape from the house where Giovanna was waiting for her reward. I took off my shoes and went out into the corridor. The door of Giovanna's room was ajar and, judging by her loud regular breathing, she must be asleep. I went cautiously up the two flights of stairs to the second floor and, once on the other side of that door of which Dr. Muli was so proud, I put on my shoes. I went through to another landing and began slowly to go downstairs, so as to arouse no suspicion.

When I had reached the first-floor landing, an elegant young woman dressed as a nurse followed me and said politely:

"Are you looking for anyone?"

She was very pretty and I should not at all have minded finishing my ten cigarettes in her company. I smiled at her rather aggressively, and said:

"Is Dr. Muli not in?"

She looked extremely surprised and said: "He is never here at this hour."

"I wonder if you could tell me where I should be likely to find him. Someone is ill in my house and wants to see him."

She kindly gave me the doctor's address, and I repeated it several times to make her think I wanted to be sure of remembering it. I was in no great hurry to be gone but she turned her back on me impatiently. I was positively being thrown out of my prison.

In the hall the door was opened for me at once by a

woman. I had no money with me, so I muttered: "I'll give you something another time."

You never can tell what will happen in the future. Things often repeat themselves with me: it was not at all impossible that I might pass that way again.

It was a warm, clear night. I took off my hat to enjoy the free fresh air. I marveled at the stars as if I were seeing them for the first time. I felt that next day, when I was well away from that sanatorium, I should want to give up smoking. Meanwhile I got some more good cigarettes in a café which was still open, because I really could not end my career as a smoker with one of poor Giovanna's cigarettes. The waiter knew me and let me have them on tick.

When I got to my house I rang the bell furiously. The servant came to the window first, and after a certain time my wife appeared. While I waited I thought with perfect calm: it would seem that Dr. Muli really is here. But directly she saw who it was, my wife made the empty street ring with her laughter, so obviously sincere that it ought to have banished all my doubts.

When I got in I cast an inquisitive and suspicious eye round the house. I promised to tell my wife my adventures on the following day, though she seemed to think she knew all about them already.

"Why don't you go to bed?" she asked.

I replied, just as an excuse: "I believe you have taken advantage of my absence to change the position of that chest of drawers."

The fact is I often feel the furniture has been moved, and my wife very often does move it, but at that moment I was hunting in every corner to see if I could find a trace of the elegant little body of Dr. Muli.

My wife had some good news for me. On her way home from the sanatorium she had run into Olivi's son, who told her the old man was much better, after taking some medicine prescribed by a new doctor.

As I fell asleep I thought what a good thing it was I had left the sanatorium, for now I would cure myself slowly at my leisure. My son, sleeping peacefully next door, was certainly not likely to begin either criticizing me or imitating me for a very long time. There was absolutely no hurry.

The Death of My Father

MY DOCTOR has gone away on a holiday and I never asked him whether he meant me to give the story of my father's life as well as my own. If I were to describe my father too minutely, it might appear an essential condition of my cure that he should have been analyzed first, in which case all my trouble will have been in vain. However, I go boldly on, because I am convinced that even if my father did need the same treatment as me it would have been for quite a different complaint. So, to save time, I will only go into my father's story in so far as it helps me to recollect my own.

15.iv.1890—4.30 a.m. My father died. L.C.

For whoever it may interest let me explain that the last two letters stand for "last cigarette." I find this note on the fly-leaf of a volume of *Positive Philosophy* by Ostwald, over which I pored optimistically, hour after hour, but never succeeded in understanding. Probably no one will believe me, but this brief note records the most important event in my life.

My mother died before I was fifteen. I wrote some poems to her memory—not a very good substitute for tears; and in the midst of my grief I could not get rid of the feeling that the serious business of life must begin for me from that moment. My grief seemed to be the token of a new and intenser life. I was at that time genuinely religious, and this also helped somewhat to lighten the blow. I felt my mother was still alive, though very far away, and that she would rejoice in any success I might achieve. This was a very comforting conclusion. I remember my state of mind perfectly at that moment. My mother's death and the healthy emotion it caused made me feel that everything was going to get better.

My father's death, on the contrary, was an unmitigated catastrophe. Paradise had ceased to exist for me, and at thirty I was played out. Yes, it was all up with me. I realized for the first time that the most important, the really decisive part of my life lay behind me and would never return. But my grief was not so purely selfish as this would seem to suggest. No! I mourned for him and for myself, but for myself only because he was dead. Up to that moment I had passed from cigarette to cigarette, and from subject to subject at the University, with an indestructible faith in my possibilities. And I cannot help believing I should not have lost that happy and inspiring faith if my father had not died. His death destroyed the future that alone gave point to my resolutions.

How often when I look back on it, have I wondered at the curious fact that this despair about my future overwhelmed me only when my father died, and not before! All this happened fairly recently and I don't need to dream, as our psychoanalytic friends prescribe, in order to remember every detail of the tragedy and my tremendous grief. I remember everything, but I understand nothing. Up to the time of my father's death I had never devoted myself to him. I made no effort to get into touch with him; I even avoided him so far as I could without giving offense. At college they all knew him by my nickname for him: Old Silva Free-Fist. It needed his illness to draw me to him, and he was hardly ill before he was dead; the doctor at once gave him up.

When I was at Trieste we saw each other at most for about an hour a day. We had never been so much together, nor for so long, as when I was mourning for his death. If only I had been nicer to him and mourned for him less, I should not have been so ill. It was difficult for us to be together, because intellectually we had so little in common. We both looked at each other with a rather pitying smile, which in him had a certain bitterness because of his anxiety about my future. Mine, on the contrary, was all indulgence; I regarded his little weaknesses as of no importance because I attributed them chiefly to age. It was he who first expressed doubts about my strength of will—too soon, I think. I cannot help suspecting, though I have no scientific proof of it, that he lacked confidence in me just because I was his child; which, in itself, was quite enough—and here science supports me—to diminish my confidence in him.

He had however the reputation of being an able man of business; but I knew that for many years past it was Olivi who had managed his affairs. In his incapacity for business he resembled me, but it was the only thing we had in common; if it comes to comparing us, I am bound to say that of the two I was the stronger character. Everything I have put down in my notebooks proves quite clearly that I have, and have always had, a strong impulse to become better; this is perhaps my greatest misfortune. My many dreams of strength and balance can only be interpreted in this sense. All this was quite outside my father's ken. He was perfectly satisfied with himself as he was, and I doubt if he ever made any effort to improve himself. He smoked all day long and, after my mother's death, all night too when he could not sleep. He drank in moderation, as a gentleman should; just enough at dinner to be sure of falling asleep directly he put his head on the pillow. But he regarded tobacco and alcohol as wholesome drugs.

As regards women, I was told by relations that my mother had had some cause for jealousy. It seems that the quiet little woman had to interfere sometimes to keep her husband within bounds. He let himself be guided by her whom he loved and respected, but apparently she never succeeded in making him confess he had been unfaithful, so that she died in the belief that she had been mistaken. However my kind relations say that she once almost caught her husband *en flagrant délit* with her dressmaker. He pleaded a fit of distraction, and with such persistence that she at last believed him. The only consequence was that my mother never went to that dressmaker again, nor did my father. In his place I think I should have ended by confessing, but probably without giving up the dressmaker; for where I halt, there I take root.

My father, like so many family men, was an adept in the art of least resistance. He was at peace with his family and with himself. He only read safe and moral books, not out of hypocrisy but from genuine conviction. I think he really believed in those sermons, and that it quieted his conscience to feel himself sincerely on the side of virtue. Now that I am getting old and begin to approach the patriarchal state, I too feel that it is worse to preach immorality than to practice it. One may be driven to commit murder by love or hatred, but one can only advocate murder out of sheer wickedness.

We had so little in common that he confessed to me that I was one of the human beings who gave him most cause for anxiety. My pursuit of health had led me to study the human body. He, on the other hand, had succeeded in banishing from his memory all thoughts of that terrible machine. As far as he was concerned the heart did not beat, and he had no need to remind himself of valves and veins and metabolism to explain why he was alive. Only no movement! for experience taught one that whatever moved must in the end wear out. For him the earth was motionless and solid, poised between its poles. Of course he never said so, but it pained him if something was said which did not conform to this conception. He interrupted me one day in sheer disgust when I said something about the antipodes. The thought of all those people standing upside down made him feel quite sick and giddy.

He reproached me for two other things—my absent-mindedness, and my tendency to laugh about serious things. As regards absent-mindedness, the only difference between us was that he kept a notebook in which he put down everything that he wanted to remember, and looked at it several times during the day. This made him feel that he had conquered his weakness and he was no longer worried by it. He insisted on my keeping a notebook, but I only used it for putting down a few last cigarettes.

As for my supposed contempt for serious things, I think his fault was to take too many things in this world seriously. For example: when, after leaving the law for chemistry, I obtained his permission to go back again to law, he said good-naturedly: "It is quite clear to me that you are mad."

I was not the least offended, and was so grateful to

him for giving his consent that I thought I would reward him by telling him something to make him laugh. I went to Dr. Canestrini to be medically examined and get a certificate of sanity. It was no easy matter, for I had to submit to a long and minute examination. When I had got my certificate I carried it off in triumph to my father; but I could not even win a smile. In an agonized voice and actually with tears in his eyes, he exclaimed: "Ah, then you really are mad!"

This was all the thanks I got for my exhausting but innocent little comedy. He never forgave me for it, and therefore he would never laugh at it. Go to a doctor as a joke? Have a certificate stamped on purpose, just as a joke? Sheer madness!

Compared with him I felt myself strong, and I sometimes think that the loss of this weaker person with whom I could compare myself to my own advantage made me feel that my value had definitely diminished.

I had a clear proof of his weakness when that scoundrel Olivi insisted on his making his will. Olivi was in a great hurry to get a will made which appointed him guardian of my affairs, and he spent much time and energy in persuading the old man to go through all the formalities of drawing it up. At last my father gave in, but his great beaming face became quite overcast. He was always thinking about death, as if the act of making his will had brought him nearer to it.

One evening he said to me: "Do you think that death is the end of everything?"

Not a day passes but I meditate on the mystery of death, but I had not yet reached the point of being able to give him the information he wanted. I invented, to please him, a very cheerful view of our life beyond the grave.

"I think that pleasure will survive, but that there will be no more need for pain. Perhaps death will remind us of the pleasures of love. It must surely be accompanied by a feeling of happiness and repose, after the continuous work of building up the body. Death must surely be the crown of life!"

It was a complete fiasco. We had just had dinner and were still at table. My father got up without a word, emptied his glass and then said:

"This is not the moment to philosophize, especially with you!" And out he went.

I followed him sadly. I should have liked to have stayed with him and tried to distract him from his gloomy thoughts. But he sent me away, saying that I reminded him of death and the pleasures he used to enjoy.

He could not get his will out of his mind till he had spoken to me about it. Whenever he saw me he thought about it. One evening he burst out with:

"I must tell you I have made my will."

Hoping to rid him of his obsession, I at once overcame the surprise this news caused me and said:

"I shall never have to bother about one, for I hope to outlive all my heirs!"

My laughing at such a serious matter upset him at once, and restored to him all his old desire to punish me so that he found it easy enough to tell me the fine trick he had played me in making Olivi my guardian.

I must confess that I behaved very dutifully. I refrained from making the smallest objection, so anxious was I that he should not again fall a prey to such melancholy thoughts. I said that whatever he might appoint I should submit to.

"Perhaps," I added, "my conduct will be such that you will feel called upon in time to make a new will."

This pleased him because he saw that I anticipated a long life for him—a very long one indeed. But he exacted from me an oath that, supposing he did not alter his will, I would not try to interfere with the powers he had given Olivi. I took an oath, since my word of honor did not satisfy him. I was so docile and accommodating that when I am tortured by the thoughts that I did not love him enough before he died, I always try to call up that scene. To be frank I must say that it was fairly easy for me to resign myself to his will because at that time I positively welcomed the idea of being obliged not to work.

About a year before he died I was able to interfere efficaciously in the interest of his health. He confided to me that he did not feel well, and I persuaded him to go and see a doctor and to let me go with him. The doctor wrote a prescription and told us to come back in a few weeks' time. My father refused to, saying that doctors and gravediggers were both equally odious, and he would not take his medicine because that also reminded him of doctors and gravediggers. He stopped smoking for a few hours, and for one whole meal drank no wine. When he decided to give up this treatment he felt much better, and seeing him so cheerful I thought no more about it.

After that he sometimes seemed to be depressed; but I should have been more surprised if he had been cheerful considering how old and lonely he was.

One evening toward the end of March I came home a little later than usual, for the rather trivial reason that I had run into a learned friend who had insisted on treating me to his ideas on the origins of Christianity. It was the first time that I had ever been asked to give a thought to the subject, and I only submitted to the long lecture to please my friend. It was raining a little and very cold. Everything seemed dreary and dismal, including the Greeks and Hebrews my friend was discussing, but I put up with his tiresome lecture for a good two hours. My usual weakness! I am so bad at refusing anyone anything that I don't mind betting I might at any moment be persuaded, if you tried hard enough, to take up astronomy—for a short time at least.

I came in at the garden gate from which a short carriage drive leads up to the house. Our servant Maria was at the window looking out for me, and when she heard me coming she called out in the dark:

"Is that you, Mr. Zeno?"

Maria was one of those servants who are a thing of the past. She had been with us for fifteen years. She put aside part of her wages monthly into the savings bank, to provide for her old age; but she never profited by her economy, for soon after my marriage she died, still in our service.

She told me that my father had come in several hours before, but that he had insisted on waiting dinner for me. When she had urged him to begin without me, he had spoken rather sharply to her and sent her away. Then he had inquired for me several times, and seemed to be worried because I did not come in. Maria hinted that my father probably was not feeling very well. She said he had difficulty in speaking and seemed short of breath. The fact is she was alone with him so much that she often got it into her head that he was ill. The poor woman had not much to think about, alone in that house, and she assumed that we should all die before her, as my mother had done.

I hurried to the dining-room, curious to see what was the matter, but without feeling any particular cause for alarm. My father rose hastily from the sofa on which he was lying and welcomed me joyfully; but his greeting left me rather cold for I thought it was meant as a reproach. It was however quite sufficient to reassure me, because joy always seems to be a token of health. I could not discover any trace of the difficulty in speaking or breathing which Maria had mentioned. Instead of scolding me he only apologized for being so obstinate.

"You must forgive me," he said gaily. "You and I are alone in the world, and I wanted to see you before going to bed."

If only I had behaved simply and embraced him—my dear father who, because he was ill, had become so tender and affectionate. But instead I began coldly to diagnose the situation: Why has old Silva suddenly grown so lamb-like? Can it be that he is ill? I looked at him suspiciously and all I could find to say, in a tone of reproach, was:

"But why did you keep dinner back all this time? You could have had yours and then waited for me."

He laughed gaily and said: "It is more fun to eat when there are two of us."

I thought his cheerfulness was a sign that he was hungry; my mind was quite at rest, and I sat down to dinner. My father shuffled to the table in his slippers, rather insecurely, and sat down in his usual place. He sat and watched me eating, only taking a few mouthfuls himself, and then pushing his plate away as if he could not bear the sight of it. But there was still the same smile on his old face. Only I remember, as clearly as if it were yesterday, that several times when I looked straight at him, he turned his face away. That is supposed to be a sign of insincerity, but I now know that it is a sign of illness. A sick creature will not let one look it straight in the eye, lest one should detect its weakness there. He was still waiting for me to tell him how I had spent all those hours he had been expecting me. And seeing how much he wanted to hear, I stopped eating a moment and said coldly that I had been busy discussing the origins of Christianity.

He looked puzzled, and said rather doubtfully:

"Are you occupied with religion too, then?"

I saw that it would have been a great consolation to
him if I would have consented to talk to him about it.
But so long as my father was alive (no longer) I always
felt contrary, and I replied in one of those well-worn
phrases, which you may hear any day in the cafés near the
university:

"I look upon religion simply as a phenomenon to be
studied like any other."

"Phenomenon?" he repeated in bewilderment. He
searched for a reply and opened his mouth in readiness to
make it. Then he hesitated and looked at the second
course, which Maria was just handing to him; but he
would not touch it. So the better to gag himself he stuck
a cigar-end between his teeth, lit it, and at once let it go
out. He had thus gained time to reflect quietly. He looked
at me fixedly for a moment and then said:

"You don't mean to laugh at religion?"

And I, who have always been the perfect type of
Bohemian student, answered with my mouth full:

"I don't laugh at it, I study it!"

He said nothing, but went on staring at the cigar-end,
which he had put down on a plate. I understand now why
he said that to me. I understand now everything that
passed through his already clouded mind, and I only
wonder why I understood so little at the time. I think it
was because I lacked the sympathy which makes one understand so many things. Later on it was easy enough. My
father avoided saying anything which might shock my
skepticism, for he could not face a direct conflict at that
moment; but he thought he might venture cautiously on a
flank attack, as more suited to the resources of an invalid.
I remember how he caught his breath, and what difficulty
he had in getting his words out. Preparing for a battle is
very exhausting. But I felt that he would not be content to
go to bed until he had put me in my place, and I resigned
myself to the discussion, which after all never came. Still
staring at his now extinguished cigar-end, he said:

"I feel that I have much experience and a great knowledge of life. One cannot have lived all these years in vain.
I know a great many things but, alas, I don't know how to
make you understand them. How I wish I could! I feel that
I can see the meaning of things to a certain extent and can
also distinguish between what is true and what is false."

It was no good arguing about it. I went on eating and muttered, without much conviction: "Yes, Father."

I didn't want to offend him.

"It is a pity you came in so late. Earlier in the evening I was less tired and could have explained it to you much better."

I thought he wanted to begin worrying me again about coming in late, and I suggested we might put off discussing things till next day.

"It is not a matter of discussing things," he said in a dreamy voice. "It is about something quite different—something that it is impossible to discuss, but which you will understand directly I have told you. But it is so difficult to talk about."

My suspicions were aroused. "Don't you feel well?" I said.

"I can't really say I feel ill, but I am very tired and shall go to bed at once."

He rang the bell and called for Maria at the same time. When she came he asked if his room was quite ready. He got up at once and went toward the door, dragging one foot after the other. As he passed me he bent down and offered me his cheek to kiss, as he did every evening.

When I saw how insecurely he walked my old doubts returned and I asked him again if he felt unwell. We both repeated the same question and answer several times, he assuring me that he was not ill, but tired. Then he added:

"Now I shall think over what I want to say to you tomorrow. I know I shall be able to convince you."

I felt quite moved. "Father," I said, "I shall be delighted to listen to you."

When he saw how ready I was to profit by his experience he seemed to hesitate about leaving me; surely he ought to take advantage of such a favorable moment. He passed his hand over his forehead several times and sat down on the chair he had leaned on when he offered me his cheek to kiss. He sighed.

"It is curious," he said, "I can't find anything to say, absolutely nothing."

He looked round as if he was hoping to get from outside what he could not find within himself.

"Yet there are so many things I know. I feel as if I

knew almost everything. It must be the result of my great experience."

He already felt less acutely his inability to express himself. He smiled as if he rejoiced in the sense of his own greatness.

I don't know why I did not send for the doctor at once. I must confess with shame and remorse that I thought my father's words were inspired by a conceit that I had often noticed in him. But I could not help seeing that he was very feeble, and that alone prevented me from arguing with him. I was glad to see him so happy in the illusion that he was strong just when he was at his weakest. Besides I felt flattered by his affection and by his wanting to hand on his knowledge to me, however convinced I may have been that I had nothing to learn from him. To flatter him and set his mind at rest, I told him that he mustn't overstrain himself in trying to find the exact words he wanted on the spot, because the wisest men often store up in the corner of their brain things that they find too complicated to express, and trust to time for them to become simpler.

He replied:

"What I am after is not at all complicated. It is only a matter of finding a single word, and I know I shall find it. But not tonight, for I shall sleep right through now and not be troubled by the least little thought."

But he still did not rise from his chair. He kept gazing at me and said at last, hesitatingly:

"I am afraid I shall not be able to tell you what I really think because you always make game of everything."

He smiled at me as if he wanted to beg me not to take offense at his words, got up from his chair, and held out his cheek to me a second time. I made no attempt to convince him by argument that there are many things in this world that one can and ought to laugh at; instead I tried to reassure him by kissing him warmly on both cheeks. Perhaps my gesture was too emphatic, for he at once escaped from my embrace, looking more troubled than ever; but he certainly understood that I wanted to show him sympathy, for he waved his hand to me affectionately.

"And now to bed!" he cried merrily, and went out of

the room, followed by Maria.

When I was left alone (how strange it seems) I did not give my father's health a thought, but found myself respectfully regretting that an intelligent man like my father, with such high ideals, should not have had the opportunity of a better education. As I write now, having very nearly reached my father's age, I know for a fact that it is perfectly possible for someone to be conscious of possessing a very lofty intellect even though that consciousness is the only proof he has of it. It is rather like this: you take a deep breath and are filled with a sense of the wonder and greatness of Nature as she is revealed to us, whole and immutable; and in doing that you participate in the mind that planned the whole of creation. I thought that last lucid moment in which my father became conscious of intellectual power, originated in a sudden religious awakening, and that it was my telling him about my study of the origins of Christianity which induced him to speak to me about it. But I know now that this feeling was a symptom of hemorrhage of the brain.

Maria came in to clear away and told me that she thought my father had gone to sleep at once. So I went to bed too, quite reassured. Outside the wind howled and moaned. From my bed it sounded like a lullaby, which grew farther and farther away as I sank deeper into sleep.

I don't know how long I had been asleep when I was wakened by Maria. It appears that she had been to my room to call me several times before and then had run away again. I was conscious of a certain disturbance in the depths of my sleep; then through my half-open eyes I recognized the old woman dancing about the room; and finally I realized what was happening. She was trying to wake me, but by the time I was really wide awake she had left the room. The wind was still trying to sing me to sleep, and to tell the truth I felt profoundly annoyed at being snatched from my dreams so brutally, as I went along to my father's room. I reflected that Maria was always thinking my father was in danger. I determined to remonstrate with her if this was another false alarm.

My father's bedroom was not very big, and it was over-furnished. When my mother died he tried to help himself to forget by moving into another room, but he took with him all the old furniture from the bigger room. The room was all in shadow, only dimly lighted by a small gas-jet above the low table by his bed. Maria was supporting my father, who was lying on his back with the upper part of his body projecting from the bed. His face, which was covered with perspiration, glowed red in the gaslight. His head was leaning against Maria's faithful breast. He was groaning with pain and his mouth hung open helplessly, while the saliva trickled from his chin. He was gazing motionless at the opposite wall, and took no notice when I came in.

Maria said she had heard him groaning and had arrived just in time to prevent him from falling out of bed. At first, she said, he had been rather restless, but now he seemed to have quieted down; only she did not dare to leave him alone. I think she wanted to apologize for having waked me, but I at once realized that she had acted rightly. She went on crying all the time she was talking to me. I did not cry; on the contrary I told her to control herself and not add to the horror of that hour by weeping. I had not really grasped yet what had happened. The poor creature did her best to calm her sobs.

I put my face close to my father's ear and said in a loud voice:

"Why are you groaning, Father? Do you feel ill?"

I think he heard me, for his groans became fainter, and he turned his eyes from the wall facing him as if he were trying to look at me; but he could not quite turn them so far. I shouted the same question in his ear three times, and always with the same result. My courage soon broke down. My father was already closer to death than he was to me; my cries could no longer reach him. Terror seized me, and immediately the words we had exchanged only the evening before came back to me. So few hours had passed, yet he was already on his way to discover which of us was right. How strange! My sorrow was accompanied by remorse. I hid my face in my father's pillow and burst into the same hopeless sobs for which I had chidden Maria.

It was now her turn to calm me, but she went a strange way about it, talking of my father as if he were already dead, though he lay groaning with his eyes wide open.

"Poor dear," she said. "To think of his dying like that, with all his fine thick hair too." She stroked it as she spoke.

It was true; my father's head was covered by a great mane of curly white hair, whereas mine, at thirty, was already very thin.

I had quite forgotten that there were such things as doctors in the world, and that sometimes they were supposed to be able to save one. I had already seen death on that face contorted with pain, and I had given up hope. It was Maria who first thought of the doctor, and she went to wake the gardener to send him to the town.

I stayed alone for about ten minutes, which seemed an eternity, supporting my father. I remember I tried to put into my hands all the tenderness with which my heart was suddenly filled. He could no longer hear my words. What could I do to make him feel how much I loved him?

When the gardener came I went to my room to write a note, and had great difficulty in framing the few words necessary to give the doctor an idea of the case so that he might know what medicines to bring with him. I kept seeing before me the imminent and certain death of my father, and asking myself: "What is there for me to do in the world now?"

Then followed several long hours of waiting. I have a fairly clear remembrance of those hours. It soon became unnecessary to support my father, for he lay back quite unconscious on the bed. His groaning had ceased; he seemed to have lost all sense of everything. His breathing was hurried; half unconsciously mine became so too. It was impossible for me to go on breathing long at that pace, so I allowed myself short intervals of rest, hoping thereby that I might induce a quieter heart-beat in my patient. But it hurried on and never tired. We tried in vain to make him take a spoonful of tea. His torpor became less profound when it was a question of defending himself against our interference. He kept his teeth resolutely shut. His obstinacy did not leave him even in a state of unconsciousness. Long before dawn the rhythm of his breathing changed. It fell into periods alternating between what seemed almost like the breathing of a healthy man and bursts of hurried respiration, with sometimes a long terrible interval when it seemed to stop altogether, which made Maria and me feel that death must be close at hand. But then the sequence of periods would begin again, a colorless music, infinitely sad. That noisy, uneven breathing seemed to become part of the room. From that time and for long, long afterwards it was always there.

I flung myself on a sofa, while Maria sat up on a chair near the bed. My bitterest tears were shed on that sofa. Tears throw a veil over our faults and allow us to accuse Fate without fear of contradiction. I wept because I was losing my father for whom I had always lived. It did not matter that I had been so little with him. Had not all my efforts to become better been made in order to give satisfaction to him? It is true that the success I strove for would have been a personal triumph for me as against him who had always doubted me, but it would have been a consolation to him as well. And now he could wait no longer and was going away convinced of my incurable incapacity. The tears I shed were indeed bitter.

While I sit writing, or rather engraving these tragic memories on my paper, I realize that the image that obsessed me at the first attempt to look into my past—the image of an engine drawing a string of coaches up a hill—came to me for the first time while I lay on the sofa listening to my father's breathing. That is just what engines do when drawing an enormous weight: they emit regular puffs, which then become faster and finally stop altogether; and that pause seems dangerous too, because as you listen you cannot help fearing that the engine and the train must go tumbling head over heels down into the valley. How curious that is! My first real effort to remember had carried me back to the night that was the most important in my life.

Dr. Coprosich arrived at the house before it grew light, accompanied by a male nurse, who was carrying a box of drugs. He was obliged to come on foot because he had been unable to find a carriage, on account of the violent storm.

I received him in tears, and he was very kind to me, and urged me not to give up hope. But I may as well say at once that from the moment of our first meeting there are few men who have aroused in me such violent antipathy as Dr. Coprosich. He is still alive, though very decrepit; and he is greatly esteemed by everybody in the town. When I see him tottering along through the streets to get a little air and exercise, all my former dislike revives.

At that time the doctor cannot have been more than forty. He had devoted himself to the study of legal medicine, and though he was notorious as being a very patriotic Italian, the Imperial Courts of Justice entrusted him with the most important missions. He was a thin, nervous type. The real insignificance of his face was disguised by his baldness, which made him appear to have a very lofty brow. Another defect also added to his importance; when he took off his spectacles (as he constantly did when meditating on anything), his myopic eyes looked round or above his interlocutor, and were strangely like the colorless eyeballs of a statue, threatening or perhaps ironical. His eyes became very disagreeable then. But directly he put on his eyeglasses (as he always did for the least word) they became at once the eyes of any honest bourgeois, submitting whatever he says to a careful examination.

He sat down to rest for a few minutes in the hall. He asked me to describe exactly what had happened from the moment of the first alarm till his arrival. He removed his eyeglasses and fixed his uncanny eyes on the wall behind my back. I tried to give an exact account, which was not very easy considering the state I was in. I remembered that Dr. Coprosich could not bear people who know nothing about medicine to use medical terms, as if they were pretending to some knowledge of the subject. And when I happened to mention "stertorous breathing" he put on his spectacles in order to say: "Go slow with your definitions. We shall soon see what the trouble is." I told him of my father's strange demeanor, of his anxiety to see me and of his anxiety to get to bed. I did not repeat to him my father's strange speeches; perhaps I was afraid I should have to repeat my answers too. But I told him what difficulty my father had had in expressing himself; and how he seemed to be revolving something in his mind which he could not succeed in formulating. The doctor, putting on his great spectacles again, exclaimed triumphantly:

"I know what was going on in his head." I knew too, but I didn't say so for fear of making him angry: it was the cerebral hemorrhage.

We went into the sick man's room. The male nurse helped him to turn over in all directions that poor lifeless body, for what seemed to me a century. He examined him thoroughly, and tried in vain to make the patient help himself a little.

"That will do," he said after a time. He came up to me with his spectacles in his hand, and his eyes on the floor, and said:

"You must be brave. It is a very serious case."

We went to my room, and he washed his face and hands. He was without his spectacles of course, and when he raised his head to dry it, it looked like the strange little head of an amulet, carved by an unskillful hand. He said he remembered that we had been to see him several months ago, and he expressed surprise that we had not been again. He imagined that we had left him for another doctor; he had stated very clearly then that my father ought to have treatment. He was terrifying, scolding me there without his glasses. He raised his voice and demanded an explanation. His eyes roved everywhere in search of it.

Of course he was quite right and I deserved his scolding. Also I don't think it was that which made me hate Dr. Coprosich. I tried to excuse myself by telling him how my father hated doctors and drugs; I wept as I spoke and the doctor generously tried to calm me by saying that even if we had called him in earlier his knowledge would only have availed to delay the catastrophe, not to avert it.

But as he proceeded to inquire into the causes leading up to my father's illness, he found occasion to reproach me. He wanted to know if my father had complained of his health during the last months, whether he had eaten and slept well. I was not able to tell him anything definite; I had not even noticed whether my father's appetite was good or bad, though we had had our meals together day after day. I was overwhelmed by a sense of guilt, but the doctor did not press his questions. I told him that Maria always thought my father was dying, and that I had laughed at her for it.

He stood drying his ears and gazing up at the ceiling.

"He will probably recover consciousness, in part at least, in the course of the next few hours," he said.

"Is there any hope then?" I exclaimed.

"None whatever!" he answered dryly. "But leeches have never been known to fail in a case like this. He will certainly become partly conscious, but will probably lose his reason."

He shrugged his shoulders and put the towel back in
its place. That shrugging of his shoulders seemed to suggest
that he had not much opinion of his own work, and I felt
encouraged to speak. I was terrified at the thought that my
father might become conscious only to realize that he was
dying, but if I had not seen the doctor shrug his shoulders
I should not have dared to express my fears.

"Doctor!" I implored. "Doesn't it seem to you wicked
to let him recover consciousness?"

I burst into tears. My nerves were so shaken that I felt
a perpetual desire to cry, and I gave way to it now unrestrainedly; I wanted him to see me crying, thinking he
would the more readily forgive me for desiring to criticize
him.

He said to me very kindly:

"There, there, you must try to control yourself. Your
father will never be sufficiently conscious to realize his
condition. He is not a doctor. One has only not to tell him
that he is dying, and he will never find out. But something
worse may happen to him; he may go mad. I brought a
strait-jacket with me in case that should happen, and the
nurse will stay here."

More terrified than ever I begged him not to apply the
leeches. Whereupon he calmly told me that the nurse had
already applied them, because he had told him to before
leaving my father's room. Then I flew into a rage. Could
anything be more wicked than to force a desperately ill
person to come to, when there was not the smallest chance
of saving his life and only misery lay before him; perhaps
too the unspeakable torture of a strait-jacket? In an absolute fury, but still crying piteously all the time, as if
imploring for mercy, I declared that it seemed an unheard-of cruelty not to let a condemned man die in peace.

I hate that man because he then got angry with me
too. And for one thing I can never forgive him. He got so
excited that he forgot to put on his spectacles, and yet
succeeded in discovering exactly where my head was, and
fixing it with his terrible eyes. He said it looked as if I
wanted to cut the slender thread of hope which still existed. He said it crudely, just like that. Here I joined battle
with him. Weeping and shouting with rage I protested
that only a few seconds before he had said himself that
there was absolutely no hope for saving my father. I refused

to let my house and its inmates be made use of for such an experiment. There were plenty of places in the world where they specialized in it!

He replied very severely, and with an almost menacing calm:

"I was explaining to you the scientific standpoint in such a case, but who knows what may happen in half an hour's time or, let us say, by tomorrow? If I have succeeded in keeping your father alive I have left a loophole for any contingency."

Then he put on his glasses, and with the manners of a pedantic official went on to make countless other demonstrations of the important role a doctor might sometimes play in the economic fortunes of a family. One half-hour of life, more or less, might alter the whole character of a patrimony.

If I went on crying now it was because I pitied myself for having to listen to such stuff at a moment like that. I was exhausted and in no mood to argue. So it was too late to stop them applying the leeches!

The doctor has a great deal of power beside a sick bed, and I treated Dr. Coprosich with all respect. Perhaps that was why I did not dare to propose a consultation, a thing for which I reproached myself for many a long year. My remorse is dead now, together with all the other matters I have to relate; so I can speak of them as coldly as if they had happened to a stranger. All that remains to me of those days is my hatred of the doctor, and that will never die.

After a little while we went into my father's bedroom again. We found him lying on his left side. They had put a bandage on his forehead to cover the wound that the leeches had made. The doctor wanted to try at once whether he had recovered consciousness, and shouted in his ear. My father made not the faintest movement.

"So much the better!" I said courageously, but still in tears.

"They cannot fail to take effect," remarked the doctor. "Can't you see that his breathing has become different?"

It was quite true that his breathing, which was now uniformly quick and labored, no longer had that periodic character which had frightened me so much, earlier.

The nurse said something to the doctor to which he

assented. It was about trying on the strait-jacket. They took
the horrible thing out of the bag, and between them raised
my father, forcing him to sit upright on the bed. Then
suddenly he opened his eyes. They were dim, and still un-
accustomed to the light. I was in an agony of fear lest he
should wake up and see everything. But instead of that
when his head fell back on the pillow his eyes closed too,
like those of certain dolls.

The doctor was triumphant:

"There, that is quite different," he said in a low voice.

Yes, it was quite different, and for me it meant something horribly threatening. I kissed my father warmly on
the forehead, and said to him in my secret heart:

"Oh, may you sleep till eternal sleep overtakes you!"
And so I prayed that my father might die. The doctor,
however, guessed nothing, for he said cheerfully:

"You must admit that you are glad to see him come
to."

Dawn had come by the time the doctor went away—
an overcast, hesitating dawn. The wind seemed to me less
violent though it still blew in gusts, and blew the frozen
snow about.

I went with the doctor as far as the garden. I behaved
to him with exaggerated politeness so that he should not
guess what I really felt toward him. My face expressed only
consideration and respect. It was not till I saw him going
down the garden path to the gate that I allowed myself a
grimace of disgust. He looked such an insignificant black
little thing in the snow, staggering down the path, and
occasionally stopping, as each fresh gust smote him, in
order to withstand it better. But the grimace was not
enough; I felt the need of violent movement after my long
effort at self-control. I walked up and down the path for
several minutes in the cold, with nothing on my head,
stamping my feet furiously in the deep snow. But I don't
really know whether my childish fury was directed against
the doctor or against myself. Myself perhaps first, because
I had desired my father's death, but had not dared to say
so. It was true that I had desired it solely out of filial
affection, but the fact that I had remained silent about it
made it a crime which weighed heavily on my mind.

The sick man was still asleep. He said only a few words
which I could not hear, but he said them in a calm,

confidential tone, contrasting strangely with his hurried
breathing, which gave such an impression of unrest. Would
he soon be conscious again and realize the worst?

Maria and the male nurse were both sitting by his
bed. I felt confidence in the latter, and was only irritated
by a certain air of exaggerated conscientiousness. He rejected Maria's proposal to give the invalid a spoonful of
broth, a remedy in which she had great faith. The doctor
had not said anything about giving him broth, and the
nurse wanted to wait for his next visit before venturing
on anything so important. I thought him much more
overbearing than was necessary. Poor Maria did not press
the matter, nor did I. But I made another grimace of disgust.

They persuaded me to lie down now, so that I could
sit up with the hired nurse during the night. Two were
enough at a time if the invalid needed anything, and we
could take it in turns to rest on the sofa. I lay down and
fell asleep at once, losing consciousness completely without
the faintest flicker of a dream.

Last night, however, after I had spent the whole of
yesterday in trying to recall what I have here set down, I
had an exceedingly vivid dream which with one enormous
bound carried me back over the years to the very time I
have been speaking of. I saw myself and the doctor standing in the room where we had been discussing the leeches
and the strait-jacket. The room looks quite different now
because it is my wife's and my bedroom. I was instructing
the doctor in the various steps he should take to cure my
father, while he, spectacles in hand, and with a distracted
look, was shouting that it was not worth while doing all
these things. I did not see him as he is now, old and decrepit, but keen and vigorous as he was then. This is
what he was saying: "We must not apply leeches; they will
only recall him to life and suffering." I meanwhile was
banging a book of prescriptions with my fist and shouting:
"Bring leeches! I will have those leeches! And the strait-
jacket too!"

Apparently I made a noise in my dream, for my wife
woke me up in the middle of it. Distant shades! It seems
one can only recapture you by an optical illusion which
turns you upside down.

My sleeping so peacefully is the last thing I can re-

member about that day. Then followed several weary days
which seem to me now to have been all exactly alike. As
the weather improved they said that my father's condition improved too. He could walk across the room now by
himself, and began his daily progress from bed to sofa, in
search of air. Sometimes he would watch for a few minutes
through the closed windows the sunlit, dazzling snow which
still covered the garden. I would go in from time to time
expecting to find that return of consciousness prophesied
by Coprosich, and resolved to overcloud it again by discussion. But though my father's eyesight and hearing
seemed to improve daily there was no real return of consciousness.

All the time my father was ill my heart was filled with
a strange mixture of grief and resentment. The principal
element in this resentment was my rage against Coprosich,
which only grew greater the longer I tried to conceal it. But
I also felt furious with myself for not daring to renew my
discussion with the doctor, and tell him that I did not care
a fig for all his science, and that I hoped my father would
die and be saved all that suffering.

And finally I began to feel resentment against my
father. Anyone will understand who has tried watching
day after day, for weeks on end, by the bed of somebody
who is ill, when one knows nothing about nursing and is
therefore obliged to be a passive spectator. I felt the need
of a real rest in order to clear up my mind and take some
of the sting out of the grief I felt on my father's account
and on my own. Instead of which I was obliged to be constantly fighting with him, now forcing him to take his
medicine and now preventing him leaving the room. And
conflict always produces anger.

One evening Carlo, the nurse, called me in to see a
further improvement in my father. Greatly excited I rushed
in, fearing that the old man had become conscious of his
condition and would upbraid me for it.

My father was standing in the middle of the room in
his underclothes, with his red silk night-cap on his head.
He still had great difficulty in breathing, but from time
to time said a few words quite intelligibly. Just as I went in
he said to Carlo:

"Open!"

He wanted him to open the window. Carlo replied

that he could not because it was too cold. For a little while my father forgot what it was he had asked. He sat down in an armchair by the window and stretched out his legs so as to be more comfortable. When he saw me he said:

"Have you been asleep?" I don't think he heard my reply. This was not the kind of recovery I had feared. When you are actually dying you have other things to do than to think about death. His whole being was concentrated on the effort to get his breath. Instead of listening to my answer he shouted to Carlo again:

"Open!"

He could not rest. He got up from the chair and tried standing. Then with a great effort, and with the help of the nurse, he lay down on the bed, lying first for an instant on his left side, and then changing almost immediately to his right, for he knew that he could hold out in this position for several minutes on end. Then he called the nurse again to help him to his feet, and went back to the arm-chair, where he remained sitting much longer than before.

The same day, on one of his frequent journeys from the bed to the armchair, he stopped in front of the glass and looked at himself in it for quite a long time. Then he murmured:

"I look like a Mexican!"

It must have been to break the awful monotony of his journey to and from the armchair that he started trying to smoke that day. But he got no further than filling his mouth once with smoke and puffing it out again, exhausted.

Once Carlo called me in during a moment of complete consciousness:

"Am I seriously ill then?" he had asked in a terrified voice; but it was only one brief flash followed by a moment's delirium. He sat up in bed and thought he had just woke up, and that he was spending the night in an hotel in Vienna. It was probably the longing to cool his burning mouth which made him dream of Vienna where there is such lovely water and so cold. He went on to speak of the delicious water which awaited him at the nearest fountain.

He was a restless patient, but otherwise very good. I was continually afraid of his becoming irritable when he discovered how ill he really was, so that his gentleness did nothing to diminish my fatigue; but he always patiently accepted any new suggestion that was made to him, because he was always hoping to get relief from one of them. When the nurse offered to go and get him a glass of milk he accepted with genuine delight. But he was soon as eager to get rid of the milk as he was to have it, and because it was not taken from him after he had had one small sip, he threw it on the ground.

The doctor never showed any sign of being disappointed by the invalid's condition. Every day he noticed a slight improvement, but he regarded the catastrophe as inevitable. One day he arrived in his carriage and was in a great hurry to be off again. He told me to persuade my father to lie down as much as possible, because a horizontal position was better for the circulation. He spoke to my father about it too, who heard what he said and promised to do so with an air of complete understanding, but nevertheless remained standing in the middle of the room and seemed to fall back at once into a state of absent-mindedness, or rather into that pre-occupation with his lack of breath which I described above.

The following night I experienced for the last time the fear of that much-dreaded return of consciousness. He was sitting by the window in an armchair, and gazing through the panes out on to the clear starlit sky. His breathing was still labored, but he was so absorbed in watching the sky that it did not seem to trouble him. Perhaps it was his efforts to get his breath which made him seem to nod his head as if in sign of assent.

I thought with horror: Now at last he is considering the problem he has always avoided. I tried to discover which exact point of the sky it was that he was gazing at. There he sat, upright, with the intense and concentrated effort of someone who is trying to peer through a window too high up. I thought he was looking at the Pleiades. During his whole life he had probably never gazed into the distance for so long on end. Suddenly he turned his whole body toward me, still sitting upright in his chair.

"Look! Look!" he said, with a stern, commanding air. He returned once more to his study of the sky, and then said to me again:

"Did you see? Did you see?"

He tried to go back again to the stars, but he could not: he sank exhausted into the armchair, and when I asked

him what it was he had wanted to show me, he did not
seem to remember that he had wanted to show me anything—he probably did not even hear me. The word he
had been searching for, which he so much wanted to confide to me had escaped him forever.

The night was long, but not particularly fatiguing
either for me or for the nurse. We let the sick man do as
he liked, and he went on walking about the room in his
queer costume, quite unconscious that he was waiting for
death. Once he tried to go out in the passage, where it
was very cold. I would not let him and he obeyed at once.
Another time when his nurse, who had heard the doctor's
orders, tried to prevent him getting up, my father rebelled.
He shook off his stupor and wept and swore as he struggled
to raise himself. I insisted on his being allowed to move
about exactly as he pleased. He quieted down at once, and
returned to his life of silence and his vain pilgrimage in
search of relief.

When the doctor came he allowed himself to be
examined, and even tried to do as he was told and to take
a deep breath. Then, turning to me, he said:

"What is he saying?"

He forgot me for a moment, but soon came back
again:

"When can I go out?"

The doctor, encouraged by his docility, urged me to
tell him that he ought to lie down more. My father only
listened to voices he knew, like mine and Maria's and the
nurse's. I had no faith in the value of that prescription,
but I repeated it to him and put a touch of severity into
my tone.

"Yes, yes," my father agreed, and at once got up and
went to the armchair.

The doctor watched him and murmured with resignation:

"It is clear that it relieves him a little to change his
position."

I went to bed soon afterwards, but I could not close
my eyes; I was probing the future, and trying to discover in
it some motive for continuing my efforts at self-improve-
ment. I cried a great deal, more on my own account than
for my poor father who roamed his room perpetually in a
vain effort to find peace.

When I got up Maria went to lie down, and I joined the nurse at my father's bedside. I was very tired and depressed, and my father was more restless than ever.

Then came that terrible, unforgettable scene which threw its shadow far into the future, and deprived me of all my courage and of all joy in life. The intensity of my grief was only mitigated when time had blunted all my feelings.

The nurse said:

"What a good thing it would be if we could persuade him to stay in bed. The doctor attaches so much importance to it."

I had been lying down on the sofa. I got up at once and went over to the bed where my father was lying at the moment, struggling more than ever to get his breath. I was resolved to insist on his remaining on the bed for at least half an hour, as the doctor had ordered. Surely it was my duty to do so.

Suddenly my father started struggling to escape the pressure of my hands which were holding him down, and began edging himself toward the other side of the bed. I kept my hand firmly on his shoulder and forced him down, while at the same time I ordered him in a loud voice not to move about. He obeyed for a few seconds, startled by the sternness of my voice. Then he exclaimed:

"I am dying!"

And he sat straight up. I in my turn was startled by his cry and relaxed the pressure of my hand, so that he succeeded in sitting on the edge of the bed, exactly facing me. I think he was furious at finding himself held down by force, even for a moment, and that he had the impression that it was I who was depriving him of the air he needed so much, just as I was shutting out the light by standing, while he was sitting down. With a supreme effort he struggled to his feet, raised his arm high above his head, and brought it down with the whole weight of his falling body on my cheek. Then he slipped from the bed on to the floor and lay there—dead!

I did not realize he was dead, but my heart contracted with grief at the thought of the punishment that the dying man had tried to administer to me. I raised him with Carlo's help and got him back on to the bed. Then, crying like a child who has been punished, I shouted in his head:

"It was not my fault! It was that cursed doctor who wanted to make you lie down!"

It was a lie. Then I promised, like a child, never to do it again:

"I will let you do exactly what you like."

The nurse said:

"He is dead."

They had to use force to get me to leave the room. He was dead and it was impossible for me to prove my innocence.

When I was alone I tried to recover myself. I began reasoning: it was out of the question that my father, who was not in his right mind, could have taken such perfect aim at my cheek with the direct intention of punishing me.

But how could I ever know for certain that my reasoning was just? I even thought of consulting Coprosich about it. He, as a doctor, might be able to throw some light on a dying man's ability to plan and execute a design like that. Perhaps I had only been the victim of a supreme effort on my father's part to recover his breath. But I never spoke to Coprosich about it. I could not bear to go and tell him what sort of a parting I had had from my father, especially as it was he who had actually accused me of not showing him enough kindness.

It was another terrible blow to me when, later in the evening, I heard Carlo say to Maria in the kitchen:

"You should have seen how the old man raised his arm and gave his son a great blow in the face. It was the last thing he did." Carlo had seen it then, so of course Coprosich would hear all about it.

When at last I went back to the death chamber I found they had already dressed the corpse. His beautiful white hair had been brushed, no doubt by the nurse. Death had already stiffened the body, which lay there proud and menacing. His large, shapely, powerful hands were livid, but were disposed so naturally that they seemed ready to grasp and punish. After that I felt that I could not bear to see him again.

At the funeral I tried to recall my father as I had always known him since childhood, indulgent and weak; and I persuaded myself that the blow he had given me when he was dying could not have been intentional. I became gentle and kind, and the memory of my father was always with me and grew ever dearer to me. It was like a delightful dream; now that we were in perfect agreement, I was the weak one and he the strong.

I returned to the religion of my childhood and held to it for a long time. I imagined that my father could hear what I said, and I was able to tell him that it had not been my fault, but the doctor's. The lie was no longer of any importance because now he understood everything and so did I. For some time I continued these conversations with my father, which were as sweet and secret as an illicit love; to everyone else I went on laughing at religious practices, though in reality—I will confess it here—I daily with my whole heart commended my father's soul to the care of some unknown being. It is the essence of true religion that one does not need to make a loud profession of it in order to get the consolation which at certain moments one cannot do without.

The Story of My Marriage

IN T H E minds of middle-class young men life is associated with a career, and in early youth that career is usually Napoleon's. They do not of course necessarily dream of becoming Emperor, because it is possible to be like Napoleon while remaining far, far below him. Similarly, the most intense life is summarized in the most rudimentary of sounds, that of a sea-wave, which from the moment it is born until it expires is in a state of continual change. I too, like Napoleon and like the wave, could at any rate look forward to a recurring state of birth and dissolution.

My life seemed only able to supply one note without any variation, a fairly high note for which some people envied me, but nevertheless terribly monotonous. During my whole life my friends have never changed their opinion of me, and I think that since I attained years of discretion my conception of myself has not changed very much either.

Perhaps it was the tedium of producing and hearing that solitary note which put into my head the idea of getting married. Those who have not experienced it are inclined to think marriage more important than it really is. The mate you choose renews, for better or for worse, her own race in your children, but Mother Nature who ordains it thus, and yet cannot lead us straight to the goal (because when we get married it is not of children that we are thinking), persuades us that our wife will bring about our own renewal—a curious illusion which the facts in no way support. In fact one may live together quite unchanged, except that one may come to feel dislike for a being so different from oneself or envy for a being so superior.

The odd thing about my matrimonial adventure is that it began by making the acquaintance of my future father-in-law, and feeling a great admiration and affection for him before I knew that he had daughters of a marriageable age. But obviously it was no conscious purpose which drove me toward a goal of which I was completely ignorant. I deserted a girl who at one moment I thought would have suited me, and attached myself wholly to my future father-in-law. I almost feel inclined to believe in fate.

The desire for novelty which I secretly cherished in my soul found satisfaction in Giovanni Malfenti, who was so entirely different from me and from anyone whose friendship I had enjoyed up to that time. I had a considerable degree of culture owing to my having studied at the university; and still more owing to my long, and I think very instructive period of doing nothing. He, on the other hand, was an important business man, ignorant and pushing. But his ignorance gave one an impression of quiet strength which fascinated me. I loved to watch him and envied him for what he was.

Malfenti was about fifty, with a constitution of iron; a huge, tall man weighing more than two hundred pounds. The few ideas that he kept in his great head had been weighed, analyzed, and sifted by him with such care and lucidity, and their application to the numerous cases that arose each day so perfectly thought out that they seemed to have become part of himself, like his limbs or his character. I was lacking in ideas like that and I clung to him in the hope of enriching myself. Olivi had advised my going to the Tergesteo,* for he said it would be a good preparation for commercial life for me to frequent the Bourse, and that I might be able from thence to give him some useful tips. I sat down at the table presided over by my future father-in-law, and there I remained; for it seemed to me that I had at last discovered a true chair of

* The Bourse of Trieste.

commerce, such as I had been in search of for a very long time.

He soon noticed my admiration for him and responded with an affection that at once struck me as paternal. Did he know from the very beginning how things were going to turn out? When, in the enthusiasm produced in me by his great activity, I declared one evening my intention of getting rid of Olivi and managing my affairs myself, he strongly dissuaded me and even seemed rather alarmed at my proposal. He had nothing against my devoting myself to commerce, but I must always remain in close touch with Olivi, whom he also knew.

He was very ready to help me, and went so far as to write with his own hand in my notebook three commandments that he held should suffice to make any business prosper:

(1) It is not essential to work yourself, but you are lost if you can't make others work for you.

(2) There is only one great cause for remorse—to have failed to look after one's own interests.

(3) Theory is very useful in business, but only when the business has already been settled.

I knew these and ever so many other wise sayings by heart, but they were never any use to me. When I admire anyone I at once try to be like him. So I began to imitate Malfenti. I soon began to feel myself as astute as he was, and once I even thought I was the sharper of the two, for I fancied I had discovered a weak point in his way of carrying on business, and decided to tell him of it at once in order to win his respect. At the Tergesteo one day I heard him calling someone a blockhead to his face, and went up to his desk and began taking him to task. I explained to him that he was making a mistake in proclaiming his cunning far and wide. The really cunning business man, I said, ought to aim at appearing as stupid as possible.

He laughed at me. On the contrary, he said, his reputation for cunning was most useful to him. A great many people came to ask his advice and brought him all kinds of fresh news, while the sound advice he gave them was based on experience dating from the Middle Ages. Sometimes the people who brought him information ended by buying his goods. At this point he would begin to shout, for he had at last discovered the final argument that was to convince me: if you wanted to buy or sell profitably you always went to the man who had the greatest reputation for cunning. All you could hope for from your stupid man was to cheat him of his profit, but his goods were always sure to cost more than the other's because he had probably been cheated when he bought them in the first instance.

I was the person whom he thought most of in his little circle at the Tergesteo. He confided to me his business secrets, and I never betrayed them. He had chosen his confidant so well that he twice succeeded in cheating me after I became his son-in-law. The first time his sharpness cost me a lot of money, but as it was Olivi who was taken in I did not mind so much. Olivi had sent me to get some tips from him, which I did. But they turned out so badly that Olivi never forgave me, and afterwards whenever I was about to open my mouth to give him a new tip he would ask: "Who did you get that from? Your father-in-law?" In order to defend myself I was obliged to begin defending Giovanni, and I ended by feeling that I had been the cheater instead of the cheated: a very agreeable sensation.

But on the other occasion I was the victim, though I could not even then bear any ill-will to my father-in-law. Sometimes he provoked my envy, sometimes my mirth. My misfortune seemed to me a perfect illustration of his principles; never had he explained them to me so well. He laughed about it too with me. He said he was only laughing because he found my folly so comic. Once however he did confess to having played a trick on me. It was at the wedding of his daughter Ada (not, alas, to me) after he had drunk some champagne, which had an exciting effect on his great body accustomed only to drink pure water.

Then he revealed what had happened, shouting in order to overcome his mirth, which almost prevented him from speaking:

"And then out came that decree! It knocked me flat, and I was just working out how much it would cost me when in came my son-in-law. He said he wanted to take up commerce. 'Here's a splendid chance for you,' I said. He flung himself on the document and signed it right away, lest Olivi should arrive and interfere; and the deed was done!" Then he began singing my praises. "He knows the classics by heart. He knows who said this and who said that. But he doesn't know how to read the newspaper!"

It was quite true. If only I had seen that decree, which had appeared in an inconspicuous place in the five newspapers I read every day, I should not have fallen into the trap. But even so I should have had to take in at once the whole bearing of the new law, which was not such an easy matter, for it concerned the reduction of a customs tax which in its turn would send down the value of certain goods.

The following day my father-in-law denied having made such a confession. The whole business assumed the same aspect it had before the wedding breakfast. "Wine is a great inventor," he calmly said, and maintained that the decree had not been published till two days after he had concluded the affair with me. He said it was clear that if I had seen it I should have realized its import. I felt flattered by this, but it was not said to spare my feelings, for he assumed that everyone who read the papers was bound to keep his own interests in mind all the time. But when I read the papers I at once became metamorphosed into public opinion, and if I see that a tax has been reduced my thoughts turn at once to Cobden and Liberalism. This seems to me so uplifting an idea that I have no room left for my own particular merchandise.

Once I really did succeed in winning his admiration, though unfortunately on account of my least admirable qualities. He and I had both had shares for some time past in a sugar factory, which was supposed to be going to work miracles. The shares, however, began to go down, only a little, but quite regularly, and Giovanni, who had no idea of swimming against the stream, sold his and advised me to sell mine. I entirely agreed, and decided to order my broker to do so, and I made a note of it in the little book that I had lately started for that purpose. But no one looks in his pocket during the daytime, and for several days on end I kept coming across my entry in turning out my pockets before going to bed, when it was of course too late to do anything. Once I could not help calling out from sheer annoyance, and so as not to have to explain to my

wife I told her I had bitten my tongue. Next time in my
rage at such incompetence I bit my hand. "Look out for
your foot," said my wife laughing. By this time I had got
so used to it that I ceased mutilating myself. I only stared
in stupefaction at the accursed little book that was too
thin to make itself felt during the day, and then forgot all
about it till the following evening.

One day a heavy shower drove me to shelter at the
Tergesteo. There I happened to meet my broker, who told
me that during the last week those shares had almost
doubled in price.

"I'll sell them now," I cried, triumphantly.

I hastened at once to my father-in-law, who had already heard of the rise in price of the shares and was
lamenting having sold his and, a little less perhaps, having
persuaded me to sell mine.

"Patience!" he said, laughing. "It's the first time you
have lost in consequence of taking my advice."

The other affair had not been by his advice, but only
at his suggestion, which according to him was quite a
different matter.

I laughed heartily.

"But I didn't take your advice!" I was not content
with my good luck. I wanted to take credit for it. I told
him I was going to sell my shares next day, and assuming
an air of great importance I tried to make him believe that
I had received information that I had forgotten to hand
on to him, and which had induced me not to follow his
advice!

He looked extremely offended and turned away as he
answered:

"Anyone with a head like yours has no right to go into
business. And when you have played a caddish trick like
that on anyone, the least you can do is not to confess it.
You have much to learn, young man."

I hated to see him angry. It was much more amusing
to have him score off me. I told him exactly what had
happened.

"You see it is precisely someone with a head like mine
who ought to go into business."

His good humor returned immediately, and he laughed
with me.

"It is not really a profit but a compensation, in your case," he said. "That head of yours has already cost you so much that it is only fair you should recover some of your losses."

I don't know why I have spent so much time describing my quarrels with him, for there were very few of them. I was so fond of him that I always wanted to be with him, in spite of the fact that he had the habit of shouting in order to think more clearly. My tympanum managed to withstand his vociferation; if he had shouted less his immoral theories would have been more offensive, and if he had had a better education his force would not have seemed so impressive. Though I was so different from him I think he returned my affection. I should feel more certain of it, though, if he had lived longer. He went on lecturing me after my marriage, and he interspersed his instructions with outbursts of violence and sudden insults which I accepted mildly and was sure that I deserved.

I married his daughter. Mother Nature guided me mysteriously, and you will see with what violence she imposed her commands. Sometimes I study my children's faces, and try to find, besides the small chin—a sign of weakness—and the dreamy eyes that I bequeathed to them, some traces of the brute force of the man I chose to be their grandfather.

I wept at my father-in-law's grave, though his final farewell to me had not been too affectionate. On his death-bed he told me he admired my damn good luck, which enabled me to go about just as I liked while he was crucified on his bed. I asked him in surprise what I could have done to make him want me to be ill. And this is what he replied:

"If I could get rid of my illness by giving it to you, you may be sure that I would do so at once, and twice over! I have got none of your humanitarian bees in my bonnet!"

There was nothing offensive in what he said; he only wanted to repeat the other occasion when he had landed me with worthless goods. The loss of my second father was a terrible one for me, caveman, ignorant, fierce fighter though he was, for these very qualities showed up the better my own weakness, culture, and timidity. Yes, it is true I am timid! I should never have realized it but for

studying Giovanni so closely. How much better I might
have known myself today if I had been able to have him
always by me!

I soon perceived that at his desk in the Tergesteo,
where he took pleasure in revealing himself exactly as he
was, and even rather worse, Giovanni made certain reservations. He never spoke about his home life, except when
absolutely obliged, and then very quietly, in a much lower
voice than usual. He had a great respect for his home and
felt, no doubt, that not everyone who sat with him at that
table was worthy to hear anything about it. All that I could
discover was that he had four daughters, whose names all
began with the same initial, the letter A; he said that this
was so convenient because anything stamped with that initial could pass from one to the other without any alteration
being necessary. Their names, which I immediately committed to memory, were Ada, Augusta, Alberta, and Anna.
I was also told that they were all good-looking. That initial
seemed to me more significant than it really was. I dreamt
about those four girls linked together so closely by their
names. I almost felt they were a bunch of flowers. But that
initial meant something else too. My name is Zeno, and
I felt as if I were about to choose a wife from a far country.

It was perhaps only chance that the first time I called
at the Malfentis I had just ended an old love affair with a
woman who deserved, I think, rather better treatment.
But if it was chance it was a curious one. I decided to break
with her on quite frivolous grounds. The poor girl thought
that making me jealous was a good way of getting me to
propose to her. But the fact that I suspected her was
enough to make me break with her altogether. She was not
to know that I was obsessed at that moment with the idea
of marriage, and that I could not make up my mind to
marry her just because she would not have seemed enough
of a novelty. The suspicion she had tried to arouse in me
by artificial means was a proof of the superiority of matrimony, which does not admit of such suspicions. When I
realized that my suspicions were groundless it occurred to
me that she was too extravagant. Today, after twenty-four
years of honest matrimony, I am no longer of that opinion.
It was fortunate for her that I broke with her, for a few
months later she married someone who was very well off.

She married before I did, and almost immediately after my wedding I met her in my own house, for her husband was a friend of my father-in-law. We met frequently, but for some years—in fact during our youth—we were rather cold to each other and never made any allusion whatever to the past. The other day, however, she suddenly said, with a youthful blush on her face which was framed by gray hair:

"Why did you give me up?"

I spoke the truth because I had no time to invent a lie:

"I really don't remember, but there are so many other things in my life which I have forgotten too."

"I am sorry," she said, and I was already beginning to bow in expectation of a compliment. "Now that you are old I find you most entertaining." I straightened myself up with a jerk. There was nothing to say thank you for.

One day I heard that the Malfenti family had come back to town after an unusually long summer holiday in the country. I did not have to take any steps to get invited to the house, for Giovanni forestalled me.

He showed me a letter from an old friend of his, asking for news of me. We had been together at the university and I had been devoted to him so long as I thought he was going to become a great light in the scientific world. But I had lost all interest in him since he had become instead the head of a great cement firm, and now I never saw him.

I remember that first visit as if it were yesterday. It was a cold, dark autumn afternoon; and I even remember the relief of taking off my overcoat in the warm atmosphere of the house. I felt as if I were coming safely into port. I still cannot help wondering at my blindness, which I regarded then as clairvoyance. I was in pursuit of health and respectability. It is true that four girls were included under the initial A, but I at once subtracted three of them, and in my mind submitted the fourth to a searching examination. I could not, however, have really told you which qualities I demanded from her and which I abominated.

I was shown into an elegant drawing-room, furnished in two different styles—Louis Quatorze and Venetian—the latter containing a good deal of leather stamped in gold. There was in fact a profusion of gold. The room was di-

vided in two, and in the window-half Augusta sat reading.
She shook hands with me, seemed to know my name, and
said that they were expecting me, as her father had said
that I should be coming. Then she went to call her mother.

Well, that was the end of one of the four girls with
the same initial, as far as I was concerned. How could
they have called her pretty? The first thing that I noticed
about her was that she squinted, and so badly sometimes
that if one had not seen her for a while that squint seemed
to sum up her whole personality. Her hair was not very
thick and of a dull shade of blondness without any lights
in it; and though she had not exactly a bad figure she was
rather broad for her age. In the few moments I remained
alone I thought to myself: "If all the others are like this
one . . . !"

Soon after, the bunch of girls was reduced to two, for
the one who now came in with her mother was only eight
years old. She was a charming child with long, curly golden
hair hanging loose over her shoulders. Her round, sweet
baby face was like one of those pensive angel faces painted
by Raphael—so long as she did not speak!

Of my mother-in-law I feel, like many another, a slight
reluctance to speak freely. I have been fond of her for many
years now, because she is my mother, but I am telling an
old story in which she did not play a friendly part toward
me. I intend, however, not to say a single disrespectful
word about her in this notebook, though she will never
see it. Besides, her intervention was so brief that I have almost forgotten it; just a little push which, administered at
the right moment, was enough to make me lose my balance. I might have lost it even without her intervention,
and who knows whether she was really responsible for
what actually happened? She is too well brought up ever to
drink too much and so let me into her secrets, like her husband. That sort of thing could never happen to her, so I am
not really very sure about the facts of my story, nor whether
it was because she was so designing or because I was so stupid
that I married the very one of her daughters I least wanted
to.

I may say, in passing, that at the time I first called on
her my mother-in-law was still a good-looking woman.
She dressed expensively, but with quiet elegance and no

display. Everything about her was harmonious and subdued.

The mutual understanding between my parents-in-law was just such a picture of married bliss as I had dreamed of. They were perfectly happy together; he shouted at her and she smiled back at him with a smile that expressed at the same time her agreement and her sympathy. She loved her big husband, and he probably won her heart and kept it by his business ability and extraordinary success. It was admiration far more than self-interest which bound her to him, an admiration that I shared and could therefore readily understand. An immense vitality gave a perpetual impetus to his life, though exercised in so restricted a sphere; a kind of cage containing merchandise, with two hostile parties contracting for it, and perpetually weaving fresh combinations and patterns. He told her everything about his business, and she was too tactful ever to give him any advice, knowing well that it would only distract him. He needed her silent sympathy and sometimes would hurry home during the day, merely in order to monologize aloud, but quite under the impression that he went to ask his wife's advice.

I was not surprised to learn that he was faithless to her, and that she knew all about it and bore him no ill will. I had been married just a year when Giovanni told me one day, in a great state of excitement, that he had lost a very important letter, and wanted to have a look through the papers he had given me in the hope that he might find it among them. A few days later he told me gleefully that he had found it in his own pocketbook. "Was it from a woman?" He nodded, and congratulated himself on his good fortune. Shortly afterwards, when my mother-in-law and my wife accused me of having mislaid some papers, I remarked that I was not so lucky as my father-in-law, whose papers found their way back into his pocketbook of their own accord. My mother-in-law laughed so heartily that I felt certain it was she who had replaced the missing paper. Evidently it made no difference to their relationship. Everyone has to deal with his love affairs in his own way. And I must say that I don't think these two chose by any means the most foolish.

I was received very kindly. Signora Malfenti apologized

for bringing little Anna with her, saying it was the hour
when she always looked after her. The child gazed at me
with her great serious eyes. When Augusta returned and
sat down on a little sofa facing the one on which I was
sitting with her mother, the child went and nestled in her
sister's lap, watching me all the time with an undivided
attention that amused me, because I could not guess what
was going on in her little head.

The conversation was not very lively at first. Signora
Malfenti, like all properly brought up people, was rather
dull when you met her for the first time. She would go on
asking about the friend who she pretended had introduced
me to the house, and whose Christian name I could not
even remember.

At last Ada and Alberta came in. I breathed again.
They were both lovely, and brought into the drawing-room
a radiance which had been quite lacking till then. They
were both dark, tall, and slender, but very different one
from the other. The choice I had to make was not difficult.
Alberta could not have been more than seventeen years old.
Though she was dark she had, like her mother, a pink
transparent skin, which added to her childish appearance.
Ada, on the contrary, was already a woman. Her eyes
shone gravely out of the pallor of her face, framed by
thick curly hair that was gracefully though severely arranged.

It is difficult to discover the first beginnings of a sentiment that was later to become so passionate, but I am
certain that in this case the so-called *coup de foudre* was
lacking. But the absence of that lightning flash was com-
pensated by my immediate conviction that she was the
woman I wanted for my wife, the woman who was to
guide me to moral and physical health in the holy monog-
amy of marriage. Looking back I am surprised that the
coup de foudre should have been lacking and that I should
have had that conviction instead. Men usually do not
seek in a wife the qualities they both adore and despise
in a mistress. So I suppose all Ada's grace and beauty was
not revealed to me at first, and I was charmed and delighted with qualities that I myself endowed her with,
such as seriousness and energy; the very qualities, slightly
modified, which I already loved in her father. If, as I still
believe, Ada really did possess these qualities as a girl, I

can account myself a good observer, though a rather blind one. The first time I saw Ada I was only conscious of one desire: to fall in love with her, because that was the first step necessary to marrying her. I applied myself to it with the energy that I always devote to measures of hygiene. I don't really remember how long it took me; perhaps I succeeded in the relatively short period of my first visit.

Giovanni had evidently talked about me a lot to his daughters. They knew, among other things, that I had deserted law for chemistry, and gone back again to law. I tried to explain to them that if a man confined himself to only one subject the greater part of knowledge remained hidden from him. And I said:

"Were it not that I was obliged to take life seriously [I did not add that it was only my decision to marry which had made me realize this necessity] I should have gone on from subject to subject."

Then to make them laugh I said it was odd that I always gave up a subject just before the examinations came on.

"Mere chance," I added with a smile intended to suggest that I was not speaking the truth. The truth was that I had changed my subject at every imaginable time of the year.

And so I set out to win Ada, and persisted in trying to make her laugh at me, forgetting that what I had first chosen her for was her seriousness. I am rather fantastic, it is true, but to her I must have seemed positively unbalanced. It was not entirely my fault, as may be seen from the fact that Augusta and Alberta, whom I had not chosen, judged me quite differently. But Ada, who indeed was quite serious enough to be already casting round her beautiful eyes in search of a man with whom to build her nest, was incapable of falling in love with anyone who made her laugh. She did laugh of course a great deal, too much in fact, and her laughter covered with ridicule the person who had provoked it. This was a bad trait in her and ended by bringing her great trouble, but at first it was damaging only to me. If only I could have learnt when to have held my tongue things might have gone differently. I might at least have given her an opportunity to talk herself, so that I could have seen what she was really like and protected myself against her.

The four girls were seated on the sofa. They were rather cramped, though Anna was sitting in Augusta's lap. They looked charming sitting together like that. I observed them with secret satisfaction, because I was well on the way to falling in love. Yes, they really were charming! Augusta's rather mouse-colored hair showed up to greater advantage the rich brown of the others.

I had been talking about the university, and Alberta, who had only one more year at school, told me about her work. She complained that she found Latin so difficult. I said I was not surprised, because it was a language unsuited to women; so much so that I thought that even among the ancient Romans the women had talked Italian. For my part, I said, Latin had always been my favorite subject. I was foolish enough soon afterwards to quote something in Latin which Alberta was obliged to correct. It was really most unfortunate, but I made light of it and told Alberta that when she had been two or three years at the university she would have to look out for her Latin quotations too.

Ada, who had just been spending several months in England with her father, said that lots of girls there knew Latin. Then in her grave and not at all musical voice, which was rather lower than one would have expected in such a delicate creature, she described how entirely different English women were from Italian. They were always forming societies for philanthropic, religious, or economic purposes. Her sisters encouraged her to talk because they wanted to hear again things that at that time seemed very strange to girls in a town like ours. So Ada told us about women who became presidents or journalists or secretaries or political agitators, and who would go up on the platform and address hundreds of people without blushing and without losing their head if anyone interrupted or questioned their statements. She told it all quite simply without any emphasis, and with no idea of making us laugh or exciting our astonishment.

I liked her simple way of talking all the more because I myself could not open my mouth without misrepresenting things or people, for otherwise I should have seen no use in talking at all. Talking seemed to me an event in itself which must not be hampered by any other events

But I had a particular dislike for perfidious Albion,

and I showed it without fear of offending Ada who, by the way, had shown neither dislike nor love for England. I had spent several months there, but I never got to know anyone in good society because en route I had lost the letters of introduction with which some business friend of my father had provided me. So I only frequented a few French and Italian families in London, and had come to the conclusion that all really nice people in London had come from abroad. My knowledge of English was very limited. With the help of my friends I arrived at understanding a certain amount about English life, but above all I was given to understand that they hated anyone who was not English.

I described to the girls how unpleasant it was to have to live among enemies. I should have stood it out, however, and managed to endure England for the six months prescribed by my father and Olivi, who wanted me to study business methods in England (which I never did because all their business seems to be carried on in secret corners), had I not been the victim of a most unfortunate accident. I had gone into a book-shop to buy a dictionary. On the counter was stretched a huge and magnificent Angora cat whose soft fur seemed to invite caresses. Well! Just because I stroked it very gently the treacherous beast sprang at me and gave me a horrible scratch on the hand. From that moment I found England unendurable, and the very next day I was in Paris.

Augusta, Alberta, and Signora Malfenti burst out laughing. But Ada was absolutely bewildered and thought she must have misheard me. Surely I had meant it was the bookseller who scratched me? I had to tell the whole story again, which is always tiresome because one never tells it so well the second time.

The learned Alberta came to my aid. The Ancients, she said, also allowed themselves to be guided by animals in making any important decision.

I refused to accept her aid. There was nothing oracular about that cat; it was fate itself.

Ada opened her eyes and insisted on further explanations. "Do you mean to say that cat symbolized for you the whole English race?"

How unfortunate I was! Though the story was quite true, it had seemed to me as instructive and interesting as if it had been invented to point a moral. It was easy enough to understand, if one reflected that in Italy, where I know and love so many people, that cat's action would not have acquired such significance. But I did not point this out. I said instead:

"I am sure no Italian cat could have been capable of such an action."

Then Ada laughed too, until I thought she would never stop. My success was really too great, for I played such a poor part in the story, and I only made the adventure seem more ridiculous by adding further explanations:

"Even the bookseller was amazed at the cat's behavior, because it was generally so friendly to everyone else. There was no getting over it; it happened to me just because it was me, or perhaps because I was Italian. *It was really disgusting.* There was nothing for it but flight."

Then something happened which really ought to have opened my eyes and saved me from myself. Little Anna, who all this time had been sitting motionless with her eyes fixed on me, suddenly said out loud what Ada had been thinking. She cried out:

"But he's mad, isn't he? Quite, quite mad!"

Signora Malfenti scolded her:

"Will you be quiet? Aren't you ashamed to break in like that when grown-up people are talking?"

The scolding only made it worse. Anna burst out again:

"He *is* mad! He talks to cats! You ought to get some rope and tie him up at once!"

Augusta, blushing with annoyance, got up and carried her off, telling her that she was very naughty and at the same time apologizing to me. But when they had got as far as the door the spiteful little creature managed to catch my eyes, made a horrid face at me, and called out again:

"They'll come and tie you up, you see if they don't!"

The onslaught had been so sudden that it took me quite a few moments to recover myself. But I was somewhat relieved to notice that Ada suffered at seeing her own feelings expressed for her in this way. The child's impertinence had drawn us together.

I laughed heartily as I told them that I had at home a stamped certificate guaranteeing that I was perfectly sane in every respect. And so I came to tell them about the trick

I had played on my father. I suggested bringing along the certificate to show to little Anna.

When I said I must be going they would not hear of it. They wanted me to forget first the scratches I had received from their own kitten. They begged me to stay on a little and offered me a cup of tea.

I think I realized from the first that if I wanted Ada to like me I ought to be rather different from what I was; but I thought I should have no difficulty in becoming what she would like me to be. We went on talking of my father's death and I thought if I showed her what a great grief it was to me she would sympathize with me. But in my desire to become like her I very soon became unnatural and, as you will see, only succeeded in estranging her still more. I said that the pain one suffered at a loss like that was so great that if I had children I should try to make them love me less, so that when I died their sorrow would be less unbearable. I was a little embarrassed when they asked what steps I proposed taking to attain this object. Ill-treating them? Beating them? Alberta said, laughingly: "The safest way would be to kill them yourself!"

I saw that Ada was afraid of displeasing me; so she remained silent. But not all her good will could do more for me than that. At last she said she was sure it was out of kindness that I wanted to arrange my children's life for them, but she did not think it was right to live by preparing yourself for death. I stuck to my idea, and asserted that death was really the great organizing force of life. I was always thinking about death and so I had only one sorrow: the certainty that I must die. Everything else became so unimportant that I could welcome it with a smile, even laugh at it. I think my reason for talking in this way was that I wanted to show them I had a sense of humor, which had often before made me popular with women. She looked thoughtful and confessed with some hesitation that she did not like that way of looking at things. If you make life of little value its balance becomes more disturbed than Mother Nature has ordained. She was really saying that I did not suit her, but to me it seemed that I had scored a success, since I had succeeded in making her thoughtful.

Alberta quoted an ancient philosopher whose view of life, she said, was rather like mine, and Augusta added that laughter was a splendid thing. Her father laughed a great deal too.

"Yes, when business goes well," said Signora Malfenti.

At last that memorable visit came to an end.

It is the most difficult thing in the world to make exactly the marriage you want; as you may see from my own case, where my resolution to get married was made long before my choice of a bride. Why didn't I go about and meet a great many more girls before choosing one? No. I really felt I should dislike seeing too many women, and I did not want to tire myself. When I had chosen a girl I might at least have examined her more closely in order to discover whether she was prepared to meet me half-way, as is the custom in novels with a happy ending. But I straight away chose a girl with a very deep voice and rather rebellious though severely dressed hair, and thought that so serious a young lady would surely not refuse a rich man of good family who was intelligent and not bad-looking. It is true that we disagreed over the very first words we exchanged, but I reflected that discords resolve themselves into harmonies. I even thought, I must confess: She shall stay just as she is, for that is how I like her; but if she wants it, I will change to please her. I was, on the whole, very modest, for it is undoubtedly easier to change oneself than to re-educate someone else.

It did not take long for the Malfenti family to become the center of my life. I spent every evening with Giovanni who, after he had introduced me into his household, had become more friendly and confidential than ever. His great friendliness gave me courage. At first I only called on his wife and daughters once a week, then several times, and at last I took to going every afternoon and spending several hours there. I had no lack of pretexts for establishing myself in the house, and I think I can honestly say that a good many were offered me. Sometimes I brought my violin and had some music with Augusta, who was the only one in the house who played the piano. It was a pity Ada did not play. It was also a pity that I played the violin so badly, and most unfortunate that Augusta was not a great musician. In every sonata we played I was obliged to cut out some passage that was too difficult for me, because, as I quite untruthfully said, I had not touched the violin for so long. An amateur pianist almost always plays better than an amateur violinist, and Augusta's technique was quite good; but though I did not play nearly as well as she did, I was dissatisfied with her playing and inwardly thought: "If I could play as well as you, I would certainly play better." While I was busy judging Augusta others were doing the same by me and, as I discovered later, none too favorably. Augusta would have liked to have some more practice at our sonatas, but I noticed that Ada was bored by it, and I pretended two or three times to have forgotten to bring my violin. After that Augusta did not mention it again.

But alas, it was not only the time I was in their house that I spent with Ada. Very soon the thought of her accompanied me all day long. She was the woman I had chosen, therefore she must be mine, and I endowed her with every ideal quality to make my life's prize more beautiful. All the qualities lacking in myself, and which I longed to possess, I gave to her; she was to become not only my wife but a second mother to me, who would equip me for a full virile life, encourage me to fight and help me to be victorious.

In my dreams I made her more beautiful too, physically. I have run after a good many women in the course of my life and succeeded in winning a fair number of them. In my dreams I possessed them all. I do not of course make them more beautiful by actually altering their features, but I do as an artist friend of mine, a very subtle painter, who when he is painting the portrait of a beautiful woman calls up vividly to his mind some other exquisite object, like fine porcelain for instance. It is a dangerous proceeding, for it is not only confined to dreams, and the lady continues in real life to keep something of the fruit, the flower, or the porcelain with which you adorned her.

It is not easy to relate my courtship of Ada. There was a long subsequent period of my life in which I tried to forget my stupid adventure. I felt so thoroughly ashamed of myself that I longed to protest loudly that it could not have been I who had made such a fool of myself. Who else then could it have been? But the mere fact of protesting gave me a certain amount of relief. If I had behaved like that ten years ago, when I was twenty, it would not have been so bad. But to be stricken with folly, just because I had decided to marry, seemed really too unjust.

That I, who had had every sort of experience, and had
carried through my adventures in a spirit of reckless daring,
should be reduced to trying to touch my lady's hand without her noticing it, like any timid schoolboy, and then
almost worshipping my own hand for having been hallowed
by such a contact! This was the purest adventure of my
life; and yet, though I am old now, I still remember it as
the most shameful. All that stuff was out of place, it came
at the wrong time; it was like a boy of ten going back to
his nurse's breast. Disgusting!

I simply can't explain why I kept hesitating to propose
to her, and did not insist on her making up her mind
whether she would have me or not. I walked straight from
my dreams into that house; I counted the stairs up to the
first floor and said to myself: If they are even that is a
proof that she loves me. It was an uneven number: forty-
three. Yet each time I went to her with the same assurance,
and each time I talked about something quite different.
Ada had never had any opportunity of rejecting me, but
still I did not speak. I think in Ada's place I certainly
would have given that boy of thirty a good kick and shown
him the door.

In a certain sense I was not an exact replica of the
twenty-year-old inamorato who waits mutely for his beloved
to throw her arms round his neck. I expected nothing of
the kind. I meant to speak to her, but later. If I waited so
long it was because I was so unsure of myself. I was always
waiting to become nobler and stronger, more worthy of my
divine mistress. This might always happen from one day to
another. Why not wait?

But I am ashamed not to have realized earlier that I
was heading for a disaster. I had to deal with a most single-
minded nature, but by continually dreaming about her I
had transformed her into a consummate flirt. My fierce
resentment when she at last made me understand she did
not want me was quite unjust. But I had so closely inter-
woven dreams with reality that it was hard for me to
believe she had actually never even kissed me.

It is a great sign of inferiority in a man not to understand women. I had never made a mistake before, and I
think I deceived myself about Ada because my relations
had been false with her from the start. I approached her
not in order to win her, but with the direct intention of

marrying her, which is an unusual way for love to take; a wide and comfortable way perhaps, but it does not lead to the goal, though very near it. Love approached in this way lacks its chief characteristic: the subjection of the female. The male sets about his task idly, and this inertia may spread to all his senses, including those of sight and hearing.

I took flowers every day to each of the three girls, and regaled them with my eccentricities; above all I was guilty of inconceivable levity in telling them the story of my life.

Everyone remembers his past with greater vividness as the present becomes more important. Dying men in their last delirium are supposed to see their whole life spread out before them. My past clutched at me now with the violence of a last farewell, because I had the feeling that I was leaving it far behind me. And I was always telling the sisters about this past, encouraged by the eager attention of Augusta and Alberta, which covered up, I fancy, Ada's indifference, though of this I am not quite sure. Augusta, who was of a sweet disposition, was easily moved, and Alberta listened to the recital of my student scrapes with cheeks flushed with desire to take part herself in similar adventures.

It was long afterwards that Augusta told me that none of them had believed my stories to be true. Augusta liked them all the more on that account for, as my invention, they seemed to her to belong to me more than if fate had actually inflicted them on me. Alberta delighted in the parts she thought untrue because they seemed to her to contain excellent suggestions. The only one who was really outraged by my lies was the serious Ada. With all my efforts I only succeeded in doing as the famous marksman, who really did hit the center of the bullseye, but only of the target next to the one he was aiming at.

And yet my anecdotes were for the most part true. I don't quite remember in which part, for I told them to so many other girls before Malfenti's daughters that without any conscious alteration on my part they constantly suffered slight modifications tending to make them more interesting. They began to be true from the moment when it would have been impossible for me to tell the story differently. I am no longer interested in proving their truth. I should be sorry to undeceive Augusta, who likes to believe

that I invented them. As for Ada, I believe she has now
changed her opinion and believes them to be true.

My entire failure with Ada became clear the moment
I made up my mind to speak openly to her. I was very
surprised and at first incredulous. She had never said a
single word that might have revealed her dislike, and I shut
my eyes to all those small acts that could not be interpreted
as showing sympathy. And then I had never spoken the
necessary word, and was thus able to persuade myself that
Ada did not know that I was there all ready to marry her,
and might suppose that I, the eccentric and unscrupulous
student, was after something quite different.

The misunderstanding continued because of my too
definitely matrimonial intentions. I had come by now to
desire Ada with my whole heart; my fancy had made her
cheek still smoother, her hands and feet still smaller, and
her waist still more slender; I desired her as my wife and
as my mistress. But one's first step in approaching a woman
is the decisive one.

On three consecutive days I found myself received
only by the other two girls. Ada's absence was explained
the first time by a duty visit, the second by her not feeling
well; and on the third occasion no excuse was given at all,
until in some alarm I asked for one. Augusta, to whom I
happened to have addressed myself, made no reply. Alberta,
whom she had looked at, as if invoking her help, answered
for her: Ada had gone to see an aunt.

My breath failed me for a moment. It was clear that
Ada wanted to avoid me. Till the day before I had borne
her absence patiently, and had even prolonged my visit in
the hope that perhaps she would come in. But on this last
day I stayed a short while longer, unable to say a single
word; till at last, pleading a sudden headache, I got up to
go. It is curious that my first feeling, on becoming conscious of Ada's determination to avoid me, was one of
anger and contempt. I even thought of appealing to
Giovanni to call his daughter to order. A man who is bent
on marrying can even stoop to such an action as that,
reverting to the customs of his ancestors.

Ada's third absence was to become still more significant. I discovered by chance that she was in the house, but
shut up in her room.

I must say that there was one other person in the

house whom I had not succeeded in winning over: and this was little Anna. She no longer attacked me when the others were there, because they had taken her severely to task for it. Sometimes she even came in with her sisters and stayed listening to my stories. When I was going away she would join me at the door and ask me prettily to bend down to her; then, rising on the tips of her toes, she would put her mouth right up to my ear and say in a whisper, so that nobody else could hear:

"But you're mad, you are quite mad!"

The comic part is that when the others were there the little hypocrite treated me very politely. If Signora Malfenti was in the room she would climb up on to her knee, and her mother would say, caressing her:

"How good my little Anna has become, hasn't she?"

I did not contradict her and the good little Anna went on calling me mad. I smiled a sickly smile that might have been interpreted as gratitude. I hoped the child would not dare to tell her elders how rude she had been to me, and nothing would have induced me to tell Ada what her sister thought of me. In the end that child quite embarrassed me. If my eye caught hers while I was talking to the others I at once tried to look somewhere else, and it was difficult to do it naturally. I know I blushed; I felt the child's innocent judgment might do me harm. I took her presents, but could not succeed in taming her. She must have been conscious of her own power and of my weakness, and when anyone else was there she would scrutinize me impertinently. I think we all have delicate spots in our conscience as we do in our bodies, which we keep covered and prefer not to think about. We do not know exactly what they are, but we know they are there. I was obliged to look away from that infant's penetrating gaze.

But on this particular day, when I was leaving the house alone and quite cast down, and she ran after me as usual and wanted me to bend down and listen to the familiar compliment, I turned on her a face of such genuine madness, and clutched the air with such threatening fingers that she ran away screaming and crying.

And that was how I came to see Ada, for it was she who ran out when she heard the child screaming. The little girl explained between her sobs that I had threatened her because she said I was mad:

"But he *is* mad, and I am going to say so. What harm is there in it?"

I paid no attention to the child, I was so taken aback to see that Ada was in the house. So her sisters had lied, or rather Alberta had, for Augusta had only done it vicariously through her. During the second in which I guessed the truth, I saw everything quite clearly. I said to Ada:

"I am glad to see you. I understood you had gone to see your aunt."

She did not reply at once, because she was bending over the weeping child. Her delay in giving me the explanation I felt I deserved made the blood rise violently to my head. I could not find a single word. I took a step forward as if to go out at the front door, and if Ada had not spoken I should have gone away and never come back again. I was so angry that it seemed to me the easiest thing in the world to give up the dream I had cherished for so long.

But before I could get out she stopped me and said, blushing, that she had just come back as her aunt was not at home.

It sufficed to calm me. How sweet she looked, bending in such a motherly way over the child, who still went on crying! Her body was so flexible that it seemed to become smaller in order to fit the child's small body. I stood gazing at her, and again considered her entirely mine.

I felt so much at peace that I wanted to make her forget the resentment I had shown just now, and I was infinitely polite both to her and Anna; I laughed and said:

"She so often calls me mad that I wanted to let her see what a mad man really looks like. Please forgive me. And you mustn't be frightened, Anna dear, for I am quite a kind madman."

Ada was very polite too. When the child still went on crying she scolded her and asked me to forgive her. If Anna had got cross and run away I should probably have proposed; I should have uttered a phrase, which is doubtless to be found in some grammars of a foreign language, so well adapted is it for simplifying one's life, if one happens to be living in a foreign country and does not know the language: "May I ask your father for your hand?" It was the first time I had wanted to get married, so that I was really in quite an unknown country. Hitherto my way of approach to the women I had had to do with had been quite different. I had put my hands on them at once without asking anyone's permission.

But I could not bring myself even to pronounce those few words. They ought to take a certain time to say, and they ought to be accompanied by an appealing expression of the face which it would be difficult to assume after my encounter with Anna, and one might say with Ada too; besides I could hear Signora Malfenti approaching from the far end of the passage, attracted by the child's screams.

I put out my hand, which Ada at once shook warmly, and said:

"Good-by, till tomorrow. Say good-by to your mother for me."

I could hardly bear to let go of that hand which lay so trustfully in mine. I felt that by going away then I was losing a unique opportunity, for at that moment Ada was ready to treat me with the utmost courtesy in order to make up for her sister's unkindness. I followed the impulse of the moment, bent down and touched her hand with my lips. Then I hastily opened the door and went out, while Ada, whose left hand was engaged in holding Anna, still clinging to her skirts, went on holding out her right hand, which my lips had touched, and gazing at it in amazement as if she wanted to see if anything were written on it. I don't think Signora Malfenti saw what had taken place.

I stood a few moments on the steps, rather startled by what I had done, which was quite unpremeditated. Was it still possible for me to go back to the door I had shut behind me, ring the bell and ask to see Ada, and speak the words she had looked for in vain on her hand? I did not think so. I should have been lacking in dignity if I had shown too much impatience. Besides, when I announced that I was coming back I had really prepared her for my declaration of love. It only rested with her to give me an opportunity to make it. At last I had stopped telling stories to the three girls in a bunch and had kissed the hand of one of them.

But the remainder of the day passed uneasily enough. I was restless and anxious. I said to myself that my uneasiness was due only to my impatience to get my adventure cleared up. I tried to persuade myself that if Ada were

to refuse me I should calmly set about looking for another
wife. My attachment to her was a deliberate resolve on my
part, and I had only to make another in order to cancel it
completely. I did not grasp the fact that there were no
other women in the world for me at that moment, that it
was only Ada I wanted.

The night that followed seemed to me to be terribly
long; I hardly slept at all. Since my father's death I had
given up my night life, and it would have been incongruous
to return to it now that I had made up my mind to get
married. So I went to bed early, longing for sleep, which
alone obliterates time.

By daylight I had placed the blindest confidence in
Ada's explanation of her absence from the drawing-room
on three successive occasions during my visit, a confidence
based on the sound conviction that the serious young
woman I had chosen would be incapable of a lie. But
during the night my faith in her diminished. I began to
wonder whether it was not I myself who had told her of
the excuse Alberta had made about her visit to her aunt,
when Augusta had refused to answer. I could not quite
remember what I had said to her—my head had been in
such a whirl—but I thought it had probably been I who
provided her with an excuse. That was a pity. If I had not
done so perhaps she would have invented some other
excuse and I, if I had caught her lying, should have known
exactly what to think.

I had occasion to discover the immense importance
that Ada had assumed for me, because in order to try and
calm myself I found myself saying that if she would not
have me I would give up all idea of marrying. So that her
refusal would change the whole of my life. And I went on
dreaming, comforting myself with the thought that her
refusal would probably be a stroke of good luck for me.
I called to mind the saying of the Greek philosopher that
repentance awaited the married man as much as the unmarried. I had not yet quite lost the capacity for laughing
at my adventure; the only capacity I lacked was that of
going to sleep.

I fell asleep just as it was beginning to get light.
When I woke up it was already so late that only a few
hours now divided me from the moment when I might
again present myself at the Malfentis. So there was really

no need for me to go on exercising my fancy on the question of the state of Ada's mind. But it is difficult to restrain oneself from brooding on a matter that concerns one so nearly. Man would be a more fortunate animal if he could. While I was occupied in dressing, which I did that day with exaggerated care, I could think of only one thing: Had I done well in kissing Ada's hand, or had I done ill in not kissing her also on the lips?

That very morning I had an idea that did me, I think, a good deal of harm, in that it robbed me of the small amount of manly initiative remaining to me in my queer adolescent condition. A painful doubt occurred to me; supposing Ada were forced to marry me by her parents without loving me at all, even perhaps disliking me? I was quite sure that all the other members of her family, Giovanni, her mother, Augusta, and Alberta, were very fond of me. It was only Ada about whom I was not so sure. The usual popular novel began to take shape in my mind, about the girl who is forced by her family to marry a man she hates. But of course I should never have consented to that. That was another reason why I must speak to Ada alone at once. The phrase I had prepared would be no use at all. I must look into her eyes and say: "Do you love me?" And if she said yes I should fold her in my arms, and should know by the beating of her heart if she were telling the truth.

So it seemed to me that I was prepared for any emergency. Yet I was suddenly to find myself confronted with an examination for which I had forgotten to revise the very text I was to be examined on.

Signora Malfenti received me alone, and made me sit down in a corner of the big drawing-room. She at once began a lively conversation, and did not allow me a moment's breathing space to ask for news of her daughters. For this reason I was rather distrait and kept repeating my lesson to myself so as to have it all ready at a favorable moment. Suddenly I was called to attention as by a trumpet call. The Signora was about to make a speech! She assured me of her and her husband's friendly feelings toward me, and of the affection all the family felt for me, including little Anna. We had known each other for such a long time. We had seen each other every day for the last four months.

"Five!" I hastened to correct her, for I had been counting them up during the night, and remembered that my first visit had been in the autumn, while now it was well on into the spring.

"Yes! Five!" said the lady, lingering over the words as if she were trying to visualize my arithmetic. Then she added with an air of reproach: "I feel that you are compromising Augusta."

"Augusta?" I repeated, thinking I could not have heard correctly.

"Yes!" she said decidedly. "You are putting ideas into her head, and compromising her."

I ingenuously betrayed my real feelings:

"But I hardly ever see Augusta."

She made a gesture of surprise and, as it seemed to me, of pained surprise.

Meanwhile I was thinking hard in order to arrive at some explanation of what seemed to be a mistake, but a mistake of which I at once realized the significance. I looked back over the last five months, and saw myself day after day engaged in watching Ada. I had played with Augusta, and it is true that I had talked to her occasionally instead of to Ada, because she was always ready to listen to me; but I only talked to her hoping that she would hand on my stories, sealed with her approval, to Ada. Ought I to speak plainly to the lady and tell her of my intentions with regard to Ada? But only a short time before I had made up my mind to speak first to Ada herself and discover what she really felt toward me. Perhaps if I had spoken openly to Signora Malfenti things would have turned out differently and, not being able to marry Ada, I should not have married Augusta either. I let myself be guided by the resolution I had made before seeing Signora Malfenti, and received her extraordinary statements in silence.

I was thinking hard, but somewhat confusedly. I wanted to understand; I felt I must find out quickly what she was driving at. If you open your eyes too wide you don't see so well. The possibility of their wanting to turn me out of the house did occur to me, but I thought I might dismiss it. I was innocent, for I had not paid court to Augusta, whom they wanted to protect. But perhaps they were only attributing to me these designs on Augusta in order not to compromise Ada. But why should they want so much to protect Ada, who was no longer a child? I had never even stroked her hair except in my dreams. In reality I had only just touched her hand with my lips. I dreaded their forbidding me to come to the house, because before leaving it I must speak to Ada. I said in a trembling voice:

"Tell me what I ought to do so as not to offend anyone."

She hesitated. I would rather have had to deal with Giovanni, who always thought at the top of his voice. Then she said firmly, but with an effort to appear polite which revealed itself in her tone:

"It would be better if you came here less often for the present; let us say two or three times a week, instead of every day."

I am certain that if she had told me rudely to go away and never to come back, I should have clung to my purpose and implored her to put up with me for two or three days more, so that I might clear up my relations with Ada. But her words, which were so much milder than I expected, gave me courage to show my resentment:

"If you wish it I will never set foot in this house again."

The result was what I had hoped. She protested, saying again how fond they all were of me, and begging me not to be angry with her. I magnanimously promised all she wanted: to refrain from coming to the house again for four or five days, and after that to come only two or three times a week; but above all not to bear her any illwill. When I had promised this I made as though I would carry it out at once and rose to go. The Signora laughingly protested:

"There can be no fear of your compromising *me*, so you may stay on a little."

When I asked her to excuse me on account of an engagement that I had only that instant remembered (the truth being that I was longing to be by myself in order to reflect on my extraordinary adventure), she positively begged me to remain, saying that she would look on it as a proof that I was not angry with her. So I stayed on, though I was on thorns at having to listen to her empty

chatter about the latest fashions, which she did *not* intend
to follow, about the theater and the dry weather that had
ushered in the spring.

But I was soon glad I had stayed on, for I began to
feel I needed a further explanation. I interrupted her unceremoniously with the question:

"Does the whole family know that you have asked me
to stay away from the house?"

At first she seemed to have already forgotten our pact.
Then she protested:

"Stay away from the house? But only for a few days,
you know. I shall say nothing about it to anyone, not even
my husband, and I should be grateful if you would use a
like discretion."

I promised that too; I even promised that if any of
them asked me why I did not come so often I would invent
some excuse or other. For the moment I believed what she
had said, and pictured Ada being surprised and distressed
by my unexpected absence. A flattering picture!

I went on sitting there in the hope that I might have
some fresh inspiration, while the lady meandered on about
the cost of provisions, which had lately gone up so terribly
in price.

Instead of a fresh inspiration their Aunt Rosina
arrived. She was a sister of Giovanni, older than him and
much less intelligent. But she had certain moral traits in
common with him which were sufficient to make one
recognize her as his sister. She had the same sense of her
own importance and of what was owing to her; but the
effect was rather comic, since she had no means of imposing herself. She also had the same bad habit of raising
her voice on the slightest provocation. She held that she
had so many rights in her brother's house that for a long
time, as I afterwards learned, she regarded his wife as an
interloper. She was an old maid and lived with one servant
whom she always spoke of as her greatest enemy. When
she died she asked my wife to keep an eye on the house till
this servant had left it. Everyone in Giovanni's house stood
in awe of her and put up with her tyrannies as best they
could.

I still did not take my leave. Aunt Rosina liked Ada
the best of all her nieces. I felt a desire to win her good
will, and sought for an amiable remark to address to her.

I vaguely remembered that the last time I had seen her (or caught a glimpse of her, for I had not then felt the need of looking closely at her) her nieces had remarked, directly she left, that she was not looking very well. I remembered one of them saying: "It's the temper she flies into with her servant that gives her that bilious complexion."

I had found what I wanted. Looking affectionately into the old woman's face, I said:

"You are looking much better, Madam."

I ought never to have said it. She stared at me in astonishment and remarked stiffly:

"I am always quite well. Why should I look better?"

She wanted to know when I had seen her last. I could not remember the date exactly, but I reminded her we had spent a whole afternoon together, sitting with her nieces in the drawing-room, but not in the half where we were sitting now, in the other half. I wanted to show her how much interest I took in her, but she demanded so many explanations that it became terribly tedious. I grew ashamed of my deception and began to feel uncomfortable.

Signora Malfenti smilingly intervened:

"But you don't mean to suggest that Aunt Rosina has got fatter?"

The devil! So that was what had made the old lady angry. She was almost as big as her brother, but was still hoping to get thin.

"Fatter? Of course not. I only meant that the Signora was looking much better in the face."

I tried to preserve an affectionate demeanor, and was obliged forcibly to restrain myself from being rude to her. Aunt Rosina did not appear to be satisfied even then. She had not been ill for a long time and could not understand why she had struck me as looking unwell. Signora Malfenti humored her:

"On the contrary, it is characteristic of her that she always looks the same," she said turning to me. "Don't you agree?"

I did agree; it was quite obvious. But I took leave at once. I held out my hand very cordially to Aunt Rosina, hoping to put her in a good humor, but when she took it she looked the other way.

I had hardly crossed the threshold when my state of

mind altered completely. What a relief! I was no longer
obliged to speculate on Signora Malfenti's intentions, nor
make an effort to please Aunt Rosina. I firmly believe that
but for the intervention of Aunt Rosina that old schemer
Signora Malfenti would have achieved her end, and that
I should have left the house perfectly satisfied with my
treatment. I descended the steps by leaps and bounds.
Aunt Rosina had provided a kind of commentary on
Signora Malfenti, who proposed to me that I should keep
away from her house for several days. Too kind of you, my
dear lady! I would oblige her beyond her expectations; she
should never see me again! They had all of them tortured
me, she, the aunt, and Ada. By what right? Because I
wanted to get married? But I had quite given up that idea.
Liberty was too sweet!

I roved about the streets for a long while, a prey to
the violence of my feelings. Then I felt the need of an even
greater liberty. I must find a way of sealing my resolution
never to set foot in the house again. I rejected the idea of
writing a letter of farewell. My scorn would be more ef-
fectual if I did not communicate my intentions of breaking
with them forever. I would simply forget to call on
Giovanni and his family.

I hit on what seemed to me a discreet and pleasant, if
slightly ironical way of confirming my purpose. I hastened
to a florist and selected a magnificent bouquet of flowers,
which I addressed to Signora Malfenti, accompanied by my
visiting-card, on which nothing was written except the date,
which I should never forget and which probably Ada and
her mother would never forget either. May the fifth, the
anniversary of Napoleon's death.

I arranged for it to be sent at once. It was extremely
important that it should arrive that same day.

And what next? I had done absolutely everything,
there was nothing more to do. Ada was shut up away from
me, with all the rest of her family, and I should be obliged
to go on doing nothing, waiting for one of them to come
and find me and give me an occasion to do or say something different.

I went straight to my study and shut myself in to
reflect. If I had given way to my torturing impatience I
should have returned at once to the house, even at the risk
of arriving there before my bouquet of flowers. It was easy

to invent an excuse. I might even have forgotten my umbrella!

But I did not want to do anything of the sort. In sending the bouquet I was making a magnificent gesture that I must not go back on. It was for me to stand firm; the next move was for them.

The solitude of my study from which I had hoped to get relief only served to throw light on the cause of my despair, which was so acute as to drive me to tears. I was in love with Ada! I could not be sure yet whether that was the right word, so I went on with my analysis. I not only wanted to possess her, I wanted her for my wife. I wanted her, with her cold face and angular body, and her serious nature, which could not and never would appreciate my humor. I should not try to make her; I would give it all up for her, and she would inspire me to live an intelligent and industrious life. I wanted the whole of her, I expected everything from her. I came to the conclusion that it was the right word after all; I loved Ada.

I felt as if I had arrived at something very important which would guide me on my way. No more hesitations! I no longer even cared whether she loved me. I must try and win her, and since Giovanni disposed of her, there was no longer any point in my speaking to her about it. I must get it all settled and leap at once into felicity, or else forget it all and be cured. Why must I endure this suspense? If I learned, and I could only learn it from Giovanni, that Ada was definitely lost to me, at least I should no longer have to contend with time, which would then flow peacefully on without my having to urge it forward. Something settled is always calm because it is dissociated from time.

I at once went in search of Giovanni. I had to make two journeys; one to his office, which is in the street we still call New House Street, because it was called so by our ancestors. It is close to the shore and overshadowed by tall old houses. Toward sunset there is very little traffic in it and I could get along at a good pace. All I thought of as I hurried along was to frame as briefly as possible the phrase I had to address to him. It would be enough to tell him briefly of my determination to marry his daughter Ada. It was not my business to explain, or to win him over. As a business man he would know what to answer as soon as

I had stated my case. The only thing I debated was
whether I had better, on an occasion like this, talk in
dialect or in the literary language.

But Giovanni had already left his office and gone on
to the Tergesteo. I made my way there, but more slowly,
for I knew that I should have to wait some time before I
could speak to him alone. When I reached Via Cavana
I had to slacken my pace still more, because of the crowd
in the narrow street. And it was while I was fighting my
way through the crowd that I suddenly saw, as in a vision,
the certainty that I had been seeking for so many hours.
The Malfentis wanted me to marry Augusta, and they did
not want me to marry Ada, for the simple reason that
Augusta was in love with me and Ada was not. She could
not be, for otherwise they would not have intervened to
separate us. They told me I was compromising Augusta,
but in fact it was she who was compromising herself by
loving me. I saw it all quite clearly in a flash, as if one of
the family had told me. And I guessed that Ada had agreed
to my being forbidden the house. She did not love me and
never would, at least so long as she thought her sister did.
So in the crowded Via Cavana I had arrived more quickly
at the truth than in the solitude of my study.

Today, when I look back on those five memorable
days that led up to my marriage I am shocked to think I
was not at all moved to find that poor Augusta was in love
with me. Now that I was banished from the house I knew
that I was madly in love with Ada. Why did it give
me no satisfaction to realize that Signora Malfenti had
banished me in vain since I was still present in the house,
and in the closest vicinity to Ada, namely in Augusta's
heart? I felt it as a fresh insult that Signora Malfenti
should have exhorted me not to compromise Augusta,
meaning that I was to marry her. I felt all the contempt
for the plain sister which I could not admit that the pretty
sister, whom I loved, felt for me.

I quickened my steps, but I turned aside from the
Tergesteo and made my way home. I no longer had any
need to speak to Giovanni. I knew exactly what I must do;
I knew it with a despairing certainty that perhaps would
give me peace at last by releasing me from the too slow
march of time. Besides, it would be dangerous to talk to
anyone so tactless as Giovanni. Signora Malfenti had

spoken so obscurely that it had taken me till Via Cavana to grasp her meaning. Her husband was capable of behaving very differently. He might easily say straight out: "Why do you want to marry Ada? Just think it over. Hadn't you better marry Augusta instead?" I remembered an axiom of his by which he might easily be guided in this case. "One must always explain the matter clearly to one's adversary, for only so can one be sure of understanding it better than he." And then? An open rupture would be sure to follow. Well then, time could move at whatever pace it pleased; I should no longer have any reason to interfere with it; I should have come to a full stop!

I remembered another of Giovanni's axioms, and clung to it because it gave me occasion to hope. I managed to cling to it for five days, during which my passion was transformed into a disease. Giovanni used to say one must never be in a hurry to liquidate a business if, there was nothing to be gained by it; sooner or later every business will liquidate itself, as is proved by the fact that in the course of the world's long history so few questions have been left unsettled. So long as one leaves it unliquidated, there is always a chance of it turning out to one's advantage.

I did not choose to recall other axioms of Giovanni which took the opposite point of view; I preferred to cling to this one. I had to cling to something. I made an iron resolution not to budge from my position till something fresh had intervened to turn things in my favor. And it was perhaps because the consequences of this were so fatal to me, that I refrained for a long time from forming any fresh resolution.

I had hardly taken my resolution before a note arrived from Signora Malfenti. I recognized her handwriting on the envelope, and before opening it I flattered myself that my iron resolution had been quite enough to make her repent of having ill-treated me, and to run after me instead. When I found it contained nothing but the letters p.r. (*pour remercier*), which meant that she was thanking me for the flowers I had sent her, I flung myself on my bed in desperation and drove my teeth into the pillow-case, as if to chain myself to it and prevent myself from running away to break my resolution on the spot. What ironic calm those initials aroused in me! Much greater than that expressed

by the date on my visiting-card, which was intended to
convey a resolution and also a reproof. "*Remember*"
Charles I had said before they cut off his head, and he
must have noted the date of that memorable day! I too
had exhorted my enemy to remember and to fear!

Those five days and nights were horrible, and I
watched the dawn and sunset that marked their beginning
and their end and brought nearer the hour when I should
be free to fight again for my love.

I went on preparing myself for the conflict. I knew
now what my mistress wanted me to be like. I will remember the resolutions I made then, partly because I have
made very similar ones more recently, and also because I
have kept the sheet of paper on which I noted them down.
I resolved to become more serious. That meant that I must
not tell any more of those comic stories, which showed me
in an unfavorable light and made my dear Ada despise me,
though they endeared me to the plain Augusta. I also
resolved to go to my office at eight every morning (it was a
long time since it had seen me), not in order to argue with
Olivi about my rights, but in order to work with him and
qualify, all in good time, to manage my affairs myself. This
change was to be effected later on, at a calmer moment,
just as I was going later on to give up smoking; i.e., when
I had recovered my freedom, for there was no reason to
make the horrible moment still more horrible. Ada must
have a perfect husband. Among other things I resolved to
devote myself to serious reading, to fence for half an hour
daily, and to ride twice a week. Twenty-four hours a day
were none too long.

During my brief exile I was continually beset by the
most violent jealousy. It was a heroic purpose to determine
to cure all one's faults and prepare for the conquest of Ada
after so few weeks. But meanwhile? While I was subjecting
myself to the most rigid discipline was it likely that all the
other males in the town would lie low and refrain from
trying to carry off my lady? There was sure to be one
among them who would not stand in need of so much
discipline in order to be favorably received. I knew or
thought I knew that when Ada found someone she felt
would suit her she would consent at once, without waiting
to fall in love. Everytime I met a well-dressed, healthy-
looking man who appeared to be at peace with himself and

the world, I hated him because I thought he would do for Ada. The chief thing I remember about those days is the jealousy that settled like a black cloud on my life.

It would be unjust to laugh at my hideous fear lest Ada should be stolen away from me, now that one knows what really did happen. When I live again through those hideous days I must needs wonder at my prophetic soul.

I walked several times beneath her windows at night. In the rooms above they were apparently enjoying themselves as of old when I was there. At midnight or a little sooner, the lights went out in the drawing-room. I hurried away, fearing lest one of the guests might catch sight of me as he left the house.

Not an hour during those days but I was tortured with impatience. Why did no one ask after me? Why did Giovanni make no move? Surely he must have wondered not to see me either at his house or at the Tergesteo? Had he agreed too then that I was to be banished? Often in the middle of my walk, at night or during the day, I would rush home to make sure that no one had called to inquire about me. I felt I could not go to bed till I had made sure, and I would wake poor Maria up to ask her. I would often stay at home for hours on end so as to be more easily accessible. But nobody called to inquire, and I should certainly still be a bachelor if I had not decided to make a move myself.

One evening I went to my club to gamble. It was many years since I had done so, because of a promise I had made my father. I felt my promise ought not to hold any longer, because my father could not have foreseen my present painful circumstances and my urgent need to procure myself some diversion. First I won a considerable sum of money, which however gave me no pleasure, because it seemed like a compensation for my misfortune in love. Then I lost, and was no better pleased, because I thought I was as unlucky at the gaming-table as I was in my love affairs. I soon took a dislike to gambling; it was unworthy of me and of Ada. So pure had I become through my love for her.

My dreams of love had been rudely shattered by the harsh realities of those last few days. And now in my sleep I dreamed quite differently too; of victory instead of love. Once Ada visited me in my dreams. She was dressed like

a bride and went with me to the altar, but even after that
I did not embrace her. I was her husband and had the
right to ask her how she could have allowed me to be
treated like that. I did not try to exercise any other rights.

In my desk I have come upon some rough copies of
letters to Ada, Giovanni, and Signora Malfenti. They belong to that time. I wrote to Signora Malfenti simply to
say that I wanted to take leave of her before setting out
on a long journey. I cannot however remember that I ever
thought of doing so. I could not think of leaving the city
while I was still uncertain whether someone might not
come and look for me. How terrible if they had come and
not found me. I never sent any of those letters. I think I
must have written them only so as to put my thoughts
down on paper.

For some years past I had looked on myself as ill, but
only in a way which made others suffer more than me. It
was now that I began to suffer from a really painful illness,
a mixture of unpleasant bodily sensations that caused me
extreme misery.

It began in this way. One night at about one o'clock,
unable to sleep, I got up and walked through the mild
night air till I reached a café in a suburb where I had
never been before and where it was unlikely I should meet
anybody I knew. I was glad of that, because I wanted to
continue an imaginary discussion I had begun with Signora Malfenti in bed, and which I did not want anyone to
interfere with. Signora Malfenti had begun to make fresh
charges against me. She said I was playing cat and mouse
with her daughters; the fact of course being that if I had
attempted anything of the sort it would have been with
Ada alone. I broke out into a cold sweat at the mere
thought of their saying such a thing about me at the
Malfentis', perhaps at this very moment. The absent are
always wrong, and they might have taken advantage of my
absence to plot against me. When I got into the bright
light of the café I found it easier to defend myself. It is
true that I should have liked to touch Ada's foot with
mine, and I did once think I had succeeded in doing so
with her approval. But then I discovered that it was only
the wooden leg of the table I was pressing, and of course
it could not protest.

I pretended to interest myself in a game of billiards.

A man who was leaning on a crutch came in and sat down beside me. He ordered a lemon squash, and the waiter looked at me for my order, so I also absent-mindedly ordered a lemon squash, though I can't endure the taste of a lemon. While he was fetching it, the crutch, which was leaning against the sofa we were sitting on, slipped to the ground and I instinctively bent down to pick it up.

"Why it's Zeno!" exclaimed the poor cripple, recognizing me just as he was about to thank me.

"Tullio!" I cried in surprise, and stretched out my hand. We had been at school together and had not seen each other for some years. All I knew about him was that after he had left school he had gone into a bank, where he had a good position.

But I was so distrait that I promptly asked him why it was that his right leg was shorter than his left, so that he needed a crutch.

He good-humoredly said that he had had rheumatism six months ago, which had caused the trouble in his leg.

I at once suggested to him a number of cures. It is the best way of simulating keen sympathy without much trouble to oneself. But he had tried them all. Then I made a further suggestion:

"Why are you not in bed at this hour? I don't think it can be good for you to expose yourself to the night air."

He laughed good-naturedly and said that he did not think the night air could do me much good either, and maintained that even if one had not got rheumatism one might easily get it. Even the Austrian Constitution, he said, allowed the right to go to bed in the early hours of the morning. Besides, contrary to the general opinion, cold and heat had nothing to do with rheumatism. He had studied his illness, in fact he did nothing whatever but study its cause and cure. He had got long leave from the bank for that very purpose, though it was supposed to be for his treatment. Then he told me about the strange treatment he was undergoing. Every day he had to eat an enormous quantity of lemons. He had already swallowed thirty that day, but he hoped with practice to arrive at a very much higher figure. He told me that lemons were good for a number of other diseases too. Since he had begun taking them he suffered much less from the effects of over-smoking to which he was a victim.

I had cold shivers at the thought of so much acid, but this was at once succeeded by a more cheerful view of life; I did not like lemons, but if they could procure for me immunity from the results of doing all the things I most enjoyed I would have eaten quite a number. Complete freedom consists in doing what you want on condition that you do something else as well which you like less. True slavery is being forced to abstain: Tantalus, not Hercules.

Tullio pretended to be anxious to hear my news. I was determined not to tell him anything about my unhappy love affair, but I had to find an outlet somehow. I gave him such an exaggerated account of my bodily symptoms (which I am sure were very slight) that I ended by having tears in my eyes, while Tullio began to feel better and better at the thought that I was worse than he was.

He asked if I was working. It was always said in the town that I did nothing, and I was afraid he was going to begin envying me, whereas at the moment I felt it was essential that I should be pitied. So I lied to him. I told him that I worked in my office about six hours daily, and that my father's affairs had been left in such confusion that I was obliged to work six hours more at them after I got home.

"Twelve hours," remarked Tullio, with a contented smile; and he proceeded to offer me what I most needed: his pity. "I must say I don't envy you."

The conclusion was obvious, but I was so much touched by it that I could hardly restrain my tears. I felt unhappier than ever, and in such a morbid state of self-pity one may easily fall a prey to unwholesome suggestions.

Tullio and I began talking again about his illness, which was his principal distraction. He had studied the anatomy of the leg and foot. He told me with amusement that when one is walking rapidly each step takes no more than half a second, and in that half second no fewer than fifty-four muscles are set in motion. I listened in bewilderment. I at once directed my attention to my legs and tried to discover the infernal machine. I thought I had succeeded in finding it. I could not of course distinguish all its fifty-four parts, but I dicovered something terrifically complicated which seemed to get out of order directly I began thinking about it.

I limped as I left the café, and for several days afterwards walking became a burden to me and even caused me a certain amount of pain. I felt as if the whole machine needed oiling. All the muscles seemed to grate together whenever one moved. A few days later my first trouble got better, but was followed by a much more serious one, which I shall have cause to speak of soon. Even today, if anyone watches me walking, the fifty-four movements get tied up in a knot, and I feel as if I shall fall down.

Ada was responsible for this trouble too. Many animals fall a prey to the hunter or to other animals when they are in love. I fell a prey to disease. I am certain that at any other time I might have heard about the infernal machine without it doing me the slightest harm.

A few words on a sheet of paper I have kept remind me of another curious adventure of that time. Besides a note of a last cigarette, and an expression of faith in my capacity to recover from the disease of the fifty-four movements, there is also an attempt at poetry about a fly. If I had not known I should have supposed those verses were produced by a respectable old maid who calls the insect she sings of "thou"; but as I know them to have been by me I can only suppose that anyone is capable of anything if I was capable of them.

This is what gave rise to the verses. One night I had gone home late and, instead of going at once to bed, I went into my study and lit the gas. A fly, attracted by the light, began to torment me. I aimed a blow at it, but only a light one, for fear of dirtying myself. I forgot all about it, and then saw it slowly recovering on the table. It was standing right up, and seemed taller than before because one of its legs was paralyzed by the blow and it could not bend it. It was industriously cleaning its wings with its two hind legs. It tried to move, but fell over on its back. Then it picked itself up again and returned obstinately to its task.

I wrote those verses in my surprise at discovering that the fly's tiny pain-racked organism was acting on two mistaken assumptions. First of all, in cleaning its wings so persistently the insect showed that it did not know which was the wounded limb. Secondly, its persistent efforts showed that it assumed health to be the portion of everyone, and that though we have lost it we shall certainly find it again. These errors are quite excusable in an insect that only lives for one season and has no time to learn by experience.

Then Sunday came. It marked the fifth day since my last visit to the Malfentis. Though I work so little, I have always felt a great respect for this holiday, which divides life into short periods that make it endurable. My plans underwent no change, but I decided they did not count for that day, and that it was permissible for me to see Ada. I did not propose to endanger my plans by writing, but I thought I ought to see her because there was always a chance of things having altered in my favor, and then it would have been a great pity to go on suffering needlessly.

So at midday, as fast as my poor legs would carry me, I hurried into the town, by the way that I knew Signora Malfenti and her daughters must take coming back from mass. It was a lovely sunny day, and as I walked along I thought of the longed-for discovery that was perhaps awaiting me in the town—Ada's love!

It was not to be, but for a moment I had the illusion of it. Fortune favored me in an incredible manner. I suddenly found myself face to face with Ada, and she was alone. I staggered and my heart beat violently. What must I do? According to my resolution I ought to have stood aside and let her pass, with a measured bow. But my mind was slightly confused because of the other resolutions I had made earlier, one of which was to speak openly to her and learn from her lips what my fate was to be. I did not stand aside, and when she greeted me as if we had only parted five minutes ago, I joined her and walked along beside her.

She said:

"Good morning, Signor Cosini! I am in rather a hurry."

And I:

"May I walk with you a little way?"

She smilingly agreed. Ought I to speak now? She added that she was going straight home, so I realized that I had only five minutes to do it in, and I wasted part of that time by calculating whether it would be long enough for the important things I had to say. Better not speak at all than to only half speak. I was also rather confused by the fact that at that time it was considered compromising for a girl to be seen about in the streets alone with a young man. Yet she let me walk with her. Was not that enough to satisfy me? Meanwhile I watched her and tried to feel again in its entirety the love that had been overcast by anger and doubt. Should I recover my dreams? She seemed to me neither big nor small, so harmonious were the lines of her figure. My dreams revived in all their force, even while she walked a living reality by my side. They were the form desire took with me, and I felt intense joy at their return. Every trace of bitterness vanished from my mind.

But suddenly a modest voice from behind said:

"May I join you, Signorina?"

I turned indignantly. Who had dared to interrupt the explanations I had not even begun? A beardless youth, dark and pale, was gazing anxiously at her. I in my turn looked at Ada, in the vain hope that she would invoke my aid. She had only to make a sign and I should have flung myself on that individual, and demanded an explanation of his audacity. Better still if he had insisted! My pain would have vanished instantly if I had been free to abandon myself to a display of brute force.

But Ada gave me no such sign. With a sudden smile which changed slightly the outline of her face and mouth, and even the color of her eyes, she stretched out her hand to him:

"Ah, Signor Guido!"

That Christian name was painful to me; only a few minutes before she had called me by my surname.

I looked at Signor Guido more closely. He was dressed with the utmost elegance, and was carrying in his gloved right hand a walking-stick with a very long ivory handle, which I would not have been seen with even if they had paid me so much per mile. It was not surprising if such a person seemed to me a danger to Ada. There are plenty of *louche* figures who dress exactly like that, and carry precisely similar canes.

Ada's smile forced me back into the world of conventional relationships. She introduced us. And I was obliged to smile too! Ada's smile was like transparent water stirred by a slight breeze. Mine was also like the movement of water, but when a stone has been thrown into it suddenly.

His name was Guido Speier. My smile became more spontaneous, because I at once saw an opportunity for saying something disagreeable to him:

"Are you German?"

He replied politely that he knew his name might make one think so, but documents showed that his family had been Italian for several centuries. He talked Tuscan fluently, whereas Ada and I were confined to our inelegant dialect.

I looked at him closely in order to take in better what he was saying. He was a very handsome young man. His slightly open lips revealed a set of perfect white teeth. He had bright, expressive eyes, and when he took off his hat I could see that his brown curly hair covered the entire space provided for it by Nature, whereas a great part of my own head had been usurped by my forehead.

I should have hated him even if Ada had not been there, but my hatred distressed me, and I tried to get rid of it. "He is too young for Ada," I thought. And I said to myself that the familiarity and kindness of her greeting was probably due to her father's instructions. Perhaps he was important in Malfenti's business, and I had noticed in such cases that all the family were obliged to collaborate. I said:

"Are you settling in Trieste?"

He said he had been there a month and was starting a business. I breathed again! Perhaps I had guessed rightly.

I limped as I walked, but as nobody took any notice I did not make much of it. I kept looking at Ada and tried to forget everything else, including our companion. I like to live in the moment, and I never give the future a thought, unless it casts its shadow too obviously over the present. Ada was walking between us, and her face wore a vague unchanging expression of happiness which was almost a smile. That happy look was new to her. For whom was her smile intended? Might it not be for me, whom she had not seen for so long?

I listened to what they were saying. They were talking about spiritualism, and I suddenly discovered that Guido had introduced table-turning into the Malfenti household.

I was burning to assure myself that the sweet smile

that played about Ada's lips was intended for me, and I leapt into the thick of the discussion with an impromptu spirit story. No poet can ever have improvised verses on a given scheme of rhymes better than I invented then. Without any idea how I should make it end, I began by saying that I believed in spirits too after what had happened to me the day before in that very street—no, it was the street running parallel, which we could see through the next turning. I went on to say that Ada had known Professor Bertini, who had died a short time ago in Florence, where he had settled on his pension. We had seen a short notice of his death in the local paper, but I had completely forgotten this, so that when I thought of Professor Bertini it was walking through the Cascine, taking his well-earned rest. Yesterday—I pointed out the exact spot in the street parallel to the one we were walking in—I was accosted by a gentleman who seemed to know me and whom I felt I knew. He had a curious swaying walk like that adopted by certain women in order to progress more easily.

"Of course it may have been Professor Bertini," said Ada, laughing.

I was encouraged by her laugh, and went on:

"I knew him, but I could not remember who he was. We talked about politics. It *was* Bertini; it was his bleating voice, and no one else could have talked such nonsense."

"His voice too!" exclaimed Ada, still laughing, and looking at me anxiously to hear the end.

"Yes, it could only have been Bertini," I said, feigning terror with all the art of the consummate actor the world has lost in me. "He pressed my hand when he said good-by, and went away with the same swinging gait. I followed him a certain distance, racking my brain to think who it could be. It was only when I had lost him from sight that I realized I had been talking to Bertini; Bertini who had been dead a whole year!"

Soon after, she stopped at the door of her house. She shook hands with Guido and said she was expecting him that evening. Then she nodded to me and said that if I was not afraid of being bored she hoped I would come too for some table-turning.

I did not thank her. I made no reply. I wanted to look into the invitation more closely before accepting. It had sounded to me like an act of enforced politeness. Well, perhaps the holiday was going to end for me with this meeting. But I did not want to seem rude, and thought I would leave it open whether or not I accepted the invitation. I asked after Giovanni, saying I wanted to speak to him. She replied that I should find him at his office, where he had been obliged to go for some important business.

Guido and I stood for a few seconds looking after the elegant figure disappearing through the porch. I don't know what Guido's thoughts were at the moment. As for me I felt extremely unhappy. Why had she not invited me before inviting Guido?

We walked back together almost to the point where we had met Ada. Guido was polite and easy in his manner, a thing that I most envied in other people; he spoke again of the story I had invented, which he evidently took seriously. The only true part of the story however was this: there was in Trieste, even after Bertini's death, someone who talked a great deal of nonsense, appeared to walk on the tips of his toes, and had an odd way of talking. I had only recently got to know him, and he had for the moment reminded me of Bertini. I was quite content that Guido should rack his brains over my invention. I had made up my mind that there was no point in my hating him, since he was no more than an important business connection as far as the Malfentis were concerned; but I loathed his ultra-elegance and his walking-stick. In fact, I found him so unsympathetic that I was dying to get rid of him. I listened to his final remarks:

"The person you talked to might easily have been much younger than Bertini, have walked like a grenadier, and had a manly voice, the only resemblance between them being that they both talked nonsense. Yet this would have been quite sufficient to fix your thoughts on Bertini. But to admit that, one would have to assume that you are very absent-minded."

I was not going to make it easy for him:

"Absent-minded?" I said. "What an idea! I am a business man. What would become of me if I were absent-minded?"

Then I reflected I was wasting my time. I wanted to see Giovanni. As I had seen the daughter I might as well see the father too, though he was so much less important.

I should have to make haste if I wanted to find him still in his office.

Guido went on prosing about what part in a miracle should be attributed to the inattention of the miracle-worker or of those who are present at it. I wanted to get away, and was anxious to appear at least as much at my ease as himself. This caused me to interrupt him rather brusquely, and to say almost rudely:

"For me miracles exist or they do not. There is no need to make them more complicated than they are. Either you believe them or you don't; in either case it is very simple."

I so little wanted to show how much I disliked him, that my words were intended as a kind of concession, seeing that I am a convinced positivist and have no belief in miracles. But it was a concession made very ill-humoredly.

I limped more than ever as I went away, and hoped that Guido would not find it necessary to look back.

I felt it essential to speak to Giovanni. I should be able to learn from him what I ought to do about accepting Ada's invitation. His attitude would make it quite clear whether I might go or whether I ought not rather to remember that Ada's invitation was directly contrary to Signora Malfenti's wishes. I must know exactly where I stood with these people, and if I could not settle the question on Sunday, then I must devote Monday to it as well. I was going on breaking my resolutions, but without being conscious of it. In fact I thought I was carrying out a resolution that I had only arrived at after five days' meditation.

Giovanni called out a loud and cheerful greeting which did me good, and invited me to sit down in an armchair facing his desk.

"Only five minutes! I'll be with you at once! But you're lame?" he added inquiringly.

I blushed. But I was in a mood for improvisation. I said I had slipped coming out of a café, and described the café where the accident had happened. I was afraid he might attribute my tumble to the fact that my mind was clouded by alcohol, and I added the humorous detail that when I fell I was with somebody who limped and was afflicted with rheumatism.

An employee and two porters were standing by Giovanni's table. Some errors needed verifying in a consignment of merchandise, and Giovanni had made one of his violent interventions in the management of his warehouse, which he rarely interfered with, wanting, as he said, to keep his mind free for what no one else could do instead. He talked louder than ever, as if he wanted to engrave his commands on the ears of his dependents. I think it was a question of deciding just how business was to be carried on between the office and the warehouse.

"This paper," shouted Giovanni, passing from his right hand to his left a paper he had torn out of a book, "will be signed by you, and the employee who takes it will give you an identical one signed by him."

He fixed his interlocutors, sometimes through his glasses, and sometimes above them, and shouted at them again:

"Do you follow?"

He was about to begin his explanations all over again, but I had already wasted too much time. I had a curious feeling that if I were to make haste I should have more chance of winning Ada, though it soon occurred to me with a sense of surprise that no one was expecting me, and that I had nothing to hope for, nor was there anything for me to do. I advanced with outstretched hand, and said to Giovanni:

"I am coming to you this evening."

He at once turned to me, while the others stood aside.

"Why haven't you been to see us all this time?" he said simply.

I was overcome by a sudden surprise. That was the very question I had a right to expect from Ada, but which she had not asked me. If no one else had been there I should have told Giovanni quite plainly that his question had proved to me his innocence of any share in what I now felt to be a plot against me. He alone was innocent and deserved my confidence.

Perhaps I did not see things quite so clearly all at once, as is proved by the fact that I could not even wait until his underlings had gone away. I also wanted to discover whether perhaps Ada had been prevented from asking her question by Guido's unexpected arrival.

But Giovanni was in such a hurry to return to his work that he put a stop to further conversation.

"We shall see each other then this evening. You will hear a violinist such as one does not often hear. He calls himself an amateur only because he has too much money to make a profession of it. He is going into business." He shrugged his shoulders contemptuously. "I am fond of business myself but, if I were in his place I wouldn't sell anything but notes. I don't know if you know him; his name is Guido Speier."

"Really? Really?" I said, pretending to be interested. I shook my head and opened my mouth, and in fact set in motion every part of me which my will could control. So that Adonis could play the violin too! "Really? Is he as good as that?" I hoped that Giovanni was joking, and that his exaggerated praise was only ironical. But he continued shaking his head to express his admiration. I held out my hand.

"Au revoir!"

I limped to the door. I felt a doubt as to whether after all I had better refuse the invitation, in which case I ought to tell Giovanni. I had turned to go back, when I noticed that he was watching me very attentively, and was even leaning forward in order to see me better. This was more than I could bear, and I left the room.

A violinist! If it was true he played as well as that, then I was lost. If only I had not played the instrument myself or had never been induced to play it at the Malfentis'! I had taken my violin there not in order to win their hearts by my playing, but as a pretext for prolonging my visits. What a fool I had been! I might have found plenty more pretexts that would have given me away less.

No one could say I have any illusions about myself. I know that I have a great feeling for music, and that there is no affectation about my preference for classical music; but my very feeling for music warned me years ago that I should never be able to play so as to give pleasure to anyone else.

I could play well if I were not ill, but I am always pursuing health even when I am practicing balance on the four strings of a violin. There are certain slight inhibitions in my organism which are more obvious when I play the violin, and therefore easier to deal with. Even the most undeveloped being, if he knows the difference between groups of three, four, and six notes, can pass rhythmically and accurately from one to the other just as his eye can pass from one color to another. But in my case, after I have been playing one of those rhythmic figures it clings to me and I can't escape from it, but get it mixed up with the following figure so that I play it out of time. If I am to play the notes right I am compelled to beat time with my feet and head; but good-by to ease, serenity and music! The music that is produced by a well-balanced physique is identical with the rhythm it creates and exploits; it is rhythm itself. When I can play like that I shall be cured.

I thought for the first time that I would acknowledge myself defeated, leave Trieste, and go off in the hope of finding distraction. I had nothing else left to hope for. Ada was lost to me. I was sure of that now! Didn't I know quite well that she would only marry a man after she had thoroughly weighed and tested him, just as if she was awarding him an academic honor? It seemed absurd, because really the violin ought not to loom so large in one's choice of a husband; but this was no help to me. I felt how important his playing was. It was like the birds choosing their mate for his song.

I crept into my lair, while the others went on enjoying their holiday. I took my violin from its case, uncertain whether to break it in pieces or play on it. Then I tried it as if I were bidding it a last farewell, and finally began practicing the immortal Kreutzer Sonata. How many miles my bow must have traveled in this very room, and now I began to drive it along mechanically over many more!

Anyone who has practiced much on those few cursed strings will know that so long as one is by oneself every little effort one makes seems to produce a corresponding progress. If it were not so who would ever submit to such unending hard labor, as severe as if one had been so unfortunate as to commit a murder? After a short time it seemed to me that my battle with Guido was not hopelessly lost. Who knows whether my violin after all might not intervene successfully between Ada and Guido?

This was not due to conceit, but to my usual incurable optimism. Every fresh misfortune that threatens, annihilates me in the first moment, but I very soon recover, in the sure faith that I shall be able to circumvent it. In this case all that I had to do was to take a more lenient view of my capabilities as a violinist. In all the arts sound judgment is the result of comparison, and that was lacking here. Besides, one's own violin resounds so close to one's ear that it reaches the heart very quickly. At last, somewhat exhausted I left off playing, and said to myself:

"Bravo, Zeno, you have earned your reward."

Without a moment's hesitation I made my way to the Malfentis'. I had accepted the invitation, so I was obliged to go. It seemed to me a good omen that the parlor-maid should receive me with a friendly smile, and inquire whether I had been ill, that I had not been there for so long. I tipped her. The family she represented had made the inquiry through her mouth.

She showed me into the drawing-room, which was immersed in complete darkness. When I came into it from the full light of the hall, I could not see anything for a moment and did not dare to move. Then I discovered several figures sitting round a table at the far end of the room, at some distance from me.

Ada's voice greeted me and seemed to me in the darkness more sensuous than usual, a soft, almost caressing voice:

"Sit down over there, and don't disturb the spirits!"

If it were to go on like this I certainly would not disturb them.

Then a voice sounded from another part of the table, it might belong to Augusta or Alberta:

"If you want to take part in the evocation of the spirits, there is a corner over here."

I was determined not to be kept out of it, so I advanced resolutely to the place from which Ada's greetings seemed to have come. I knocked my knee against the corner of the Venetian table they were sitting at, which seemed to be nothing but corners. It was extremely painful, but I would let nothing stop me, and pressed on to occupy the seat that somebody offered me, I did not know who. It was between two of the sisters, and I imagined the one on my right to be Ada, and the one on my left Augusta. In order to avoid coming into contact with the latter I pushed my chair closer to the other.

But I thought I might have made a mistake about my right-hand neighbor, so in order to hear her voice I asked:

"Have you had any message yet from the spirits?"

Guido, who was apparently sitting opposite, interrupted me. He called out imperiously: "Silence!"

Then more gently:

"Collect yourselves and concentrate all your thoughts
on the dead person you want to summon."

I have no objection to anyone making attempts to spy
on the world beyond the grave. In fact I was irritated at not
having introduced table-turning myself, since it was such a
success at Giovanni's house. But I didn't see why I must
obey Guido's orders, and therefore I made no effort to concentrate. Besides I had reproached myself so often for allowing things to reach this point, without having had any
explanation with Ada, that now I had her next to me, and
in the dark too, I was determined to settle it once and for
all. I was only restrained by the delicious sense of having
her so close after I had feared to lose her forever. I preferred to breathe the fragrance of the soft texture of her
dress which was touching me, and I thought that, close
as we now were together, my feet must be actually pressing
hers. I knew she always wore patent-leather shoes in the
evening. It was almost too much for me after such long
torture.

Guido was speaking again:

"I do beg you to concentrate. Implore the spirits you
have invoked to manifest themselves by moving the table."

I was glad that he was still busying himself about the
table. It was clear now that Ada had resigned herself to
bearing almost my whole weight! She must love me or
she would not have stood it. At last the hour of explanation had arrived. I removed my arm from the table and put
it gently round her waist:

"I love you, Ada!" I said in a low voice, putting my
face close to hers so that she could hear better.

The girl did not reply at once. Then she murmured in
a faint voice—but Augusta's:

"Why have you not been here for so long?"

Surprise and disappointment made me almost fall out
of my chair. I at once felt that though I must banish this
tiresome girl from my life, I must treat her with the consideration that a perfect gentleman like me owes to the
woman who loves him, even though she be the ugliest of
God's creatures. For she certainly loved me! In the midst

of my suffering I felt her love. It could only have been love that suggested to her not to tell me that she was not Ada, and to ask me the question I had been waiting for in vain on Ada's part, and which she had evidently determined to ask me directly she saw me again.

I obeyed my instinct not to answer her question, but after a moment's hesitation I said to her:

"I am glad to have confided in you, Augusta, for I know how kind you are."

I recovered my balance on my three-legged stool. An explanation with Ada was out of the question, and there remained nothing else to explain to Augusta. Further misunderstanding was impossible between us.

Guido admonished us again:

"If you won't keep quiet there is no point in us all sitting here in the dark."

He could not know it, but I needed a little darkness in order to withdraw from the crowd and recover my self-control. I had discovered my mistake, but the only balance I had yet recovered was on my chair.

I would speak to Ada, I thought, but in the light. I suspected that it was not she on my left hand, but Alberta. How could I ascertain this? My uncertainty almost made me fall over on the left, and in order to recover my balance, I leaned on the table. They all began shouting: "It's moving, it's moving!" My involuntary act would perhaps solve the question. Where did Ada's voice come from? But Guido, drowning everyone else's voice with his own, imposed the silence that I should have liked to impose on him. Then in a changed voice, a voice of supplication (idiot!), he conversed with the spirits he imagined to be present:

"I beg you tell us your name, using the letters of our alphabet."

He provided for everything; he was afraid the spirit might use the Greek alphabet!

I went on with the comedy, still trying to pierce the darkness in search of Ada. After a little hesitation I made the table rise seven times, so that the letter G was obtained. The idea seemed to me a good one, and though the letter U which followed necessitated countless movements, I dictated Guido's name letter by letter quite clearly. I have no doubt that in dictating his name I was inspired by the desire to relegate him to the spirit world.

When Guido's name was completed Ada at last spoke:
"Could it be an ancestor of yours?" she suggested.
She was sitting next to him. I should have liked to move
the table so much that it went between them and divided
them.

"It may be," said Guido. So he believed himself to
have ancestors! But this did not alarm me. His voice was
transformed by genuine emotion, which gave me the satisfaction a fencer must feel when he discovers his opponent
to be weaker than he supposed. He was not conducting
these experiments in cold blood. He really was an idiot!
Most forms of weakness arouse my compassion, but not
his.

Then he addressed himself to the spirit:

"If your name is Speier make only one movement;
otherwise move the table twice." Since he was so anxious
to have ancestors I obliged him by making the table move
once.

"My grandfather," murmured Guido.

Then the conversation with the spirit proceeded more
briskly. The spirit was asked if it had anything to tell us.
It replied yes. About business or other things? About business. I chose this reply simply because it required the table
to be moved once only. Guido asked if it had good or bad
news to give us? The bad news was to be indicated by two
movements and, this time without any hesitation, I tried
to move the table twice. But in the second movement I
encountered some opposition, and concluded there must
be someone present who wanted the news to be good. Ada
perhaps. To produce the second movement I positively
flung myself on the table and won easily! The news was
bad!

But the second movement was so violent, on account
of the opposition it had met with, that everyone was
thrown from his seat.

"Very strange," muttered Guido. Then he shouted
decisively: "Stop! Stop! Someone present is fooling us!"

Almost everyone gladly obeyed, and in a moment the
drawing-room was flooded with light from many different
points. I thought Guido looked pale. Ada was deceived in
that young man, and I was determined to open her eyes.

Besides the three girls and Signora Malfenti, there

was another lady in the drawing-room the sight of whom caused me embarrassment and agitation, for I thought it was Aunt Rosina. For different reasons I greeted both ladies very formally.

The amusing part is that I alone remained sitting at the table, beside Augusta. That again was compromising, but I could not persuade myself to join all the others who crowded round Guido. He was engaged in explaining with great vehemence how he had come to realize that the table was not being moved by a spirit, but by a malicious mortal made of flesh and blood. Not Ada, but he himself had tried to curb the table's eloquence.

He said:

"I held the table back with all my force to try to prevent it moving a second time. Someone must have actually flung himself on it to overcome my resistance."

A nice kind of spiritualism! So a powerful effort could not be due to a spirit!

I looked at poor Augusta to see what impression my declaration of love to her sister had made on her. She was very red but she smiled on me benevolently. It was only then that she admitted having heard my declaration:

"I won't tell anyone," she said, in a low voice.

That pleased me very much.

"Thank you," I murmured, pressing her hand, which was not very small but well modeled. I felt I should like to be a good friend to Augusta, though before that I should never have thought it possible to become friends with anyone who was ugly. But I felt a certain affection for her waist, round which I had so lately held my arm and which I had found smaller than I expected. Her face was really quite pretty, but for that eye which had gone off on a path of its own. I had certainly exaggerated her deformity and assumed that it went through her whole body.

They had brought Guido some lemonade.

I joined the group that surrounded him, and ran into Signora Malfenti, who was just leaving it. I laughed and said to her:

"Does he need a cordial?" She made a rather contemptuous movement and said with decision:

"He doesn't seem like a man!"

I flattered myself that my victory might have definite

consequences. Ada could not set up her opinion against her mother's. It immediately had the effect it could not fail to have on a man of my temperament. All my ill will vanished and I wanted to spare Guido any further suffering. The world would certainly be less disagreeable if there were more people like me in it.

I sat down beside him, and without taking any notice of the others, I said:

"You must forgive me, Signor Guido. The trick I played on you was in bad taste. It was I who made the table declare that it had been moved by a spirit who bore your name. I would never have done it had I known that your grandfather bore the same name."

Guido's face, which cleared at once, betrayed how much importance he attached to my statement. But he would not admit it and merely said:

"These ladies are too kind! I don't need comforting. The matter is of no consequence whatever. Thank you for your frankness, but I had already guessed that some-one had stepped into my grandfather's shoes."

He smiled with self-satisfaction and added:

"You must be pretty strong! I might have guessed that the table must have been moved by the only other man present." I had, indeed, shown myself to be stronger than him, but I was soon to feel myself weaker. Ada eyed me with animosity, and with flaming cheeks began to attack me:

"I am very angry that you should have taken it upon yourself to play such a trick."

My breath failed me and I stammered out:

"It was only a joke! I never really thought that any of you took the table-turning seriously."

It was rather late in the day to attack Guido, and besides I might have known, if my ear had been more sensitive, that in any conflict between him and me he was bound to be victorious. Ada's anger was very significant—how was it I did not guess that she was wholly his? But I persisted in the idea that he was not worthy of her, because he was not the sort of man her serious eye was looking for. Had not even Signora Malfenti seen it too?

They all defended me and made my situation worse. Signora Malfenti said laughingly:

"It was only a joke, and it came off very well." Aunt

Rosina's huge body was quivering with mirth, and she cried out admiringly:

"Splendid! Splendid!"

I could have wished Guido were less friendly. As a matter of fact all he cared about was to be sure the bad news rapped out by the table was not a spirit communication. He said:

"I don't mind betting you didn't move the table on purpose to begin with. You probably moved it the first time unintentionally, and then perhaps you decided to be malicious and move it on purpose. So that there was something in it up to the moment when you let your inspiration lead you away so violently."

Ada turned and looked at me curiously. She was betraying her excessive devotion to Guido by forgiving me just because he had done so. I refused to allow it.

"No, no!" I said emphatically. "I was tired of waiting for the spirits, and amused myself by taking their place."

Ada turned her back on me in such a way that I felt I had received a box on the ear. The very curls on her neck seemed to me to express disdain. As usual, instead of keeping my eyes and ears open I was entirely occupied with my own thoughts. I was oppressed by the fact that Ada was compromising herself dreadfully. It caused me as much pain as to hear my mistress had been unfaithful to me. In spite of the affection she showed to Guido I thought she might still be mine, but I felt I should never be able to forgive her attitude. Perhaps I think too slowly to follow the events that go on developing, without waiting for the impression previous events have made on my brain to be canceled. I felt compelled to go straight on in the path my resolution had marked out for me. It was sheer blind obstinacy. I also found it necessary to strengthen my resolution by renewing it. I went up to Augusta, who was watching me anxiously with an encouraging smile on her open face, and said to her gravely and earnestly:

"This is perhaps the last time I shall enter your house, for I am going to propose to Ada this very evening."

"You mustn't do that," she said, imploringly. "Don't you see what has happened? I should hate you to have to suffer."

She continued to intervene between Ada and me. I replied defiantly:

"I shall speak to Ada because it is my duty. It is all the same to me what she replies."

I went off, limping again, toward Guido. When I had joined him I lit a cigarette, looking at myself in the glass meanwhile. I saw that I was very pale, which for me is sufficient ground for becoming paler still. I made an effort to recover my composure and to appear unconcerned. The absence of mind produced by this double effort made me take up Guido's glass unconsciously. Once I had it in my hand I could find nothing better to do than to empty it.

Guido began to laugh:

"Now you will know all my thoughts, for I have been drinking out of that glass."

I have always disliked the taste of lemon. This particular one seemed to me positively poisonous; first because I felt that in drinking out of his glass I had come into horrible contact with Guido, secondly because I was struck at the same moment by the expression of angry impatience on Ada's face. She at once called the servant and ordered another glass of lemonade, and insisted on its being brought, though Guido said he was not thirsty.

Then I felt genuine compassion for her. She was compromising herself more and more.

"Forgive me, Ada," I said gently, looking at her as if I were awaiting an explanation. "I did not mean to offend you."

Suddenly I was afraid my eyes would fill with tears. I wanted to save myself from appearing ridiculous, and cried:

"I have squirted some lemon in my eye!"

That enabled me to cover my eyes with my handkerchief, and I had no further need to restrain my tears so long as I succeeded in not sobbing.

I shall never forget what I endured in the darkness behind my handkerchief. It hid not only my tears, but also a moment's utter madness. I thought: I will tell her everything, she will understand me and love me, but I will never, never forgive her.

I removed the handkerchief from my face so that everyone could see the tears in my eyes; I tried to laugh and to make everyone else laugh too. I said:

"I guarantee that Signor Giovanni sends home citric acid for making lemon squash with!"

Giovanni arrived at that moment and greeted me with his customary cordiality. This comforted me a little, but it did not last long, because he said he had come back earlier than usual in order to hear Guido play the violin. He broke off to ask why I was crying. They told him what I had said about him and the lemon squash, which amused him.

I was hypocritical enough to join Giovanni in begging Guido to play to us. I reminded myself that I had actually come there that evening to hear Guido play. And the odd thing is that I hoped to mollify Ada by asking him to do so. I looked at her in the hope that for the first time that evening we should be in complete accord. Strange! Wasn't I going to speak to her and refuse to forgive her? But all I saw was her back and the disdainful curls on her neck. She was hastening to take the violin out of its case.

Guido asked for a quarter of an hour's quiet first. He seemed to hesitate. During all the years I have known him since, I have found that he always hesitated before doing the simplest thing he was asked to do. He would only do what pleased him, and before granting any request he proceeded to probe the remotest corners of his mind to determine whether he wanted to do it or not.

This was the happiest quarter of an hour for me on that memorable evening. My whimsical chatter amused everyone, including Ada. It was certainly the result of my excitement, but also of the supreme effort I made to conquer the victorious violin that kept coming nearer and nearer. That short period of time which I succeeded in making so amusing for the others was remembered by me as a time of desperate conflict.

Giovanni was saying that on his way home in the tram he had witnessed a painful scene. A woman had tried to get out of it while it was still going, and had fallen and hurt herself. Giovanni gave a rather exaggerated account of his anxiety when he saw the woman was intending to jump out; he saw at once that if she jumped like that she must fall and would probably be run over. It had been very painful to look on and not be in time to save her.

I had an inspiration. I said I had discovered a remedy for the attacks of giddiness from which I used to suffer. When I was watching an acrobat perform his feats at too great a height, or saw some elderly or not very agile per-

son jump out of a tram that was moving, I overcame my
anxiety by willing them to come to grief. I even varied the
formula that I used in praying they might fall and break
their bones. This had a wonderfully calming effect on me,
enabling me to contemplate an accident with complete
indifference. If my prayers were not fulfilled I was still
more pleased.

Guido was charmed by my idea, which he regarded
as a psychological discovery. He analyzed it as he liked to
do with every trifle; he was longing for an opportunity to
try my remedy. But he had one objection to it; he thought
that bad wishes probably increased the number of disasters
in the world. Ada laughed with him and even gave me a
look of approval, which I, like a great donkey, felt quite
happy about. I thus made the discovery that it was not
true I could not forgive her, and of this I was very glad.

We all laughed a good deal, like children at play
together. It happened that I was left alone for a few minutes in that part of the drawing-room where Aunt Rosina
was sitting. She was still discussing the table-turning. She
was rather fat, and sat motionless in her chair, not even
looking at me as she spoke. I contrived to make signs to
the others that I was bored, and they all looked at me and
laughed themselves, without being seen by the aunt.

To increase their mirth it occurred to me to say to
her without further preamble:

"But you look much better, Signora, than when I last
saw you—quite rejuvenated."

If she had got angry that might have been something
to laugh at. But instead of this she was simply delighted
and said that she was in fact much better after her recent
illness. I was so surprised by her reply that my face must
have taken on a rather comic expression, for everyone
burst out laughing again. Soon after the riddle was explained. I discovered that she was not Aunt Rosina at all,
but Aunt Maria, a sister of Signora Malfenti. So that one
source of misery had been removed from that drawing-
room, though not the chief.

The moment came when Guido asked for his violin.
He said on that occasion he would do without the piano
accompaniment to the Chaconne. Ada held out his violin
to him with a welcoming smile. He took it without looking at her; but he looked at the violin as if he would like

to shut himself up with it and his inspiration. Then he placed himself in the middle of the room, turning his back on most of the company, passed his bow lightly over the strings to see if they were in tune, and played a few arpeggios. He broke off a moment to say with a smile:

"It's pretty bold of me, considering I haven't touched the violin since the last time I played here."

Charlatan! He turned his back on Ada. I watched her anxiously to see if she were hurt. But she did not seem to be. She had leaned her elbow on the table and sat with her chin resting on her hand, all attention.

And then, facing me, the great Bach appeared in person. Never, before or since, have I felt so intensely the beauty of that music, which seemed to have grown out of the four strings like a Michelangelo angel out of a block of marble. It produced quite a new state of mind in me, so that I sat gazing ecstatically upward, as if at some revelation. In vain I strove to keep that music at a distance. In vain I thought: "Beware! the violin is a siren and you need not have the heart of a hero in order to make others weep with it!" The music took me completely by storm. It seemed to express all the suffering of my mind and body and to soothe it with smiles and caresses. But it was Guido speaking! I tried to escape from the music, saying to myself: "To play like this you only need a great sense of rhythm, a sure hand, and a capacity for imitation. I have none of these things, which is not a sign of inferiority, but merely my misfortune."

While I protested, Bach swept on unerring as fate. The passionate melody on the high strings dropped suddenly to the *basso ostinato*, the beauty of which always takes one by surprise, however well one knows it. And the rhythm of every note was perfect! A second later, and the melody would have dissolved before the echoing harmony could reach it, a second earlier and it would have been overpowered and drowned. Nothing of that sort happened to Guido; his arm did not tremble, even in the presence of Bach; which was really a sign of inferiority, I thought.

As I write this today, I have abundant proof that what I thought then was true, but it is no satisfaction to me to have seen it so clearly. At the moment I was full of hatred that even that mighty music was powerless to subdue. Very soon the daily business of life was to efface it altogether, without any resistance on my part. Yes, ordinary everyday life can do many such things; but woe to the genius who should discover this!

Guido's masterly performance came to an end. Nobody applauded except Giovanni, and for a few moments nobody spoke. Then, alas, I felt the need to say something. I can't imagine how I dared, in front of those people who had heard *me* play. It was as if my violin, which so vainly strove to produce music, had suddenly found a tongue, and begun to criticize that other instrument through which music flowed like light, air, and life.

"Magnificent!" I said. The word sounded more like condescension than applause. "But I don't understand why, toward the end, you played those notes staccato, though Bach has marked them legato."

I knew every note of the Chaconne. There had been a time when I thought my progress depended on my undertaking such Herculean tasks, and for months on end I would spend my time studying certain of Bach's compositions note by note.

I knew that everyone in the room was regarding me with contempt and dislike. But I went on, as if by talking I thought I could overcome their hostility.

"Bach," I added, "uses such humble means to attain his end that an artificial bowing like that is quite out of place."

I was probably right, but the fact was that I should have been quite incapable of using that style of bowing even if I had wanted to.

Guido's reply was as impertinent as my criticism had been.

He said:

"Perhaps Bach wasn't familiar with that means of giving expression. I make him a present of it!"

He dared to put himself above Bach, and no one protested; whereas they laughed at me, who had merely ventured to put myself above Guido.

Then something happened, unimportant in itself, but crucial for me. From a fairly remote part of the house came the sound of little Anna screaming. It appeared later that she had cut her lip. They all hurried out of the room, leaving me alone with Ada, to whom Guido had trusted his precious violin before following the others.

"Shall I take the violin?" I asked, seeing her hesitate as to whether she should go too. I had not had time to grasp that the longed-for moment had arrived at last.

She hesitated, but her distrust of me won the day. Holding the violin still closer she said:

"No. There is no need for me to go too. I don't expect Anna has really hurt herself. It takes nothing to make her cry."

She sat down, still holding the violin, and by doing so she seemed to be inviting me to speak. Besides, how could I have gone home without speaking to her? What should I have done all the long night through? I pictured myself tossing from side to side in bed, or roaming about the streets in search of distraction. No! I must not leave that house without obtaining the assurance I needed for my peace of mind.

I tried to be as simple and brief as possible. I was also compelled to be, for I could hardly breathe. I said:

"I love you, Ada. May I speak to your father?"

She sat staring at me in horror and amazement. I was afraid she was going to begin screaming too, like her little sister. I knew that her calm eye and delicately molded face had had no experience of love, but never had I seen them so remote from it as at that moment. She began to say something that sounded like an introduction to something else. But I wanted a definite answer: yes or no! Perhaps the fact that she appeared at all undecided, offended me. I wanted to force her to make up her mind quickly, by refusing to allow her time to think it over.

"Surely you must have understood!" I said. "You couldn't have thought I wanted to make love to Augusta!"

I wanted to speak emphatically, but in my flurry I put my emphasis in the wrong place, and ended by pronouncing poor Augusta's name with a tone and gesture of contempt.

This sufficed to relieve Ada's embarrassment. She let everything pass except the insult to Augusta.

"Why do you think yourself better than Augusta? I don't for a moment suppose that Augusta would consent to be your wife!"

It was only then that she remembered I was waiting for an answer.

"As for me . . . I wonder that such a thing entered your head."

The sharp tone of her reply was meant to avenge Augusta. In my great distress of mind I thought that the meaning of the words was inspired by the same thought; I believe if someone gave me a box on the ear I should begin analyzing the cause. So that I tried again to persuade her:

"Think it over, Ada. I am not a bad man. I am rich. I am rather eccentric, but I can easily cure myself of that."

Ada spoke more gently, but she still insisted on talking about Augusta.

"You think it over too, Zeno; Augusta is a good girl and would make you an excellent wife. I can't answer for her, but I think . . ."

It was very sweet to me to hear my Christian name pronounced by Ada for the first time. Was she not really inviting me to speak more plainly? Perhaps I had lost her, or at least she would not consent to marry me at once, but meanwhile it was my duty to prevent her from compromising herself still further with Guido; I ought to open her eyes to the danger. I behaved diplomatically, and told her first of all that I admired and respected Augusta, but that it was quite out of the question that I should marry her. I repeated it twice to make sure she had understood. "I could not marry her." I hoped in this way to mollify Ada, who had thought at first that I wanted to insult Augusta.

"Augusta is a dear, good, charming girl; but she is not suited to me."

Then I went ahead too fast, because I had heard a noise in the passage and was afraid I might at any moment be interrupted.

"Ada, that man is not worthy of you. He is a fool! Didn't you notice how upset he was by the answers at the table-turning? Did you see his walking-stick? He plays the violin well, but so do monkeys sometimes. He betrays his stupidity in every word he utters."

She listened with the air of someone who had difficulty in grasping what is being said to her. Then she sprang to her feet, still holding the violin and bow, and interrupted me with a shower of abuse. I did my best to forget her words, and succeeded. I only remember that she began by asking me in a loud voice how I dared to speak like that about herself and Guido! I looked very surprised, because I thought I had only been talking about him. I forgot all her scornful words, but not the beauty of her noble face, glowing with health and anger, its lines rendered more precise, almost sculptural, by the fire of her indignation. That I could never forget, and when I think of my youth and my love, I see again Ada's lovely face at the moment when she banished me definitely from her life.

They all came back into the room with Signora Malfenti, who was holding Anna in her arms, still crying quietly. No one noticed Ada or me, and without saying good-by to anyone I left the room; I took my hat from the hall without anybody trying to stop me, oddly enough. Then I stopped myself, remembering that it would be very bad manners to go away without saying good-by formally to everyone. The truth no doubt is that what prevented me leaving the house was my consciousness that a night even worse than all the five previous nights awaited me. I had obtained certainty, and now felt the need of something else: peace, peace with every man. If I could banish all bitterness from my relations with Ada and the others I thought I should be able to sleep better. Why must there be that bitterness? There was no reason really for my being angry with Guido, who, even if it was through no merit of his own, could not be blamed because Ada preferred him to me.

She was the only one who had noticed me going out into the hall, and when she saw me coming back she looked anxiously at me. Was she afraid I should make a scene? I wanted to reassure her at once, so I went and stood beside her and whispered:

"Forgive me if I offended you!"

She took my hand and pressed it reassuringly. It was a great comfort to me. I shut my eyes for a moment in order to be alone with my own soul and feel the peace that her pressure gave me.

Fate willed that while all the others were still busy trying to comfort the child, I found myself sitting by Alberta. I had not seen her, and only realized her presence when she said to me:

"She did not hurt herself at all. It is a pity father is here, for whenever he sees her crying he gives her an expensive present."

I stopped analyzing myself, because I suddenly saw myself whole! If I wanted to have peace I must ensure that I should never be banished from that drawing-room. I looked at Alberta. She was very like Ada. She was a little smaller and still had something childish about her whole person. She would often shout rather, and laugh so loudly that her little face became quite puckered up and red. Oddly enough, just at that moment I called to mind an axiom of my father's. "Choose a young wife, it will be easier for you to educate her to suit you." This decided me. I again looked at Alberta. I undressed her in imagination, and the soft young body I pictured delighted me. I said:

"Listen, Alberta! I've got an idea. Has it ever occurred to you that you are old enough to get married?"

"I don't want to get married!" she replied, smiling and looking kindly at me, without blushing or appearing at all embarrassed. "I want to go on studying. Mother wants me to as well."

"But you could go on studying just as well if you were married."

I had what seemed to me rather a bright idea:

"I think of going on studying too when I am married."

She laughed heartily, but I saw I was wasting my time; this sort of nonsense was not the way to win a wife and peace of mind. One must take it seriously. It ought to be easy in Alberta's case, for her reception was very different from Ada's.

I was quite in earnest. I felt I ought to tell my future wife everything. I said to her in a tone full of feeling:

"I have just made the same proposal to Ada as I now make to you. She refused me with scorn. You can imagine what a state I am in."

These words, which were accompanied by a gesture of profound depression, were really a kind of final declaration of love to Ada. I was getting too serious, and added in a lighter tone:

"But I think if you consent to marry me I should be perfectly happy, and forget everything and everyone for you."

She became very serious and said:

"Don't be offended, Zeno, for I should hate to hurt your feelings. I respect you very much. I think you're a very nice fellow, and you understand lots of things without having learnt them, whereas my professors only know what they have learnt. But I don't want to get married. I may change my mind, but at the moment I have only one ambition: to become a writer. You see how I trust you. I have never told anyone else and I hope you won't give me away. On my side I promise I won't ever tell anyone of your proposal."

"You can tell anyone you choose," I interrupted angrily. I felt again that I was in danger of being banished from that house, and I hastened to put up my defense. There was only one way of taking down Alberta's pride in having refused me, and directly I saw it I adopted it. I said:

"I shall now propose to Augusta and tell everyone I married her because both her sisters refused me!"

I laughed with extravagant good humor as I reflected on the strangeness of my proceeding. The wit on which I prided myself so much was manifesting itself in deeds instead of words!

I looked round to try and find Augusta. She had gone out into the passage with a tray on which was a glass half full of a soothing drink for Anna. I ran after her, calling her by her name, and she leaned against a wall and waited for me. I stood facing her, and said without a moment's hesitation:

"Listen to me, Augusta! Would you like us to get married?" It was a very rough-and-ready proposal. I was proposing to marry her, and yet I never asked what she thought about it, nor did it ever occur to me that anyone would have the right to ask me for an explanation. I was only doing what they all seemed to expect of me!

The eyes she lifted to me were wide with astonishment. This seemed to make her squint more than ever. Her soft, pale face first grew paler, then suddenly became red all over. She clutched at the glass to steady it on the tray. In a voice I could hardly hear, she said:

"You are joking, it is unkind of you."

I was afraid she was going to cry, and the odd idea came to me that I might comfort her by telling her my own troubles.

"I am not joking," I said, gravely and sadly. "First I

proposed to Ada, who refused me angrily; then I asked
Alberta to marry me, and she refused me too, with fine
speeches. I don't bear either of them any ill will. But I am
very, very unhappy."

She grew calmer as she saw my grief, and looked
tenderly at me. She was evidently thinking hard. Her look
was like a caress, but gave me no pleasure.

"So you want me to understand and always to remember that you don't love me?" she asked.

What did she mean by that sibylline saying? Was it
the prelude to consent?

Did she mean she would remember during all the
years she would have to live with me? I felt like someone
who has put himself in a dangerous position on purpose to
kill himself, and then has to strain every nerve in order
to save his own life. Wouldn't it have been better if
Augusta had refused me too, and I had been able to return
safe and sound to my study, which after all I had not
found intolerable even on that awful day? I said:

"It is true that I only love Ada, and now I am asking
you to marry me."

It was on the tip of my tongue to say that it was
because I could not bear the thought of never meeting Ada
again that I was willing even to become her brother-in-law.
But it would have seemed too fantastic. And Augusta
might easily think that I was making fun of her again. So
I only said:

"I can't face living alone any longer."

She remained leaning against the wall. Perhaps she
felt she needed some support, but she seemed calmer and
managed to hold the tray in one hand. Was I saved, and
must I therefore leave the house forever? Or might I stay
there on condition that I got married? I went on talking,
in my impatience to hear her reply, which was long in
coming:

"I am quite a good fellow, and I think I should be
easy enough to live with, even if it wasn't very romantic."

This was a phrase I had been preparing for Ada during
the long days before, in the hope of persuading her to say
yes, even if she did not love me very much.

Augusta sighed gently and still remained silent. Her
silence might mean a refusal, the most delicate imaginable;

I was on the point of going to fetch my hat while my head was still my own to put it on.

But Augusta had at last made up her mind, and with a dignity I have never forgotten she stood erect, no longer needing the wall to support her. So that she was now quite close, facing me in the narrow passage. She said:

"You need a woman, Zeno, to live with you and look after you. I will be that woman."

She put out her plump hand, which I almost instinctively kissed. Clearly there was no possibility of doing anything else. I don't mind confessing that at that moment a feeling of immense satisfaction pervaded me. I had no longer any decision to make. Everything was decided for me. At last I had obtained certainty.

And so I became engaged. We at once received endless congratulations. My success was something like Guido's on the violin, as far as the applause was concerned. Giovanni kissed me and was most affectionate. He said he had looked upon me as a son ever since he began to give me advice about my business.

My future mother-in-law also held out her cheek for me to kiss, which I did as lightly as I could. I should not have escaped that kiss even if I had married Ada.

"You see I guessed everything," she said, with an incredible assurance, which only went unpunished because I did not choose to protest.

Then she embraced Augusta, and the warmth of her affection was betrayed by a sob, even in the midst of her joyful outpourings. I could not endure Signora Malfenti, but somehow her tears seemed to surround my engagement, for that one evening at least, with a halo of sympathy and importance.

Alberta was radiant, and shook me warmly by the hand:

"I will be a good sister to you," she said.

And Ada said:

"Bravo, Zeno!" then in a lower voice she added: "I want to tell you this: you may think you have been too hasty, but no one has ever acted more sensibly than you have this evening."

Guido expressed great surprise.

"I realized for the first time this morning," he said,

"that you were after one or other of the sisters, but I could not discover which."

They couldn't be very intimate then, if Ada had not said anything to him about my proposal. Had I really been in too much of a hurry?

Soon after, however, Ada said to me:

"I want you to love me as a sister. Let us forget all that has happened; I shall never say a word to Guido."

It was after all very nice to have given such pleasure to a whole family; and if I was not as happy as I ought to have been, it was only because I was so tired. I felt terribly sleepy, which was a proof that I had acted with a certain amount of foresight. I was going to have a good night at last.

At supper Augusta and I received all our congratulations in silence. She felt she must apologize for not taking part in the general conversation and said:

"I can't talk. You must remember that till half an hour ago I had no idea what was going to happen to me."

She always spoke the exact truth. She did not know whether to laugh or cry, and looked at me. I tried to make my answering look into a caress, but I don't know if I succeeded.

Later the same evening, while we were still at supper, my feelings were wounded again; this time by Guido.

It appears that shortly before I had arrived to take part in the spiritualistic séance, Guido had told them what I had said that morning about not being absent-minded. They at once produced so many proofs of my having lied that in revenge, or perhaps to show that he could draw, he did two caricatures of me. The first showed me with my nose in the air, leaning on an umbrella stuck in the ground. In the second the umbrella was broken and the handle was sticking into my back. The two caricatures attained their object of making people laugh by the simple fact that the figure which was supposed to represent me, and was not really in the least like me except that he was very bald, was identical in both sketches, and might therefore be supposed to be so absent-minded that he had not even changed his position though an umbrella had run through his back.

Everyone laughed a great deal, too much I thought. I was extremely pained by this very successful attempt to pour ridicule on me. It was on this occasion that I was conscious for the first time of a stinging pain in my right forearm and hip, an intense burning sensation, a turmoil of the nerves, as if they had been seized by a kind of cramp. I held my hip in alarm and clutched at the same time at my right arm with my left hand. Augusta said:

"What's the matter?"

I said the bruise was hurting me which I had got when I fell, as I was leaving the café.

I at once made an energetic effort to get rid of the pain. I thought it would probably be cured if I could think of a way to avenge myself for the insult. I asked for a piece of paper and a pencil, and tried to draw someone being crushed by a table falling on the top of him. By his side was a stick that had fallen from his hand at the moment of the accident. No one recognized the walking-stick, so that my vengeance fell very flat. In order that they might realize for whom it was intended, and how he had got into that position, I wrote underneath it: "Guido Speier fighting with the table." As a matter of fact nothing was visible of the man under the table but his legs, which might possibly have been like Guido's if I had not intentionally made them bandy, and if the spirit of vengeance had not intervened to make my already childish drawing worse still.

The severe pain I was suffering made me work very rapidly. Never before had my whole being longed so desperately to wound someone, and if I could have exchanged the pencil, which I was incapable of using, for a saber, perhaps my cure would have been complete.

Guido laughed heartily at my drawing, then remarked quietly:

"The table doesn't seem to have done me much harm."

It was quite true it had not hurt him at all, and it was the injustice of this which stung me so much.

Ada took Guido's two drawings, saying she wanted to keep them. I looked at her reproachfully and she was obliged to avoid my eyes. I had the right to reproach her for making me suffer so much.

Augusta came to my rescue by saying she wanted me to put the date of our engagement on my drawing, for she was going to keep it too. I felt the warm blood course through my veins at this token of her affection, of which I now first recognized all the importance. But it did not put a stop to my pain, and I could not help thinking that such a mark of affection given me by Ada would have produced a flow of blood sufficient to purify my nerves from all their long accumulation of poison.

I have never got rid of that pain. In my old age I suffer less from it because I view its advent with more indulgence, and only say: "Oh, are you there again, to remind me that I once was young?" But while I was young it was a different matter; not that the pain was severe, though it sometimes prevented my moving and would occasionally keep me awake all night. It played a large part in my life, because I was always trying to get cured. Why must I bear the brand of defeat throughout my life, and become as it were a walking monument to Guido's victory? It was necessary to banish that pain from my body.

And so began my series of cures. But the irrational cause of the malady was soon forgotten, and even I soon found it difficult to retrace. This was natural, for I had great faith in the doctors who were treating me, and sincerely believed them when they told me the pain was due sometimes to imperfect metabolism, sometimes to defective circulation, to tuberculosis, and various infections shameful or otherwise. All my treatments gave me temporary relief, so that each fresh diagnosis seemed at the outset to justify itself. Sooner or later they would break down, but they generally contained some element of truth, because none of my bodily functions are ideally perfect.

Only once they went completely wrong. I had gone to a sort of veterinary surgeon who insisted for a long time on treating my sciatic nerve with blisters, till he was nonplussed one day by the pain darting suddenly from my thigh to the back of my head, which could not be connected with the sciatic nerve. Æsculapius was furious and showed me the door, and I remember that I went off not in the least angry but only interested to notice that the pain, though it had changed its position, was exactly the same as before. It was just as violent and as inaccessible as it had been in my hip. It is curious how every part of our body may be susceptible to the same kind of pain.

All the other diagnoses have proved their right to lodge in my body, and still continue to strive among themselves for mastery. There are days when uric acid bears sway, others in which it is slain, or rather cured by an inflammation of the veins. I have whole chests full of medicines, and they are the only ones that I keep tidy myself. I love my medicines, and know that even if I give one up I shall go back to it sooner or later. And I don't consider I have wasted my time. I might have been dead long ago, who knows of what ghastly disease, if my pain had not simulated each in turn so as to induce me to get cured before it had time really to take hold on me.

But though I am unable to define its real nature I know when my pain took shape for the first time. It was really on account of that drawing which was so much better than mine. That was the last drop which made the pitcher overflow! I am certain I had never felt the pain before. I tried to explain its origin to a doctor, but I could not make him understand. Who knows? Perhaps psycho-analysis will bring to light all the changes that took place in my body during those days, and especially during the few hours immediately following my engagement.

Few hours! They seemed more than a few. When the party broke up Augusta said to me gaily:

"Till tomorrow then!"

This pleased me because it showed that I had attained my end, that nothing was over, but would go on just the same tomorrow. She looked into my eyes, and was cheered to find them respond warmly to her invitation. I went down the stairs, which I no longer counted, saying to myself:

"Who knows? Perhaps I do love her after all."

This uncertainty has never left me during the whole of my life, and today I am compelled to believe that true love is compatible with such a doubt.

But even after I had left the house I was not allowed to go home and enjoy the fruit of my evening's activity in a long, restoring night's sleep. Guido thought he would like an ice, and asked me to go with him to a café. He took my arm in a friendly way, and I responded with like good will. He was a very important person to me, and I felt I could refuse him nothing. My fatigue, which ought really to have driven me to bed, made me more submissive than usual.

We went into the very same place where poor Tullio had infected me with his disease, and sat down at a table a little apart from the others. On the way there my pain, which I little thought was to be my life's companion, had

been very bad, and I was glad to sit down, for this seemed
at first to relieve it.

I found Guido's company almost intolerable. He inquired with great curiosity into the story of my love for
Augusta. Did he suspect I was deceiving him? I told him
brazenly that I had fallen in love with her at first sight, on
the occasion of my first visit to the Malfentis. The pain I
was suffering made me talkative, as if I were endeavoring
to shout it down. But I talked too much, and if Guido had
really been listening he would soon have discovered that
I was not so much in love with Augusta as all that. I spoke
of the most conspicuous thing in her body, namely her
squint, which somehow made one expect that all other
limbs would be slightly crooked too. Then I tried to explain
why I had not proposed sooner. Guido was perhaps
surprised to see me turn up at the last minute only in order
to get engaged? I said emphatically:

"The Malfenti girls are used to a great deal of luxury,
and I could not make up mind whether I ought to take on
such a responsibility."

I was vexed at having dragged Ada in too, but there
was no help for it now; it was so difficult to keep Augusta
apart from Ada! I lowered my voice so as to keep myself
more under control and went on:

"I had to work things out first. I knew the money I
had was not enough. So I began thinking how I could
increase my business." I think I went on to say that it took
time to work it all out, and that was why I had kept away
from the Malfentis for five days. By dint of exercise my
tongue was beginning to arrive at a certain degree of
sincerity. I was almost in tears, and pressing my thigh with
my hand I murmured:

"Five days is a long time."

Guido said he was glad to discover I was so cautious.
I remarked dryly:

"A cautious person is not necessarily more popular
than a scatterbrain."

Guido laughed.

"Curious," he said, "that the cautious person should
feel obliged to defend the scatterbrain."

Then he passed directly to telling me in a very matter-
of-fact way that he was about to ask for Ada's hand. Had
he dragged me to the café just to listen to his confession,

or had he got bored by hearing me talk so long, and now felt that he must have his turn?

I feel almost sure that I succeeded in showing equal surprise and pleasure. But I very soon contrived to get my own back.

I said viciously:

"Now I understand why Ada liked your travesty of Bach so much. You played well, but you remember there used to be a notice up in the streets of medieval Florence: *'Gli otto probiscono di lordare.'* " *

The blow struck home and Guido turned red from the pain of it. He replied gently, because he now lacked the support of his small enthusiastic audience.

"Good God!" he began, in order to gain time. "Sometimes when one is playing one gives way to caprice. Very few of them knew Bach, so I thought I would modernize him a little for them."

He seemed quite content with his idea; so was I, because by making such an excuse he admitted he was in the wrong. This was quite enough to mollify me, and besides, I would not for worlds have quarreled with Ada's future husband; I told him I had rarely heard an amateur play so well.

He was not satisfied; he said he could only be considered as an amateur because he did not choose to rank as a professional.

Was that all he wanted? Very well; I agree with him: it was obvious that he could not be looked on as an amateur.

So we became friends again.

Then suddenly, out of the blue, he began talking against women. I listened to him with open mouth. Now that I know him better, I realize that he will plunge into an eloquent discussion on whatever subject, directly he feels at his ease. I had spoken earlier about the luxury the Malfenti girls were accustomed to, and he returned to the subject and went on to discuss all the other bad qualities of women. I was too tired to interrupt him. All I could do was to go on nodding my head in agreement, and even this I found very fatiguing. Otherwise I should certainly have protested. I know that I had every reason to talk against

* Roughly: *It is forbidden to commit a nuisance.*

women as represented by Ada, Alberta, and my future
mother-in-law; but he had no reason whatever for attacking
the sex that was solely represented for him by Ada, who
loved him.

He seemed to know a great deal, and tired as I was I
listened to him with admiration. It was not till long afterwards that I discovered he had adopted the genial theories
of the young suicide Weininger. While he talked I seemed
to receive a fresh revelation, as when I had heard him play
Bach. I almost wondered whether he was not trying to cure
me of my love. Otherwise why was he so anxious to convince me that women were incapable either of genius or
goodness? I think the cure might have been efficacious if
it had been administered by anyone but Guido. But I
remembered his theories and supplemented them later by
reading Weininger. They never do cure one, but it is well
to keep them in mind when one is running after women.

When he had finished his ice Guido felt the need of
a breath of fresh air, and persuaded me to join him in a
walk to the outskirts of the town.

I remember that for days past the whole city had been
longing for rain to cool the air, for the hot weather had
begun unusually early. Personally I had not even noticed
the heat. This evening filmy white clouds had begun to
collect, the kind that are popularly supposed to bring heavy
rain; but a great moon was climbing up the sky, which,
where it was still clear, was intensely blue: one of those
full-cheeked moons which, also in the popular belief, are
able to devour the clouds. In fact one could see that as
she climbed the clouds dispersed and the sky became clear.

I tried to interrupt Guido's continual chatter, which
compelled me to keep nodding my head and drove me to
distraction, by telling him about the kiss that the poet
Zamboni thought he had seen in the moon; how sweet that
kiss seemed in the moon of our dark nights, when compared with the injustice done me by Guido. As I talked,
and shook off the torpor produced by my continued assent,
my pain seemed to grow less. It was the reward of my
rebellion, and I went on developing my line of thought.

Guido was obliged to leave women alone for a while
and look up at the sky. But not for long! Directly he discovered with my help the pale woman's face in the moon
he resumed his argument with a witticism at which he

laughed loudly, though no one laughed with him in the
deserted street:

"What a lot of things that woman sees! It's a pity
that being a woman she can't remember them."

It was part of his theory (or Weininger's) that women
can never have genius because they have no memory.

We reached the bottom of the Via Belvedere. Guido
said a climb would do us good. I again consented to go
with him. At the top, by one of those impulses more
common to quite young boys, he stretched himself out on
the wall that separated the upper road from the one below.
He thought he was being very courageous to run the risk
of falling thirty feet. I was horrified at first when I saw
him in such a perilous position; then I recalled the system
I had myself evolved that very evening in a burst of
inspiration, in order to escape from my depression, and I
began to pray fervently that he might fall.

From that dangerous vantage-ground he still went on
preaching against women. He said that they always needed
toys like children, only more costly ones. I remembered
Ada saying how fond she was of jewelry, so perhaps he was
really meaning her! Then a fearful idea came to me. Why
shouldn't I make Guido fall those thirty feet? Wouldn't it
be only fair to do away with someone who was taking Ada
away from me without loving her? For a moment it seemed
to me that when I had killed him I should be able to run
straight to Ada and receive my reward. On that strange,
moonlight night I felt as if she were present and could hear
Guido insulting her. I must confess that for a moment I
really did think of killing Guido! I was standing by him as
he lay at full length on the low wall, and I speculated
coldly on how I had better take hold of him, so as to be
sure of being successful. Then I saw that I should have no
need to take hold of him at all. He was lying with his arms
folded behind his head, and it would only need a sudden
good push to throw him completely off his balance.

Then an idea came to me which seemed important
enough to be compared to the great moon climbing up the
sky and sweeping it clean. I had got engaged to Augusta
just in order to have a good night. How should I be able to
sleep if I killed Guido? This thought saved both of us. I
felt I must instantly change my position, for it was my
being above Guido which tempted me to kill him. I

dropped on my knees, and crouched so low that my head was almost touching the ground.

"Oh, the pain! The pain!" I screamed.

Guido was so startled that he sprang to his feet, begging to know what was the matter. I went on moaning in a lower tone, without paying any attention to his question. I knew why I was moaning; it was because I had wanted to kill him, and partly, perhaps, because I had not the courage to do so. The pain and my groans excused everything. It seemed to me that I was crying out that it was not my fault if I hadn't been able to do it. It was entirely the fault of my illness and this pain of mine. But as a matter of fact I distinctly remember that the pain went away completely at that moment, and that my groans were simply a piece of play-acting to which I tried in vain to give some context by remembering the pain I had suffered and attempting to reproduce its effect on me. But all my efforts were in vain; it would only return at its own time.

As usual Guido had various hypotheses ready to hand. Among others he suggested that it was probably the same pain as that which had been produced by my fall in the café. I thought the idea a good one and agreed.

He took me affectionately by the arm and helped me to rise. Then still supporting me and helping me as much as he could, he led me down the short incline. When we had got to the bottom I said I felt better and thought that with the help of his arm I might manage to go a little quicker. And so at last I was really on my way to bed! For the first time that day I experienced a genuine satisfaction in the thought that Guido was working for me; he was, in fact, almost carrying me. It was after all I who was imposing my will on him.

We found a chemist open, and he insisted on getting me a sleeping draught to take to bed. He built up a whole theory of actual pain and the exaggerated idea one had of it, the pain being increased by the sense of exasperation which it had in the first instance produced. That small bottle was the beginning of my collection of drugs, and it was appropriate that it should have been chosen for me by Guido.

To give a more solid foundation to his theory he argued that I must have been suffering from that pain for

some days past. I was sorry I could not agree with him.
I said I had felt no pain whatever at the Malfentis' that
evening. It was impossible that I should have suffered just
at the moment when my long-dreamed-of hopes were
realized.

I was anxious in all sincerity to be like what I had
claimed to be, and kept on repeating to myself:

"I love Augusta, I don't love Ada; I love Augusta, and
this evening my long-dreamed-of hopes were realized."

We continued to walk through the moonlit streets. I
think that Guido at last found my weight rather too much,
for he became silent. He suggested however seeing me
home to bed, which I refused; when at last the door of
my own house shut behind me I gave a sigh of relief. No
doubt Guido uttered a similar sigh.

I went up the stairs four at a time, and was in bed in
less than ten minutes. I fell asleep at once, and during the
short time I was awake I thought neither of Ada nor
Augusta, but only of Guido, who had been so kind and
patient. It is true I could not forget that I had wanted to
kill him such a short time before, but that was of no importance, because the thing no one knows about and which
leaves no trace does not exist.

Next day I went in some trepidation to my fiancée's
house. I was uncertain whether the pledges I had taken
the evening before had really the importance that I attached to them. I soon discovered they had for everyone
present. Augusta had by no means forgotten she was
engaged; in fact to her it seemed much more definite than
to me.

It was a tedious engagement. I felt as if I had broken
it off several times and patched it up again by a great effort,
and I am surprised that nobody seemed to notice it. I never
felt in the least as if I were going to get married, but
apparently I played the part of a fond lover to everyone's
satisfaction. I never missed an opportunity of kissing Ada's
sister and clasping her to my breast. Augusta submitted
dutifully to my embraces, and I behaved fairly well, but
only because Signora Malfenti never left us alone for more
than a few minutes at a time. My bride was much less ugly
than I had imagined, and it was by kissing her that I discovered her chief beauty: that she blushed so readily.

Whenever I kissed her a flame was lit in my honor, and I continued to kiss her more out of scientific curiosity than with the ardor of a lover.

But I felt desire for her too, which made the time pass rather less heavily. It was fortunate that Augusta and her mother did not allow my flame to burn itself out all at once, as I could often have wished. How could I have gone on living then? At least my desire gave me the same feeling of excitement each time I mounted the steps as when I had gone there, as I thought, to win Ada. When I counted an uneven number I promised myself that I would show Augusta that day what an engagement really might be. I pictured myself doing something violent which would completely restore my sense of freedom. That was all I really wanted, and it is curious that when Augusta realized what I was after she should have read it as a sign that I was passionately in love.

As far as I can remember that period was divided into two phases. During the first Signora Malfenti often used to send Alberta to chaperon us, or made little Anna and her governess do lessons in the drawing-room. Ada was never there, and I persuaded myself that I was glad of it, though I dimly remember thinking once that it would have given me great satisfaction to kiss Augusta in front of Ada. With what ardor I would have done it too!

The second phase began when Guido's engagement to Ada was made public and Signora Malfenti, like the practical woman she was, put the two couples together in the drawing-room to look after each other.

I know that Augusta professed herself completely satisfied with me during the first phase. When I was not trying to kiss her I became extraordinarily talkative. Talkativeness was an absolute necessity to me. I even invented fresh opportunities by persuading myself that as I was going to marry Augusta I ought to undertake her education. I trained her in gentleness, affection and, above all, fidelity. I don't remember exactly what form I gave to my sermons, though she has reminded me of some of them, for she never forgot them. She listened to me with the utmost deference and attention. Once in an outburst of eloquence I declared that if she ever should discover that I had been unfaithful to her it would be her duty to pay me back in the same coin. She indignantly protested that she would not even betray me with my own permission, and that if I were unfaithful to her she would only take the liberty to weep.

I think that these sermons, the content of which was really quite unimportant, nevertheless had a good effect on my marriage. They certainly had a considerable influence on Augusta's mind. Her fidelity was never put to the proof because she never knew when I had been unfaithful to her, but her affection and gentleness remained unchanged during the long years we lived together, just as she had promised me they should.

When Guido became engaged I initiated the second phase of my engagement with the following pronouncement: "Now I have completely recovered from my love for Ada." I thought up to then that Augusta's blushes had been enough to cure me, but one can never be completely cured! The memory of those blushes made me think that now the same sort of thing would go on between Ada and Guido. Surely that would be more efficacious still in putting a stop to my desire. My desire to rape Augusta belongs to the first phase. I was much less excited during the second. Signora Malfenti had certainly been wise in arranging for our supervision at the cost of so little trouble to herself.

I remember that I once began jokingly to kiss Augusta. Guido, instead of laughing at me, began kissing Ada in his turn. I thought it showed very little delicacy on his part, because he did not kiss chastely, as I had done owing to their presence, but he kissed Ada full on the mouth, caressing her with his tongue. I had got used by that time to thinking of Ada as a sister, but I was not prepared to see her being treated like that. Nor do I think I should have tolerated it if I had been her brother.

After that I never kissed Augusta again when Guido was there. Guido, however, tried on one occasion to draw Ada to him, but she resisted this time, and he never made another attempt.

I only dimly remember the many, many evenings we spent together. The scene that was repeated *ad infinitum* impressed itself thus on my mind: we were all four sitting round the delicately carved Venetian table, on which was burning an oil-lamp with a green shade, which threw everything into shadow except the embroidery on which the girls

were engaged: Ada on a handkerchief and Augusta on
something in a little round frame. I can hear Guido holding forth, and it must frequently have happened that I was
the only person he could find to agree with him. I remember too Ada's black wavy hair, on which the light fell in
such a way as to produce green and yellow tones in it.

We discussed that effect, and also the real color of her
hair. Guido, who understood painting as well, explained to
us how to analyze colors. I have never forgotten that lesson
on color, and to this day, when I want to understand the
color of a landscape, I half close my eyes until most of
the lines disappear and the lights alone remain, which in
their turn fade away into one real color. But when I undertake an analysis like this, immediately after the real images
there appears on my retina, as by a physical reaction, the
yellow and green lights in the black hair on which my eye
had its first lesson in observation.

I can never forget one evening, which was notable for
an expression of jealousy on Augusta's part immediately
followed by a serious indiscretion on mine. To tease us
Guido and Ada had retired to the far end of the drawing-
room and were sitting at the Louis Quatorze table, so that
I got a crick in the neck through turning round to talk to
them. Augusta said:

"Leave them alone; they really *are* making love!"

Without thinking of what I was saying, I replied in a
low voice that I doubted it, because Guido didn't like
women. It was a sort of excuse for having interrupted their
love-making by my conversation. But it was malicious and
indiscreet to let Augusta know how Guido talked about
women when he was alone with me, as of course he never
did with any other members of the family. The thought of
what I had said gave me a bad taste in my mouth for
several days, whereas I can truthfully say that the thought
that I had wanted to kill Guido did not upset me even for
an hour. But to kill someone, even treacherously, is more
manly than to wound a friend by betraying his confidence.

But Augusta did wrong to be jealous of Ada even then.
It was not in order to see Ada that I was twisting my neck
round like that. Guido's eloquence helped to while the
time away. I had become quite fond of him already, and
passed part of every day with him. I had a further tie of
gratitude to him for his high opinion of me, which he

communicated to the others. Even Ada would now listen to what I said with great attention.

Every evening I waited for the sound of the supper gong with a certain impatience. The chief thing I remember about those suppers is my constant indigestion. I ate too much from the sheer necessity of doing something. I made many fond speeches to Augusta, when my mouth was not too full to admit of it, and her parents might easily have got the unpleasant impression that my greediness interfered with my affection. They were surprised to find that when I came back from my honeymoon my appetite was much smaller. It disappeared directly I was no longer compelled to act a passion I did not feel. It is unpardonable to let the bride's parents see you treat her coldly just when you are supposed to be preparing to go to bed with her! Augusta particularly remembers the affectionate things I whispered to her, sitting at that table; I must have invented marvelous ones between one mouthful and another, and I am amazed when they are repeated to me, for they never sound as if I could possibly have said them.

Even my father-in-law, that rogue Giovanni, was taken in, and as long as he lived he would always quote my love for his daughter (meaning, of course, Augusta) whenever he wanted to give an example of a "*grande passion.*" He smiled beatifically, good father that he was, but he none the less rather despised me for it; because, according to him, no real man would entrust his fate to the hands of a woman, or fail to see that there were other women in the world besides his own wife. Which shows that I was not always judged quite fairly.

My mother-in-law, on the other hand, never really believed in my love, even when Augusta was gradually beginning to believe in it herself. For many years she continued to eye me distrustfully, uncertain as to the fate of her favorite daughter. That is another reason why I am certain she was really leading me on during the days that preceded my engagement. It was impossible to deceive her, for she must have known my state of mind better than I did myself.

At last came the day appointed for my marriage, and that very day a final doubt assailed me. I was supposed to be with Augusta by eight o'clock in the morning, but at a quarter to eight I was still in bed, smoking furiously, and

looking out of my window at the sun, which was shining
brightly for the first time that winter. I meditated deserting
Augusta! The absurdity of my marriage became evident
now that I no longer wanted to remain close to Ada.
Nothing tremendous could happen supposing I failed to
keep my appointment! Besides: Augusta had been a charming fiancée, but one could never know how she would
behave directly she was married. Supposing she were suddenly to call me an idiot for having let myself be caught
like that?

Fortunately Guido came in at this point, and far from
rebelling, I apologized for being late, saying that I thought
another hour had been fixed for the wedding. Instead of
reproaching me Guido started talking about himself and
telling me of the many times he had missed an appointment, out of absent-mindedness. Even in that respect he
wanted to prove himself superior to me! I had no time to
stop and listen to him: I wanted to be off. And so I actually
had to run to my wedding.

All the same I arrived very late. No one reproached
me, and all except Augusta were satisfied with Guido's
explanations. She was so pale that the color had even left
her lips. Even though I could not say I loved her I would
on no account have wished to hurt her. I tried to repair
my fault, and was so foolish as to give at least three reasons
for my being late. That was too many, and showed so
clearly what I must have been thinking about in my bed
as I lay watching the wintry sun, that our departure for
the church had to be delayed to allow time for Augusta to
recover herself.

My "yes" at the altar was very distrait, because I felt
so sorry for Augusta that I was busy evolving a fourth
explanation of my delay, which seemed to me the best of
them all.

However, when we left the church I saw that the color
had quite come back to Augusta's cheeks. I was really rather
annoyed at this, because my "yes" ought not to have been
enough to reassure her as to my love. I was quite ready to
treat her very roughly, supposing she had now recovered
sufficiently to call me a fool for letting myself be caught.
But instead of that, she took advantage of a moment when
we were left alone, to say with tears in her eyes:

"I shall never forget that you married me, though you did not love me."

I did not protest, because it was so obvious that I could not. But I embraced her tenderly and compassionately.

After that the matter was never discussed again between us, for marriage is much simpler than being engaged. Once one is married, one no longer talks about love, and if ever one feels the need to do so the senses intervene and enforce silence. But animal instinct may have become so humanized as to undergo a complicated process of falsification, and it may happen that as one bends over a woman's head one evokes a light that is not there. You close your eyes, and the woman becomes someone else, to change back to herself again when you have left her. It is to her that all your gratitude is due, especially if the effort was successful. And so, if I had to be born again (Mother Nature is capable of anything), I would willingly marry Augusta, but would never choose to be engaged to her.

At the station Ada offered me her cheek for a fraternal kiss. I had not noticed her before among all the crowd who had come to see us off, and I thought at once: "Yes, it is you who are responsible for this!" I put my lips close to her veiled cheek, taking care not to touch it with them. It was the first satisfaction I had known that day, and for one instant I realized the advantage my marriage gave me. I had avenged myself by refusing to profit by the only opportunity I had ever had of kissing Ada! But when the train had started and I was sitting by Augusta, I was not sure of having acted rightly. I was afraid I might have prejudiced my friendship with Guido. But I suffered more still as I reflected that perhaps Ada had not even noticed that I had not kissed the cheek she had held out to me.

She had noticed it, but I only discovered this some months later, when I saw her and Guido off from the same station. She kissed all the others. But to me she held out her hand, though very cordially. I shook it coldly. Her revenge came too late, for in the meantime the circumstances had completely changed. After I returned from my honeymoon we had been on the most friendly terms as brother and sister, so that her refusing to kiss me was quite inexplicable.

Wife and Mistress

At various times in my life I have thought myself to be at last on the road to health and happiness, and this faith was never stronger than during my honeymoon and the few weeks immediately following our return home. I began by making a startling discovery: I loved Augusta as much as she loved me. At first I refused to believe it. I enjoyed the passing day, but expected the next to be altogether different. But one day followed another, and they were all radiant with love and kindness— Augusta's naturally, but also, and this surprised me, my own. Every morning renewed her tender affection and my equally tender gratitude, which, if it was not love, was very like it. Who could have foreseen it, that day I went limping from Ada to Alberta to arrive at last at Augusta? I discovered that far from being a blind beast driven by another's will, I was a very clever man. When she saw my astonishment, Augusta said:

"But why are you so surprised? Didn't you know that marriage was like this? I knew it, though I know so much less than you."

I don't remember now whether it was before or after I became so fond of her that I formed the great hope that I might in the end grow like Augusta, who was the personification of health. During our engagement I had scarcely been conscious of this quality in her; I was far too busy studying first myself and then Ada and Guido. The oil-lamp in that drawing-room had never shed its rays on Augusta's modest head of hair.

I have talked a lot about her blushes. When these faded, as naturally as the colors of the dawn fade before the full rays of the sun, Augusta walked boldly along the path so many of her sisters have trodden before her on this earth; those who are content to find all their happiness in law and order, or else to renounce it altogether. Although I knew her security to be ill-founded, since I was its foundation, I loved and adored it none the less. I felt obliged to treat it with the same respect I had previously shown to spiritualism. It might be true, and so might faith in human life.

One thing I found very startling: every word and every act of hers showed that she believed in eternal life. She never said it in so many words; but she was surprised once when I, who had hated superstitions before I learned to love her, felt the need of reminding her of the shortness of life. She knew that we must all die, but, now that we were married, this did not prevent us from remaining together for ever and ever. Did she not know then that when two people are united in this world it is for such a short, infinitely short time, that one can never understand how one has become so intimate, when there were endless ages during which we had not known each other and there would be endless ages again during which we shall never meet? I understood at last the meaning of perfect health in a human being, when I realized that for her the present was a tangible reality in which we could take shelter and be near together. I tried to be admitted to this sanctuary and to stay there, resolved not to laugh either at myself or her; for my skepticism would only be a symptom of disease, and I must at least beware of infecting someone who had given her life into my keeping. It was my desire to protect her which made me behave for a while like a normal human being.

She knew all about the things that drive a man to desperation, but they seemed to change their nature when she regarded them. Even if the world does go round, that is no reason for being seasick. On the contrary, the world goes round but everything else stays in its place. And these stationary things are of immense importance; a wedding-ring, jewels and clothes—the black dress or the green, or

the walking costume, which was hung in the wardrobe
directly she got home; also her evening dress, which must
on no account be worn in the daytime, and only in the
evening if I put on dress-clothes. Then there were the
hours of meals, which must be rigidly observed, and also
bedtime. All these hours had a genuine existence and were
always in their right place.

On Sunday she attended mass, and I sometimes went
with her to see what effect the contemplation of pain and
death had on her. For her it seemed not to exist, and the
visit was a source of quiet refreshment to her for the whole
week. She used to go on certain feast-days too, which she
knew by heart. That was all; whereas if I had been religious
I should have ensured my everlasting happiness by stopping
in church all day long.

Even here below there were plenty of powers that be
to reassure her. There were Austrian and Italian officials,
who made the streets and houses safe for people to live in,
and I did my best to share her admiration for them. Then
there were the doctors, who had gone through all their
medical training in order to cure us if by some unhappy
chance we fell ill. I made daily use of the latter authorities;
she never did. And so I knew only too well how hideous
my fate would be when I should at last be struck down by
a mortal disease, while she, who was securely guarded both
above and below, firmly believed that she would find
salvation.

I am trying to arrive at the source of her well-being,
but I know that I cannot succeed, for directly I start
analyzing it I seem to turn it into a disease. And now that
I have begun writing about it I begin to wonder whether
health like hers did not perhaps need some treatment or
training to correct it. But during all the years I lived with
her such a doubt never crossed my mind.

What importance I acquired in this little world of
hers! I had to say what I thought about every proposal,
whether it concerned food or clothes, people or books. I
was obliged always to be doing something, and I must say
that I was not bored by it. I was collaborating in the building up of a patriarchal family, and I myself was on the way
to becoming the patriarch I had previously hated, and who
now stood for me for an emblem of health. It is one thing

to be a patriarch, and quite another to be called on to
revere someone else who has assumed that position. I
desired health for myself, and did not mind what happened
to those who were not patriarchs. During our honeymoon
in particular, I was prone to assume the dignified pose of an
equestrian statue.

But even on our honeymoon I did not always find it
easy to live up to the model I had put before myself.
Augusta wanted to see everything just as if she had been on
a voyage of instruction. It was not enough to have been to
the Pitti Palace, one had to go through all those innumerable galleries, stopping at least a few minutes in front
of each work of art. I refused to go beyond the first room,
and saw nothing else; but it was sufficient fatigue inventing
excuses for my laziness. I spent a whole morning in front
of the portraits of the founders of the Medici family, and
made the discovery that they were like Carnegie and
Vanderbilt. How very strange! Yet they belonged to my
own race. Augusta did not share my surprise. She knew
what Yankees were, but she did not yet quite know what
I was.

But even her strength broke down at last, and she was
obliged to give up museums. I told her how once, when I
was at the Louvrè, I got in such a rage with all these works
of art that I very nearly smashed the Venus of Milo in
pieces. Augusta said:

"It is lucky one only has to visit museums on one's
honeymoon, and then never again!"

And it is true that life lacks the monotony of museums. There come days which seem worthy of being
framed, but they are so full of conflicting sounds, of line
and color and living, burning light that they never become
tedious.

Health impels people to action, and to take upon
themselves a whole world of worries. Directly the museums
are closed one must begin buying things. Though she had
not lived in it, Augusta knew our house much better than
I did; she knew that a certain room had no looking-glass;
that another had no carpet, and that a statue would look
so well in a third. She bought a complete drawing-room set,
and from every town we visited we sent home at least one
large packing-case. I could not help thinking it would have

been much more convenient and less tiresome to buy everything in Trieste, for now we had to worry about having it sent off, insured, and passed through the Customs.

"But don't you know that all goods have to travel? Aren't you a merchant yourself?" she inquired, laughing.

There was some truth in what she said.

"Goods have to travel in order to be sold and to make a profit," I retorted. "Failing that one lets them stay where they are, and does the same oneself!"

But her enterprise was one of the things I liked best about her. It was deliciously ingenuous; for one could know nothing about the history of the world if one imagined one had made a good bargain simply by acquiring something; it is when you come to sell it that you prove the value of what you have acquired.

I thought I was on the road to perfect health. My pain was much better, and my general condition was one of continued cheerfulness. It was a duty I owed to Augusta, and which I had vowed to fulfill in those memorable days, and it remained the only oath I never broke except for a few brief moments when life laughed louder than I did. Our relationship was a happy one from the first. I was always smiling at what I thought was her ignorance, and she, who thought me so clever, at my mistakes, which she flattered herself she could have avoided. I remained outwardly cheerful even when my malady returned in full force. I continued to smile as if the pain I suffered only tickled me.

In the course of our long journey through Italy I suffered a good deal, in spite of my newly found health. We had started off without letters of introduction, and many of the strangers we found ourselves among seemed to me hostile. It was an absurd fear, but I could not get over it. I might have been attacked, insulted or, what was worse, maligned, and who would have defended me?

This fear became a positive panic, though fortunately no one, not even Augusta, found out about it. I was in the habit of buying almost every paper that was offered me in the street. One day when I was standing in front of a newsvendor's bench, it occurred to me that he might easily take a dislike to me and have me arrested as a thief, because although I had only bought one paper from him I had a number under my arm still unopened, which I had bought

from other newspaper boys. I hurried away, followed by
Augusta, to whom I gave no reason for my sudden haste.
I made friends with a coachman and a guide, feeling that
in their company I was at least sure not to be accused of
childish thefts.

The coachman and I had certain obvious points in
common. He was very fond of the Castelli wines, and said
that his feet would often swell up suddenly. He went into
hospital, and when he came out cured they strongly advised
him to give up drinking wine. So he made what he called
an iron resolution, because to guarantee its solidity he tied
a knot in his metal watch-chain. But when I knew him his
chain was hanging down on his stomach without any knot
in it. I invited him to come and stay with me at Trieste.
I described the taste of our native wine, which is so different from his, to make him feel his cure was bound to be
successful. He would not hear of it, and refused with an
expression of prophetic home-sickness on his face.

I made friends with the guide because I thought he
seemed superior to most of his class. It is not difficult to
know more history than I do, but even Augusta, with her
accuracy and her Baedeker, verified many of his statements.
He was young too, so took us at a good pace down the
streets lined with statues.

When I lost these two friends I left Rome. The coachman, who had had a great deal of money from me, evidently wanted to show me that wine went to his head
sometimes, and threw us against a very solid old piece of
Roman masonry. The guide one day took it into his head
to maintain that the old Romans understood all about
electricity and made great use of it. He declaimed some
Latin verses in proof of his statement.

At that time I was attacked by a slight illness from
which I was never to recover. It was a mere trifle; the fear
of growing old, and above all the fear of death. I think it
arose out of a kind of jealousy. I was only afraid of growing
old because it brought me nearer to death. While I was
alive I was sure Augusta would never betray me, but I
pictured to myself that directly I was dead and buried, no
sooner would she have provided for my tomb to be kept in
good order and the necessary masses said, than she would
look about for my successor, whom she would then en-
throne in the same sane and regular world as that in which

I now reigned supreme. Her splendid health would not perish just because I was dead. I had such tremendous faith in her health that it did not seem to me possible it should perish unless it were shattered into fragments by an express train.

I remember one evening at Venice we were going in a gondola along one of those canals whose profound silence is interrupted every now and then by the light and noise of a thoroughfare suddenly crossing above it. Augusta was on the look-out, as usual, and taking accurate note of everything: a fresh, green garden rising above a dirty mudbank which the retreating tide had laid bare; a campanile reflected in the turbid water; a long dark lane with lights and people at the end of it. All I could do in the darkness was to be uncomfortably conscious of myself. I reminded her how time was passing and that she would soon be taking the same honeymoon journey with someone else! I was so certain of it that I felt as if I were telling her a story that had already happened. And it seemed out of place that she should begin crying, in order to prove to me that the story was untrue. Perhaps she had misunderstood me, and thought I was accusing her of intending to murder me. Far from it! To make my meaning clearer I described the way I should probably die; my legs, in which the circulation was already poor, would become gangrened, and the gangrene would spread and spread till it reached a vital organ, indispensable to keeping my eyes open. I should have to shut them, and . . . adieu patriarch! Another one would have to be produced.

She continued to sob and, amid the tremendous melancholy of that canal, her sobbing seemed to me to be very significant. Had she suddenly become aware of her own fearful strength and did it fill her with despair? In that case all humanity ought to have joined in her lamentation. But I discovered later that she had no conception of what health really is. Health cannot analyze itself even if it looks at itself in the glass. It is only we invalids who can know anything about ourselves.

It was on that occasion that she told me how she had loved me even before we met. She had loved me from the first moment that her father had mentioned my name and spoken of me in the following terms: "Zeno Cosini, a naïve youth who pricks up his ears when he hears of anything doing in business, and at once puts it down in a notebook that he promptly loses." If I didn't notice her confusion at our first meeting it must have been because I was feeling rather confused myself.

I remembered how when I first saw Augusta I had been quite put off by her plainness, seeing that I had fully expected to find there four lovely girls whose names began with A. I now discovered that she had loved me for a long time. But what did that prove? I could not alter my opinion. I was sure that if I died she would choose someone else. When she had become calmer she leaned closer to me and suddenly asked me, laughing:

"Where should I turn for my second husband? Don't you see how ugly I am?"

Yes, I should probably be allowed a certain time in which to putrefy peacefully.

But the fear of growing old never left me, and always on account of my fear of handing over my wife to someone else. That fear was not diminished even when I was unfaithful to her, and was not increased by the thought of losing my mistress for the same reason. That was quite a different matter, totally unrelated to the first. When the fear of death assailed me I turned to Augusta for comfort, as children hold out the hand they have hurt to their mother to be kissed. She always found some fresh words of comfort. On our honeymoon she promised me thirty more years of youth; nor does she promise less today. I knew only too well that those weeks of happiness during our honeymoon had brought me sensibly nearer to the terrifying specter of death. Augusta might say what she would, my account was soon settled: every week I drew nearer to that one week.

When I saw that I was falling a prey too often to the same distress of mind, I thought I must not wear her out by continually repeating the same things to her, so to let her know that I wanted comforting I would only murmur: "Poor Cosini!" She knew then exactly what was troubling me and hastened to envelop me in the warmth of her affection. So I always succeeded in being comforted by her even when the cause of my distress was quite different. One day, when I was feeling quite ill at the thought of

having been unfaithful to her, I murmured by mistake:
"Poor Cosini!" I was glad that I had, for it was infinitely
sweet to be comforted by her even in a case like that.

On our return from the honeymoon I had the pleasant
surprise of living in a warmer, more comfortable house than
I had ever known before. Augusta introduced all the con-
veniences which they had in her own house, but a great
many others as well, which she herself invented. The bathroom, which within living memory had always been at the
end of a long passage, about half a mile from one's bedroom, was now next door and contained a great supply of
taps. Then she had turned a tiny room next to the dining-
room into a coffee-room. The floor was covered with rugs,
with several great leather armchairs, and here we spent half
an hour every day after our meals. Contrary to my wishes
it had every convenience for smoking. Even my little study,
though I tried to keep it as it was, underwent several
changes. I was afraid I should hate it if any changes were
made in it, but I found, on the contrary, that only now
had it become habitable. Augusta had arranged the light so
that I could read sitting at the table, lounging in the armchair, or lying on the sofa. There was a music-stand too for
my violin, with a little lamp of its own which shone on
the music without hurting one's eyes. There too, against
my will, I was surrounded by every convenience for smoking
comfortably.

All these improvements necessitated a good deal of
building and a certain amount of disorder which was
disturbing to our peace. For Augusta, who was working for
eternity, the brief inconvenience no doubt did not matter,
but it was a very different thing for me. I strongly opposed
the idea of putting up a private laundry in the garden,
which would actually have involved building a little house.
Augusta assured me that a home laundry was essential to
the children's health. But as there were no children yet,
I didn't see why I must be inconvenienced by them before
they arrived. In any case she brought into the old house
a feeling of the open air; her love was like the swallow's,
whose first thought is for its nest.

But I played the lover too, and used to bring her home
flowers and jewelry. My life had been entirely changed by
marriage. After a few feeble efforts I gave up trying to
dispose of my time as I pleased, and kept to the most rigid

time-table. In this respect my education made great strides.
One day, soon after our return from the honeymoon, I
innocently let myself be persuaded not to go home to
lunch, and after eating something at a bar stayed out till
the evening. When I got home I found Augusta had had
no lunch herself, and was quite faint from hunger. She did
not reproach me, but I could not make her see that she
had done wrong herself. She declared, quietly but firmly,
that if I didn't let her know I wasn't coming back she
would always wait lunch for me, even till dinner. That was
no joke! Another time a friend persuaded me to stay out
till two in the morning. I found Augusta sitting up for me,
with her teeth chattering because the stove had gone out.
She caught a slight chill in consequence, which stamped
that lesson on my mind.

One day I decided to make her a splendid present: I
decided to work! She wanted me to, and I also thought
that work would be good for my health. It is natural that
someone who has no time to be ill actually is less ill. So
I went to business, and if I did not persevere it was really
not my fault. I went with the best intentions and in the
most humble frame of mind. I never suggested taking over
the management of the business; all I wanted was to be
allowed to keep the register. That huge book, with its rows
of neat entries like street after street of houses, filled me
with respect, so that my hand trembled as I wrote in it.

Olivi's son, a well-dressed youth who wore glasses and
was learned in all the commercial sciences, took over my
education, and I have nothing to complain of as to his
thoroughness. He bored me a good deal with his science of
economics and theory of supply and demand, which seemed
to me much more obvious than he would admit. But he
showed a certain respect for his employer, which I welcomed all the more as it was clear he could not have learnt
it from his father. Respect for property was, no doubt, part
of his science of economics. He never upbraided me for
the frequent mistakes I made in the entries; but he was
inclined to attribute them to ignorance, and gave me explanations, which were superfluous.

Unfortunately, seeing business done gave me the
desire to do some on my own account. Instead of the
register it was always my own purse that I saw before me,
and when I entered something to a client on the debit

side I felt as if I were wielding the croupier's shovel and collecting the money scattered over the table.

Young Olivi showed me the letters as they came in, and I read them very carefully with the idea that I should probably understand them better than anyone else. One day a quite ordinary offer aroused my passionate interest. Even before reading it I was conscious of a sensation very like the secret presentiment that sometimes comes to me at the gaming-table. That presentiment is difficult to describe. It consists in a certain expansion of the lungs, which makes one breathe the air with rapture, however smoky it may be. But there is something else; you know in a flash that everything will go well with you directly you double your pool. It takes some practice to appreciate this at once; one needs to have left the gaming-table with empty pockets, and the horrible sense of having missed one's opportunity; then one never lets it slip again. And if you have once missed it there is no more hope for that day; for the cards avenge themselves on you. But it is much more excusable to miss it sitting at the gaming-table than sitting peacefully in front of the register. Something at once cried out in me: "Buy that dried fruit immediately!"

I discussed it modestly with Olivi, though of course I did not mention its being an inspiration. Olivi replied that he only took on that sort of thing at somebody else's risk, in the hope of a small profit. He thus completely excluded the possibility of inspiration from my affairs, and reserved it entirely for a third party.

During the night my conviction only grew stronger: there could be no doubt about my having a presentiment. My breathing became so violent that it actually prevented my getting off to sleep. Augusta saw I was worried about something and insisted on knowing the reason. She at once shared my inspiration, and even went so far as to murmur sleepily:

"Aren't you the master?"

Next morning, before I went out, she said to me thoughtfully: "It is no good upsetting Olivi. Would you like me to speak to father about it?"

I said no, for I knew that Giovanni did not set much store by inspirations either.

I arrived at the office fully determined to fight for my idea, if only to avenge myself for having slept so badly.

The duel lasted till midday, after which the offer no longer held good. Olivi obstinately refused to consider it and silenced me with the usual remark:

"Perhaps you wish to curtail the authority with which your dear father entrusted me."

I was furious, and went on turning over the leaves of my register, fully resolved never to interfere again in business. But the taste of the sultana remained in my mouth and I inquired daily at the Tergesteo what the price of it was. I thought of nothing else. It rose very, very slowly, as if it were gathering itself together for a spring. Then in a single day it went up with an enormous leap. The vintage had been very poor and they had just realized the fact. What a strange thing inspiration is! I had not foreseen the poor vintage, only the increase in price. The cards were avenging themselves. Meanwhile I had lost all interest in my register and all respect for my teachers, especially as Olivi did not seem to be quite so confident now that he had acted wisely. It was my turn to laugh, and chaffing Olivi became my principal occupation.

The same offer was made to us again, this time at almost double the price. To put me in a good humor Olivi asked my advice, whereupon I triumphantly replied that I would never dream of eating raisins at that price. Olivi was offended and muttered:

"I am only abiding by the system I have followed all my life." And he went off to try and find a buyer. He found one for a much smaller quantity, and, still with the best intentions, came back and said to me hesitatingly:

"Shall I provide the stock for this small amount, do you think?" I was still in a bad temper, and replied shortly:

"I should have done that before selling it, if I had been you."

Olivi ended by losing all confidence in his own judgment, and left the sale uncovered. The raisins went on rising, and we lost as much as it was possible to lose on such a small sale.

Olivi got angry with me and declared that he had gambled only to please me. The old humbug forgot that I had told him to back the red, and that he had backed the black instead. Our quarrel was irreconcilable. Olivi appealed to my father-in-law saying that between us he and I would ruin the business, and that if my family preferred,

he and his sons would retire and give me a free hand. My
father-in-law at once declared in favor of Olivi. He said to
me:

"This business of the dried fruit is very instructive.
You two men will never be able to work together. Now
which of you is going to retire? The one who might have
done one good stroke of business if he had been left to
himself, or the one who has been running the whole
business alone for fifty years?"

He even persuaded Augusta to make me promise not
to busy myself with my own affairs in future.

"Your kindness of heart and simplicity seem to dis-
qualify you for business," she said. "Stay at home with
me."

I retired to my tent, or rather I should say my study,
in high dudgeon. I amused myself with reading and playing
for a while, but then I felt the need of a more serious
occupation and very nearly took up chemistry and law
again. Finally, I don't quite know why, I devoted myself
to the study of religion. I felt as if I were resuming the
study I had begun just at the time of my father's death.
Perhaps this time I was impelled by a strong desire to get
into touch with Augusta and become perfectly healthy like
her. Going to mass with her was not enough; I must get
there in other ways, such as reading Renan and Strauss,
the first with great enjoyment, the second as a punishment.
I only mention it here to show how great was my desire to
come nearer to Augusta. She had no idea of it when she
saw me with a critical edition of the Gospels in my hand.
She preferred indifference to scientific interest, and was
therefore incapable of appreciating the greatest mark of
affection I had yet shown her. She used to interrupt her
toilette or her household duties in order to look into my
room and greet me; but when she saw me bending over
those texts she would make a face and say:

"Are you still doing that stuff?"

Augusta's religion did not take time to acquire or put
into practice. You bowed your knee and returned to ordinary life again immediately! That was all. Religion for me
was a very different thing. If I had only believed, nothing
else in the world would have mattered to me.

I must confess that boredom sometimes visited my

perfectly appointed study—or was it worry, that although
I really felt the strength to work I kept on waiting for life
to set me some task? Whilst waiting, I often went out and
spent several hours at the Tergesteo or in some café. I lived
in a perpetual state of sham activity which bored me extremely.

The visit of a college friend, who had been obliged to
return in hot haste from a little village in Styria to be
treated for a serious complaint, decided my fate, though it
did not at first seem very significant. He came to call on
me after spending a month in bed in Trieste, during which
time his acute nephritis had become chronic and probably
incurable. But he believed himself to be better and was
looking forward to going almost at once, before the spring
was over, to a milder climate where he hoped to be completely restored to health. Perhaps it was staying too long
in our raw climate which finally proved fatal to him.

The visit of that man, who was at once so dangerously
ill and so cheerful and bright, seems to have brought me ill
luck. But I may be wrong; perhaps it only marked a stage
in my life through which it was necessary for me to pass.

My friend Enrico Copler was surprised to find that I
had heard nothing about him or his illness, though
Giovanni must surely know of it. But since Giovanni had
become ill himself he had had no time for anyone else,
and he had not said a word to me about it, though whenever we had a sunny day he would come to my house and
sleep for several hours in the open air.

I used to spend very lively afternoons with my two
invalids. We talked about their various complaints, which
is an invalid's chief distraction and a rather pleasing subject
to those who happen to be in good health. Their only
difference was that Giovanni was obliged to be out in the
open air, whereas the other was forbidden it. A little wind,
however, soon removed this obstacle by obliging Giovanni
to stay indoors with us in my warm, cozy little room.

Copler told us that his illness did not cause him any
pain though it made him very weak. It was only now he
was better that he realized how ill he had been. When
he talked about the medicines he had been ordered to take,
my interest was at once aroused. Among other things his
doctor had suggested something that was supposed to

produce sleep without any of the poisonous effects of sleeping-draughts. Was not this the very thing I needed myself?

When my poor friend heard that I needed medicine too he flattered himself for an instant that I might be suffering from his complaint, and advised me to have myself thoroughly examined and analyzed.

Augusta laughed heartily and declared that I was only a *malade imaginaire*. Then something that looked like anger passed over Copler's emaciated face. With a sudden virile impulse he shook off his physical disabilities and attacked me with great vehemence.

"*Malade imaginaire?* Well, I prefer to be a real one. In the first place a *malade imaginaire* is ridiculous and pitiable; and then nothing can cure him, whereas in the case of a real invalid like me there is always some drug that can be found to meet the case."

He seemed to speak like a healthy man, and I must confess that his words caused me some pain.

My father-in-law supported him energetically, but his scorn could not wither the most imaginary of invalids; it was so evidently dictated by the envy of a sick man for a sound one. He said that if he were as well as I was he would soon be at his business again instead of worrying his neighbors with complaints about his health, especially now that he had succeeded in reducing his stomach. He did not know that this very reduction was regarded as an unfavorable symptom.

Copler's attack had the effect of making me really look ill and care-worn. Augusta felt she must come to my assistance. She began stroking my hand as it lay on the table, and said that I worried no one with my malady, and she wasn't even sure that I believed in it myself, for otherwise I shouldn't have so much *joie de vivre*. This reduced Copler to the state of inferiority to which his health condemned him. He was quite alone in the world, and if he could compete with me as regards disease he could not produce any example of affection such as Augusta felt for me. He felt the need of a sick-nurse acutely, and was forced to confess to me later on how much he envied me on that account.

The discussion was resumed, though more calmly, during the next few days, while Giovanni was asleep in the garden. And Copler, after thinking it over, had come to the conclusion that the *malade imaginaire* was a real invalid, and perhaps more fundamentally and actually so than the others; for his nerves were in such a bad state that they registered disease when there was none, whereas their normal function was to give the alarm by a message of pain, so that one might at once hasten to defend the part that was in danger.

"Yes!" I said. "For example, with one's teeth, where you only feel pain when the nerve is uncovered, and you have to destroy it in order to cure it."

We finally agreed that one sort of invalid was as good as the other. In the case of Copler's nephritis, just what he had lacked and in fact still did, was that warning from the nerves, whereas mine, it seemed, were so sensitive that they already gave warning of a disease from which possibly I was going to die only twenty years later. They might in fact be called perfect nerves, their only disadvantage being that there were very few days when they left me in peace. Having succeeded in classing me among the invalids, Copler felt perfectly satisfied.

I don't know why the poor man had such a mania for talking about women; when my wife was not there we talked of nothing else. He maintained that in a real illness, at least those that he knew anything about, sexual desire becomes weaker, which was the body's way of defending itself; whereas in an imaginary malady due only (according to our diagnosis) to overactivity of the nerves, sex was pathologically strong. My experience seemed to corroborate his theory and we pitied each other. I don't know why I didn't want to tell him that for a long time now I had not been conscious of any abnormality of the sort. I might at least have confessed that I believed myself to be convalescent, if not quite well, so as not to wound his feelings, and because it is difficult ever to say you are well, seeing how complicated an organism our body is.

"Do you really desire all the pretty women you see?" asked Copler again.

"Not quite all!" I murmured, anxious to show him that I was not so ill as all that. I certainly no longer desired Ada, whom I saw every evening. As far as I was concerned she was forbidden fruit. The rustling of her skirts left me cold, and even if I had been allowed to lift them myself

I should have felt the same. It was lucky I had not married her. I took this indifference for a genuine manifestation of health. Perhaps my desire had exhausted itself by its very violence. But I felt the same indifference toward Alberta, charming as she looked in her neat school dress. Was the fact that I possessed Augusta enough to quench my desire for the whole Malfenti family? That really would have been highly moral!

Perhaps I refrained from talking about my virtue because I was always betraying Augusta in imagination; even while I was talking to Copler I thought, with a quiver of desire, of all the women I was giving up for her. I thought of all the women who were walking along the streets, and whose secondary sexual organs, just because they were hidden, became so important, whereas they disappeared altogether in the woman you possessed, as if the very fact of possession had atrophied them. My desire for adventure was still strong; the kind of adventure which begins by admiring a shoe or a glove or a skirt; anything that hides and alters a woman's shape. But this desire of mine was not really a guilty one. Copler did wrong in forcing me to analyze it, for to explain to somebody how he is made is only another way of authorizing him to do as he likes. Copler, however, went further, though of course it was impossible for him to foresee where his words or his actions would lead me.

Copler's words are so firmly fixed in my memory that when I go back over them they call up again all the feelings, things, and people that were associated with them. I had accompanied my friend down the garden, for he was obliged to be indoors before sunset. From my villa, which is on a hill, we had a view over the harbor and the sea, a view that is spoilt now by subsequent building. We stood for a long time watching the sea, stirred by a faint breeze which broke the calm light of the sky into a myriad shades of rose. The soft green of the Istrian peninsula was reposeful to look on, as it spread in a vast bow into the sea, shadowy but solid. The moles and breakwaters, stretching in stiff, repeated lines, looked small and insignificant, and the water in the little bays between lay dark and still because no breeze stirred it, or perhaps because it was muddy. In all that vast panorama peace seemed to have no place beside the endless movement of the rosy waters, and dazzled with the light, we soon turned from the sea to where night was already falling on the little terrace in front of the house.

In a great armchair outside the porch, with a cap on his head and the collar of his fur coat turned up, my father-in-law lay sleeping, with a rug wrapped round his legs. We stood and watched him. His mouth was open, his lower jaw hung lifelessly down, his breathing was noisy and hurried. His head was continually dropping on his chest, and each time he would raise it again without waking up. When he did so there was a slight flutter of his eyelids as if he wanted to open his eyes in order to recover his balance, and the rhythm of his breathing changed each time his sleep was interrupted.

It was the first time I had fully realized the serious nature of my father-in-law's illness, and I was profoundly moved.

Copler said to me in a low voice:

"He ought to be treated. He is probably suffering from nephritis too. He is not really asleep; I know that state quite well. Poor devil!"

He ended by recommending me his own doctor. Giovanni heard us and opened his eyes. He looked less ill at once and began teasing Copler:

"Are you wise to be standing about in the open air like that? I don't think it can be good for you."

He thought he had had a good sleep, and was quite unconscious that he had been short of breath with that great ocean of air in front of him. But his voice was hoarse and he had to stop talking and gasp for breath; his face was ashen and when he got out of his armchair he was cold as ice. He was obliged to go indoors. I can see him now walking across the terrace with his rug under his arm, panting as he waved us a laughing salute.

"There is a real invalid for you!" said Copler, who could not escape from his *idée fixe*. "He is dying and he doesn't even know he is ill."

I too thought that the genuine invalid did not seem to suffer much. My father-in-law and Copler have been lying these many years past in the cemetery of S. Anna, but one day not long ago, as I was walking past their graves, I could not help thinking that the fact that they had lain so long under their tombstones did not invalidate the thesis propounded long ago by one of them.

Before leaving his former abode Copler had wound up his affairs, so that like me he had nothing to do. But he could not keep quiet, and directly he was out of bed in the morning he began busying himself about other people's affairs, partly because he had none of his own to busy himself with, and partly because other people's seemed to him much more interesting. He would laugh at himself for this, but I was soon to discover what an agreeable flavor other people's affairs may have. He was a philanthropist, and as he had decided to live on the interest of his capital he could not afford the luxury of being charitable entirely at his own expense. So he would organize subscription-lists and take toll of his friends and acquaintances. He entered it all in a perfectly business-like way, and I regarded that book as his viaticum, and could not help thinking that if I had been in his place, with no family of my own and obviously destined not to live long, I should have swelled the funds with some of my capital. But he was the man of health *imaginaire* and would never touch anything but the interest, refusing to admit that he had only a short future before him.

One day he asked me for a few hundred kronen, to buy a piano for a poor girl who was already in receipt of a small monthly pension subscribed by me and a few other people at Copler's request. I could not refuse, but rather ungraciously remarked that it would have been lucky for me if I had stayed at home that day. I am subject to attacks of avarice from time to time.

Copler took the money with a few words of thanks, but soon afterwards my comment took effect, and a very important one. He came to tell me that the piano had arrived, and that Carla Gerco and her mother begged I would go and see them, so that they might thank me. Copler was afraid of losing a client, and hoped to bind me to him by letting me taste the sweets of gratitude for favors received. I tried to relieve his anxiety by assuring him that I was convinced he dispensed his charity admirably, but he insisted so much that at last I consented to go.

"Is she pretty?" I asked, laughing.

"Very pretty indeed," he replied, "but she is too hard a nut for us to crack."

It was curious that he must class my good teeth with his bad ones like that. He dilated on the honesty of the unfortunate family we were going to visit, telling me that the father had died several years ago, and that though they were miserably poor they had always earned their living respectably.

It was an unpleasant sort of story. An icy wind was blowing and I envied Copler his fur coat. I had to hold my hat on, otherwise it would have blown away. But I was in a good humor, because I was going to receive the gratitude my beneficence had earned me. We went on foot through the Corsia Stadion and the Giardino Pubblico. I had never been in this part of the city before. We entered one of those houses that our forefathers used to build as a speculation forty years ago, at a little distance from the town, which promptly surrounded them; it was modest, but better in appearance than those that are put up today for the same purpose. The staircase occupied a very small space and was therefore very steep.

We stopped on the first floor, which I reached a good while before my companion, who climbed very slowly. I was surprised that two of the doors opening on the landing had Carla Gerco's visiting-card nailed on them, while the third bore a visiting-card with another name on it. Copler explained that the Gercos had the kitchen and bedroom on the right side, and only one room on the left, which was Carla's studio. They had sub-let the middle part of their flat, so that the rent cost them very little; but there was the inconvenience of always having to cross the landing to get from one part to the other. We knocked at the door on the left—the studio—where mother and daughter, who expected us, were waiting to receive us. Copler introduced us. The mother, a timid little woman with snow-white hair, who had on a rather threadbare black dress, made a little speech, which she had evidently prepared beforehand; they felt honored by my visit and thanked me for my generous gift. After that she did not open her mouth again.

Copler stood by like a schoolmaster at an official examination, listening to the recital of the lesson he had taken such pains to teach. He corrected the poor woman, saying that I had not only given the money for the piano, but that I contributed to the monthly allowance that he paid out to them. He was a lover of accuracy.

Signorina Carla got up from the chair she was sitting on beside the piano, gave me her hand, and said simply: "Thank you!"

Anyway that was shorter. I was feeling rather over-come by my philanthropic role. I was behaving quite like a real invalid in busying myself in other people's affairs. What would that charming girl see in me? A person to be respected, no doubt, but hardly a man! She really was very charming. I think she wanted to look younger than she was, for her skirt was shorter than usual at that time, unless she was using up indoors one that she had worn before she had finished growing. Her head was that of a young woman and, judging by the care with which her hair was done, a young woman anxious to please. Her thick brown locks were arranged so as to cover her ears and part of her neck. I was so overwhelmed by my own dignity and so afraid of Copler's inquisitorial gaze that I could not look at her properly. But now I know everything about her. Her speak-ing voice was musical, and with an affectation that had become second nature to her she was wont to pause on the syllables as if she wanted to caress the sounds she made. On account of this, and of her very broad pronunciation of certain vowels—unusually broad even in Trieste—there was something rather foreign in her way of talking. I discovered afterwards that some singing-masters, when they are teach-ing voice-production, alter the value of the vowels. It was certainly the direct opposite of Ada's pronunciation. Every sound she uttered seemed a caress.

Carla kept smiling during the whole of our visit, perhaps under the impression that she had stamped a look of gratitude on her face. It was rather a forced smile, perfect as an expression of gratitude. When, several hours later, I began dreaming about Carla, it seemed to me that joy and sorrow conflicted in her face. But when I knew her better I found nothing of all this, and was forced to recog-nize once again that feminine beauty can simulate feelings that are wholly foreign to it, just as the canvas on which is painted a battle scene has nothing heroic about it.

Copler seemed as pleased about his introduction as if the two women had been the work of his own hands. He described them to me: they were always cheerful and industrious and contented with their lot. He made a little speech that might have come out of a lesson-book, and my mechanical nods of agreement seemed to prove that I had learnt my lessons and therefore knew all about poor, virtuous women who are left without any money.

Then he asked Carla to sing something. She refused at first, saying she had a cold. She wanted to put it off until another day. I thought she was probably afraid of our criticism and sympathized with her, but as I wanted to prolong the visit I joined Copler in begging her to sing. I added that I did not know if I should be able to come again as I was very busy. Copler, who knew that I had nothing on earth to do, gravely confirmed my statement. It was clear to me at once that he would rather I did not see Carla again.

She still tried to get out of it, but Copler insisted in such a way as positively to command her, and she obeyed. How easy it was to force her!

She sang *"La mia bandiera."* I sat on my soft sofa listening to her, and wishing with all my heart to be able to admire her. How wonderful it would be to discover she was a genius! But I was unpleasantly surprised to find that when she sang her voice lost all its musical quality. The effort of singing changed it completely. Carla could not play either, and her wooden accompaniment made the poor music seem still more feeble. I reflected that I was listening to a student and must consider whether she had enough voice. More than enough! In that small room I was almost deafened by it. So as to be able to encourage her to go on, I decided that it was only because she had been badly taught.

When she stopped I joined in the wordy applause that Copler was pouring out. He said:

"Imagine the effect of a voice like that if it was accompanied by a good orchestra."

There was certainly truth in that. Her voice needed a powerful orchestra. I was able to say sincerely that I hoped to have the privilege of hearing her sing again in a few months' time, and that then I should be able to say more about the value of her method. I added, less sincerely, that a voice of that quality deserved to be trained by a first-class teacher. Then in order to eliminate anything that might have seemed unappreciative in my first remarks, I began philosophizing on the necessity of finding a superlatively good method for a superlatively good voice. That superlative covered a multitude of sins. But when I was alone I wondered why I had found it so necessary to be sincere with Carla. Was I in love with her then, already? But I hadn't even looked at her properly!

On the rather smelly staircase Copler said again: "Her voice is too big. It is only good for opera." He could not know that I had already divined something quite different: her voice was suited to a small space where one could enjoy to the full its naïve quality, and dream of putting into it life and suffering—of making it into a work of art.

When we parted Copler said he would let me know when Carla's singing-master was giving a public concert. He was as yet very little known in the town, but was certain to become very famous. Copler was quite positive about this though the master was already fairly old. Apparently fame was to come to him now because Copler had got to know him. Dying men's illusions! Copler's and the singing-master's!

Curiously enough I felt I must tell Augusta all about my visit. You might think I did it as a precaution, seeing that Copler knew about it and I did not feel inclined to swear him to silence. But I was only too glad to talk about it. It was a great relief to me. Up to now I had nothing to reproach myself with, unless I had hidden it from Augusta. So that now I was completely innocent.

She asked me about the girl, and whether she was pretty or not. I found it difficult to answer: I said I thought the poor girl looked rather anemic. Then I had a bright idea:

"Supposing you were to interest yourself in her a little?"

Augusta had so much to do in her new house and in looking after her family, who were continually calling on her now her father was ill, that she thought no more about it. But my idea was really a good one.

Copler heard from Augusta that I had told her about our visit, and that made him forget the qualities he had attributed to the *malade imaginaire*. He said to me before Augusta that he must soon pay another visit to Carla. He evidently trusted me completely.

Having nothing to do I at once felt a desire to see Carla again. I did not dare go, however, lest Copler should hear of it. I might easily have found an excuse. I might have gone to offer her more money, without Copler knowing, but I should have had to be sure first that she would see it was to her advantage not to give me away. And supposing that real invalid should turn out to be her lover? I knew nothing at all about real invalids and it might very well be a habit of theirs to make other people support their mistresses for them. In that case a single visit to Carla would be enough to compromise me. I could not endanger the peace of my own little family; or rather, it was in no danger at all unless my desire for Carla should increase.

It did in fact increase continually. I already knew her far better than when I had shaken hands with her and said good-by. I particularly remembered the brown lock that hung down her snow-white neck and which I should have to push away with my nose before I could kiss the skin that was hidden by it. All that was needed to rouse my desire was to remind myself that on the first floor of a certain house in my little town a lovely girl was on show, and that it was only a short walk for me to go there and take her! Under such circumstances it became exceedingly difficult to fight against temptation, because one had to keep renewing one's fight every hour of every day, in fact so long as that girl was still living on her first floor. Carla's long vowels called to me, and perhaps it was their sound which had persuaded me that once I had overcome my own resistance I had no other to fear. But of course it was possible I was mistaken and that Copler knew more about it. This possibility helped to weaken my resistance, seeing that poor Augusta might still be saved from an infidelity on my part by Carla herself, whose duty as a woman it was to resist me.

Why did my desire for Carla make me feel such remorse, when it seemed to have come just in time to save me from the boredom which at that moment threatened me? It in no way damaged my relations with Augusta—rather the reverse. I not only spoke to her with my customary affection but lavished on her also expressions of tenderness which were springing up in my mind for that other woman. There had never before been such abundance of tenderness in my house, and Augusta seemed blissfully

happy. I was always punctual in my observance of what I
called the family time-table. I have such a tender conscience that I was always trying by my present behavior to
diminish the remorse I must feel in the future.

That I really did make some effort to resist is proved
by the fact that I did not reach Carla in one bound, but
by slow degrees. I began by going alone several days running to the Giardino Pubblico, sincerely intending to revel
in the green, which seems lovelier still by contrast with the
gray streets and houses that surround it. Then, not being
lucky enough, as I had hoped, to run into her by chance, I
left the garden intending to take a turn beneath her
windows. I did so with a degree of emotion that was like
the exquisite delight of a youth who encounters love for the
first time. It was so long now since I had been cut off, not
from love but from the paths that lead to love.

I had hardly got outside the Giardino Pubblico before
I found myself face to face with my mother-in-law. A
curious suspicion arose in my mind. What was she doing
there so early in the morning, such a long way from our
part of the town? Could it be that she was being unfaithful
to her sick husband? I at once discovered that I had
suspected her unjustly; she had been to the doctor, hoping
to be comforted by him after a bad night by Giovanni's
bedside. The doctor had tried to reassure her, but she was
so upset that she left me almost immediately, without even
remembering to be surprised at finding me in a place that
was usually only visited by old men, nurses, and children.

But the sight of her was sufficient to revive all my
feelings of attachment to my own family. I walked home
with a firm step, keeping time to it with the words: "Never
again! Never again!" Meeting Augusta's mother at that
moment, weighed down by grief, had brought all my duties
home to me with renewed force. I had had a good lesson
and it sufficed for the whole of that day.

Augusta was not in; she had gone to see her father and
was spending the morning with him. She told me at lunch
that they had been discussing whether they ought not to
postpone Ada's wedding, which was fixed for the following
week. Giovanni, however, was feeling better. He apparently
had eaten too much the night before at supper, and his
consequent indigestion had made his complaint seem
worse.

I told Augusta I had already had news of him from her mother, whom I had met by chance in the Giardino Pubblico. She did not express any surprise at my going there, but I felt the need of some explanation. I told her that I had for some time past taken a fancy to the Giardino Pubblico. I liked sitting on a seat and reading my paper there. I added:

"That Olivi did me a bad turn when he gave me so much time to waste!"

Augusta, who felt rather guilty about it herself, became quite pensive, and looked penitently at me. But I was really feeling in the best of spirits. I had nothing whatever to reproach myself with, for I spent the whole afternoon in my study, and could really flatter myself that I was cured of any wayward desire. I was engaged in reading the Apocalypse.

Although it was now officially understood that I was allowed to go to the Giardino Pubblico every morning, my strength to resist temptation had become so great that when I went out the next day I actually turned in the opposite direction. I had to go and buy some music, as I wanted to try a new violin method that had just been recommended to me.

Before going out I heard that my father-in-law had passed a very good night and was going to drive to see us in the afternoon. I was as glad on Guido's account as on my father-in-law's, because now he would be able to get married. Everything was going well; I was out of danger and so was my father-in-law.

But it was that very music which led me back to Carla. Among the methods I was shown was one that had got in by mistake, but was really a singing method. I read the title carefully: "Complete Treatise on the Art of Singing (Garcia School), by E. Garcia (son), with a Report on the Memorial Presented to the Paris Academy of Science."

I let the shopman attend to other clients while I began reading the pamphlet. I confess to have read it with the same excitement that a depraved youth might feel in reading a pornographic book. Yes. That was the way to approach Carla. It was just the book she needed and it would have been a sin on my part not to introduce her to it. I bought it and went home.

Garcia's book was in two parts: theoretical and practical. I went on reading it with the intention of becoming so familiar with it that I should be able to give good advice to Carla when I next went to see her with Copler. Meanwhile I should have gained time, and could continue to enjoy my sleep in peace, and look forward at the same time to the adventure that lay before me.

But it was Augusta herself who precipitated matters. She interrupted my reading by coming to say good morning to me, bent over me, and touched my cheek with her lips. She asked me what I was reading and, hearing that it was a new method, assumed it was for the violin and did not stop to look at it more closely. After she had gone I exaggerated the danger I had been in, and thought that prudence demanded I should no longer keep the book in my study. I ought to convey it at once to the person it was destined for, and so I came to plunge straight into my adventure. I had found something better than an excuse for doing what I wanted to do.

I no longer had any hesitation. Directly I reached the landing I turned to the door on the left. But outside the door I stopped a moment and listened to the strains of "La mia bandiera" echoing triumphantly down the stairs I felt as if Carla had gone on singing the same thing all the time I had been absent. I smiled to myself, feeling a great affection and longing for her childishness. Then I opened the door cautiously without knocking, and went into the room on tiptoe. I could not wait; I wanted to see her at once. In that small room her voice really sounded very unpleasant. She was singing with great enthusiasm, and with much more expression than on my first visit. She was leaning well back in her chair, so as to be able to empty her lungs more completely. I could only see her head, with the great plaits wound round it, and I withdrew terrified at the thought of having been so bold. Meanwhile she had reached the last note of her song, which she seemed as if she could not bear to let go, and I was able to return to the landing and close the door behind me, without her discovering that I was there. That last note had wavered up and down till at last it was absolutely in tune. This showed that Carla was capable of hitting the right note, and it now remained with Garcia to teach her to do so more quickly.

When I felt calmer I knocked again. She at once ran to open the door, and I shall never forget how sweet she looked against the door-post, with her great dark eyes fixed on me, unable at first to recognize me in the darkness.

But I had calmed down so much that all my old doubts took possession of me. I was about to be faithless to Augusta, but I thought that, as on the previous days I had managed to be satisfied with going no farther than the Giardino Pubblico, it ought to be easier still for me to stop at the threshold, give her the compromising book and go away completely satisfied. For a brief moment I was full of good resolutions. I even called to mind some curious advice that had been offered me in order to help me give up smoking, and which might come in useful on this occasion: sometimes it was quite enough if one lit a match and threw away both match and cigarette.

It would have been very easy for me to do this, for Carla herself, when she recognized me, blushed and seemed on the point of running away. She was ashamed, as I discovered later, of being seen in the poor shabby little dress she wore in the house.

When I saw she had recognized me I began making excuses:

"I have brought you this book, because I thought it would interest you. If you prefer, I will leave it here and go away at once."

My words sounded brusque, or so it seemed to me, but their meaning was the reverse, for I had really left it to her to decide whether I should go away on the spot or stay behind and betray Augusta.

Her decision was quickly taken; she took hold of my hand to prevent my going, and pulled me into the room. Everything seemed to swim before me. I remember my excitement was due less to the exquisite contact of her hand than to that touch of familiarity which seemed at once to decide my fate and Augusta's. I really believe that I went in rather reluctantly, and when I go over the story of my first infidelity I have distinctly the sense of having been seduced.

Carla's face was really beautiful when she blushed like that. I was deliciously surprised to discover that even though she had not expected me she had hoped all the same that I would come. She said in the kindest voice:

"So you really felt you wanted to see again the poor girl who owes so much to you?"

If I had wanted to I could have taken her in my arms on the spot, but the idea never entered my head. So little did I think of such a thing that I did not even reply, because her words seemed to me rather compromising: I at once began talking about Garcia, and saying how useful she would find the book. I championed the book with such enthusiasm that I was led into saying more than I meant to. Garcia, I told her, would teach her how to produce notes that were as solid as metal and as light as air. She would learn from him that a tone ought only to represent a straight line or a flat surface, but the surface must be really flat.

My enthusiasm dried up at once when she interrupted in a tone of great disappointment:

"Then you don't like my singing?"

I was amazed at her question. I had criticized her severely, but was quite unaware that I had done so, and I denied it in perfect good faith. So effectually too, that though I was only talking all the time about singing, I felt as if I had got back again to the desire which had so irresistibly drawn me to that house. And I spoke so affectionately that I could not help betraying part of the truth:

"How can you believe such a thing? Do you think I should have come in that case? I stood out on the landing for quite a long time, because I enjoyed your singing so much. Your voice is exquisite and completely unspoilt. It is just because I think it so perfect that I have brought you something which will help it to become even more so."

How powerful Augusta's influence must have been for me to go on protesting so vehemently that it was not desire that had driven me there!

Carla listened to my flattering words, which it would have been beyond her power to analyze. She had not had much education, but I discovered to my great surprise that she had a good deal of common sense. She told me that she often wondered whether she had enough talent and enough voice to go on; she said she felt she was not making much progress. Often when she had been practicing for a certain number of hours she allowed herself to sing "La mia bandiera" for a treat, hoping to detect some fresh quality in her voice. But it was always the same; no worse, perhaps even rather good—at least so the people said who had heard her (and she flashed a mildly interrogating glance at me, as if she wanted to be reassured as to the meaning of my words, which still rather bewildered her), but she was making no real progress. Her master said that there was no such thing as slow progress in art; one reached the goal by leaps and bounds, and one fine day she would wake up and find herself a great artist.

"But it is a long business," she sighed, gazing into space, and perhaps seeing written there her long hours of boredom and weariness.

If being honest is saying what you really mean, the honestest thing I could have done would have been to advise the poor girl to give up singing and become my mistress. But I had not yet left the Giardino Pubblico so far behind me, and besides, if for no other reason, I was not so very sure of my judgment in the matter of singing. For the last few moments I had been completely pre-occupied by one person—namely that tiresome Copler who used to spend every Sunday at my villa with my wife and me. That would have been a good moment to find some excuse for asking Carla not to say anything to him about my visit. But I did not do so because I could think of no way of disguising my request. It was a good thing that I did not, for a few days later my poor friend fell ill, and died shortly afterwards.

Meanwhile I told her she would find all she needed in Garcia, and she believed me for a moment, and thought the book was going to work wonders. But only for a moment. When she found herself confronted by so many words, she very soon began to doubt whether the magic would work. I read Garcia's theories aloud in Italian, then I explained them in Italian or, if that were not sufficient, translated them into the dialect of Trieste; but she did not feel anything moving in her throat, and that was where she would have had to feel it if she was really to believe in the efficacy of the book. The worst of it was that it did not take long to convince me that in my hands the book was not worth much. When I had read those sentences over three times and still did not know what to make of them, I avenged myself by criticizing the book freely. Surely Garcia was wasting his time and mine in trying to prove that since the human voice could produce a variety of sounds it could

not therefore be considered as one instrument. In that case
you might as well say that the violin was a conglomeration
of instruments. Perhaps it was foolish of me to make any
criticism openly before Carla, but if one wants to win a
woman it is difficult not to take advantage of any occasion
that offers for showing one's superiority. She did in fact
admire me for it, but literally pushed away the book, which
was our Galeotto, but which did not go with us to our sin.
I could not consent to banishing it so soon, but put it off
till my next visit. After Copler died we needed it no longer.
He was the only link between Carla's house and mine, and
when he was dead I had nothing to restrain me but my
own conscience.

Meanwhile we had become fairly intimate, more so
than one might haxe expected from that half-hour's conversation. I think a common ground of criticism is a sure
step toward intimacy. Poor Carla took advantage of that
intimacy to share her troubles with me. Since Copler had
come to their aid they had lived modestly but without real
privations. The thought of what would happen to them in
the future was the poor girl's chief anxiety. Copler, it is
true, brought them their subsidy quite regularly, but he
made it clear to them that they must not count on it. He
could not hold himself responsible for the future; they
must be prepared to provide for themselves. And then he
did not give them the money for nothing; he made them
feel that he was the master of the house and must be told
of every detail of expenditure. Woe betide them if they
allowed themselves to spend money on anything not first
approved by him! Not long ago Carla's mother had been
poorly and Carla had not practiced singing for several days,
so as to be able to look after the house. When her singing-
master told him about it Copler had made quite a scene,
and flounced out of the house saying that they did not
deserve that respectable people should be bothered to contribute to their keep. For several days they went in terror
lest he should really mean to abandon them to their fate.
When he came to see them again he made a fresh agreement with them, mapped out just how many hours Carla
was to sit at the piano, and how many she was to devote
to house-work. He threatened to burst in at any time of
the day and take her by surprise.

"Of course," said the girl, "he only does it for our

good, but he gets in such a rage about nothing at all that I am certain one of these fine days, when he is in a passion, he will turn us out in the street. But now that you are interested in us too, there is no danger of that, is there?"

She pressed my hand again. When I did not reply at once she began to be afraid I was on Copler's side and added:

"Copler is always telling us how kind you are."

This last remark was intended as a compliment to me, and to Copler as well.

The unsympathetic picture she drew of Copler was new to me and actually aroused my sympathy. I wished I could have been like him, knowing as I did so well that the feeling which drove me to that house made me the exact opposite of him. It was true, of course, that it was other people's money he brought them, but he gave up his time to them, a part of his own life. It was his fatherly feelings that made him so angry with them. But I could not help wondering whether, after all, it was not his own desire which made him take all that trouble. I at once said to Carla:

"Has Copler ever asked you for a kiss?"

"Never!" replied Carla, emphatically. "If he is satisfied with my behavior he coldly expresses his approval, just touches my hand, and goes away. At other times, when he is angry, he will not even shake hands with me, and he takes no notice even if I am frightened and cry. It would be a great relief to me if I could give him a kiss when he is like that."

When she saw me laughing Carla explained herself better:

"I would gladly let an old man like that kiss me, after all that I owe to him."

That is one of the advantages of being a genuine invalid; you appear older than you really are.

I made a feeble attempt to be like Copler. Smiling, so as not to frighten the poor girl, I said that when I took an interest in anyone I also tended to become tyrannical. On the whole, I thought that if you were studying any art it was your duty to do it seriously. At last I so identified myself with the part I was playing that I even ceased smiling. Copler was quite right to be strict with a girl who had no idea of the value of time; and she must remember how many people were denying themselves in order to help her. I was really very much in earnest.

The time came for me to be going home to lunch, especially as I did not want to keep Augusta waiting, that day in particular. I stretched out my hand to Carla, and it was only then that I saw how pale she was. I tried to comfort her:

"You may rest assured I shall always say all I can to Copler and the other people in your favor."

She thanked me but still seemed depressed. I realized afterwards that when she saw me come in she at once almost guessed the truth, and thought I was in love with her and that therefore she was saved. But then—especially when she saw me getting ready to go—she thought that I too only cared about art and singing, and that therefore if she didn't sing well and make progress I should desert her.

I saw she was terribly cast down. I felt very sorry for her, and as there was no time to be lost I reassured her by employing the method that she herself had suggested as being the most efficacious. I had already got as far as the door when I drew her to me, pushing away with my nose the great lock of hair in her neck, so that I could touch her skin with my lips and even with my teeth. It seemed quite a playful kiss and she ended by laughing too, but only when I had let her go. Up to then she had remained quite still in my arms, as if overcome with surprise.

She followed me out on to the landing, and as I began to go down she asked me laughingly:

"When will you come again?"

"Tomorrow, or perhaps later," I answered, already rather doubtful. Then I said decidedly: "I will certainly come tomorrow." And anxious not to compromise myself too much I added: "We will go on reading Garcia together."

Her expression never changed during that brief space of time. She accepted my first uncertain promise, gratefully accepted the second, and even agreed to my third proposal, all with the same smile on her face. Women always know what they want. There was no hesitation on the part of Ada who rejected me, of Augusta who accepted me, or of Carla who let me do as I liked.

Directly I got into the street I felt nearer to Augusta

than to Carla. I breathed the fresh air with enjoyment and a wonderful sense of freedom. I had only been playing, and it was none the less a game because it finished on her neck under the lock of hair. Carla had accepted my kiss as a promise of affection and above all of assistance.

But at lunch that day I began really to suffer. My adventure stood between Augusta and me like a great dark shadow which it seemed impossible that she should not see too. I felt insignificant, guilty, and ill; the pain in my side seemed like a sympathetic pain, an echo of the great wound in my conscience. While I was absent-mindedly toying with my food I sought relief in an iron resolution. "I won't ever see her again," I said to myself, "and if I am obliged to see her for the sake of discretion, it will be for the last time." Not so very much was asked of me after all: only one single effort not to see Carla again.

Augusta laughingly asked me if I had been to see Olivi, that I appeared so preoccupied.

I began laughing too. It was a great relief to be able to talk. I could not say the words that would really have made me at peace with myself, for I should have had to confess and promise never to do it again, but in default of that it was a relief to be talking at all. My words flowed on; I was in the best of humors. Then I had a brilliant idea; I spoke of the little laundry she was so anxious to have and which I had refused up to now, and I gave her permission to build it at once. She was so touched by my spontaneous offer that she got up and came over to give me a kiss. That kiss obviously wiped out the other, and I felt better at once. This was how we came to have our laundry, and even today, when I pass the tiny building, I remember it was Augusta who wanted it and Carla who gave her consent.

We passed an enchanting afternoon, in quiet enjoyment of each other. My conscience only troubled me when I was alone. When Augusta was there to talk affectionately to me it was appeased at once. We went out together. We went to her mother's and spent the whole evening with her.

As often before going to sleep, I lay for some time watching my wife, who was already asleep and breathing quietly. Even when she was asleep everything about her was in beautiful order, the sheet neatly folded under her chin and her hair done in a short plait down her back.

I said to myself: "I will never make her suffer. Never!" And I quietly fell asleep. Next day I would clear up my relations with Carla, and would find some means of reassuring the poor girl as to her future, without being obliged to kiss her.

I had a curious dream: I was not only kissing Carla's neck, I was positively devouring it. But though I was inflicting terrible wounds on it in my mad lust, the wounds did not bleed and the delicate curve of her neck was still unaltered under its soft white skin. Carla, prostrate in my arms, did not seem to suffer from the bites. It was Augusta, coming in unexpectedly, who suffered. To calm her I said: "I won't eat her all up: I will leave a little for you."

I only felt the dream as a nightmare when I awoke from it in the middle of the night and was able to remember it distinctly; but while it lasted not even Augusta's presence had been able to dispel the sense of satisfaction it gave me.

Directly I was wide awake I became fully conscious of the strength of my passion and the danger it presented to Augusta and me. Perhaps another life for which I was responsible was already stirring in the womb of the woman who lay beside me. How could I tell what demands Carla might make on me if she became my mistress? She seemed to be hungry for the affection that had been denied her till now, and how could I provide for two families? Augusta asked for a useful laundry. The other would ask for something else, not less costly. I could see Carla laughing and waving her hand to me from the landing after I had kissed her. She knew that I was bound to become her prey. I was frightened, and alone in the darkness I could not help uttering a groan.

My wife woke up with a start and asked me what was the matter, and I said the first thing that came into my head, after I had recovered from the shock of being questioned at the very moment when I felt as if I had shouted my confession aloud.

"I was thinking of old age coming on."

She laughed and tried to comfort me, without being able quite to shake off her sleepiness. She repeated the same phrases that she always used when she saw me cast down by thoughts of time passing:

"Don't think about it while we are still young. . . .
Sleep is so lovely."

I obeyed her command; I thought no more about it
and went to sleep again. At night speech is like a bright ray
in the darkness. It suddenly lights up reality before which
the creations of one's fancy fade away. Why was I so afraid
of poor Carla when I had not even become her lover yet?
It was clear that I had done my best to frighten myself
about the whole situation. Even the baby that I had pictured in Augusta's womb had given no sign of life, besides
the building of the laundry.

I got up still full of the best resolutions. I hurried to
my study and put some money into an envelope, intending
to offer it to Carla at the same moment that I announced
I was going to give her up. But I was also going to an-
nounce my readiness to send her more money any time she
liked to write to an address I would give her. Just as I was
on the point of going out Augusta asked me with a charming smile whether I would mind going with her to her
father's. Guido's father had come from Buenos Aires to
take part in the wedding and she must go and make his
acquaintance. But it was not so much Guido's father as
me she was thinking about. She hoped to renew the sweetness of the day before. But things were no longer the same,
I felt. I should be doing wrong to let any time pass before
putting into practice my good resolution. Even as we
walked down the street side by side, apparently secure in
our mutual affection, that other woman already believed
me to be in love with her. That was bad. I felt that walk
to be an intolerable burden.

We found Giovanni distinctly better. But he could
not put on his boots because of a tendency to swelling in
his feet, which neither he nor I thought anything of at the
time. He was in the drawing-room with Guido's father, to
whom he introduced me. Augusta soon left us to go and
join her mother and sister.

Señor Francesco Speier seemed a man of much less
education than his son. He was a man of about sixty, short
and stumpy, with very few ideas in his head and not much
vitality; which may have been because he was rather deaf
after an illness. He mixed a few Spanish words with his
Italian: "Every time, Señor, that I come to Trieste. . . ."

The two old men talked business, and Giovanni listened attentively, because the business they were talking of was very important as regards Ada's future. I listened to them absent-mindedly. I gathered that old Speier had decided to wind up his affairs in the Argentine and to hand over all his *duros* to Guido, to be used in founding a business in Trieste; then he proposed going back to Buenos Aires to live with his wife and daughter on the small estate he still intended to keep there. I could not understand why he told Giovanni all this before me, and I still do not understand.

At a certain point it seemed to me that they had both stopped talking and were looking at me as if they expected me to give them some advice, and in order to make myself agreeable I remarked:

"Your estate can't be so very small if it produces enough for you to live on!"

Giovanni suddenly bellowed out:

"What on earth are you talking about?" The volume of his tone recalled better days, but if he hadn't shouted so, Señor Francesco would probably have taken no notice of my observation. As it was, he grew pale and said:

"I hope very much that Guido will not fail to pay interest on my capital."

Giovanni, still shouting at the top of his voice, tried to reassure him:

"Interest? I should think so indeed! And twice as much if need be. Isn't he your son?"

But Señor Francesco still seemed a little uneasy and as if he were waiting for a reassuring word from me. I hastened to give it, and repeated it several times over, because the old man seemed to be harder of hearing than before.

Then they went on talking about business, but I was careful not to interfere again. Giovanni looked at me from time to time over the top of his glasses as if to keep me under observation, and there was something menacing about his heavy breathing. He went on talking for some time, and at a certain point broke off to say:

"Don't you think so?"

I hastily agreed.

My agreement must have seemed all the more fervent on account of the fury that was gradually taking possession of me and coloring every movement I made. What on earth was I doing in this *galère*, while the time was fast slipping away for putting into practice my good resolutions? Why should they force me to neglect something that was obviously so important both for me and Augusta? I was just preparing for an excuse for going away when the ladies burst into the drawing-room, accompanied by Guido. The latter, soon after his father's arrival, had given his bride a most magnificent ring. No one took any notice of me at all, not even little Anna.

Ada had the precious stone on her finger and stood resting her arm on her fiancé's shoulder, while she showed it to her father. All the ladies were in ecstasies over it, but I could not get up any enthusiasm for rings. I did not even wear my wedding-ring, because I thought it interfered with my circulation. Without saying good-by to anyone I slipped through the drawing-room door, and was on the point of going through the front door when Augusta, who had noticed my escape, caught me up. Her appearance quite startled me. Her lips were as pale as they had been on her wedding-day just before we went to the church. I said I had an important engagement; I had remembered just in time that a few days before, for no particular reason, I had bought a pair of very weak glasses for long sight, which I had never tried since I had put them in my waistcoat pocket where I felt them now. So I told her I had an appointment with an oculist whom I wanted to examine my eyes, as they had given me some trouble lately. She replied that I could go directly I had said good-by properly to Guido's father. I shrugged my shoulders impatiently, but stayed to please her.

When I went back into the drawing-room they all greeted me politely. As I was sure that I should have no difficulty now in getting away I felt in quite a good temper. Guido's father, who did not feel at home among so many new relations, said to me:

"Shall I see you again before I go back to Buenos Aires?"

"Yes, Señor," I said. "Every time you come here you will probably find me here too."

They all laughed, and I went away in triumph, with quite a cheerful parting wave from Augusta. Now that I was properly dismissed, after submitting to all the usual formalities, I was able to go off with an easy conscience. But I had another reason for being freed from the doubts that had beset me up to that moment; if I was hurrying away from my father-in-law's house it was because I wanted to get as far away from it as possible (even as far as Carla's house). It was not the first time, I said to myself, that they had suspected me there of basely conspiring to injure Guido. It was in perfect innocence and absence of mind that I had made that remark about the estate in the Argentine, and Giovanni had immediately interpreted my words as being said on purpose to prejudice Guido's father against him. It would have been quite easy to explain to Guido, if explanation was necessary; but there was only one way of dealing with Giovanni and the rest who believed me guilty of machinations like that: I must avenge myself. Of course I did not actually go off intending to betray Augusta. But I felt justified in doing exactly as I liked now, in the light of day. Not that paying Carla a visit was as yet bad in itself, but if I had happened to run into my mother-in-law again, and if she had asked me what I was doing there I should have answered without any hesitation:

"Well, if you want to know, I am going to see Carla." This was actually the only occasion on which I went to see Carla without thinking of Augusta, so furious had my father-in-law's attitude made me!

When I reached the landing I could not hear any sound of Carla's voice. For a moment I was terrified; could she have gone out? I knocked and went in without waiting for anyone to say "Come in." Carla was there all right, but her mother was there too. They were both sewing as perhaps people often do, but as I had never seen two people sewing before. They were both working at the same big sheet, each at an opposite corner. Here had I been in such a hurry to get to Carla, and now I found her mother there as well. That was not what I had bargained for. Under the circumstances neither good nor bad resolutions could take effect. Everything must still remain in suspense.

Carla sprang up at once, looking delighted, while the old woman slowly took off her glasses and put them in their case. I meanwhile discovered a cause for indignation quite other than the real one, which was that I was prevented from at once making the situation clear. Was not this the very time which Copler had set aside for practice?

I bowed politely to the old lady, though even that act of
courtesy was quite an effort to me. I said how-do-you-do to
Carla too; but almost without looking at her. I said:

"I came to see whether we mightn't find something
else useful in that book," and I pointed to Garcia's manual,
which was lying on the table exactly where we had left it.
I sat down just where I had sat the other day and at once
opened the book. Carla began by trying to smile at me,
but as I gave no answering smile she sat down beside me
and looked over, with an air of obedient attention. She
hesitated a little; she did not quite understand. I looked at
her and saw an expression of rather contemptuous obstinacy overspread her face. That was probably how she
looked, I thought, when Copler took her to task. Only
she was not sure yet whether my scolding was going to be
the same as Copler's for, as she told me afterwards, she
remembered that I had kissed her the day before, and
thought that my anger was probably never anything so very
terrible. So she was ready at any moment to exchange her
rebellious look for a friendly smile. I may as well say here,
as I shall have no time for it later, that her conviction that
she had tied me forever to her chariot wheels by allowing
me to steal a kiss, displeased me extremely; a woman who
can think that is very dangerous. But at the moment I felt
very like Copler, full of reproaches and indignation. I began
reading aloud the very part we had read the day before,
and which I myself had disposed of. I read pedantically,
without making any comment, and pausing on what seemed
to me the most important words.

Carla interrupted me, a slight tremor in her voice:

"I think we have read that before!"

So I was obliged to contribute some remarks of my
own. It does one good sometimes to hear one's own words.
Mine not only sounded kinder than I meant them to, they
put me into a sociable mood again:

"You see, Signorina," I said, accompanying my words
with a smile that might if one chose be interpreted as that
of a lover, "I should like to go over what we have read
before going any further. We may have judged it a little
too hastily yesterday; one of my friends has just told me
that if one wishes to understand everything that Garcia
says one must study the whole book carefully."

I suddenly felt as if I must show the old lady a little

consideration too, for she had probably, in the whole course of her not very happy life, never found herself in a similar situation. The smile I gave her was more of an effort than the one I had given Carla:

"It is not very amusing," I said, "but even anyone who is not studying music may get something out of it."

I went on reading obstinately. Carla was certainly feeling happier, and something approaching a smile played about her full lips. The old woman, on the other hand, looked like a poor caged beast, and obviously only went on sitting there because she was too timid to invent an excuse for going away. For my part, I was determined on no account to betray my desire to put her out of the room. Such a step would have been much too compromising.

Carla showed more courage; she asked me with great courtesy to stop reading for a moment, and turning to her mother, told her that she need not stop and that they would finish sewing the sheet in the afternoon.

The Signora came up to me and timidly held out her hand. I shook it warmly, almost affectionately, and said:

"I can understand you don't find the book very entertaining."

It sounded as if I was sorry she was leaving us. She went away after having laid on a chair the sheet which up to then she had been holding in her lap. Carla followed her out on to the landing for a moment, to say something to her, while I was consumed with impatience to have her to myself at last. She came back, shutting the door behind her, and took her old place beside me, with that same rather fixed look in her mouth which reminded me of an obstinate child. She said:

"I always practice every day at this time. And of course just today this work must come along, and had to be done in a hurry."

"But can't you see that I don't care a fig for your singing?" I cried, seizing her in a violent embrace. I kissed her first on the mouth and immediately afterwards on the spot where I had kissed her the day before.

Then a strange thing happened. She burst out crying bitterly and tried to escape from my arms. She told me between her sobs that she had suffered too much seeing me come in like that. She was crying out of self-pity, which

one always feels when one sees another person pitying one.
It is less the pain which makes one's tears flow than the
cause of that pain. One weeps when one arraigns the world
of injustice. And it was surely unjust to force that lovely
girl to work when one might have been kissing her instead.

It did not all go quite so smoothly as I had expected.
I was obliged to explain myself, and to get on quicker I did
not allow myself time to invent, but told the exact truth.
I told her how impatient I had been to see her and to kiss
her. I had intended to come and see her early in the
morning; I had lain awake all night thinking about it.
Naturally I did not tell her what I had intended to do
when I got to her, but that was a matter of small importance. What was true was that I had felt the same
agonizing impatience to see her, whether it was to tell her
I must give her up forever or to take her in my arms.
Then I told her what had happened that morning, and how
I had been obliged to go out with my wife and see my
father-in-law, and how I had been forced to sit there hopelessly while they discussed things that had nothing whatever to do with me. And then when I finally managed to
escape by dint of tremendous efforts and come all that long
way at full speed, what do I find but an enormous sheet
filling the whole room!

Carla burst out laughing, for she saw that I was not
the least like Copler. When she laughed it was as if a
rainbow had come out on her beautiful face, and I kissed
her again. She did not return my caresses, but accepted
them submissively, an attitude I adore, because I love the
weaker sex just in proportion as they are weak. She mentioned for the first time that Copler had said how devoted
I was to my wife. The shadow of a serious purpose passed
over her face as she said:

"So we must just be good friends and nothing more."

I did not put much faith in this very wise proposition,
seeing that the mouth that uttered it made no effort to
escape from my kisses.

Carla went on talking for quite a long time. She evidently wanted to arouse my compassion. I remember everything she said, but I did not believe it till she had gone
from my life forever. All the time she was with me I feared
her, as a woman who would sooner or later take advantage

of her ascendancy over me to ruin me and my family. I
never believed her when she said she only wanted to feel
that she and her mother would lack for nothing. I know
now that she never intended to get more from me than
would suffice for their bare needs, and whenever I think
of her I blush for shame at having understood her so little
and loved her so ill. She, poor child, never got anything out
of me. I would have given her anything, because I never
try to get out of paying my debts. But I was always waiting
for her to ask me.

She told me of the desperate straits she found herself
in after her father's death. For months on end she and her
mother had been obliged to work day and night on some
embroidery a shop had commissioned them to do. She had
naïvely believed that a divine providence would send them
help, and she would sometimes stand at the window watching for it to arrive. Copler came instead. Now she was
contented with her position, but she and her mother passed
uneasy nights sometimes, thinking how precarious the help
was that they were receiving. Supposing she should discover
one day that she had no voice and no talent? Copler would
certainly abandon her. He talked of giving her a public
performance in a few months' time. Supposing it should
prove a complete fiasco?

Still with the idea of arousing my compassion, she told
me that her family's financial misfortune had also shattered
her dreams of love; her fiancé had deserted her.

I was still far from feeling pity for her. I said:

"Did your fiancé kiss you a great deal? Did he kiss
you like I do?"

She laughed because I prevented her talking. I saw my
predecessor pointing me the way.

It was long past the hour when I ought to have been
home for luncheon. And I wanted to go. It was enough
for that day. I was very far from feeling the remorse that
had kept me awake during the night, and the unrest that
had driven me to Carla had entirely disappeared. But I was
not calm. Perhaps it is my fate never to be so. I felt no
misgivings, because now Carla had promised me as many
kisses as I wanted, under the name of friendship; and
that could not injure Augusta in any way. Then I thought
I had discovered the cause of the discontent, which as usual

sent dim pains winding through my body. Carla was seeing me in a false light. Carla might despise me for being so eager for her kisses when I was in love with Augusta! Carla who admitted liking me so much because she had such need of me!

I determined to win her esteem, and said something that I shall always remember as a cowardly crime, a treason committed of my own free will, without any need and with nothing to be gained by it.

I was almost at the door when I said to Carla, with the unperturbed air of someone who feels there is something he ought just to say:

"Copler told you of my love for my wife. It is true I admire her very much."

Then I told her in every detail the story of my marriage; how I had fallen in love with Augusta's elder sister, who would have nothing to do with me because she was in love with someone else; how I had tried then to marry one of the other sisters, who also refused me, and how I had at last to resign myself to marrying her.

Carla believed it all at once. Later on I heard that Copler, who knew something about the story, had given her some rather inaccurate details, which I now corrected or confirmed.

"Is your wife very pretty?" she asked, thoughtfully.

"That is a matter of taste," I answered.

Some restraining principle was still at work in me. I had said i admired my wife, but I had not yet said that I did not love her. I had not said that I thought her pretty, but neither had I said that I might not think her so. At the moment it seemed to me that I was being very truthful; now I know that in those few words I betrayed all women and all love, both mine and theirs.

To tell the truth I was still not quite at my ease; something else was lacking. I remembered my envelope of good intentions, and offered it to Carla. She opened it and gave it back to me, saying that a few days ago Copler had brought the month's money and that she had no need of money for the moment. This only increased my anxiety, for it was an old idea of mine that a really dangerous woman will not accept a small sum of money. She saw that something was troubling me, and with a charming naïveté that I appreciate now for the first time, she asked me for a few kronen to buy some plates they had had the misfortune to break in the kitchen.

Then something happened which left an indelible trace on my memory. Just as I was going I kissed her again, and this time she returned my kisses with the utmost fervor. The poison had worked. She said naïvely:

"I love you because you are so good that you are not even spoilt by being rich."

Then she added with a slight touch of malice:

"I know now that you must not be kept waiting, but that otherwise you are not at all dangerous."

On the landing she said:

"Can I send the singing-master and Copler to the devil?"

As I ran quickly downstairs I replied:

"We will see about that."

So there was still something in our relationship which remained unsettled; everything else had been put on a perfectly firm basis.

I found this so upsetting that when I got out into the street I began going in the opposite direction to my own house. I almost felt as if I must go back again at once and explain something else to Carla: namely my love for Augusta. I easily could, because I had never said that I did not love her. Only, in telling that perfectly true story, I had forgotten to tell the end, which was that I now really loved Augusta. Carla concluded that I really did not love her, and that was why she had returned my kiss so passionately, sealing it by a declaration of love. I felt now that but for that episode it would have been easier for me to have borne Augusta's trustful gaze. And to think that so short a while ago I had been glad to hear that Carla knew of my love for my wife, and that by her own wish the adventure I had gone in search of was offered me in the form of friendship flavored with kisses!

I sat down on a seat in the Giardino Pubblico, and absent-mindedly traced the date with my stick on the gravel. Then I laughed bitterly; I knew that that date would by no means mark the end of my betrayals. In fact only the beginning. Where could I find strength not to go back to the woman I desired so much, and who was waiting for me? Besides, I had already incurred a debt, a debt of honor. I had taken her kisses, and all that I had been allowed to give in return was the cost of some crockery! I was actually bound to Carla now by an unpaid debt.

We had a gloomy luncheon. Augusta did not ask why I was so late, and I did not tell her. I was afraid of betraying myself; all the more because during my short walk from the Gardens to my house I had toyed with the idea of telling her everything, so that the story of my treason was probably written on my honest face, for all to read. That would have been the only way of saving myself. If I had told her all I should have put myself under her protection and supervision. It would have been so decisive a step that I should have been able in good faith to put down the date of that day as one on which I had made a great step toward a clean and healthy life.

We talked of various indifferent things. I tried to be gay, but I could not even pretend to be affectionate. She was utterly taken aback; she was certainly waiting for an explanation, which never came.

Then she left me, to go on with her great work of putting the winter clothes away in special wardrobes. I often caught sight of her during the afternoon at the end of the long passage, intent on her work, with the servant to help her.

I was restless, and wandered about between my bedroom and the bathroom. I should have liked to call to Augusta and tell her I loved her, which would have been quite enough for her, poor innocent! Instead of which I went on thinking and smoking.

I passed naturally through various phases. There was even a moment in which my virtuous mood was interrupted by acute impatience for the next day to come so that I might hasten to Carla again. Perhaps even this desire had some good resolution behind it. The great difficulty was to make up my mind to do my duty entirely by myself. It was unthinkable really that I should get my wife to collaborate with me by confessing everything to her. There remained only Carla on whose lips I might seal my oath with one last kiss. But who was Carla? Not even her vengeance was the greatest danger I ran with her! The very next day she would probably become my mistress; who could tell what the consequences might be? All I knew about her was what I had heard from that idiot Copler,

and a more cautious person, Olivi for instance, would never
have dreamt of undertaking any business transaction on
information supplied by him.

All Augusta's work in my house, wholesome and admirable as it was, had been wasted. The drastic cure of
matrimony, undertaken by me in my eager quest for health,
had failed. I was worse off than ever, and wedded to my
own and other people's misfortunes.

Later on, when I had really become Carla's lover, my
thoughts would go back to that melancholy afternoon, and
I could not understand why I had not been capable of the
manly resolution that would have prevented my plunging
deeper in.

I had deplored my own infidelity so much beforehand
that you would have thought I might easily have avoided
it. It is easy to laugh at anyone for being wise after the
event, but it is almost as useless to be wise before it. During those hours of torment I wrote the date of the day
in my dictionary against the letter C (Carla) with the
comment: "Last Betrayal." But my first actual infidelity,
which led to all the subsequent ones, only took place on
the following day.

Late in the afternoon, having nothing better to do, I
took a bath. I felt as if my whole body were soiled and I
must wash the dirt away. When I was in my bath I
thought: "If I am to get quite clean I should need to dis-
solve in this water." I dressed again, but was so utterly
without will-power that I did not even dry myself properly.
It was getting dusk, and I stood by the window watching
the new green leaves on the trees in my garden. I began
to shiver, and thought with a certain satisfaction that
perhaps I had got fever. It was not death I desired, but
an illness, which would serve as an excuse for doing what
I wanted or which would prevent my doing it.

After having hesitated for so long Augusta at last
came to look for me. When I saw her so gentle and so
completely without ill-feeling my shivering fit grew worse
and my teeth began to chatter. Much alarmed, she forced
me to go to bed at once. My teeth were still chattering
from the cold, but I knew now that I had not got any
fever and refused to let her send for the doctor. I begged
her to put out the light and to sit beside me without talk-

ing. I don't know how long we remained like that; I gradually got warm again and recovered a certain degree of confidence. But my mind was in such a state of confusion that when she again spoke of sending for the doctor I told her that I knew what had made me unwell and would tell her about it later on. I had returned to my first resolution to confess everything to her. There was no other way in which I could relieve my mind of its burden.

We stayed like this for some time in silence. At last I noticed that Augusta had got up from her armchair and was coming toward me. I was frightened: perhaps she had guessed everything. She took my hand and stroked it, then she laid her own hand lightly on my head to feel if it was very hot, and said at last:

"You must have known it would come! Why did it take you so dreadfully by surprise?"

These strange words puzzled me, especially as they were accompanied by a smothered sob. It was clearly not my adventure she was alluding to. For how could I have foreseen that, or that it would affect me as it had? I asked, rather abruptly:

"What do you mean? What ought I to have known would come?"

She murmured in some confusion:

"That Guido's father would come for Ada's wedding."

At last I understood; she thought that my suffering was caused by Ada's coming marriage. I honestly felt that she was wronging me; I was not guilty of such a crime as that. I felt as pure and innocent as a new-born babe, and freed at once from every pang of conscience, I sprang out of bed:

"You mean to say that you think I am ill on account of Ada's marriage?" I cried. "You must be mad! Ever since I married you I have never given her a thought. I had even forgotten that the Señor had arrived today!"

I hugged and kissed her with the utmost devotion, and with such obvious sincerity that she was ashamed of her suspicions.

Every cloud vanished from her face too and we went to supper feeling quite famished. At the table where we had sat together so miserably a few hours ago we behaved now like two friends out on a holiday.

She reminded me that I had promised to tell her what had upset me. I invented a disease that was to enable me to do whatever I wanted without feeling guilty. I told her that while I was sitting with the two old gentlemen that morning I had begun to feel profoundly depressed. Then I had gone to fetch the spectacles that the oculist had ordered me. Perhaps that emblem of old age had added to my depression. I had been walking about the streets for hours and hours. I touched on some of the fancies that had made me suffer so much before, and there was even a shadow of a confession in some of the things I said. I don't remember what connection it was supposed to have with my imaginary disease, but I reminded her how our blood kept on turning and turning, how it held us upright and made us capable of thought and action, and therefore of sin and remorse. She could not understand that I was referring to Carla, but I felt as if I had told her.

After supper I put on my spectacles and pretended to read the paper for quite a long while, but I found the glasses made everything go misty. I felt slightly excited as if I had been drinking. I said I could not understand what I was reading. I continued to play the invalid.

I hardly slept at all that night. I longed passionately to hold Carla in my arms. I desired her and her only, the girl with thick, untidy locks and a voice that was so musical when it was allowed to choose its own note. She had become more desirable still because of all I had suffered on her account. All night long an iron resolution kept me company. I would be absolutely frank with Carla before possessing her; I would tell her the whole truth of my relations with Augusta. I could not help laughing to myself, it seemed so odd to set out to win one lady with a declaration of love for another on your lips! Perhaps Carla would resume her former attitude of passivity! But what difference would that make? At the moment nothing she could do would diminish the value of her submission, and of that I felt absolutely sure.

Next morning while I was dressing, I murmured to myself the words I was going to say to her. Before she gave herself to me Carla had got to know that Augusta's character and good health (I would explain to her at length what I meant by health—that also was to be part of her

education) had succeeded in winning not only my respect
but my love.

I was so busy preparing my long and elaborate speech,
while drinking my coffee, that Augusta received no other
token of affection than a light kiss before I went out. What
matter since I was hers! I was going to Carla to kindle my
passion for *her*.

I was so relieved to find Carla alone and expecting me
that directly I got into her room I drew her to me and
embraced her passionately. I was horrified by the rigor with
which she repulsed me. She was almost violent! She would
not let me touch her, and I stood open-mouthed in the
middle of the room, a prey to bitter disappointment.

But Carla quickly recovered herself and whispered:

"Don't you see that you have left the door open and
someone is going downstairs?"

I assumed the bearing of a formal visitor till the in-
truder had passed. Then we shut the door. She grew pale
when she saw me turn the key in the lock. Now everything
was clear between us. A little while after, when I had her
fast in my arms, she murmured faintly:

"Do you want it? Do you really want it?"

It was enough. She wanted it too. I instantly replied:
"What else should I want?"

I had forgotten that there was something I wanted to
explain to her.

A little later I should have liked to begin telling her
about my relations with Augusta, as I had omitted to do it
at first. But for the moment it was not easy. If I had begun
talking to Carla about something else at a moment like
that it would have seemed as if I underrated the importance of her offering. The densest of men realize that you
cannot do a thing like that, although we all know there is
no comparison between the importance of the offering before it is made and immediately after. It would be a terrible insult to say to a woman immediately after you had
lain with her for the first time: "First of all I must explain
what I said to you yesterday." What has yesterday to do
with it? Whatever happened yesterday ought to appear
unworthy of mention, and if anyone who calls himself a
gentleman does not feel this, so much the worse for him,
and he had better take care that no one else discovers it.

Clearly I was one of those insensitive gentlemen, for I was guilty of a mistake that no one could have made who was really wholehearted. I said:

"What made you give yourself to me? What had I done to deserve it?"

Was I expressing my gratitude or trying to rebuke her? Probably I was only trying to lead the way to some explanation on my part.

She was rather surprised and looked up at me to try and read my thoughts.

"I thought it was you who had taken me," she said, smiling affectionately at me to show that she did not mean it as a reproach.

I remembered that women always insist on the fiction that they have been raped. But she soon saw she had made a mistake, for you may take things, but people must give themselves. She whispered:

"I was waiting for you. You were the knight who was to come and set me free. Of course it is a pity you are married, but as you don't love your wife I need not feel that my happiness is destroying anyone else's."

The pain in my side came on so violently that I had to let go my embrace. Then I had not overestimated the importance of my idle words! It really was that lie of mine which had induced Carla to give herself to me! If I were suddenly to begin talking now of my love for Augusta, Carla would have every right to accuse me of having set a trap for her. It was out of the question to correct or explain anything at the moment. Later on I should have the chance of telling her all about it quietly. Waiting for that moment to come made a fresh link between Carla and me.

As I lay there beside her, my love for Augusta revived in all its force. I only had one wish now: to hurry home to my wife, just in order to see her working like a busy bee, putting all our clothes away in camphor and naphthaline.

But I remained at my post, and now had to face a new difficulty; something that worried me a good deal at first, for I detected in it the menacing prophecy of a sphinx. Carla told me how, directly I had gone the day before, her singing-master had come and she had quickly shown him the door.

I could not conceal a movement of annoyance. It was

as good as tellnig Copler straight away about our affair!

"Whatever will Copler say?" I exclaimed.

She burst out laughing and hid herself in my arms, this time really on her own initiative.

"But didn't we say that we were going to show him the door as well?"

She was a darling, but she could not seduce me again. I assumed the role of a pedagogue, which suited me quite well under the circumstances, for it gave me the opportunity of venting the irritation I felt in the bottom of my heart against the woman who would not allow me to say what I wanted about my wife. Everyone must work in this world I said, for she ought to know by this time that the world is a bad place, where strength is the only thing that counts. Supposing I were to die? What would become of her? I had hinted at the possibility of abandoning her in such a way that she could not take offense; and she was in fact even touched by it. Then with the obvious intention of depressing her I told her it was enough for me to express the smallest wish—my wife at once fulfilled it.

"Very well," she said, resignedly, "we will send for him to come back." Then she tried to explain to me why she disliked him so much. Day after day she had to put up with that horrible old man, who made her repeat the same exercises over and over again, though they were absolutely useless. The only days she ever enjoyed were when the singing-master was ill. She had hoped he would die, but she never had any luck.

She became quite violent in her despair. She kept on repeating that she never had any luck; she was hopelessly unlucky, always. When she thought how she had loved me at first sight because my way of doing things, my way of speaking, the look in my eyes seemed to promise her a life less full of hardships, less dreary, less dependent on charity given grudgingly, she felt as if she must cry.

It was not long before I made acquaintance with her sobs, and they bored me. She sobbed violently, passionately, and the whole of her frail body seemed shaken to its foundations. I felt as if a sudden assault had been made on my purse and on my life itself. I said:

"Do you imagine my wife has nothing to do but sit still? Why at this very moment while we are here together her lungs are being choked with camphor and naphthaline."

Carla exclaimed between her sobs:

"How lucky she is! All that furniture, all those clothes to look after!"

I thought with irritation that she wanted me to go off at once and buy her all those things, just so that she might have a sympathetic occupation. I am glad to say I did not show how angry I felt; instead, I obeyed the call of duty which told me to caress the poor girl who had just given herself to me! I did caress her. I stroked her hair gently, and soon her sobs died down and her tears flowed abundantly and without restraint, like rain after violent thunder and lightning.

"You are my first lover," she said again. "I hope you will go on loving me."

The statement that I was her first lover, which seemed to prepare the way for a second, did not move me greatly. It came rather late in any case, for we had given up discussing the question a good half-hour ago. It seemed to contain a new threat. A woman thinks she can demand anything of her first lover. I murmured softly in her ear:

"You are my first mistress too—since I married."

The softness in my voice was intended to veil the fact that we were quits.

I left her soon after, for I would not on any account be late for luncheon. Before going I again took from my pocket what I called my "envelope of good resolutions" because it had originated in an excellent resolution. I thought I should feel freer if only I were allowed to pay. Carla again quietly refused the money, which made me extremely angry; but the only sign I gave of my wrath was that I uttered the sweetest nothings at the top of my voice. I shouted to prevent myself striking her, but I disguised my feelings well. I said that in possessing her my dearest hopes had been realized, and that now I wanted to feel her more wholly mine by being allowed to support her entirely; but that she must take care not to make me angry, for I should suffer too much. Because I was in a hurry to get away I summed up my idea in a few words; shouted like that I must say it sounded very brusque.

"Are you my mistress or not? If you are it is my business to support you."

She was so startled that she made no more effort at resistance, but took the envelope, watching me anxiously all the while, in the hope of discovering which she ought to take seriously: my angry voice or the tender words that granted her all she desired. She was a little reassured when I touched her forehead with my lips before going away. On the stairs I began to be afraid lest, now that she had the money and the assurance that I would provide for her in future, she might show Copler the door too, supposing he should happen to call that afternoon. I thought for a moment of running upstairs again to beg her not to compromise me by doing anything of the kind. But I had no time to go back, I had to hurry away at once.

I am afraid the doctor who reads this manuscript will think at once that Carla would be an interesting subject for psychoanalysis. He will think that she offered herself to me a little too soon after discussing the singing-master. I thought too at first that she expected a little too much of me in return for her love. It was a great many months before I got to know the poor girl better. She probably let me seduce her so as to escape from Copler's tedious guardianship, and it must have been a painful surprise for her to discover it was all in vain, and that she was still expected to do what she least wanted to, namely sing. Even while she still was lying in my arms she was told that she had got to go on singing. This aroused in her a degree of pain and anger such as could not easily find expression in words. For entirely different reasons we both said the strangest things. When she got to love me she became quite natural again, though for a while her calculations had banished her simplicity.

As I was going away I thought: "If only she knew how much I love my wife she would behave quite differently." And indeed, when she knew it she did behave quite differently.

When I got into the open air I took great draughts of freedom and did not suffer at all from the thought of having compromised her. There was still time before tomorrow came, and I thought I might find some way out of the difficulties that hung over me. As I hurried home I was even bold enough to begin attacking our social system, as if that were responsible for my shortcomings. I thought it ought to be so arranged as to allow one to have intercourse occasionally with other women without having to fear the consequences. Even with women one could never love. I felt no trace of remorse. Therefore I don't think that remorse springs from regret for having done something wrong, but rather from a recognition of one's own sinful nature. The higher part of one's body bends down to observe and judge the lower, and finds it monstrous. The sense of horror it experiences at the sight is what we call remorse. In classical tragedy the victim did not return to life, and yet all remorse vanished: which meant that the deformity was cured and that it was idle to lament any longer. How could I have any room for remorse now that I was hastening with so much joy and tender affection to rejoin the wife of my bosom? I had not felt so innocent for a long time.

I was in high spirits during luncheon, and found it quite natural to behave affectionately to Augusta. There was nothing that jarred between us all day long. I did not overdo it; I behaved just as I should toward the woman whom I could honestly and securely call my own. There were times when I behaved with excessive devotion; but only when a conflict was going on in my mind between the two women, and the extravagant signs of affection I gave Augusta made it easier for me to conceal from her that the shadow of another woman lay darkly between us for the moment. Therefore I am bound to say that Augusta preferred me just when I was in fact less wholly hers.

I myself was rather surprised at being so calm, and attributed it to the fact that I had succeeded in making Carla accept the envelope of good resolutions. Not that I imagined I had settled my account with her in full. But I felt as if I had begun to pay an indulgence.

Unfortunately money remained my chief preoccupation during the whole of my affair with Carla. At every opportunity I would put some aside in a remote corner of my library, so as to be ready for any demands on the part of the mistress I so much feared. When at last Carla gave me up as well as the money, I used it to pay for something quite different.

We were to spend the evening at my father-in-law's, at a dinner to which only members of the family were invited, and which was to take the place of the traditional wedding breakfast. The wedding was to be two days later;

Guido wanted to take advantage of the improvement in
Giovanni's health in order to get married, for he did not
think it would last.

I went with Augusta early in the afternoon to call on
my mother-in-law. On the way I reminded her that she
had, only the day before, suspected me of still suffering
on account of the wedding. She was ashamed of her suspicion, and I talked a good deal about my innocence. Why,
only today I had come home quite forgetting that the
ceremonies preparatory to the wedding were to be this very
evening.

Although only the family were invited the Malfentis
wanted the dinner to be a very formal affair. Augusta had
been asked to help in getting the room ready and laying the
table. Alberta would have nothing to do with it. Not long
ago she had won a prize in a competition for a one-act
play, and was now busily engaged in reforming the National Theater. Augusta and I were given the table to lay,
with the help of a parlor-maid and one of Giovanni's office
boys, who seemed to have as much talent for arranging
things in a private house as in an office.

It was my job to fetch the flowers and help to arrange
them on the table.

"You see," I said, jokingly, to Augusta, "how I am
contributing to their happiness. If they were to ask me
to make ready the marriage-bed for them I should be just
as glad to do it!"

Then we went to look for the bride and bridegroom,
who had just returned from a formal call. They were sitting
in the most retired corner of the drawing-room, and had
probably been kissing. The bride still had on her outdoor
dress and looked extremely pretty, with a flush on her
cheeks from the warm room.

They seemed to want to hide the fact that they had
been kissing by pretending that they had been talking
about science. It was very stupid of them, in fact rather
ill-mannered. Who did they think would care whether
they kissed each other or not, that they must stop doing it
directly we came in? It did not, however, diminish my good
humor. Guido said that Ada would not believe that certain wasps were able to paralyze other insects, even much
bigger than themselves, by injecting something into them
which kept them alive and fresh, though paralyzed, so that

their offspring could use them for food. I seemed to remember too that some such monstrous fact did exist in nature, but I did not want to have to concede anything to Guido at that moment.

"Do you take me for a wasp, that you ask me about it?" I said laughing.

We left them alone to occupy themselves with more congenial matters. I was beginning to find the afternoon rather long, and should have liked to go home and sit in my study till dinner-time.

In the hall we met Dr. Paoli. who had just come from my father-in-law's bedroom. He was a young doctor who had already succeeded in building up a good practice. He was very fair, with the pink and white complexion of a boy. But he had a powerful physique and his remarkable eyes gave a rather imposing air of gravity to his whole person. His spectacles made them seem bigger than they really were, and when he looked at things he seemed to hold them with his eye as if he were caressing them. Now that I know both him and Dr. S. (the psychoanalytic man) so well, I feel as if the latter gazed at things with a conscious purpose, whereas Paoli gazes at them out of sheer, inexhaustible curiosity. Paoli observes his patient in every detail, and not only him but also his wife and the chair he is sitting on. God knows which of the two does more harm to his patients! During my father-in-law's illness I used often to go and see Paoli, to try and induce him not to let the family know how imminent the catastrophe was which threatened them, and I remember that one day he gave me a much more searching look than I cared for, and said, smiling:

"How you adore your wife!"

He was a good observer, for as a matter of fact at the moment I was adoring my wife, because she suffered so much during her father's illness, and because I was betraying her daily.

Paoli told us that Giovanni was even better than the day before. He said that there was no longer any cause for anxiety, as the time of year was favorable to his recovery, and he thought the bride and bridegroom might safely start on their honeymoon.

"Of course," he added, cautiously, "I mean barring

unforeseen complications." His qualifying clause was justified; unforeseen complications actually did take place:

Just as he was saying good-by he remembered that we knew someone called Copler, on whom he had been called to give an opinion only that day. He found him suffering from paralysis of the intestines, which had started with frightful toothache. He took a very serious view of it, but qualified it as usual by saying: "If he lives through the night there is still hope for him."

Augusta's eyes at once filled with tears of pity, and she begged me to go off at once and visit our poor friend. After a moment's hesitation I willingly enough agreed to do so, for I was suddenly filled with the thought of Carla. How hard I had been on the poor girl! Now that Copler was removed, there she was alone on her landing with no fear of her compromising me, because she would be cut off from all means of communication with the world I moved in. It was important that I should go and see her at once, to cancel the impression she must have received from my harshness that morning.

But I took the precaution of going first to Copler's. I must at least be able to tell Augusta I had seen him.

I already knew the humble, but clean and comfortable apartment where Copler lived in Corsia Stadion. An old pensioner had let him three of his five rooms. He opened the door to me himself. He was a heavy man with red eyes, who snorted as he paced uneasily up and down the short dark passage. He told me that the doctor who was in charge of the case had only just gone, and that he had said Copler was dying. The old man talked in a low voice, as if he were afraid of disturbing the peace of the dying, and panted heavily as he talked. I lowered my voice too. People do that in token of respect, but perhaps the dying would rather be accompanied on their last journey by loud, clear voices that would remind them of life.

The old man told me that a nurse was looking after the invalid. He made me stand reverentially outside the door for some time. Copler, with the death-rattle in his throat, was measuring out his last hours of breath. His noisy breathing consisted of two sounds; one hesitating, as if produced by the air he breathed in; one hurried, when he expelled the air from his lungs. Was he in a hurry to die?

A pause always followed these two sounds, and I thought that when that pause grew longer the new life would have begun.

The old man wanted me to go in, but I refused. I had been looked at reproachfully by too many dying people already.

I did not wait for the pause to grow longer, but hurried off to Carla. I knocked at the door of her studio, which was locked; but there was no answer. In my impatience I kicked the door, and then someone opened the front door of the flat, behind me. It was the voice of Carla's mother which said:

"But who is it?"

The old woman leaned out timidly, and when she had recognized me by the dim light that came from her kitchen, I saw that her face, in its frame of snow-white hair, became red all over. Carla was not in, and her mother offered to go and fetch the key of the studio, so that she could receive me in the only room, she said, which was worthy of me. But I told her not to trouble, and went into the kitchen and sat down on a wooden chair. A meager coal fire was burning on the hearth, under a saucepan. I told her not to interrupt cooking the supper on my account. She reassured me. She said she was cooking beans and that one could never cook them too much. To see such poor food, in a house of which I was the sole support, moved me and calmed the irritation I felt at not finding my mistress waiting for me.

The old woman remained standing, though I kept asking her to sit down. I told her at once that I had come to bring her daughter some bad news: Copler was dying.

The old woman let her arms drop to her side, and she immediately sank into a chair.

"My God!" she murmured. "What will become of us?" Then she remembered that it was worse for Copler than for her, and added compassionately:

"Poor gentleman! He was so good too!"

The tears were already streaming down her cheeks. She was clearly unconscious of the fact that unless the poor man had died he would have been turned out of her house that very day. This tended to reassure me. How discreet everyone was!

I tried to calm her by saying that I would go on doing for them exactly what Copler had done up to then. She pretended that she was not so much crying for herself as at the thought of their benefactor's death; she knew there were so many kind friends willing to help them.

She wanted to know what he was dying of. I told her how his last illness had begun, and recalled the discussion I had had with him a little time before about the utility of pain. Here were the nerves of his teeth becoming uneasy and calling for help, because about three feet away from them his bowels had ceased to function. I was so indifferent to the fate of the friend whose death-rattle I had heard only a short while before, that I went on playing with his ideas. If he had been there to hear I should have said that it was very easy to understand by analogy how the nerves of a *malade imaginaire* might suffer from an illness that had broken out a few kilometers away.

The old woman and I did not find much to say to each other, and I finally agreed to go and wait for Carla in her studio. I took up Garcia and tried to read a few pages. But I was not very interested in singing.

The mother soon joined me. She could not understand why Carla had not come back. She told me that she had gone out to buy some plates, which they badly needed.

My patience was almost exhausted. I said crossly:

"Why did you break the plates? Couldn't you have been more careful?"

Anyway I succeeded in getting rid of the old woman, who went off muttering:

"Only two. . . . I broke them myself."

This amused me for a moment, because I knew they had all been broken, and not by the old woman at all, but by Carla. Afterwards I discovered that Carla was not very nice to her mother, and that the poor old woman was terrified of saying anything about her to her protectors. Apparently she had once, in all innocence, told Copler how Carla hated her singing lessons. Copler scolded Carla, who was furious with her mother about it.

When at last my exquisite mistress came I surprised her by the violence of my passion. She murmured with delight:

"Fancy my having doubted your love. I have been

haunted all day by the idea of committing suicide, because
I had given myself to someone who was so unkind to me
directly afterwards."

I explained that I often got terrible pains in the head
quite suddenly; and on subsequent occasions when, if I
had not made a great effort, I should have hurried away
to Augusta on the spot, I had only to talk of those pains
in the head and I succeeded in controlling myself. I was
making progress! Meanwhile Carla and I mourned Copler
together; we actually mingled our tears over him!

But Carla was by no means indifferent to the sad end
of her benefactor. She became quite pale when she talked
about him.

"I can't help it," she said. "I am made like that. It
will be ever so long before I shall dare to be left alone.
I was frightened enough of him when he was alive."

And for the first time she timidly proposed my
spending the whole night with her. It was the last thing
I wanted to do; I could not bear the thought of spending
another half-hour in that room. But I was anxious not to
let the poor girl read my thoughts, of which I was
thoroughly ashamed, and began making objections on the
ground of her mother being there. She curled her lip dis-
dainfully and said:

"We could bring the bed in here; mother would never
spy on me."

I told her about the wedding banquet to which I had
to go, but I also felt I must tell her that I should never be
able to spend the night with her. Thanks to the resolution
I had just made always to be kind to Carla, I managed to
keep out of my voice any touch of harshness, but I felt that
any other concession, either actual or promised, would
have seemed like a fresh betrayal of Augusta, which I could
not bring myself to commit.

It suddenly became clear to me what it was that
bound me most closely to Carla; my resolution always to be
kind to her and the lies I told about my relations with
Augusta, which in course of time I must gradually modify
till I had done away with them altogether. I began that
very evening, but as cautiously as possible, for what I had
obtained in consequence of my lie was still too fresh in my
mind. I told her that I had a strong sense of duty to my
wife, who was a most admirable woman and certainly

deserved to be loved better. I could not bear her to know
that I had been unfaithful to her.

Carla kissed me and said:

"That is how I like you best; I knew you were good
and kind the first moment I saw you. I will never try to do
anything that would hurt the poor thing."

I didn't at all like Augusta being called a "poor thing"
—but I was grateful to poor Carla for demanding so little.
It was a good thing that she did not hate my wife. I
wanted to show my gratitude to her, and cast round in my
mind for some token of affection. At last I hit on it. I
made her a present of a "private laundry" in that I allowed
her not to send for the singing-master again.

This was the signal for an outburst of tenderness on
Carla's part which I found rather trying but bore with
fortitude. Then she told me that she had never wanted
to give up singing. She sang all day long, but in her own
way. She wanted me to hear her sing something on the
spot. But I would not hear of it, and took my leave rather
unceremoniously. Probably it made her contemplate suicide
that night too, but I never gave her time to tell me about
it.

I went back to Copler first, for I had to take Augusta
the latest news of the invalid, to make her believe that I
had been spending all those hours by his bedside. Copler
had been dead about two hours; he died almost immediately after I left. I went into his room accompanied
by the old pensioner, who had spent the whole time pacing
up and down the little passage. The corpse, already dressed,
was lying on the bare mattress of the bed. A crucifix was
placed between his hands. The pensioner told me in a low
voice that all the proper formalities had been performed
and that a nephew of the dead man was coming to watch
by the corpse.

I was now free to leave him, knowing that all my poor
friend needed had been done for him, but I stayed watching him for a few minutes. I should have liked to screw
one genuine tear of compassion from my eyes for the poor
man who had waged so valiant a fight against disease, before he would consent to make peace. "It is very sad!" I
said. He had been brutally killed by an illness for which so
many drugs exist. It seemed such a mockery. But I could
not shed a tear. Copler's emaciated face had never seemed

so strong as it did now in the rigidity of death. It looked as if it had been hewn out of colored marble, and no one guessed that it was on the brink of decay. That face seemed still to have an expression of life; perhaps it disapproved of me, the *malade imaginaire*, or of Carla who would not learn singing. I shuddered for a moment, thinking I heard again the death-rattle of the dead man. But I resumed the dispassionate study of his face when I realized that what I took to be a death-rattle was only the pensioner's heavy breathing, which emotion made more labored.

The pensioner accompanied me to the door, and begged me to say a good word for him if I knew of anyone wanting apartments:

"You see I have done all I could even in a situation like this; I have done my duty and a great deal more too."

He raised his voice for the first time, and there was a note of resentment in it, no doubt against poor Copler for having left his room without giving due notice. I went off as fast as I could, promising to do all that he asked.

When I reached my father-in-law's house I found that they had sat down to dinner. They asked for news at once, and so as not to damp the spirits of the company I said that Copler was still alive and that there was therefore room for hope.

I thought the party seemed very dull. Perhaps I got this impression from seeing my father-in-law condemned to a plate of soup and a glass of milk, while all around were feeding on the choicest dainties. He had plenty of time at his disposal and employed it in watching the others eat. When he saw Señor Francesco eating hors-d'œuvres he muttered:

"To think that he is two years older than me!"

And when Señor Francesco reached his third glass of white wine he growled:

"That is the third! May it turn to gall in his stomach!"

This pious hope would not have troubled me if I myself had not been eating and drinking at the same table, and had not realized that every mouthful of wine I drank would have a like blessing bestowed on it. So I began eating and drinking secretly. I took advantage of a moment when my father-in-law's great nose was hidden in his glass of milk, or when he was answering some remark that had been addressed to him, to swallow huge mouthfuls of food and gulp whole glasses of wine. Alberta, simply in order to be funny, warned Augusta that I was drinking too much. My wife threatened me laughingly with her finger. She meant no harm, but it had the unfortunate result of making my efforts to eat secretly useless too. Giovanni, who had almost forgotten my existence, flung me, over his glasses, a veritable look of hate. He said:

"I have never abused food or drink. Anyone who eats or drinks to excess is no man but a . . ." And he went on repeating the last word, which was not exactly complimentary.

The wine I had drunk made that offensive word, at which everybody laughed heartily, rankle in my breast, and I felt a quite unreasoning desire to avenge myself. I attacked my father-in-law at his weakest point—his illness. I shouted that the contemptible person was not one who ate or drank to excess, but one who submitted tamely to the doctor's orders. If I had been in his place I should have acted very differently. At my own daughter's marriage, my affection for her, if nothing else would have made me refuse to have my eating and drinking interfered with.

Giovanni wrathfully observed:

"I should like to see you in my shoes!"

"Isn't it enough to see me in my own? Do I give up smoking by any chance?"

It was the first time I had succeeded in boasting of this weakness of mine, and I at once lit a cigarette in illustration of my words. They all laughed, and told Señor Francesco how my life was full of last cigarettes. This one was not going to be the last, and I felt strong and combative. But the others soon withdrew their support when I proceeded to pour some wine into Giovanni's big drinking-water glass. They were afraid he would drink it, and shouted at him to stop him, till at last Signora Malfenti managed to get hold of the glass and take it away.

"So you want to kill me, do you?" asked Giovanni mildly, looking curiously at me. "The wine has not done *you* much good." He had made not the slightest effort to drink what I had poured out for him.

I felt thoroughly depressed and in the wrong. I could almost have flung myself at my father-in-law's feet to implore his forgiveness, but I knew that would probably also have been inspired by wine, and crushed the impulse. It

was a pity, for in asking for forgiveness I could have
confessed my fault, and the dinner would have lasted long
enough to give me a chance of repairing that first unfortunate joke. There is a time for everything in this world.
Not all drunkards fall immediately under the influence of
wine. When I have drunk too much I go on analyzing my
fellow-creatures just as I do when sober, and probably with
the same result. I now continued my self-analysis in order
to discover how I could have hit on the horrible thought of
doing harm to my father-in-law. I discovered that I was
tired, absolutely dead tired. If they had known what a day
I had been through they would have made some excuse for
me. I had twice seduced and violently abandoned one
woman, and twice returned to my wife only to deny her
twice. It was fortunate for me that some train of thought
suddenly brought to my mind the corpse over which I had
vainly tried to shed tears. If this had not banished my
thoughts about the two women I should have ended by
speaking of Carla. Have I not always had a great desire for
confession, even when wine has not made me more ex-
pansive still?

So I spoke about Copler instead, for I wanted them all
to know that I had lost a great friend that day. They would
be more ready to excuse my behavior.

I cried out that Copler was dead, stone dead, and that
I had not told them before so as not to cast a gloom over
the party. And now at last, strange to say, I felt the tears
rising and had to turn my eyes away so as to hide them.

They all laughed, because they did not believe me; so
with an obstinacy which too much wine tends to produce
I proceeded to describe his death:

"He looked like a figure of Michelangelo, as if he had
been hewn out of a block of marble."

There was a general silence, interrupted by Guido,
who exclaimed:

"So you no longer care whether you depress us or
not?" His reproof was deserved. I had again failed to keep
a resolution. Perhaps I might still save the situation!

I began laughing immoderately and cried out:

"I've caught you! He is still alive, and getting better."

They all stared at me in the utmost amazement.

"He is better," I said gravely; "he recognized me and
even smiled at me."

They all believed me, but were extremely indignant. Giovanni announced that if he had not been afraid of straining himself, he would have flung a plate at my head. It was of course unpardonable of me to harrow the party by inventing such a piece of information. If it had been true there would have been no harm in it. Wouldn't it be better for me to tell them the truth even now? Copler was dead, and directly I was left alone I should find plenty of tears to shed for him; I felt they would flow abundantly now. I tried to find words, but Signora Malfenti, with her air of *grande dame*, interrupted me:

"Let us leave that unfortunate Copler in peace," she said. "Tomorrow will be time enough for us to think about him."

I instantly obeyed, even to the point of dismissing the dead man from my thoughts as well. "Farewell," I said to him. "Wait for me! I will come back to you later on."

The time had come for the toast. The doctor had given Giovanni permission to drink a glass of champagne for the occasion. He gravely watched them pouring out the wine, and refused to touch it with his lips till the glass was quite full. When he had proposed their health in plain and simple terms, he drained it to the dregs. With a malicious glance at me he said that the last drop had been dedicated to my health. I crossed my fingers under the table to avert his wish, which I knew boded me no good.

I have no very clear memory of the remainder of that evening. I know that at Augusta's instigation they said lots of nice things about me, and quoted me as a model husband. I was quite restored to favor; even my father-in-law became more conciliatory. He said, however, that he hoped Ada's husband would prove as good a one as me, and at the same time a better business man; and above all someone who . . . and he hunted about for the right word. He could not find it, nor did anyone press for it. Not even Señor Francesco, who as he had only seen me for the first time that morning, could not be expected to know much about me. I was not at all offended. The consciousness that one has great wrongs to repair subdues one's pride a good deal. I was ready to accept insults readily, so long as they were accompanied by an affection that I knew I did not deserve. My mind, confused as it was by wine and fatigue, played cheerfully with the idea of the perfect

husband which had been conjured up, and saw no reason
why that husband became less perfect by having committed
adultery. One had just got to be good, and again good:
nothing else mattered. I kissed my hand to Augusta who
returned my greeting with a grateful smile.

Seeing I was drunk, it occurred to some of the guests
that it might be amusing to call on me for a toast. I accepted, because at that moment it seemed to me that it
would set my feet firmly on the right path if I were to
make my good resolutions in public. Not that I had any
doubts of myself, for at that moment I really felt I did
correspond to their description of me, but I should be
better still, I thought, if I were to state my good resolutions
in front of so many people who would act, as it were, as
my witnesses.

And this was how I came only to talk about Augusta
and myself in my toast. For the second time that day I told
the story of my marriage. In telling it to Carla I had misrepresented it, because I had not said anything about
loving my wife; now I misrepresented it in the other
direction, by saying nothing at all about the two people
who played such an important part in the story—Ada and
Alberta. I told of my hesitations and scruples, which I now
bitterly regretted because they had robbed me of months
of happiness. Then, out of gallantry, I attributed like
hesitations to Augusta, which she laughingly denied.

I had some difficulty in finding the thread again. I
related how we had at last come to the honeymoon, and
how I had made love to her in all the museums of Italy.
I was so up to my neck in lies that I even threw in that
mendacious detail, though it served no purpose whatever.
And yet they say, "*In vino veritas.*"

Augusta broke in a second time to put things right,
and said that she had been obliged to avoid museums,
because of the danger the masterpieces were in at my
hands. She did not see that she thereby threw doubt on
the whole story, and not only one detail of it! If there had
been an acute observer present he would at once have
drawn his conclusions as to the kind of love I proposed
making in such surroundings.

I resumed my long, rambling speech, telling about our
arrival home, and how we had both set to work making

improvements in the house, putting in this and putting in that—among other things a laundry.

Augusta, still laughing, broke in again:

"This party is not being given in honor of us, you know, but for Ada and Guido! Try and talk about them!" This sally was received with clamorous applause. I laughed too, seeing how I had been instrumental in bringing about that state of noisy mirth which is *de rigueur* on such occasions. But I could not think of anything else to say. I felt as if I had been talking for hours. I swallowed down several more glasses of wine, one after the other.

"To Ada!" I stood up in my place for a moment, to see whether she was crossing her fingers under the table.

"To Guido!" and emptying my glass I added:

"With all my heart!" forgetting that I had omitted this little coda with the first glass.

"To your first child!" I should have gone on drinking glass after glass to each of their children in turn, if they had not ended by stopping me. I was quite ready to drink all the wine there was left on the table to those poor innocents.

Then everything became still more dim. I only remember clearly that my chief concern was not to appear drunk. I sat upright and said very little. I mistrusted myself; I felt obliged to analyze every word before I uttered it. I was afraid to take part in the general conversation because it gave me no time to clear up my thoughts. I thought I would start a topic myself, and said to my father-in-law:

"Have you heard that Extérieur have gone down two points?" I was talking of something I knew nothing whatever about; in fact I was only repeating what I had heard on the Bourse; all I wanted was to show that I was not drunk, by talking about business, which one generally forgets all about under those conditions. But it was clearly a more serious matter for my father-in-law, who called me a bird of ill-omen. I had no luck with him that day.

Then I turned to my next-door neighbor, Alberta. We began talking about love. She was interested in it only in theory, and for the moment I was not very interested in it in practice either. So it was nice to talk about it. She asked me to tell her my ideas about it, and I immediately discovered one which seemed to me to grow out of that day's experience. A woman, I said, varied in value much more than any share on the Bourse. Alberta misunderstood me, and thought I meant what is of course a commonplace, that a woman of a certain age has quite a different value from a young woman. I tried to explain myself more clearly; a woman might be worth a great deal at a certain hour in the morning, nothing at all at midday, and twice as much in the afternoon, whereas perhaps in the evening her value might be actually negative. I explained what I meant by a negative value; a woman might be said to have it when a man began calculating what he would be willing to pay if she would go a very, very long way off.

The poor playwright could not see that there was any truth at all in my discovery; whereas I, who had fresh in my mind the fluctuations in value that Carla and Augusta had undergone this very day, was sure of it. But when I wanted to make my meaning still clearer, the wine I had drunk tripped me up and I made a terrible *faux pas*.

"Imagine," I said, "that your value is *x*; if you let me press your foot with mine, your value would be at least twice as great."

I at once suited the action to the words.

She blushed scarlet and at once removed her foot, saying, in an attempt to be witty:

"But this is practice, not theory. I shall appeal to Augusta."

I must confess that I also found that pressure anything but theoretical, but I protested with the most innocent air in the world:

"It is pure theory, and nothing else, and it shows you have a low mind if you look at it in any other way."

Fancies which spring from wine are as real as actual events. For a long time Alberta and I were unable to forget that I had touched a part of her body with the definite intention of experiencing pleasure from the contact. The act had become significant by being talked about, and the words by being put into practice. . . . So long as she remained unmarried she always greeted me with a smile and a blush; afterwards, with an angry blush without the smile. Women are made like that. Each day, as it comes, provides them with a new interpretation of the one that went before. Their life can never be at all monotonous. As regards myself, the interpretation of my action always remained the same: the theft of a small thing possessing great charm. It was Alberta's fault that for a certain length of time I tried to make her remember that act of mine; whereas later on I would have paid a good deal to have it quite forgotten.

I remember that before I left the house something much more serious happened. I remained alone for a moment with Ada. Giovanni had gone to bed early, and the guests were taking leave of Señor Francesco, whom Guido was to accompany to his hotel. I stood gazing at Ada. She was dressed all in white lace, with bare neck and arms. For a long time I remained silent, though I wanted to say something to her, but everything that rose to my lips seemed inadequate when I came to analyze it. I remember I wondered whether it would be permissible for me to say to her:

"I am so delighted you are going to get married, and that you are marrying Guido, who is such a great friend of mine. Now at last all is over between us." It was a lie of course, for everyone knew that all had been over between us now for some months, but I thought it would sound very flattering, and a woman who is dressed as beautifully as that deserves to have compliments paid her, if she can appreciate them. But after reflecting on it for some time, I decided to say nothing. In the sea of wine in which I was floating I found at last a plank that saved me. I thought it would be wrong of me to jeopardize Augusta's affection only in order to please Ada, who did not love me. But in the agitation of the moment, even after I had made the effort of suppressing those words, I gave Ada such a look that she rose and left the room after turning round in alarm to see what I might be doing, and ready perhaps to run away if necessary.

One remembers a look one has cast at another person, as well as, or even better than one's own words. A look is even more important than a word, because if you hunt the whole dictionary through you will never be able to undress a woman with a word. I know now that the look I gave Ada contradicted the words I had pictured myself saying to her, and thereby simplified them. Through her eyes I had tried to pierce her clothes and her skin. And it had quite clearly meant: "So will you come to bed at once?"

Wine is a great danger not because it brings the truth to light; but, on the contrary, because it reveals what is past and forgotten and plays no part in one's present conscious will. All the fantastic ideas one toyed with in the more or less recent past, and has long since forgotten, come crowding to the surface; it traces afresh what one had erased, and reads whatever is still perceptible in our hearts. If one has made a mistake in endorsing a check, it is easy enough to correct it; but in the heart those erasures are impossible. Our whole life-history is written there, and wine proclaims it abroad, regardless of the emandations of time.

Augusta and I took a carriage home. I thought it my duty to kiss and embrace my wife in the dark, because I had often done so on similar occasions, and was afraid that if I did not she might think things had changed between us. Nothing whatever had changed between us: that also was proclaimed by the wine! She had married Zeno Cosini, and he was sitting by her, just the same as ever. What did it matter if I had had other women that day? Their number had been augmented by the wine I had drunk, and included now Ada or Alberta, I could not remember which.

I remember that just as I was falling asleep I saw Copler's marble face on his death-bed. He seemed to ask for justice, that is to say for the tears I had promised him. But he did not get them even then, for sleep took hold of me and completely annihilated me. I had only time to say to the phantom: "Wait just a little while, I shall be with you very soon!" I never was with him again in any form, for I did not even go to his funeral. We had so much to do at home, and I outside as well, that there was no time to think of him. We talked about him sometimes, but only as a joke, remembering how many times my wine had killed him off and resurrected him again. He became in fact quite a proverb in the family, and when the papers, as often happens, announced the death of someone and later corrected the announcement, we still say: "Like poor Copler!"

Next morning I got up with a slight headache. The pain in my side worried me rather too, probably because while the effect of the wine lasted I had not felt it at all, and had already lost the habit of it. But I was not really depressed. Augusta cheered me by saying that it would have been dreadful if I had not come to the wedding dinner, because before I arrived it had seemed like a funeral. So I need not reproach myself for having behaved badly. But there was one thing I felt later would never be forgiven me: the look I had given Ada!

When we met in the afternoon Ada gave me her hand with an air of anxiety which increased my own. Perhaps the fact that she had fled from me the day before weighed on her conscience. It was certainly very rude of her, but it was also extremely rude of me to have looked at her like that. I remembered exactly how I had moved my eyes, and quite understood it would be a thing one could not forget if one had happened to experience it. I must make up for it now by the most correct brotherly behavior.

They say that if you are suffering from having drunk too much the best cure is to drink still more. So I went that morning to Carla to recover my spirits. I went to her with the definite desire to live more intensely, which is what drives one back to drink, but on the way there I felt that I should like quite a different kind of intensity from the day before. I made several resolutions as I went along, all of them rather vague but very honorable. I knew that I could not abandon her at once, but I would approach that highly moral act by slow degrees. Meanwhile I would continue to talk to her about my wife. I had another envelope of money ready in my waistcoat in case of emergency.

I reached Carla's house. A quarter of an hour later she made me a reproach that lingered in my ears for a long while afterwards: "How roughly you make love." I don't remember having been particularly rough just then. I had begun talking to her about my wife, and the praises I gave Augusta had sounded to Carla's ears like reproaches to herself.

Then it was Carla's turn to wound me. To pass the time I told her how uncomfortable I had been at the banquet, especially on account of a toast I had proposed, which was in terribly bad taste. Carla remarked:

"If you loved your wife, you wouldn't propose toasts in bad taste at her father's table."

And she gave me a kiss, as if to reward me for loving my wife so little.

But the desire for a greater intensity of life, which had already driven me to Carla, soon made me feel that I wanted to return to Augusta, the only person to whom

I could talk about my love for herself. I had already had too much of the wine I had taken for a cure, and now I wanted quite a different kind of wine. But my relations with Carla were destined to become tenderer that very day, and finally to be crowned by the sympathy which, as I discovered later, the poor girl deserved. She had often suggested singing me a little song on which she wanted my criticism. But I was tired of her singing; even its simplicity no longer had any charms for me. I told her that since she refused to practice it was not worth while her singing any more.

I had insulted her badly and she felt it very keenly. She was sitting beside me, and kept her eyes fixed on her hands, which were clasped on her knees, so that I should not see that she was crying. She repeated her reproach:

"How unkind you must be to someone you don't love if you are so unkind to me."

In spite of everything I am really very good-natured. So I allowed myself to be moved by Carla's tears, and begged her once more to deafen me with her great voice in that little room. It was her turn to show reluctance now, and I was obliged to threaten to go away if she did not sing. I must confess that I thought for the moment I was going to recover my freedom, but hearing my threat my humble slave went at once with downcast eyes to the piano. She sat quite still for a moment to recover herself, and passed her hand over her brow as if to chase away a cloud. She succeeded in doing so with a quickness that surprised me; and when she uncovered her face again it bore no trace of her former grief.

A great surprise awaited me. Carla recited her song; she did not shout it, she spoke it. She told me afterwards that it was her master who made her shout like that; now that he had been dismissed the shouting had gone too. This is how the little Triestine song began:

> Pazzo l'amor xe vero
> Cossa ghe sce de mal
> Vola che a sedes' ani
> Sto la come un cocal. . . .

It was a kind of spoken confession. Carla's eyes sparkled with wickedness, and expressed even more than

the words. There was no fear of the drum of one's ear
being broken, and I went quite close to her, surprised and
delighted at the change. I sat down beside her, and she
recited the canzonetta as if she were addressing it directly
to me, half closing her eyes and telling me in the sweetest,
purest tone of voice that her sixteen years cried out for love
and liberty.

I had for the first time an opportunity of studying
Carla's face. It was a pure oval, only broken by the deep
and beautiful curve of her eyebrows and the faint line of
the cheek-bones, and made purer still by its snowy whiteness, now that her face was turned toward me and the
light, instead of being half in shadow. Her skin seemed
almost transparent, yet scarcely a trace of the delicate veins
appeared in it, and something in its soft lines called up all
my instincts of love and protection.

I was ready to offer it all to her now unconditionally,
even at the very moment when I most wanted to go back
to Augusta; for Carla seemed only to ask for a fatherly love,
which I could give her without any infidelity. What a
satisfaction for me! I could stay there with Carla, giving all
that the oval of her face demanded, and at the same time
I could feel myself near Augusta!

My love for Carla became more tender, more refined.
Henceforward I need not run away if I felt aspirations
toward honesty and purity: I had only to turn the conversation into another channel.

Was it my discovery of her oval face which gave me
this new sensation of happiness, or her musical talent? Her
talent was undeniable. The strange dialect folk-song ends
with a verse in which the woman declares that she is old
and abandoned, and seeks no other liberty now than to die.
Carla put an extraordinary amount of temperament into
her rendering of the poor verses. In her it was youth
disguised as age which continued to proclaim its rights
from a new point of view. When at the end she found me
full of admiration she too for the first time seemed to feel
a genuine liking as well as love for me. She knew that her
little song had pleased me more than the style that her
singing-master had taught her.

"It is a pity," she added sadly, "that unless one sings
in *cafés chantants* it is impossible to make enough to live."

It was easy for me to convince her that this was not
true. There were plenty of great artists in the world who
recited instead of singing.

She made me tell her their names. She was enraptured
when she discovered how important her art might become.

"I know," she naïvely said, "that this way of singing
is much more difficult than the other in which you only
have to shout at the top of your voice."

I smiled and did not discuss the matter further. Her
art was certainly difficult too, and she realized it because it
was the only art she had any knowledge of. That little song
had cost her a great deal of study. She had said it over and
over again, correcting the intonation of each word and
each note. Now she was studying another, but would not
know it for several weeks yet, and till then she did not
want me to hear it.

There followed enchanting moments in that room,
which up to then had only been the scene of violent love-
making. A new career was opening before Carla, a career
that would perhaps take her off my hands. It was very
much what Copler had dreamt of for her! I suggested
finding a master for her. At first the word frightened her,
but she consented at once when I told her that she would
be perfectly free to dismiss him if she did not like him and
found him of no use.

I got on very well with Augusta too that day. My
mind was as easy as if I had just returned from a walk
instead of from Carla's house; I felt, no doubt, just as poor
Copler did on the days when he left the house without
having had any reason for being angry. I had the delicious
sensation of having reached an oasis. It would have been
terribly bad for my health if my long affair with Carla had
been one perpetual excitement. From that day things went
on more quietly, as if as a result of the aesthetic beauty we
enjoyed together; with only an occasional interruption that
sufficed to arouse afresh my love for Carla and also for
Augusta. Every visit I paid to Carla meant of course that
I was unfaithful to Augusta, but all was soon forgotten in
a health-giving bath of good resolutions. And there was
nothing brutal or sadistic now in my good resolutions, as
when I had felt a passionate need to tell Carla I would
never see her again. I had become gentle and protective;
my thoughts turned again to her career. Giving up a

woman each day in order to run after her the next would have been an altogether too exhausting process for my poor heart to bear. As it was, Carla remained in my power, and I was able to influence her now in one direction, now in another.

It was some time before my good resolutions were strong enough to induce me to scour the city in search of a teacher who would do for Carla. I toyed with the good resolution while continuing to do nothing about it. Then one fine day Augusta told me she was going to become a mother; whereupon my resolution grew to gigantic proportions and Carla had her teacher.

One reason why I had waited so long was that it was clear that Carla, even without a master, would be capable of working seriously at her new art. Each week she had a new song to recite to me, carefully thought out both as to expression and articulation of the words. Perhaps certain tones ought to have been lighter, but no doubt she would find the right balance in time. One decisive proof that Carla was an artist was the way she went on perfecting her songs without letting go of what was best in her first conception. I often used to make her recite her earliest songs again, and there was always some new touch that was very much to the point.

Seeing how ignorant she was, it was remarkable that in spite of her efforts to give the utmost expression to the song she never introduced a false or exaggerated note. Like a true artist she added a small stone to the building daily, without destroying what was there already. The song was not stereotyped, only the sentiment that inspired it. Before she began singing Carla used always to pass her hand over her face, and that moment's quiet sufficed to plunge her in the drama she had to create. Nor was the drama always puerile. The ironic mentor of

Rosina te xe nata in un casoto

must not be taken too seriously. The speaker seemed to wish it to be treated as an everyday story. Carla had a different conception of it but she arrived at the same conclusion:

"My sympathy is with Rosina, for otherwise the song would not be worth singing," she said.

It sometimes happened that Carla would quite unconsciously rekindle my love for Augusta and my remorse on her account. In fact it happened whenever she did anything that seemed to aim at undermining the unassailable position held by my wife. She was still as anxious as ever to have me to herself for one whole night; she confided to me that it seemed to her something was wanting in our intimacy because we had never slept together.

As I wished to get into the habit of treating her more gently I did not absolutely refuse to do what she wanted, but it almost always seemed to me that it would be impossible to do so unless I could make up my mind to find Augusta looking out of the window, after having sat up for me all night. Besides, would it not be a fresh infidelity to my wife? Sometimes, especially when desire had driven me to Carla, I felt inclined to satisfy her, but almost immediately afterwards the difficulty and impossibility of the situation was borne in on me. So that for a long time the idea remained in abeyance, neither realized nor actually dismissed. It was understood that we had agreed sooner or later to spend a whole night together; and there was every facility now for doing so, for I had persuaded the Gercos to give notice to the tenants who lived in the middle part of their flat, cutting it in two; so that Carla at last had a bedroom to herself.

Soon after Guido's wedding my father-in-law had the attack that finally killed him, and I was foolish enough to tell Carla that my wife was obliged to spend the night at her father's bedside, so as to allow my mother-in-law to get a little rest. Having done so there was no way of getting out of it; Carla insisted on my spending that night with her—the very night that was to be so painful for my wife. I had not the courage to refuse, and agreed with a heavy heart.

I prepared for the sacrifice by not going to see Carla in the morning, so that I rushed round to her in the evening full of unsatisfied desire, saying to myself that it was childish to think I was being more unfaithful to Augusta just because at that moment she was obliged to suffer owing to quite a different cause. I even felt impatient with poor Augusta for delaying me while she explained to me where to find everything I might need for supper, for the night and for breakfast the next morning.

Carla received me in her studio. Soon after, the old woman who was at once her mother and maid-of-all-work, served us a delicious little meal, which I supplemented with what I had brought for dessert. Then she came in and cleared away, and I should have been only too glad to go to bed at once; but it was really too early, and Carla persuaded me to let her sing first. She went through the whole of her repertory, and that was the part of the evening I enjoyed most, for the excitement with which I waited for the moment when I might enjoy my mistress added to the pleasure I always took in listening to her recitations.

"The audience would load you with flowers and applause," I said, forgetting that it would be impossible for a whole audience to share my present state of mind.

We went to bed at last in a small, bare room, meanly furnished. It looked like part of a passage, divided in two by a wall. I was not at all sleepy, but even if I had been, I reflected with horror that it would have been impossible to sleep in such a stuffy place.

Carla's mother called to her in a timid voice. She went to the door to answer, and half closed it again behind her. I heard her asking the old woman crossly what she wanted. The other said something I could not hear, and then Carla cried out angrily, as she slammed the door in her mother's face:

"Leave me alone, I've told you I am going to sleep here tonight!"

Then I discovered that Carla, who was afraid of the dark, always slept in her old bedroom with her mother, where there was another bed, and that the bed we were sleeping on was generally empty. It was of course fear that had made her try to get me to desert Augusta. She admitted with a malicious satisfaction, which I did not share, that she felt safer with me than with her mother. That bed, all alone there in the little room next door to the studio, gave me food for reflection. I had never seen it before. I felt jealous! And I did not at all like the way Carla had spoken to her mother. How different from Augusta, who had denied herself my company in order to wait on her parents. I am particularly sensitive to any lack of consideration in children toward their parents. How patiently I put up with my own dear father's whims!

Carla was quite unconscious both of my jealousy and

my unfavorable criticism of her. I suppressed any inclination to show that I was jealous, for I felt I hardly had the right to be so, seeing that I had spent a good part of my time in wishing that someone would take my mistress off my hands. And there was no point in showing the poor girl that I despised her just when I was again toying with the idea of giving her up finally; though I despised her all the more for the very reasons that a short time ago would have made me still more jealous. The important thing was to get away as quickly as possible from that horrible little room containing barely three cubic feet of air, and overheated into the bargain.

I can't remember exactly what excuse I made for going away almost at once. I threw on my clothes in frantic haste. I think I said something about having forgotten to give my wife a key, so that she would not be able to get in, supposing she needed something from the house. I showed her the key, which was really the one I always carried about in my pocket, but which I produced as a tangible proof of the truth of my statements. Carla did not attempt to keep me; she dressed too, and came with me to light me down the stairs. In the darkness I thought I felt her cast searching glances at me now and then, and wondered in some anxiety whether she was beginning to understand me. It was not so easy, seeing how good I was at pretending. To show my gratitude to her for letting me go I touched her cheek with my lips several times and pretended to be still under the influence of the emotion that had driven me to her. That I acted well was obvious from the results. Carla had told me shortly before, in an access of lyrical enthusiasm, that the ugly name of Zeno which my parents had given me was not worthy of me. According to her I ought to have been called Dario, and when she said good-by to me at the foot of the dark staircase, that was the name she called me by. But I felt that I could not endure her for another second, and fled with the key still in my hand. I had almost come to believe myself that it really was the one I said it was.

The night was intensely dark, but the darkness was broken from time to time by dazzling flashes of lightning. Thunder rumbled far away in the distance. The air was very still and as suffocating as in Carla's room. Even the few drops that fell at intervals were warm. Evidently a

storm was threatening, and I ran at full speed. By good
luck I found a lighted entrance still open in the Corsa
Stadion and took shelter there just in time. Immediately
afterwards the deluge came. The downpour of rain was
lashed by a furious wind that seemed to bring the thunder
along with it until it was almost above one's head. I
shuddered to think how compromising it would be for me
to be found struck dead by lightning at that hour in the
Corsa Stadion. Fortunately my wife knew that I was a man
of strange tastes who might even take it into his head to
walk as far as that at night, so probably an excuse would be
found.

I had to stay in that entrance for over an hour. I kept
on thinking that the weather was going to get better, but
each time the rain came on again with greater fury. And
now it had turned to hail.

The porter of the house came to keep me company in
the entrance, and I had to give him something for keeping
the outer door open a little longer. Then a gentleman
joined us, who was dressed in white and dripping with
water. He was old and thin and withered. I never saw him
again, but I cannot forget the light in his black eyes and
the vitality that emanated from each point of his small
person. He swore at the weather for making him so dirty.

I have always loved talking to people I don't know. I
feel quite safe and sound with them; it is quite a rest to be
with them. If only I take care not to limp I am all right.

When at last the rain began to give over I went as
quickly as I could, not to my own house but to my father-
in-law's. I felt at that moment that it was my duty to be on
the spot in case I was needed.

My father-in-law was asleep and Augusta, who had
her sister to help her, was able to join me. She said it was
so nice of me to have come, and flung herself weeping into
my arms. She had seen her father suffer horribly.

She noticed that I was quite wet. She made me sit
down in an armchair and covered me with some rugs. Then
she sat down beside me for a little while. I was very tired
and found it hard work to keep awake, even during the
short time she was with me. I felt very innocent in not
having been unfaithful to the extent of staying away from
home all night. Innocence was so delightful that I tried to
increase the sensation of it. I began putting a few words

together which sounded like a confession. I said I felt weak
and guilty but, seeing that she looked at me inquiringly at
this point as if in need of an explanation, I drew in my
horns again and began talking about the sense of sin which
I had in every word I spoke or breath I drew in.

"That is what the monks believe," said Augusta.
"Perhaps it is for the sins we have unconsciously committed that we are being punished now."

The words were well suited to her tears, which continued to flow. It seemed to me that she had not quite
understood the difference between my way of thinking and
that of the monks, but I did not want to discuss it, and to
the monotonous accompaniment of the wind, which had
now risen, I soon fell into a long, refreshing sleep, my mind
quite eased by my attempted confession.

When the question of the singing-master came up
again I arranged everything within a few hours. I had made
up my mind some time who it was to be, and to tell the
truth I chose him because his fees were lower than those
of any other teacher in Trieste. I thought it better not to
come into it myself, so I sent Carla to call on him. In fact
I have never seen him, but I know a great deal about him
now and he is one of the people in the world whom I most
respect. He is evidently a very simple-minded, healthy
creature, which is strange in an artist who lives so entirely
for art as Vittorio Lali. I must say that I envy him for
being such a genius and at the same time so healthy.

I at once noticed a change in Carla's voice; it became
softer and at the same time surer and more flexible. We
were so afraid that he might force it, like the teacher whom
Copler had chosen. He may have adapted himself to
Carla's wishes, in any case he always kept to the style of
singing which she preferred. It was only some months afterwards that I found she had departed from it slightly as her
feeling became finer. She no longer sang Triestine or
Neapolitan canzonettas, but old Italian songs; and from
them she passed to Mozart and Schubert.

I remember specially a cradle song attributed to
Mozart, and sometimes when I am most conscious of the
sadness of life, and think regretfully of the fragile girl who
was my mistress but whom I never loved, the cradle song
rings reproachfully in my ears. I see again Carla in her role
of mother, summoning her sweetest tones to woo her baby

to sleep. But she, who was unforgettable as a lover, was too bad a daughter ever to become a good mother. She could sing like a mother though, and that was a gift that covered a multitude of sins.

Carla told me her singing-master's story. He had studied for several years at the Vienna Conservatoire and had then come to Trieste, where he had the good fortune to work for our best composer, who was stricken with blindness. He took down all his compositions to dictation, and was treated by him with the confidence that all blind people feel the need of reprosing absolutely in anyone on whom they are dependent. So he got to know his ideas and schemes, which though they were mature remained always eternally youthful. He soon became familiar with every kind of music, and knew just what Carla needed. She described his appearance to me: he was young and fair and rather solidly built, negligently dressed with a soft shirt that sometimes might have been cleaner, a large flowing tie that must once have been black, and a shabby broad-brimmed hat. He was a man of few words, according to Carla; and I think she was speaking the truth, for a few months later when he became more confidential she told me at once. He was entirely absorbed in his work.

Fresh complications very soon set in. It was with a feeling of bitter jealousy, as well as love, that I went to see Carla in the morning, though it passed off somewhat during the day. I could not believe that the young man would not take advantage of such an easy prey. Carla appeared surprised at my thinking of such a thing, but her surprise made me think it all the more. Had she forgotten already what had happened between her and me?

I arrived one day wild with jealousy, and frightened her so much that she offered at once to dismiss the singing-master. I don't think that it was only because she was afraid of losing my support, for she showed me many genuine signs of affection at that time, which sometimes made me intensely happy, and, when I was in another frame of mind, irritated me because I felt them to be directed against Augusta; and yet, however much I wanted to, I could not dissociate myself from them. I was embarrassed by her suggestion, which I felt I could not accept whatever mood I might be in at the moment. I felt the need of keeping the channel open between my two states of being, and I did not want to curtail in any way my freedom to pass from one to the other at will. Though I could not accept her suggestion it made me realize that I must be more careful, and I resolved, however jealous I might feel, not to show it. My love became more and more a source of irritation to me, and I ended by feeling Carla to be an inferior being, whether I desired her or not. At times I did not care whether she was unfaithful to me or not; she seemed quite unimportant. When I was not hating her I no longer remembered her existence. I belonged to the sphere of health and respectability wherein Augusta reigned supreme, and I returned to her body and soul as soon as I could escape from Carla.

Carla was in reality absolutely sincere, so that I know exactly for how long I could call her completely mine—and it was a very long time. My periodical jealousy was no doubt the expression of an obscure sense of justice. What I deserved actually did happen. The singing-master fell in love first. The first intimation I had of it was something that Carla triumphantly repeated to me, as a sign that she had scored her first artistic success as an artist and earned my congratulations. He said that he enjoyed teaching her so much that if at any time she could not afford to pay for more lessons he would go on giving them to her gratis. I felt inclined to box her ears, but I soon recovered and pretended to be as glad as she was about her success. She forgot the grimace I had made on hearing the news (like when one bites into a lemon), and accepted my tardy praise quite calmly. He had told her all his private affairs, which were nothing very much: music, poverty, family worries. His sister had been a great trouble to him, and he had succeeded in making Carla take a great dislike to a woman she had never seen. I thought her dislike very compromising. They sang together songs of his own composition, which I thought very poor both when I was in love with Carla and when I found her a burden. Perhaps they were good all the same, but I have never heard anyone speak of them since. He later conducted an orchestra in the United States, and it may be that they sing those songs over there.

But the day she told me that he had asked her to marry him and that she had refused I passed two horrible half-hours; the first because I was so furious with the singing-master that I should have liked to wait till he came in order to kick him out; the second because I could see no means of reconciling the continuation of my liaison with Carla's marriage, which I yet felt to be a much more satisfactory and moral solution of our relationship than the career that Carla had pictured starting in my company.

Why did the God-forsaken teacher want to take fire so soon? During the year that our liaison had lasted, so much had adjusted itself between Carla and me; even my frown had vanished when I said good-by to her. If I still reproached myself I felt hardly any remorse, and though Carla would still have been right in saying that I made love roughly she seemed to have got used to it. This was not so difficult for her, for I had never again treated her with the brutality of the first days of our liaison, and having endured that, the rest must have seemed to her comparatively mild.

So that even if Carla no longer meant very much to me I could easily foresee that I should be by no means content to come to see my mistress and not find her. Of course it would be wonderful to be able to go back to Augusta without having enjoyed the usual interlude with Carla, and at that moment I felt quite equal to doing so. But I should have liked to have given it a trial first. The resolution I made was more or less as follows: Tomorrow I will beg her to accept his proposal but I will prevent her doing so today. And by a great effort I continued to behave as a lover. Now that I am able to look back on every phase of my adventure, I see that it looks as if I wanted to make another man marry my mistress and yet keep her for myself, as somebody much more experienced and of a much colder temperament than myself might have done. But I was far from being as immoral as that, and such a design never entered my head. I wanted her to marry the singing-master, but to postpone her decision till tomorrow. It was only now that what I persist in calling my state of innocence came to an end. I could no longer adore Carla for a short time every day and then hate her for twenty-four hours on end; or wake every morning as innocent as a new-born babe, and pass the day in wonderment at the adventures it brought, though it was just like all the other days, and I ought to have known those adventures by heart.

This was no longer possible. I saw before me the prob-

ability of losing my mistress forever unless I could overcome my desire to get rid of her. I instantly overcame it.

And so it came about that just the very day when she
had ceased to matter anything at all to me, I made Carla
a scene that in its falsity and jealous rage resembled the
scene I had made Augusta that night in the carriage. But
on this occasion I was not drunk with wine; I was only
genuinely moved by the sound of my own words. I told her
I loved her, that I could not live without her, but that I
did not see how I could ask her to sacrifice her whole life
to me, when I had nothing to offer in comparison with
what she offered me.

It struck an altogether new note in our relationship,
already rich in passionate experiences. She listened enraptured to my words, and it was a long time before she made
up her mind to tell me that I need not worry about Lali
being in love with her, because she did not care for him
in the least.

I thanked her with the same ardor as before, though
I was no longer moved by it myself. I felt a certain weight
on my chest; evidently I was more deeply involved than
ever. Instead of diminishing, my feigned ardor increased
in order to give me the opportunity to say a word of eulogy
for poor Lali. I did not want to let him go; I wanted to
reserve him—but for the following day.

When we had to consider the question of keeping him
on or of dismissing him as a singing-master, we were in
complete agreement; I had no wish to rob her of her career
as well as of a husband. She admitted that she thought a
great deal of him as a teacher; at every lesson she realized
more how much she needed his help. She begged me not
to worry, and to have complete confidence in her; assuring
me that she loved me and me only.

Evidently my adultery was growing in scope and importance. I had now become bound more closely than ever
to my mistress. New links had become forged in our relationship, which threatened to invade a territory reserved
hitherto to my married love. But directly I got home my
new affection for Carla was diverted into an increasing tenderness for my wife. For Carla I felt nothing but profound
mistrust. Who knows what truth there was in that proposal
of marriage? I should not have been surprised if one

fine day Carla had presented me with a son who had a great gift for music. I again made iron resolutions, which I took with me to Carla, forgot while I was with her, and remembered again almost before I left her. The resolutions existed for their own sake, and had no practical results whatever.

And for the time being everything remained as before. The summer passed away, and carried off my father-in-law. I found plenty to occupy me in Guido's new house of business, where I did more work than I had ever done before, not excepting my varied studies at the University. I will say more later about this new activity of mine. The winter went by, and the first green leaves that opened in my garden found me more sure of myself than those of the year before. My daughter Antonia was born. Carla's master was still at our disposition, but Carla would not hear of marrying him at present, and I still wanted to put it off too.

But events that seemed at the time to be of no importance produced very serious results in my relations with Carla. They passed almost unobserved at the time, and it was only their consequences that drew my attention to them.

It was just at the beginning of spring that I consented to go for a walk with Carla in the Giardino Pubblico. I felt it to be terribly compromising for me, but Carla was so anxious to walk in the sunshine leaning on my arm that I at last consented. We were not to be allowed to spend even a few moments together as husband and wife, for even this attempt ended badly.

We sat down on a seat, the better to enjoy the sudden warmth; the sun for the first time seemed to be entering again into his kingdom. On weekday mornings the garden was deserted, and I thought if we sat still we should run still less danger of being seen. But we had not been sitting long when I saw Tullio approaching, with slow but mighty strides, leaning on his crutch. (He was the individual of the fifty-four muscles.) He sat down beside us without looking at us. Then he raised his head, his eyes met mine, and he said:

"Well, how are you after all this long time? Are you less busy than you were?"

He had sat down quite close to me, and after I had recovered from my surprise my first instinct was to pre-

vent him catching sight of Carla. But directly he had
shaken hands with me he asked:

"Is that your wife?"

He waited for me to introduce him.

I had to give way.

"Signorina Carla Greco, a friend of my wife's."

Then I went on lying, and Tullio told me afterwards
himself that my second lie sufficed to make everything clear
to him. I said with a forced smile:

"The young lady sat down beside me too, without
seeing me."

It is important to remember, if one is going to tell lies,
that one must only tell essential ones if one wants to be
believed. When we next met, Tullio said to me with his
native common sense:

"You explained too much; I guessed at once that that
charming young lady was your mistress."

I had already lost Carla, and it was a satisfaction to be
able to tell Tullio that he was right, but that she had, alas,
given me up. He did not believe me, for which I was
grateful to him. I thought his incredulity was somehow a
good omen.

That meeting in the garden produced in Carla an ill-
humor that I had never seen in her before. I know now
that her rebellion dated from that moment, but I did not
notice it at once because I had turned my back on her in
order to listen to Tullio telling me about his illness and
the various cures he had tried. I afterwards discovered that
no woman can consent to be slighted in public, whatever
treatment she may put up with in private. She vented her
wrath on the poor cripple rather than on me, refusing to
reply when he spoke to her. I could not listen to him
either with any patience, for at the moment I could not interest myself in his cures. I looked hard at him and tried
to read in his little eyes what he was really thinking
about our meeting. I knew he had retired, and that having nothing to do all day he might easily amuse himself by
gossiping about us in the narrow circle of Triestine society,
which was all that existed in those days.

After reflecting on it for some time Carla got up as if
to leave us. She murmured good-by and began to move
away.

I knew she was angry with me and, while still reckoning with Tullio's presence, I tried to snatch an opportunity for reconciling myself with Carla. I asked her to allow me to accompany her as I was going in the direction of her house. Her cold good-by had sounded like a final farewell, and this was the first time I feared she would leave me for good. Such a cruel threat quite took my breath away.

But Carla did not know herself where she was going with such a firm step. She was giving vent to a momentary exasperation, which would soon have passed.

She waited for me and we walked along side by side without speaking. When we got home she burst into a flood of tears, which distressed me less, because they forced her to take refuge in my arms. I explained to her who Tullio was and what harm his tongue might do me. As she still went on crying in my arms I ventured on a firmer tone: Did she want to compromise me? Had we not agreed to do all in our power to give as little suffering as possible to the poor woman who was my wife and the mother of my child?

Carla seemed to agree, but she wanted to be alone to recover herself. I went away in quite good spirits.

It must have been this adventure that made her keep wanting to appear in public as my wife. It seemed that as she did not want to marry the singing-master she was bent on making me fill a good part of the place that she had refused him. She kept on plaguing me to take two seats at the theater, which we were to occupy as if by chance, both coming in by different doors and sitting down next to each other. But I would only consent to go with her several times to the Giardino Pubblico, which marked the limit of my excursions on foot; only now I arrived from the opposite direction. I would never go beyond. My mistress was beginning to resemble me a little too much. For no reason at all she would break out into sudden bursts of anger. She soon came to her senses again, but the fear of these outbursts sufficed to make me very docile and attentive to her. I would often find her dissolved in tears, and could never succeed in getting any explanation of the cause of her grief. Perhaps it was my fault for not insisting enough on her telling me. When I got to know her better, that is to say when she left me, no further explanation was necessary. Necessity had compelled her to fling herself into that adventure with me, though I was not really what she wanted. In my arms she had become a woman and, as I like to think, an honest woman. Naturally this is not to be attributed to any merit of mine, especially as I had nothing but disappointment in the end.

She developed a new caprice, which at first surprised me and then moved me deeply; she wanted to see my wife. She swore she would not go near her and that she would take care not to be seen by her. I promised her that if I happened to hear my wife was going out at a particular time I would let her know. She must not see my wife near my villa, which was in a lonely spot where every passer-by attracts attention, but in one of the crowded streets of the city.

About this time my mother-in-law had some disease of the eyes which obliged her to keep a bandage over them for several days. This bored her terribly, and to see that she obeyed the doctor's orders exactly, her daughters took it in turn to sit with her; my wife in the morning and Ada from four o'clock in the afternoon. I don't know even now what led me to indicate Ada to Carla as my wife. No doubt after the singing-masters' proposal I felt the need of attaching her more closely to me, and I may have thought that the lovelier my wife seemed to her the more she would love the man who, in some sort, had sacrificed such a woman to her. Augusta was at that time no more than a splendidly healthy nursing mother. Perhaps I was guided to a certain extent by considerations of prudence. I had good reasons to fear Carla's capricious humor, and if she had let herself be carried away into some indiscretion before Ada it would not have mattered so much, seeing that I already had sufficient proof that Ada would never try to damage me in Augusta's eyes.

If Carla had compromised me with Ada I should have told the latter the whole story, and not without a certain secret satisfaction.

But my stratagem had results that I could never have foreseen. Feeling slightly anxious as to how things had gone, I went to see Carla earlier than usual next morning. I found her quite changed from the day before. The pure oval of her face wore an expression of great seriousness. I was going to kiss her but she repulsed me at first, then let

me just touch her cheeks with my lips to induce me to
listen to her quietly. I sat down at the table facing her.
She took up a sheet of paper on which she had been writing till I came in, and put it with some deliberation
among some music that was lying on the table. I took no
notice of the sheet of paper and it was only later that I
learned it was a letter to Lali.

I know now that up to that moment Carla's soul had
been torn by doubts. She gazed at me questioningly with
her serious eyes; then she turned toward the window, as if
she sought to be alone with herself and to look into her
own heart. Perhaps if I had been quicker to divine what
was going on in her mind I might even then have kept
my exquisite mistress for myself.

She told me about her meeting with Ada. She had
waited for her outside my mother-in-law's house, and
when she came out had recognized her at once.

"Nobody could have mistaken her. You had described
her chief features to me. Oh, how well you know her!"

She was silent for a moment, trying to control the tu-
mult of her senses, which made it difficult for her to speak.
Then she went on:

"I don't know what has happened between you, but I
don't want ever again to betray that woman. She is so
beautiful and so sad! I shall write to the singing-master today, saying that I am willing to marry him!"

"Sad?" I exclaimed in astonishment. "You must
have made a mistake, or she may have had a shoe that
pinched her at that moment."

Ada sad! Why, she was always laughing and smiling;
even that very morning when I had seen her at my house.

But Carla knew more about it than I did.

"A shoe that pinched her! She had the carriage of a
goddess walking on the clouds!"

She told me with evergrowing agitation that she had
even had a few words addressed to her—ah, such sweet
ones—by Ada. The latter had dropped her handkerchief
and Carla had picked it up and given it back to her. Her
brief words of thanks had moved Carla to tears. Something
else had also happened between the two women. Carla
maintained that Ada had noticed she was crying and had
given her a parting look of tender sympathy. Everything
was plain to Carla; my wife knew that I was unfaithful to

her, and was suffering. That was why she had decided not to see me any more, and to marry Lali.

I did not know what to say in my own defense. It would have been easy for me to talk about Ada as if I disliked her, but not about my wife, who was so busy doing her duty as a good mother that she did not perceive what was going on in my mind. I asked Carla if she had not noticed a certain hard look in Ada's eyes, and that her voice was low and harsh without any touch of gentleness. If only I could have had Carla's love again, there on the spot, I would gladly have attributed many other failings to my wife; but how could I, seeing that for about a year now I had been praising her to the skies before my mistress?

I got out of it another way. I was so deeply moved myself that the tears rose to my eyes. I felt I was greatly deserving of pity. Without at all intending it, I had fallen head-first into a dilemma from which I could see no way out. It was intolerable to have Ada and Augusta mistaken for each other like that. The real facts were that my wife was not at all beautiful, and that Ada, who so keenly aroused Carla's compassion, had treated me very badly. Carla was really unjust in her judgment of me.

My tears softened Carla a little toward me.

"Dear Dario," she said, "it does me good to see you cry. There must have been some misunderstanding between you two, and it has got to be cleared up. I don't want to be too hard on you but I have made up my mind never to betray her again. I am determined she shan't have to cry because of me. I swear it!"

In spite of having sworn it, she did betray Augusta one last time. She wanted to part from me forever with a final kiss, but I would only allow this kiss to take one form, otherwise I should have parted from her full of resentment. So she submitted. We both murmured: "For the last time."

It was an exquisite moment. That resolution taken by both of us in common had the power to wipe out all our guilt. We were innocent and happy. Kind fate had requited me with one moment of perfect bliss.

I felt so happy that I went on with the comedy up to the moment of saying good-by. We were never to see each other again. She refused the envelope that I always carried

in my pocket, and would not even accept any momento
from me. Every trace of our past must be banished from
the new life on which we were entering. Then I consented
to kiss her on the forehead like a father, as she had wanted
me to at first.

On the stairs I had a sudden misgiving that the matter
was becoming too serious. If I could have known that she
would still be at my disposition the next day I should not
have been troubled so soon with thoughts of the future.
She watched me go downstairs from her landing, and I
called up to her, laughingly:

"Till tomorrow!"

She gave a start of shocked surprise and went away,
saying:

"Never again!"

All the same I felt relieved to think I had dared to say
something that left the way open for a last embrace, if I felt
the desire for it. With nothing I wanted to do and no
business to attend to, I spent the whole day with Augusta
and in Guido's office. My complete idleness gave me the
opportunity to see more of my wife and child than usual.
I was not only kind to them but played a father's part in
the direction of the household, giving orders and looking
into everything. As I was going to bed I said to myself:

"Every day ought to be like this."

Before we went to sleep Augusta felt she must confide
a great secret to me; her mother had told her only today.
A few days ago Ada had come upon Guido kissing one of
the maids. Ada would have preferred to have taken a high
line about it, but the girl had been insolent and she had
sent her away on the spot. Yesterday they had all been
anxious to hear what Guido would do about it; if he had
complained Ada had intended to ask for a separation. But
Guido had laughed and protested that Ada had made a
mistake; he had nothing against her being sent away as he
could not bear the girl, he said. The matter appeared to
have been smoothed over.

I was very curious to know whether Ada really had
been wrong when she surprised her husband in that position; was there any possible room for doubt? For after all
when two people are kissing each other they are in quite a
different position from when one is tying the other's shoe-

laces. I felt in the best of humors. I even felt the need of displaying a very calm and equable mind in my judgment of Guido. Ada was certainly of a jealous temperament, which might have made her see them nearer together than they really were, and doing something quite different.

Augusta said sadly that she was sure Ada had not made a mistake, and that it was excess of affection which made her take another view now. She added:

"She would have done better to have married you!"

I was feeling more and more innocent, and boldly replied:

"We have yet to see whether I should have made a better bargain if I had married her instead of you!"

As I was dropping off to sleep I murmured:

"What a scandal! Deceiving his wife in her own house!"

I had sufficient decency to reproach him only with that part of his conduct which I had no need to reproach in myself.

Next morning I rose with the ardent hope that the first day at least would be exactly like the preceding one. Probably Carla would not feel any more bound than myself by the delicious resolutions we had taken in common the day before, and I for my part felt completely free. They had been too pleasant to be binding. But my anxiety to know what Carla really thought about it made me hasten to see her. What I hoped was that I should find her in the mood for forming a fresh resolution. So life would flow on, rich in enjoyment but more still in efforts to get better; a great part of each day would be devoted to well-doing, only a small part to regrets. I felt a certain anxiety, it is true, because during the whole of this year, which for me had abounded in resolutions, Carla had only formed one: to show me she loved me. She had kept hers, and it was rather difficult for me to argue from this whether or not she would find it easy to keep a new resolution that was the direct opposite of the old.

Carla was not at home. I was terribly disappointed and bit my nails in mortification. The old woman made me go into the kitchen. She said that Carla would be back before night. She had told her that she would be feeding out, so there was not even the usual small fire on the hearth.

"Didn't you know?" asked the old woman, her eyes wide with astonishment.

I muttered absent-mindedly, and with a heavy heart:

"I knew yesterday. But I wasn't sure whether Carla's plans held good for today or not."

I went away after having said good-by as graciously as I could. I ground my teeth, but in secret. It took me some time to pluck up sufficient courage to be angry in public. I went to the Giardino Pubblico and walked about for half an hour, to give myself time to think things over. They had become so clear as to baffle me altogether. Suddenly, piteously, I found myself forced to keep a resolution like that. I felt ill, really ill. I limped along, trying in vain to contend with my bodily distress. I sometimes have attacks like this; I can breathe perfectly well, but I count each breath I draw, because each requires a special effort of the will. I have the feeling that if I were not careful I should die of suffocation.

At that hour I ought to have gone to the office, or better still to Guido's. But I had not the strength of mind to leave that spot. What should I do if I did? How different today was from yesterday. If only I had known the address of that wretched singing-master who by dint of singing at my expense had carried off my mistress!

I ended at last by going back to the old woman. I might be able to think of some message that would induce Carla to see me again. The problem was how to get hold of her, and that as quickly as possible. The rest, I felt, would not present any great difficulty.

I found the old woman sitting by one of the windows of the kitchen, busy darning a stocking. She took off her spectacles and eyed me curiously and half timidly. I hesitated a moment and then said:

"You know that Carla has decided to marry Lali?"

I felt as if I were telling myself the news for the first time. It is true that Carla had told me twice, but the day before I had not paid much attention to her. Her words had struck my ear, and so clearly that I recalled them perfectly; but they had slipped off again without penetrating my mind. Now, for the first time, they reached my vitals and I writhed with pain.

The old woman looked at me, and she too seemed

to hesitate. She was obviously afraid of committing some indiscretion with which she would be reproached afterwards. Then she burst out in great delight:

"Has Carla told you that? Then it must be true. I think she is quite right! What do you think about it?"

She laughed with joy, the horrid old witch; and I had always imagined she knew all about my liaison with Carla. I longed to hit her, but contented myself with saying that I should have preferred to wait till the singing-master had attained a better position. For my part I thought they were being too hasty.

In her joy the old woman became quite talkative for the first time. She did not agree with me. If one married young one must make a career for oneself afterwards. Why must one always make it first? Carla needed so little. And the training of her voice would cost less too, as it was her singing-master she was going to marry.

These words, which might be interpreted as a reproof to my avarice, gave me an idea that struck me at the time as magnificent, and relieved my mind for the moment. The money that I still always carried in an envelope in my breast-pocket must have reached by now a considerable sum. I took it out and handed it to the old woman, asking her to give it to Carla for me. Perhaps I felt the need of making my mistress some proper return, but my chief desire was to see her and possess her again. Carla would surely see me again in either case, whether she wanted to return the money or whether she found it more convenient to keep it; then she would feel that she must say thank you for it. I breathed again: it was not the end of everything!

I told her mother that the envelope contained the remains of the money collected among his friends by Copler, which he had entrusted to me. Then, with my spirits quite restored, I asked her to tell Carla that I should always be a good friend to her and that she was to come to me in case she ever needed help. This enabled me to give her my address: I gave Guido's office.

I went away with a much lighter step than I had come. But that day I had a violent quarrel with Augusta. It was all about nothing. I said the soup was too salt, while she maintained it was not. I suddenly got into a violent rage because I thought she was laughing at me, and pulled the cloth toward me with a jerk, so that everything was scattered on the floor. The baby, who was in the nurse's arms, began to howl; which humiliated me very much because I thought it was trying to reproach me too. Augusta grew pale as only she knew how, took the baby in her arms and left the room. I thought this was really going too far; was I to be left to eat my food alone like a dog? But she returned almost at once without the baby, put the cloth to rights, and sat down again in front of her plate. She took up some soup in her spoon as if she were going to begin eating again.

I was inwardly swearing, but I had come to look upon myself as a plaything in the hands of the uncontrolled forces of nature. Nature found no difficulty in accumulating them, and less still in unchaining them on the world. My curses were directed against Carla, who pretended to be acting entirely in the interests of my wife. It was all her fault that I had behaved like this!

Augusta has her own method of dealing with me when I am in this condition, a method from which she has never departed. She does not argue, or weep or protest. When I began humbly apologizing, she only wanted to explain one thing: she had not laughed, she had only smiled, as she had done so many times before when I had seemed to like it.

I was properly ashamed of myself. I begged Augusta to have the baby brought back, and took it in my arms and played with it for a long time. Then I made it sit on my head, and dried my eyes—wet with the tears Augusta had not shed—with its little frock that hung down over my face. I played with the baby because I knew that without having to make any more excuses for my conduct I was really making it up to Augusta; and sure enough her cheeks had already resumed their normal color.

The day, after all, ended well, the afternoon being very much like the preceding one. It was almost as good as if I had found Carla in her usual place that morning. I felt the same sort of stimulus. I kept on telling Augusta how sorry I was, because I wanted to induce her to put on her motherly smile again when I said or did anything ridiculous. I could not have borne it if she had felt constrained to adopt a certain attitude toward me, or if my conduct had obliged her to repress a single one of those tender smiles of hers, which seemed to me the kindest and most final judgment that anyone could pass on me.

In the evening we talked again about Guido. He had apparently entirely made his peace with Ada. Augusta wondered how her sister could be such a saint. This time it was my turn to laugh, for she had evidently forgotten how very charitable she was herself. I said to her:

"Supposing I were to do the same thing in our house, wouldn't you forgive me?"

She hesitated a moment and then exclaimed:

"We have our child, but Ada has no children to bind her to that man."

She did not like Guido; I sometimes think that she continued to bear him a grudge for having made me suffer.

A few months later Ada presented Guido with twins, and Guido could never understand why I congratulated him so warmly. According to Augusta's theory, now that he had children he could amuse himself as much as he liked with the maids without danger to himself.

Next morning when I went to the office and found on my desk an envelope in Carla's handwriting, I breathed again. So nothing was at an end, and I was still to be provided with all the elements essential to my life. In a few brief words Carla gave me an appointment for eleven o'clock in the Giardino Pubblico, by the entrance opposite her house. We were not to meet in her room, it is true, but somewhere very near to it.

I could not control my impatience, and arrived at the rendezvous a quarter of an hour too soon. If Carla had failed to appear at the appointed place I decided I would go straight to her house, which would have been much more convenient.

It was another of those delicious spring days, fresh and soft and luminous. When I left the noisy Corsa Stadion and went into the garden, the silence seemed almost rural, hardly broken by the faint rustling of leaves in the mild breeze.

As I walked quickly toward the other gate of the garden, I saw Carla coming to meet me. She had my envelope in her hand, and advanced toward me without a smile of greeting, and with a stern, fixed expression on her pale face. She had on a simple dress of rather loosely woven linen with a blue stripe in it, which suited her very well. She seemed to be part of the garden. Afterwards, during the times when I felt I hated her most, I accused her in my own mind having put on that dress so as to make herself more desirable at the very moment she meant to refuse herself to me. But she was really clothed in the first fine day of spring. Besides, one must remember that the personal adornment of my mistress had played a very small part in our long but hurried liaison. I had always gone straight to her studio, and modest women when they are at home always dress very simply.

She gave me her hand, which I pressed, saying:

"Thank you for coming!"

How much better it would have been if I had remained as unexacting as that during the whole interview!

Carla seemed to me to be very agitated, and when she spoke a nervous tremor passed through her, and her lips trembled. Sometimes when she was singing that movement of the lips prevented her from producing the tone she wanted. She said:

"I wish I could please you by accepting this money from you, but I can't, I simply can't. Please take it back again."

When I saw that she was almost in tears I did what she wanted at once, and took the envelope from her. Long after I had left her I found it still in my hand.

"Do you really want to have nothing more to do with me?"

I asked her this, quite forgetting that she had already answered me the day before. But was it likely that she would continue to withstand me, when I desired her so much?

"Zeno," she replied in a softer tone, "didn't we promise never to see each other again? It is because of that promise that I have taken certain vows, which you had already taken before you met me. They are as sacred as yours, and I hope by now your wife knows that you belong entirely to her."

She was evidently still troubled by the thought of Ada's beauty. If I could have been sure that this was the real reason she had given me up I might have been able to avert it. I might have told her that Ada was not my wife and have shown her the cast in Augusta's eye and her spoilt figure. But the vows she said she had taken were more important still, and I was obliged to discuss them with her.

I tried to talk calmly to her, though my lips were trembling too—but with desire. I said she did not seem to know how much she meant to me, and that she had not the right to dispose of herself like that. The scientific proof of what I wanted to say passed through my mind—to wit, Darwin's famous experiment on an Arab mare—but thank God I don't think I mentioned it. But I am sure I talked about animals and their physical fidelity, babbling on incoherently. I abandoned the more difficult arguments, which were beyond us both at that moment, and said:

"What vows can you have taken? And how can they be of any importance compared to a love like ours, which has bound us for over a year?"

I seized her roughly by the hand, for I felt the need of some violent movement to take the place of the words I could not utter.

She snatched her hand away from me as resolutely as if it were the first time I had dared to take hold of it.

"But," she said as solemnly as if she were taking an oath, "I have taken the most sacred of all vows, and with a man who did exactly the same to me."

There was no longer any room for doubt. The blood that suddenly colored her cheeks was driven there by anger against the man who had never taken any vows toward her. And she proceeded to make her meaning still clearer:

"Yesterday we went for a walk together, with my mother, and we walked through the streets arm in arm."

She was running away from me, that was clear; farther and farther away. I began running madly after her, making hasty leaps like a dog who has had tasty bits of meat taken away from him. I seized her hand again and cried:

"Very well, we will walk hand in hand from one end of the town to the other. In that unusual position we will go right down the Corsa Stadion, along the Volti di Chiozza, and on and on down the Corso to Sant' Andrea; and we will come back to our room quite a different way, so that the whole city may have a chance of looking at us."

For the first time I was proposing really to give up Augusta! And I was glad I was going to get free, for it was she who was really robbing me of Carla.

She again released herself from my grasp and said coldly:

"That is about the same route we took yesterday."

I made another leap:

"But does he know everything? Does he know you gave yourself to me yesterday?"

"Yes," she answered proudly. "He knows everything, everything."

I felt I was lost, and like a dog who, when he can no longer get the desired morsel, worries with his teeth the person who has refused it him, I exclaimed in my rage:

"That bridegroom of yours must have an excellent digestion. He can swallow me today, and tomorrow he will swallow whatever you like to give him."

I hardly knew what I was saying. I only know I was crying out with pain. But her face assumed an expression of indignation of which I should hardly have thought her soft gazelle-like brown eyes would have been capable.

"You dare say that to me? Why haven't you got the courage to say it to him?"

She turned her back on me and walked swiftly toward the gate. I was already regretting my words, but was stupefied to discover that I was no longer allowed to speak roughly to Carla. This discovery rooted me to the spot. It was only when the little figure in blue and white had already reached the gate with rapid steps that I decided to run after her. I had no idea what I should say to her, but we could not part like that.

I caught her up just as she was going in at the front door, and said out of the fullness of my heart:

"Are we really going to part like this, after having loved each other so much?"

She continued to walk on without answering me, and I followed her up the stairs. Then she looked at me with the same hostile eye and said:

"If you want to see my fiancé, come in with me. Don't you hear? That is him playing the piano."

Then I heard the syncopations of Schubert's "*Gruss*" arranged by Liszt.

Although I have never at any time practiced with a saber or swordstick, I am not at all a timid man. The intense desire that had moved me up to that moment suddenly died down; all that remained of the male in me was my combativeness. I had imperiously demanded something that I could not have. To put myself less in the wrong it was essential for me to fight, otherwise the memory of that woman, threatening to have me punished by her fiancé, would be too atrocious.

"Very well, then!" I said. "If you allow me I will come with you." My heart was beating fast, not from fear but because I was afraid I might not behave properly.

I continued to walk upstairs beside her. But suddenly she stopped, leaned against the wall and began crying silently. The strains of Schubert's *"Gruss,"* on the piano I had paid for, still floated down to us. Carla's tears made it seem much more moving.

"I will do whatever you like," I said. "Do you want me to go away?"

"Yes," she murmured, hardly able to articulate that one short word.

"Good-by," I said. "Since you wish it, good-by forever."

I went slowly downstairs, whistling the tune of Schubert's song. Was it a dream, or did she really call after me: "Zeno"? At that moment I would not have stopped even if she had called me by her strange pet name, Dario. I was longing to get away and return, pure again, to Augusta. Even a dog, prevented by kicks from approaching the female, runs away perfectly pure for the time being.

Next day when I was again reduced to the state I had been in on my way to the Giardino Pubblico, I simply felt that I had been a cad; she had called me, even though not by my pet name, and I had not answered. It was my first day of unhappiness, and was followed by many in which I suffered bitter pangs of loneliness. I could not understand why I had gone away like that, and concluded it must have been because I was afraid of that man or of a scandal. I felt now that I would gladly compromise myself to any extent, as for instance when I had suggested to Carla that we should take the long walk together in the town. I had lost a favorable moment, and I knew well enough that with certain women those moments only come once. Once would have been enough for me.

I decided to write to Carla immediately. I could not let pass a single day without trying to get into touch with her again. I wrote and rewrote that letter, trying to put into a few words all the understanding of which I was capable. I rewrote it so many times partly because writing was a great comfort to me; it gave me just the outlet I needed. I asked her to forgive me for getting so angry, telling her that my great love would take a long time to calm down. I added: "Every day that passes brings me a fresh grain of peace." I wrote these sentences several times over, grinding my teeth as I wrote. I went on to say that I could not forgive myself for having spoken to her like that, and that I felt the need of asking her forgiveness. I could not, alas, offer her what Lali offered, and what she so richly deserved.

I pictured the letter making a great impression on her. Since Lali knew all about it Carla would be sure to show him the letter and Lali might easily feel that it was a great advantage to him to have a friend of my standing. I even dreamed of our having a very agreeable life together à trois, for my love was so great at the moment that I should have felt it an alleviation of my lot to have even been allowed to pay court to Carla.

On the third day I received a short note from her. In it she called me neither Zeno nor Dario. She only said: "Thank you! I hope you will be happy too with your wife, who so much deserves to be happy!" She was, of course, speaking of Ada.

The favorable moment had not lasted, and it never does last with women unless you take hold of them by the hair of their head. My desire had taken the form of mad rage. Not with Augusta! My mind was so full of Carla that I felt quite remorseful, and all the time I was with Augusta I wore a forced, idiotic smile which she took to be genuine.

But something must be done. I could not just wait and go on suffering like this day after day! I did not want to write to her again. It is a waste of time to cover paper with ink for a woman. I must find something better than that.

With no definite plan in my mind I made my way to the Giardino Pubblico. Then, much more slowly, I went on to Carla's house, and when I had reached the landing knocked at the kitchen door. I would have preferred if possible not to meet Lali, but I felt I should not mind running into him. It would be just the climax I was needing.

The old lady was by the hearth as usual, where two good fires were burning. She was surprised to see me, but the kind old thing at once made me welcome, and said laughingly:

"Well I *am* pleased to see you! You had got so used to coming to see us every day that it's no wonder you can't get out of it as soon as all that."

It was easy enough to set her talking. She told me that Carla and Vittorio were very much in love with each other. He and his mother were coming to dinner that very day. She added, laughing:

"I shouldn't wonder if he didn't soon persuade her to go with him to his singing lessons. He has such a lot to give every day. They can't bear to be separated for a moment."

She laughed with motherly pride to think they were so happy. She told me they were going to be married in a few weeks' time.

I had a bad taste in my mouth and was on the point of going away. But I refrained, in the hope that the old woman's gossip might suggest something to my mind, or give me some sort of hope. The last mistake I had made with Carla had been just that—that I had run away before having studied every possible loophole that might be offered me of staying.

For a moment I really did think I had got an idea. I asked the old woman if it was her intention to act as her daughter's servant for the rest of her life. I said I knew that Carla was not very nice to her.

She went on with what she was doing at the fire, but listened to me while she worked. She was extraordinarily frank with me, though I had done nothing to deserve it. She complained that Carla lost patience with her over every little trifle. She tried to excuse herself.

"I know I get older every day," she said. "And I forget everything. It is not my fault!"

But she hoped things were beginning to go better. Carla was much less bad-tempered now that she was happy. And then Vittorio had treated her with great respect from the very first. She went on making a paste of flour and fruit into various shapes while she talked.

"It is my duty to stay with my daughter," she said. "I can't do otherwise."

I took some pains to make her change her mind. I said she might very well escape from such slavery. Could not I help her? I would continue to pay her the monthly allowance that had hitherto been paid to Carla. It had become a necessity to me to support somebody! I wanted to keep the old woman, because she seemed to me to be part of her daughter.

She expressed her gratitude warmly. She said how good it was of me, but she laughed at the idea of leaving her daughter. She could never dream of such a thing. This was a hard saying for me, and left me with a terrible weight on my mind. I had got to return then to my state of loneliness, where there was no Carla and no way by which I could return to her. I remember I made one last effort to deceive myself into thinking that a way might still be open. Before going away I told the old woman that if she were at any time to change her mind she had only got to let me know.

I left the house full of scorn and indignation, feeling as if I had been maltreated by the very people to whom I was intending to show kindness. The old woman had insulted me by bursting out laughing like that. Her laughter still sounded in my ears, and meant much more than that she had mocked at my last proposal.

I did not want to go back to Augusta feeling like that. I knew exactly what would happen. If I had gone I should have behaved badly to her and she would have avenged herself by that strange pallor which made me feel so unhappy. I preferred to walk up and down the streets with a rhythmic tread that I hoped might produce a little order in my thoughts. And that order did in fact come. I ceased lamenting my fate, and saw myself as if I had been projected by a great light on the wall in front of me. I did not want Carla, but only her embrace, and preferably her final embrace. The thing was ridiculous! I bit my lips, hoping the pain might give some sort of substance to my ludicrous fancy. I knew myself thoroughly, and it was inexcusable that I should suffer so much when I had such a unique opportunity for freeing myself. Carla had ceased to exist just as I had so often wished she might.

Such was my lucidity of mind that when a little later, in an out of the way part of the town which I found my way to at random, a woman of the streets accosted me, I unhesitatingly went with her.

I got home very late for luinch, but was so nice to

Augusta that her spirits rose at once. But I could not bring myself to kiss my child, and for several hours was incapable of eating anything. I felt unclean! I did not feign sickness, as I had done on several other occasions to conceal my misdeeds and remorse. I thought I should never again find comfort in any resolution, and for the first time I failed to make one. It took me a good many hours to recover the accustomed rhythm that might bridge the gulf between my gloomy present and the bright future.

Augusta noticed that something had happened to me. She said, laughing:

"One can never be bored if one is with you. Every day you become a different man."

It was true! That woman in the suburban street was quite different from any other, and I had her in my blood.

I spent the whole afternoon and evening with Augusta. She was very busy, and I stayed beside her doing nothing. I felt as if I were being carried along by a stream of clear water: my respectable home life.

I abandoned myself to the stream, which carried me along but did not purify me. On the contrary it only emphasized my stain.

Naturally during the long night that followed I formed a fresh resolution. The first was the most iron of all. I determined to buy a pistol, and shoot myself directly I found myself turning toward that part of the town. This resolution made me feel better, and less disgusted with myself.

I never groaned in bed; instead I imitated the regular breathing of someone who is asleep. I returned to my old idea of making a confession to my wife, just as when I had been on the point of committing adultery with Carla. But this confession would have been much more difficult to make, not so much on account of the gravity of my offense as of the complications that had preceded it. Face to face with a judge like my wife, I should have had to plead attenuating circumstances, and this I could only have done if I had been free to tell her of my unexpected and violent rupture with Carla. But in that case I should have been obliged to have gone back over the whole story of my infidelity, and confess everything to her.

By a process of self-analysis my resolutions became more and more reasonable. I thought I could prevent a

similar thing happening again by taking immediate steps to
form another liaison like the one that was just at an end,
and which it was obvious I could not do without. But the
thought of another woman alarmed me considerably. Too
many perils threatened me and my little family. There was
not another Carla to be found in the world, and I shed
bitter tears at the thought of what I had lost; she was so
sweet and good, and had even tried to love the woman I
loved. She had only not succeeded because I had shown
her another woman instead, and precisely the one I did
not love!

A Business Partnership

I T W A S Guido who wanted me to join him in his new commercial undertaking. I was dying to do so, but I never allowed him to guess how much I wanted it. It was natural that having nothing to do, the idea of working with a friend should have been sympathetic to me. But there was something besides. I had not yet given up hopes of becoming a good man of business, and I thought I should learn more by teaching Guido than by taking lessons from Olivi. Many people can only learn by listening to themselves, or at least cannot learn anything by listening to others.

I had other reasons for wishing to ally myself to Guido. I wanted to be of use to him. In the first place I was very fond of him, and although he made a show of being strong and sure of himself, he seemed to me a weak creature who was in need of the protection I was so anxious to give. Further, I sincerely felt, not only on Augusta's account but on my own, that the closer my relationship to Guido, the more evident would appear my absolute indifference to Ada.

I was only waiting for a word from Guido in order to put myself entirely at his disposal, and if he did not call upon me sooner it was because he assumed I had a distaste for business, as I always refused to have anything to do with it in my own family.

One day he said to me:

"I have been all through the Higher School of Commerce, but I still don't find it so very easy to arrange properly all the details necessary in order to guarantee the sound running of a business. Of course no business man need really know anything, but if he wants his goods weighed he has only to get a weighing-machine, if he wants to go to law he consults a solicitor, if he wants to know how his accounts stand he calls in an accountant. But it seems hard to have to hand over one's accounts straight away to a stranger."

It was the first open allusion to his proposal that I should join him; to tell the truth my experience of accounts was confined to the few months during which I had kept Olivi's register, but, on the other hand, I was certainly the only accountant who was not a stranger to Guido.

Our first frank discussion of the possibility of going into business together was when I went with him to choose the furniture for his office. He ordered two writing-desks for the manager's room. I asked him, blushing, why he had ordered two? and he replied:

"The second one is for you."

I felt so grateful to him that I could almost have hugged him.

After we had left the shop Guido, with a touch of embarrassment, explained to me that he was hardly in a position yet to offer me a post in his business. He had ordered a desk to be put in his room for me in the hope that I might come and keep him company sometimes if I felt so inclined. He didn't want to bind me to anything, and he must be free too. If his business went well he intended to ask me to become a partner in it.

When he talked about his business Guido's handsome face became very serious. He appeared to have already thought out all the transactions he proposed to engage in. He took a long view, right over my head, and I was so much impressed by his seriousness of purpose that I came to see things with his eyes, the financial operations, that is to say, which were to make his fortune. He was content neither to walk in the path so successfully trodden by our father-in-law, nor in the humble path of "safety first" pursued by Olivi. According to him they were quite out of date in their methods. One must strike out quite a new path, and he wanted me to be connected with him because he thought the old men had not had time to ruin me yet.

I quite agreed with him. I felt I had scored my first commercial success, and I again blushed with pleasure. It was really out of gratitude for his good opinion of me that I went on working for him for two years with varying degrees of energy, and with no other reward than the glory of a desk in the manager's room. This was the longest time I had ever spent up to now at the same occupation. But I cannot boast of it, because all my energy produced no results either for Guido or me, and in business, as everyone knows, you can only judge by results.

I preserved my faith in the undertaking for about three months, just time enough for getting it started. I knew it would devolve on me to arrange such details as the correspondence and the accounts, as well as keeping an eye on the business generally. But Guido kept a great ascendancy over me; in fact so much so that I was nearly ruined by him, and was only saved by my lucky star. He had only to beckon, for me to rush to him at once. I still wonder at it even now, after having had time to think it over for the greater part of my life.

I have decided to write about those two years, because my devotion to him seems to me a clear symptom of disease. What reason had I for attaching myself to him in order to learn big business, and then for remaining attached to him in order to teach him the details? What reason had I for being so satisfied with my position just because I thought my great friendship for Guido showed that I did not care about Ada? Who obliged me to do this? Was not our mutual indifference sufficiently demonstrated by the existence of the children we both produced so regularly? I did not dislike Guido, but he was certainly not the friend I should have chosen. I saw his faults so plainly that I was irritated by his way of thinking, even when I was not put off by some act of weakness on his part. I sacrificed my freedom to him for years and allowed him to place me in the most odious position, simply in order that I might help him. It was either a real manifestation of disease or of great benevolence, both of which qualities are closely related to each other.

This remained true, even though with time we developed a strong affection, as often happens between people

who see each other every day. My feeling for him was very
strong indeed. When he disappeared I went on missing him
for a very long time: in fact my whole life seemed empty,
so great a part of it having been usurped by him and his
affairs.

I can't help smiling when I remember what a muddle
we made of our first transaction, the buying of furniture.
We had saddled ourselves with the furniture, but could not
make up our minds where to have the office. There was a
difference of opinion between Guido and me about the
choice of an office, which considerably retarded our getting
one. In the case of my father-in-law and Olivi, I had seen
how important it was to have your warehouse near to the
office if you were to keep it under proper supervision.
Guido protested with a sort of disgust:

"Those offices down in the town stink of fish and
skins!"

He asserted that it would be quite easy for him to
keep control of the warehouse from a distance, but meanwhile he delayed about taking one. One fine day the firm
from which he had bought the furniture informed him
that if he did not fetch it away it would be thrown into
the street, whereupon he dashed off to take an office—the
best that had been offered him—with no warehouse near
it, and in the very middle of the town. And so it came
about that we never had a warehouse at all.

The office consisted of two very large, well-lit rooms
and a small room without windows. A notice was pinned
on the door of the uninhabitable room with "Accountant's
Office" inscribed on it in large letters. One of the other
doors bore the inscription "Counting-house," and the third
rejoiced in the very English appellation of "Private." Guido
had studied business in England too and had brought back
several useful ideas. The "Counting-house" had of course
a magnificent iron safe and the customary grid. Our room,
marked "Private," was a luxurious apartment upholstered
in brown velvet and furnished with two desks, a divan and
several very comfortable armchairs.

Next came the purchase of books and various smaller
articles of furniture. In this department my position as
director was undisputed. I had only to give an order and
the things arrived. I would really have preferred a rather
less implicit obedience, but it was my job to decide exactly

what was necessary in an office. It was then that I began to discover the fundamental difference between Guido and myself. All the knowledge I had acquired was used by me for talking, and by him for action. When he had acquired all the information I could give him he would buy. It is true that he sometimes decided to sit still and do nothing at all—neither buy nor sell—but even this impressed me as the act of someone who is very sure of himself. I should have been much more troubled by doubts, even if it had been a question of doing nothing.

I was very cautious about the purchases I made. I hurried off to Olivi to take the measurements of the duplicating-machine and account-books. Young Olivi showed me how to open the accounts and explained to me about bookkeeping with double entries, all of which is easy enough to learn, but rather difficult to remember. When the weighing-machine arrived he promised he would explain this to me as well.

We were not yet very clear as to what we were going to do in the office (for I now know that Guido was equally ignorant) and we had great discussions about the proper conduct of the business. I remember we spent several days in discussing where we should put the other employees and whether we really needed them at all. Guido proposed putting as many as possible in the room labeled "Counting-house." But Luciano, the office-boy, who was for the moment our only employee, said that only those who were actually connected with the Counting-house ought to be in that room. It was hard to reconcile ourselves to taking lessons from the office-boy! I had an inspiration: "I seem to remember that in England they pay everything by check."

I had been told so by someone in Trieste.

"Bravo," said Guido. "I remember it too now. It is odd that I should have forgotten!"

We began explaining to Luciano in great detail that it was no longer the custom to use coins in dealing either in large or in small sums of money. People are accustomed to doing all their business by check, whatever the amount may be. Our victory was complete, and Luciano was silenced.

He was to learn a great deal from Guido. Our office-boy has now become a highly respected man of business in

Trieste, but he still greets me with a deferential smile.
Guido spent a part of each day in teaching Luciano, then
me, and finally the lady member of the staff. I remember
that for some time past he had entertained the idea of
doing business on commission, so as not to risk his own
money. He explained the essentials of that sort of business
to me, and as I grasped it too readily he proceeded to
explain it to Luciano, who would listen to him as long as
he liked with the keenest attention, his great eyes lighting
up his boyish face. No one could say that Guido wasted his
time with him, for Luciano is the only one among us who
has made a success in that kind of business. And yet they
say that science always wins!

Meanwhile the pesos began arriving from Buenos Aires.
That was a serious matter. At first I thought it would be
quite simple, but the Trieste market was not accustomed to
that exotic coinage. We had to call in young Olivi again,
who showed us how to get our money changed into the
native currency. But at a certain point Olivi thought he had
taught us enough, and left us to our own devices; and
Guido remained several days with his pockets bulging with
kronen, till at last we found our way to a bank and were
able to exchange our uneasy burden for a check-book,
which we soon learned to make use of.

Guido felt it his duty to point out to Olivi that in
helping him he was running the risk of being cut out by
him.

"But I promise I will never compete against my young
friend's firm," he added.

The young business man, who had quite a different
conception of trade, replied:

"My God! I should be only too thankful if there were
more people dealing in our particular goods. We should be
much better off."

Guido listened open-mouthed, at once grasped the
idea with his usual facility and proceeded to propound it
to anyone he could get to listen to him.

In spite of the Higher School of Commerce, Guido
had no very definite idea of credit and debit. When I
opened our capital account and entered our expenses, he
watched the proceedings with the utmost astonishment.
Later on he became so versed in bookkeeping that the first
thing he did when any business proposition was put before

him, was to analyze it from a bookkeeper's point of view.
It really looked as if a knowledge of bookkeeping had made
him see the world in quite a new light. He saw debtors and
creditors everywhere, even when two people were only
fighting or kissing each other.

On his first entry into business he used the utmost
caution. He turned down many business propositions, and
continued to do so for six months, with the calm air of one
who knows better.

"No!" he would say; and the monosyllable always appeared to be the result of careful calculation, even though
he had never set eyes on the goods in question. All his
meditations were directed toward discovering exactly how
a certain transaction would figure in the accounts, whether
successful or unsuccessful. As bookkeeping was the last
thing he had learnt it filled his whole horizon and colored
all he saw.

I am sorry to have to speak so ill of my poor friend,
but I must tell of things as they were, if only to understand
myself better. I remember the intellectual effort that went
into lumbering up our poor little office with a mass of
worthless stuff which entirely prevented any proper work
being done. Once when we were about to start business
on commission we sent out by post about a thousand
circulars. Guido argued as follows:

"What a lot of stamps we should save if we could
know beforehand how many people will take any notice of
them!"

The remark was in itself quite harmless, but Guido
was much too pleased with it, and began throwing the
sealed circulars up into the air, and would only send those
that fell with the address uppermost. This experiment
reminded me of something rather like it which I had done
in the past, but I don't remember having carried it to such
a pitch. I naturally did not pick up or post the ones he
rejected, for I could not be sure that he had not really had
an inspiration, and in that case it would be wrong to waste
stamps that he was obliged to pay for.

It was my good fortune not to be ruined by Guido,
and the same good fortune prevented my taking too active
a part in his affairs. I proclaim it aloud here, because there
are some in Trieste who do not believe it; during the whole
time I was with him I never intervened with any inspi-

ration, such as that of the dried raisins. I never urged him either to go in for anything in particular, or to avoid it. I was only there to admonish him to further activity and prudence. I would never have ventured to speculate with his money.

All the time I was with him I did nothing at all. I tried to put him on the right path, and perhaps I should have succeeded if I had been a little less passive. But when two people are working together it does not rest with them to decide who is to be Don Quixote and who Sancho Panza. He did all the work, and I, like a good Sancho, followed him at a leisurely pace in my account-books, after first submitting everything to a searching criticism.

Our sales on commission ended in complete failure, but without any loss to us. The only firm who sent us any goods was a stationer in Vienna, and part of what he sent was sold by Luciano, who gradually got to know how much commission we expected and managed to persuade Guido to give most of it to him. Guido finally agreed, because it was only a small amount and because the first stroke of business we had done was sure to bring us good luck. We stored the remainder of our stock of stationery and office requisites of all kinds, which we were obliged to keep and pay for, in the lumber-room. We had enough to keep a much more flourishing firm than ours supplied for a number of years.

Our bright little office in the heart of the city provided us with a delightful retreat for several years. Very little work was done there (only two business deals, I think, in empty packing-cases that we sold the same day that we acquired them, making a small profit), but there was a great deal of conversation in which Luciano joined; he got as excited talking about business as other lads of his age do about women.

At this time I found it pleasant enough to while away the time with those two innocents, because I had not yet lost Carla. I remember every hour of those days with pleasure. When I got home in the evening I had a lot to tell Augusta, and I had no need to hide from her any single thing that went on in the office, nor to falsify it in any way.

I was not the least worried when Augusta anxiously exclaimed:

"But when are you going to begin to make money?" We had not begun thinking about that yet. We knew that the first thing we had to do was to lie low and observe; to take stock of the goods, the market and all the background of business. You couldn't improvise a business house on the spur of the moment. Even Augusta's mind was set at rest by my explanations.

Soon a very noisy inmate was introduced into the office, a sporting-dog only a few months old, a lively and absorbing companion. Guido was devoted to him and ordered a daily supply of milk and meat. When I had nothing else to do or think about I used to love watching him too, dashing about the office with those four or five doggish gestures, which are so endearing because we know just what they mean. But I could not help feeling that a dog who made so much noise and brought in so much dirt was out of place in the office. It was the presence of the dog which first made me feel that Guido was not really worthy to conduct a house of business. It proved conclusively that he was entirely lacking in seriousness. I tried to explain to him that the dog could not in any way promote our business, but I had not the courage to insist on his being sent away, and Guido always had some answer ready which silenced me for the moment.

So then I thought it was my duty to devote myself to training our new colleague, and I took great pleasure in giving him a kick or two when Guido was not there. The dog howled, and at first came back to me, thinking I must have kicked him by mistake. But a second kick explained matters, and then he would go and lie down in the corner, and till Guido arrived we had peace in the office. I was sorry afterwards to think I had wreaked my vengeance on an innocent dog, but it was too late. I loaded him with attentions, but he no longer trusted me and showed clear signs of his dislike in Guido's presence. Guido said:

"It's very odd! It is lucky I know you, or I should feel rather suspicious of you. Dogs don't often make a mistake in the people they dislike."

To dispel Guido's doubts I was on the point of telling him how I had succeeded in making myself disliked by the dog.

It was not long before I fell out with Guido about

something that really ought not to have upset me so very much. The result of his passionate interest in bookkeeping was that he took it into his head to put down his private expenses with those of the office. After talking it over with Olivi I made a fuss about it, and tried to look after the interests of the old señor. It was really unheard of to put down to his account everything that Guido and Ada spent, not to mention the twins. Those were all expenses which ought to have been borne by Guido personally, not by the firm. As a compromise I suggested writing to Buenos Aires to ask Guido's father to pay him a salary. The father however refused, saying that Guido was already receiving seventy-five per cent of the profits, while he only got the remaining twenty-five. It seemed to me a reasonable enough reply, but Guido at once began writing long letters to his father, discussing the matter from a loftier point of view, as he said. Buenos Aires was a very long way off, so that the correspondence went on all the time our firm was in existence. But I won my point. Our general expenses account remained intact, and was not encroached on by Guido's private expenses, so that when our business collapsed, the whole undiminished capital went with it.

The fifth person to be introduced into our office (including Argo) was Carmen. I was present when she took up her duties with us. I had come to the office after having been to see Carla, and I was in a very serene state of mind, the sort of eight-o'clock-in-the-morning serenity that Talleyrand speaks of. I saw a young woman standing in the dark passage, and Luciano told me she wanted to speak to Guido. I had something I wanted to do so I asked her to wait outside. Guido came in soon afterwards, evidently without having seen the young woman, and Luciano gave him the letter of introduction that she had brought with her. Guido read it. Then he said sharply:

"No!" at the same time taking off his waistcoat, because of the heat. After a moment's hesitation he added:

"I suppose I had better just find out who sent her."

He had her in, and I saw her for the first time just as Guido had snatched up his waistcoat and was putting it on, with his handsome dark face and shining eyes turned toward the girl.

I am quite certain I have seen other girls just as pretty

as Carmen, but none whose beauty made so startling an appeal at the first glance. It is generally desire that makes women beautiful, but this girl stood in no need of an initial phase of that sort. I could not help smiling—even laughing —as I looked at her. She seemed to me like a shopkeeper traveling about the world to proclaim the excellence of his wares. She was applying for a post, but I felt inclined to interpose with the question: "What sort of a post? In the bedchamber?"

I saw that her face was not made up, but her coloring was so perfect, so like the bloom of a ripe fruit, that nature in her seemed to have rivalled art. Her great brown eyes refracted so much light that every movement she made with them seemed significant.

Guido made her sit down, and she kept her eyes fixed modestly on the point of her sunshade or more probably on the toes of her patent-leather shoes. When he spoke to her she raised her eyes quickly and gave him such a brilliant glance that my poor chief was quite overwhelmed. She was modestly dressed, but her modesty served no purpose, for it was completely contradicted by her body. Her shoes were the only luxurious thing about her and reminded one of the snow-white paper that Velasquez used to place under the feet of his models. In order to make Carmen stand out from her surroundings, Velasquez would probably have given her a black lacquer background.

I listened curiously to their conversation in an impersonal, calm frame of mind. Guido asked her if she knew shorthand. She admitted she did not, but said she had had a great deal of practice in writing to dictation. It was odd that such a tall graceful creature, whose movements were so harmonious, should have such a hoarse voice. I could not conceal my surprise.

"Have you a cold?" I asked.

"No!" she replied. "Why do you ask?"

She was so astonished at my question that the look she gave me was more than usually searching. She had no idea that her voice did not ring true, and I was obliged to conclude that her ear was not so perfect as it looked.

Guido asked if she knew English, French, and German. He gave her a choice of languages, as we did not yet know ourselves which one we should have most need of.

Carmen replied that she knew a little German, but only very little.

Guido never made any decision without reasoning it out. He remarked:

"We don't need German, for I know it so well myself."

The young woman still sat waiting for the final word (which I thought had been said already), and to hasten it remarked that she was taking a new situation partly because she was anxious to get experience, and that therefore she would be satisfied with quite a small salary.

One of the first effects of feminine beauty on a man is that it removes his avarice. Guido shrugged his shoulders as much as to say that he took no interest in such insignificant details, offered her a salary that she gratefully accepted, and gravely advised her to study shorthand. He gave her this advice entirely for my benefit, as he had rather committed himself by saying beforehand that the first member of the staff he engaged would be someone who had a perfect knowledge of shorthand.

That evening I told my wife about our new colleague. She was very much annoyed. Without my saying anything to suggest it she at once assumed that Guido had taken the girl into his employ in order to make her his mistress. I talked it over with her, and though I was obliged to admit that Guido did behave a little as if he were in love with her, I maintained that he would probably get over his infatuation without its having any serious consequences. The girl, I said, seemed quite respectable.

A few days later—I don't know whether it was a mere chance—Ada paid us a call at the office. Guido had not yet arrived and she stayed with me a minute, asking me at what time I expected him. Then, with a hesitating step she went into the next room, where there were at the moment only Carmen and Luciano. Carmen was busy at the typewriter, picking out the letters one by one with great deliberation. She lifted her beautiful eyes to look at Ada, who was gazing at her fixedly. How different the two women were! Carmen was, in a way, not unlike Ada, but a caricature of her. I could not help feeling that though she was more expensively dressed Ada was cut out for the part of wife and mother, while Carmen, though she was wearing an apron at the moment, so as not to dirty her dress with the typewriter, was obviously meant to be someone's mistress. I don't know whether there is anyone in the world clever enough to explain to me why Ada's beautiful eye seemed to absorb less light than Carmen's, which made it appear a real organ of observation, whereas the chief function of Carmen's was to dazzle. She bore Ada's disdainful but curious glance with perfect equanimity; I fancied there was a touch of envy in it, but I may have put that there myself.

This was the last time I saw Ada looking beautiful, as I had known her when I proposed to her and was refused. Soon after came her disastrous pregnancy, and the surgeon had to be called in to assist at the birth of the twins. This was followed almost immediately by the illness that robbed her of every vestige of beauty. That is probably why I remember this visit so well. But I also remember it because at the moment my whole sympathy was enlisted on the side of the woman whose gentle, unobtrusive beauty made so little show beside the brilliance of the other. I was not the least in love with Carmen; I only knew her magnificent eyes and splendid coloring, her hoarse voice, and the circumstances under which she had become part of our staff, for which she could not be held responsible. On the other hand I really loved Ada at that moment; and it is a strange feeling to love a woman whom one has desired passionately but never possessed, and who now means nothing to one. On the whole the situation is the same as it would have been if the woman had yielded, and it is interesting as proving once more how little importance we ought to attach to certain things that for the time being fill our whole horizon.

I wanted to cut short the painful moment, and led her into the other room. Guido, who came in shortly afterwards, grew very red when he saw his wife. Ada gave some very plausible reason for her coming, but just as she was going she said:

"Have you got a new employee in the office now?"

"Yes!" replied Guido, and to hide his confusion he asked whether anyone had called on him while he was out. On hearing there had been no one he gave a snort of disgust as if he had been expecting an important visitor, though I knew we expected absolutely no one. It was only then that he said to Ada, with an air of assumed indifference:

"We needed a stenographer."

I was extremely amused to hear him use the masculine form of the word, thus making a blunder even as to the sex of the person he needed.

Carmen's coming gave great animation to the office. I don't mean the animation of her eyes, her charming figure, and lovely complexion; I am thinking only of business. Her mere presence gave Guido an impulse to work. In the first place he was anxious to show me and everyone else that the new member of the staff was essential to him, and every day he would invent something fresh to be done, in which he also took a share. For a long time he employed all his energy in coaching Carmen, and in this he reached an incredible degree of efficiency. He had to teach her exactly how to take down the letters he dictated, and to correct the spelling of innumerable words. He was always very patient with her; nothing the girl could do in return would have been too much.

Very little of the business invented by him when he was in love bore any fruit. On one occasion he spent a lot of time arranging for the sale of an article that proved after all impossible for us to trade in. At a certain point in our undertaking we had to face a man who was overcome with fury because we were unwittingly trespassing on his preserves. He wanted to know by what right we were interfering with that article at all, and jumped to the conclusion that we were representatives of powerful competitors abroad. The first time we saw him he was beside himself, fearing the worst. When he discovered how inexperienced we were, he laughed in our face and assured us that we should never have done any good at it. He proved to be right, but it was a long time before we could bring ourselves to accept the unfavorable verdict, and not till a great many letters had been writen by Carmen. We found that the article in question was quite inaccessible, owing to the number of tariffs by which it was surrounded. I did not mention the affair to Augusta, but she spoke to me about it because Guido had told Ada, to prove to her what a lot there was for a stenographer to do. But the business we did not do was none the less important to Guido. He talked about it daily; he was convinced that such a thing could not have happened in any other town in the world. Our whole commercial life was wrecked, and any enterprising business man was strangled by it, as we now knew by experience.

In the mad, chaotic sequence of affairs which passed through our hands at that time, there was one that really did burn our fingers. It was not of our seeking either; it simply threw itself at us. We got involved in it through a certain Dalmatian called Tacich, whose father had worked in the Argentine under Guido's. He came to see us first in order to get some business tips, with which we were able to supply him.

Tacich was a handsome youth, almost too handsome in fact. He was tall and powerfully built, with an olive complexion that blended marvelously with the exquisite dark blue of his eyes, his long eyelashes, and short thick mustache with gold lights in it. He was such a perfect study in color that he seemed to be born to be Carmen's lover. He evidently thought so too, and came to see us every day. There were hours of conversation daily in the office, but it was never boring. The two men were both striving to win Carmen and, like all animals when they are in love, displayed their best qualities. Guido was rather handicapped by the fact that the Dalmatian came to his house too and knew Ada; but it was just that which did him most harm in Carmen's eyes, as I, who knew those eyes so well, at once realized. Tacich however only made the discovery much later, and to have an excuse for seeing her bought several truck-loads of soap from us instead of from the manufacturer, for which he had to pay quite a lot more. Our going into that disastrous affair at all was one of the consequences of his being in love.

His father had noticed that sulphate of copper rose in price at certain seasons of the year and fell at others. So he decided as a speculation to buy about sixty tons of it in England at the most favorable moment. We discussed the affair at great length, and put the matter in hand by getting into touch with an English firm. The son had a telegram from his father telling him that he thought the right moment had come, and saying at what price he would be prepared to deal. Tacich, who was madly in love, rushed round to the office and entrusted the affair to us, receiving for his reward a long, caressing glance from Carmen. The

poor Dalmatian gratefully treasured the glance, not knowing it was a manifestation of love for Guido.

I remember with what quiet confidence Guido took
the business in hand, and it really did not seem as if it
could present any difficulties, because in England goods
could be transmitted for transport direct to Trieste and
made over at once to our buyer, without having ever been
touched. Guido decided exactly what his profit was to be,
and fixed with my assistance the point to which our
English friend could safely go in making the purchase.
With the help of a dictionary we managed to send off a
wire in English. Directly it had gone Guido rubbed his
hands and began counting up how many kronen would rain
into our funds as the reward of so short and slight an
effort. To propitiate the gods he allotted me a small bonus;
and the same to Carmen, with a slight touch of malice,
perhaps, for having collaborated with her *beaux yeux*. We
both wanted to refuse, but he begged us at least to pretend
to accept. He said he was afraid of our putting the evil eye
on him, and to please him I at once gave in. I knew, as a
mathematical certainty, that nothing but good wishes could
come from me, but I recognized that he might think otherwise. In this world we generally like the people we don't
actually hate, but reserve our really fervent wishes for an
undertaking in which we have a personal interest.

Every detail of the business was arranged, and I remember Guido even calculating how many months he
would be able to maintain his family and the office on
what he would get from it; his two families he sometimes
called them, or, when he was very bored at home, his two
offices. It was perhaps because we had thought it all out
too much beforehand that the business was a failure. A
brief cable came from London with the one word "Booked"
and a note of the day's price of sulphate, a much higher
one than we had got from our buyer. Farewell to any
profit! We told Tacich about it and he left Trieste soon
afterwards.

Just about this time I stayed away from the office for
quite a month, and that was how it happened that a letter
sent to the firm failed to pass through my hands. It looked
inoffensive enough but was to have disastrous consequences
for Guido. In it the English house confirmed their telegram
and went on to say they would consider our order to hold

good unless we revoked it. Guido forgot all about revoking it and when I came back to the office the transaction had quite gone out of my mind. One evening a few months later Guido brought a telegram to my house which he could not understand and thought must have been sent to us by mistake, though it clearly bore the telegraphic address of which I had notified the authorities directly we were installed in our office. The telegram consisted of only three words:

SIXTY TONS SETTLED.

I understood it at once, which was not very difficult as the sulphate of copper was the only important transaction we had entered on. I said it was clear from the wire that the price we had fixed for carrying out our order had been reached, and that now we were the fortunate owners of sixty tons of sulphate.

Guido protested:

"But how can they imagine I should consent to their carrying out my order so long afterwards?"

It at once occurred to me that the letter confirming the telegram must be somewhere at the office, though Guido could not remember anything about it. In a great state of agitation he suggested hurrying off at once to the office to see if it were there; which suited me very well, as I was not at all anxious to continue the discussion before Augusta, who had no idea that I had not been to the office for a month.

We went to the office together. Guido was so upset at the thought of being forced into the first important piece of business we had done, that he would have set off for London on the spot if he could by that means have backed out of it. We opened the office door, and felt our way in the darkness till we reached our room and lit the gas. The letter was found almost immediately, and it was conceived in exactly the terms I had expected; it informed us that the order which we had never revoked had been executed.

Guido stood staring at the letter and frowning, either with rage or because he hoped, by a supreme effort of will, to destroy at a glance the fact recorded by those few simple words.

"Only to think," he said, "that two or three words were all that was needed to save us from such a loss!"

He was not reproaching me, for I had been absent from the office, and had never even seen the letter up to that moment, though I now knew exactly where it could be found. But the better to clear myself of all responsibility in the matter I said to him rather severely:

"You might at least have read all the letters carefully while I was away!"

Guido's face cleared. He shrugged his shoulders and muttered:

"It may still turn out to be a stroke of good luck."

Soon after we parted, and I went back home. But Tacich was right; in due course sulphate of copper began to go down lower and lower every day, and we had plenty of opportunity for studying the phenomenon, since we could not go back on our order and could not get rid of the sulphate at the price we had to pay for it. Our losses became heavier and heavier. The first day Guido asked my advice, and I contented myself with reminding him of Tacich's conviction that the fall in sulphate would continue for over five months. Guido laughed and said:

"It will be the last straw if I am to get someone from the provinces to run my business for me!"

I tried to make him take a different view by telling him that Tacich had for many years now spent all his time in a little town in Dalmatia watching the fluctuations in copper. I cannot therefore feel any responsibility for Guido's losses over the business. If only he had listened to me he would have been spared them.

Later on we discussed the affair again with an agent, a short, fat little man, very much on the spot, who while blaming us for making such a purchase, said that he could but share Tacich's opinion. According to him, sulphate of copper, while forming a market of its own, was affected by the price of metal in general. This interview gave Guido a certain amount of confidence. He begged the agent to keep him informed of any fluctuation in the price; he preferred to wait, he said, in order to sell not only without any loss, but with a small profit. The agent laughed a little, and in the course of conversation said something that seemed to me very true, and which I made a note of.

"It is curious how few people in the world can reconcile themselves to small losses, whereas they have no difficulty whatsoever in reconciling themselves to big ones."

Guido was unconvinced. I could not help admiring him, however, because he never told the agent how he had come to make such a purchase. I said so to him and he was pleased. He said he would have been afraid of bringing us and our goods into disrepute if he had told the whole story.

For some time after this we said no more about sulphate, till one day a letter came from London inviting payment, and asking us to give instructions about sending the goods. The mere thought of receiving and storing sixty tons made Guido's brain whirl. We tried to reckon how much it would cost to store something like that for several months. The sum was enormous! I said nothing; but the broker, who would have been quite glad to see the merchandise arrive in Trieste, because sooner or later the task of selling it would devolve on him, pointed out to Guido that what seemed such a huge sum was really not so very much when expressed in terms of percentage on the value of the goods.

This remark seemed odd to Guido and made him laugh.

"I haven't only got a hundred kilos of sulphate," he said, "I've sixty tons, worse luck!"

He might have ended by accepting the agent's calculation—evidently quite a just one, seeing that if the price rose only a little the costs would have been more than covered—had he not at that moment had a sudden inspiration. Whenever a business idea came to him quite of itself he became completely obsessed by it, and had no room in his head for any other consideration. This was his idea: the goods had been sold to him prepaid to Trieste, so the cost of transport was being borne by the sender. If therefore he were to sell the goods back to the seller, he ought to receive a much better price than he had been offered in Trieste, because the original seller would thereby save the cost of carriage.

What he said was not strictly accurate, but to humor him no one questioned it. Once he had settled the business a somewhat bitter smile spread over his face; he looked quite the philosophic pessimist as he said:

"Don't let us talk any more about it. The lesson cost us rather dear, but let us turn it to account now."

However we did talk about it again. He had lost his former splendid assurance in refusing business that offered, and when at the end of the year I called his attention to the amount of money we had lost, he muttered:

"It was that cursed sulphate of copper which ruined me! I was continually feeling that I must make good that loss."

My absence from the office had been caused by Carla having deserted me. I could not stay there and see Carmen and Guido making love to each other. They were always exchanging glances and smiling, in front of me. I took my resolution while shutting up the office, and went haughtily away without saying a word about it to anyone. I was always expecting Guido to ask me why I had deserted him in this way, and intended to tell him what I thought about him. I could be very strict with him since he knew nothing about my expeditions to the Giardino Pubblico.

It was really a form of jealousy on my part, because I looked on Carmen as Guido's Carla, a gentler and more submissive one. He had had better luck than me with his second woman, as with his first. But perhaps (and it was this that furnished me with a fresh grudge against him) he owed his good fortune to certain qualities of his which I envied, though I continued to think them inferior; his ease in playing the violin corresponded to the assurance and detachment with which he went through life. I realized now that I had sacrificed Carla to Augusta. When I went back over the two happy years Carla had given me I could not understand how it was that she—constituted as I now know her to be—could have put up with me for so long. Hadn't I insulted her daily by my love for Augusta? Guido, as I knew very well, would never be distracted in his love for Carmen by any thought of Ada. His hospitable mind could easily entertain two women at the same time. Compared to him I really felt myself to be an angel of innocence. I had married Augusta without being in love with her, yet it was impossible for me to betray her without a pang. Perhaps he too had married Ada without loving her; but though Ada meant nothing to me now, I remembered the love she had inspired in me, and I could not help feeling that if I had been in his place I should have behaved with much more consideration.

It was not Guido who came to look for me, but I who returned to the office on my own account, to try and escape from my terrible feeling of emptiness. He behaved ac-

cording to the terms of our agreement, which put me under
no obligation to take a regular part in his affairs; and when
he ran into me casually at home or elsewhere he showed
the same friendliness he had always shown (for which I
felt grateful to him), and seemed to have forgotten that
my place at the desk he had bought specially for me was
left empty. When we were together I was the only one
who felt any embarrassment. When I went back to my
post he received me as if I had only been away for a day,
expressed his delight at seeing me again, and exclaimed on
hearing that I proposed resuming my work:

"It's a good thing, then, that I didn't let anyone touch
your books!"

And indeed I found the register and my newspaper
exactly where I had left them.

Luciano said to me:

"I hope we shall get going again now that you have
come back. I think Signor Guido was discouraged by two
things he tried which did not succeed. Don't tell him that
I said anything to you about it, but see if you can't put a
little heart into him."

I very soon realized that next to no work was being
done in the office, and till the moment when our losses on
the sulphate of copper became a terrible reality we led a
positively idyllic life there. I soon perceived that Guido no
longer felt the need of supervising Carmen at her work,
and therefore concluded that the period of courtship was
over and she had become his mistress.

Carmen's reception surprised me, for she at once felt
obliged to remind me of something that I had completely
forgotten. It appeared that before leaving the office, and
during the days I ran after so many women because I could
not have the one I wanted, I had assaulted Carmen too.
She spoke of it to me, very severely and with some embarrassment; she said she was glad to see me again because
I was fond of Guido and because she thought my advice
might be useful to him, and she would like us, if I consented, to be real friends, brother and sister in fact. While
she was saying this or something like it, she held out her
hand with a friendly gesture. There was a severe expression
on her lovely, gentle face, as if to emphasize the innocence
of the relationship she was offering me.

It was only then that I remembered what had

happened, and blushed. Perhaps if I had remembered sooner I should never have gone back to the office at all. It had been just an affair of a moment, among so many others of the same sort, and if I had not been reminded of it now it would have been as if it had never existed. A few days after Carla had thrown me over I had been going through the books and asked Carmen to help me; at one point I had put my arm round her waist, so as to be able to look at the same page, and had drawn her closer and closer to me. In one bound Carmen had sprung away from me, whereupon I immediately left the office.

I might have excused myself by smiling and inducing her to smile too, for women are so prone to smile at misdeeds of that sort. I might have said to her:

"I have failed in what I tried to do, and I am sorry for it, but I don't bear you any ill-will, and will be your friend if you won't let me be anything more."

Or I might have assumed the role of a serious person, and apologized to her and Guido somewhat as follows:

"You must forgive me, and not judge me till you know the circumstances that have led me to behave like this."

But words failed me. Resentment seemed to have dried up my throat, and I could not speak. All these women who persisted in refusing me threw a sort of tragic hue over my life. I felt I had never been so unfortunate before. Instead of replying I felt more inclined to grind my teeth, a rather uncomfortable process if you are obliged to hide it. Perhaps it was disappointment at seeing a hope I had unconsciously cherished taken from me forever, which deprived me of speech. I may as well confess that I could imagine no one who would better fill than Carmen the place of the mistress I had lost; my unexacting Carla, who only asked to be allowed to live quietly at my side, till the day when she asked never to see me again. A mistress shared is the least compromising one can have. At that time I had not thought things out so clearly as I have since, but I had certain intuitions, which I now know to be true. If I were to become Carmen's lover I should be doing a good turn to Ada, without doing much harm to Augusta. The infidelity in either case would have been much less great than if Guido and I had each had a mistress to ourselves.

I gave Carmen my answer several days later, and to

this moment I still blush to think of it. The anguish of mind into which Carla's desertion had thrown me must still have subsisted for me to arrive at such a point. I feel more remorse about it than about any other action of my life. The foolish words that escape us sometimes react more violently than the most discreditable deeds due to a passionate impulse. Of course I mean by words only those that are not really deeds; I know very well that Iago's words, for example, belong to the latter kind. But deeds, including the words spoken by Iago, are committed for the sake of some hoped-for profit or pleasure, and then our whole being, even that part of us which ought to rise in judgment, joins in and bears witness in our favor. But a foolish tongue acts independently, in the interests of a small part of our being which otherwise would feel itself to be defeated, and continues to simulate fight when the fight is already over. Words are spoken with intention to wound or caress, and often they turn against the mouth that utters them and burn it.

I noticed she had lost the lovely complexion that had won her such speedy admission to our office. I would not admit that it could be bodily suffering that had caused the change in her appearance, and I attributed it to her love for Guido. We men are commonly much inclined to pity women who give themselves to other men. We never can see what advantage they hope to get from it. We may perhaps even love the man in question—as in my own case —but we never even then succeed in forgetting what is the usual end to such love-adventures. I felt genuine compassion for Carmen. I said to her:

"Since you have been so kind as to invite me to be your friend, would you allow me to give you some good advice?"

She would not, because like all women in a similar situation she was inclined to look on all advice as an act of aggression. She blushed and stammered:

"I don't understand! What do you mean?" and in order to impose silence on me added immediately afterwards:

"If I should need any advice I will certainly come to you, Signor Cosini."

So I was not allowed to give her moral advice, which was a misfortune for me. Had I done so, I should certainly have been able to be more honest with myself, even though I might have tried to embrace her again. And I should not now be blaming myself for having assumed the lying role of mentor.

For several days each week Guido failed to put in an appearance at the office, because of his passion for shooting and fishing. I, on the contrary, was very regular for some time after my return, and found plenty to do putting the books in order. I spent a good deal of time alone with Carmen and Luciano, who looked on me as their chief. Carmen did not seem to mind Guido being absent, and I supposed her love for him to be so great that she was glad to think of him enjoying himself. He must have told her beforehand the days he was not coming, for she showed no sign of waiting anxiously for his arrival. I knew from Augusta that it was quite a different matter with Ada, who complained bitterly of her husband's frequent absences. Nor was this her only grievance. Like all women who feel themselves to be unloved she put the same energy into her complaints about big or small grievances. Not only was Guido unfaithful to her, but when he was at home he was always playing the violin. That violin, which had caused me so much suffering, was a kind of Achilles' spear in the variety of its adaptations. I discovered that it had appeared in our office, where it had assisted at the courting of Carmen with exquisite variations on the *Barbiere*. And when it was no longer needed at the office it returned home, where it saved Guido from the tiresome necessity of talking to his wife.

There was never anything between Carmen and me. I very soon felt completely indifferent to her, as though she had changed her sex; rather the same as I felt for Ada. Yes, it is quite true, I felt nothing but warm sympathy for them both.

Guido overwhelmed me with attentions. I fancy that during the month I left him alone he had learnt to appreciate my company. A girl like Carmen may be a charming diversion from time to time, but one cannot stand her for days on end. He invited me to go shooting and fishing with him. I detest shooting, and resolutely refused to accompany him. But one evening, when I was feeling particularly bored, I finally agreed to go out fishing with him. Fish have no means of communicating with us and cannot

arouse our sympathy. They pant even when they are safe
and sound in the water! In fact death hardly alters their
appearance. Their pain, if it exists, is perfectly concealed
under their scales.

One day when he invited me to go out fishing the
same night, I said I must wait and see whether Augusta
could spare me that evening, and whether she would mind
me staying out so late. He told me he was going to start
off at nine o'clock from the Sartorio quay, so I said I would
be there by then if I could manage to get away. I thought
he would probably not expect to see me again that evening,
as I had so often before made a similar appointment and
failed to keep it.

But as it happened I was driven from the house that
night by baby Antonia's screams. The more her mother
kissed and caressed her the more she howled. Then I tried
my plan of shouting insults into her ear. The only result
however was to change the rhythm of her screams, for the
little monkey began to howl with terror instead. I was
about to try a more energetic method of restraint, but
Augusta reminded me just in time of Guido's invitation,
and accompanied me to the door, promising to go to bed
without me if it was very late before I got back. In her
anxiety to get me out of the house she even promised to
take her coffee alone next morning, supposing I were to
stay out all night. There is only one small difference of
opinion between Augusta and me: what is the proper way
of treating troublesome children. I always feel that a baby's
sufferings are less important than ours, and that it is worth
while making it suffer if by that means a grown-up person
can be saved a great deal of annoyance; she, however, takes
the view that having brought children into the world we
have got to put up with them.

I had plenty of time to reach our rendezvous and
strolled in a leisurely way through the town, looking at
the women and at the same time trying to think of a new
plaything that should eliminate all difference of opinion
between Augusta and me. But humanity was not sufficiently evolved to accept my new plaything! It belonged
to the distant future and was only useful to me now as
showing me on what a detail my disputes with Augusta
depended: the lack of a simple toy. It could have been very
simple; an indoor tramline and a little seat provided with

wheels to run on the line. On this little seat the child would spend its day; by pressing an electric button it would be sent screaming to the farthest end of the house, whence . its voice, weakened by distance, would float back quite pleasantly. And Augusta and I could have remained together in peace and perfect amity.

It was a starry night without a moon, one of those transparent nights that calm and tranquillize the spirit. I gazed at the stars, seeking the constellation on which my father's dying look had rested. The awful time would soon be over when children dirty themselves and scream. Then they would become like me, and I should be able to like them without constraint, as it was my duty to do. The vast and tranquil beauty of the night brought me peace; I did not even feel the need of making resolutions.

At the end of the Sartorio mole the lights of the town were cut off by a ruined building, set on the last rocks of the promontory which jut out into the sea. The darkness here was complete, and the high tide lapped its silent endless waters dimly against the mole.

I had stopped looking at the sea or the sky. A few steps away from me was a woman who aroused my curiosity by the patent-leather shoe that I saw gleaming for a moment in the darkness. During that brief moment in the dark, I felt as if I were shut into a room alone with that tall and doubtless elegant woman. The most pleasant adventures sometimes happen when one least expects them, and seeing her come deliberately toward me I had for a moment a delightful sensation, which disappeared directly I heard Carmen's hoarse voice. She pretended to be pleased when she heard I was to be of the party. But with a voice like hers, and in the dark, pretense was impossible.

I said roughly to her:

"Guido asked me to come. But I will leave you two alone if you like, and find something else to do."

She protested, saying that she was on the contrary very glad to see me again—for the third time that day. She told me the entire office was about to assemble in that small boat, for Luciano was coming too. It would be a terrible thing for our business if we were to founder! She told me of course that Luciano was coming too, in order to show me what an innocent rendezvous it was. Then she chattered ceaselessly, telling me among other things that this was the first time she had been out with Guido, and then that it was the second. She let slip casually that she found it quite pleasant to sit on the bottom-board, and I expressed surprise at her using such a nautical expression. She was obliged to confess that she had heard Guido use it the first time she had gone fishing with him.

She was evidently anxious to let me know how innocent their first outing had been.

"We went fishing that time in the morning," she said. "We were fishing for mackerel, not John Dory."

It was a pity I had no time to let her chatter a little more, because then I might have found out all I wanted to know; but at that moment Guido's boat shot out from the darkness of the Sacchetta and came swiftly toward us. I was still debating whether, as Carmen was there, I had not better go away. Perhaps Guido had not meant to invite us both together, for I remembered I had half refused his invitation. Meanwhile the boat pulled in and Carmen leaped lightly into it, refusing, dark as it was, the hand that Luciano held out for her support. As I still hesitated Guido shouted out:

"Don't let us waste any more time!"

With one bound I was in the boat. My bound was almost involuntary, and made in response to Guido's cry. I looked longingly at the shore, but that moment's hesitation made it impossible for me to spring out again, and I seated myself in the prow of the boat, which was a fairly small one. When I got used to the darkness I saw Guido facing me in the stern, with Carmen at his feet. Luciano, who was rowing, was between us. I did not feel very safe or very comfortable in that small boat, but I soon got used to it and began watching the stars, which again had a calming influence on me. It was true that with Luciano present, who was a devoted servant of our wives' family, Guido would never have risked being unfaithful to Ada, so that there was no harm in my being there too. I had a great longing to enjoy to the full the sky, the sea, and that vast quietness, but if my being there was to cause me remorse, I might as well have stayed at home and let myself be tormented by little Antonia. The fresh night air filled my lungs, and I was conscious of enjoying myself thoroughly in the company of Guido and Carmen, both of whom I really liked very much.

We passed the lighthouse and came out into the open sea. A few miles farther out shone the lights of innumerable sailing-boats; the bait they threw for the fishes was very different from ours. We passed the military baths—an enormous building, looming darkly out of the water—and began rowing up and down close to the Sant' Andrea shore. It was a favorite place for fishermen. Many other boats were moving about noiselessly close to us. Guido made ready three lines, and baited them with small crabs, with the hook through their tails. He gave us each one, saying that mine, the only one that was leaded, would attract most fish. In the darkness I could just see the hook through the tail of my crab, which still seemed to be moving the upper part of its body to and fro. It was a gentle motion and seemed to express meditation rather than bodily agony. Perhaps what produces pain in larger bodies may, in very little ones, be so refined that it is experienced merely as a fresh sensation, a stimulus to thought. I threw it into the water, lowering it about thirty feet according to Guido's instructions. Then Carmen and Guido let out their lines. Guido had an oar in the stern now, with which he guided the boat in such a way as to prevent the lines becoming entangled. Apparently Luciano was not yet quite equal to the task of guiding the boat like that. But in any case he was busy with the little net in which he was to collect the fish brought to the surface by the lines. For a long time there was nothing for him to do. Guido was very talkative. Perhaps it was his passion for giving instruction, even more than love, which attached him to Carmen. Rather than listen to him I should have preferred to go on thinking about the little animal I was holding in the water. But Guido kept calling to me and I was obliged to listen to his theories of fishing. He said we should often feel the fish nibbling at the bait, but we must be sure not to draw in our lines till we felt a pull. Then we must be ready to give a jerk, which would embed the hook firmly in the fish's mouth. Guido's explanations were, as usual, very long. He wanted to explain quite clearly exactly what sensation we should feel in our hand when the fish nibbled the bait. And he went on with his explanations long after Carmen and I knew by experience the almost audible contact of the fish's mouth with the bait. Several times we were obliged to draw in our lines and bait them afresh.

The reflective little crab had been swallowed down in the jaws of a cautious fish who had learnt how to avoid the hook.

There were beer and sandwiches on board, and Guido's inexhaustible chatter lent flavor to our picnic. He was talking now of the immense riches that lay at the bottom of the sea. He did not mean, as Luciano thought, the fishes, nor the treasure that man has spilt into the sea, but the gold that is dissolved in sea-water. Suddenly he remembered I had studied chemistry, and said:

"You ought to know something about that gold."

I did not remember much, but I accepted his statement, and hazarded a suggestion, the truth of which I felt to be rather doubtful. I said:

"Sea-gold is the most costly of all to collect. In order to get a single one of those dispersed napoleons you would have to spend five."

Luciano, who had turned eagerly toward me for confirmation of the rumored riches over which we were floating, turned his back in disgust; he no longer took any interest in that kind of gold. But Guido agreed with me, and thought he remembered hearing that the price of sea-gold was exactly five times higher than that of ordinary gold, as I had just said. His confirmation of my statement (which I knew to be a fiction of the brain) was meant as high praise. He clearly did not look on me as at all dangerous and felt no shadow of jealousy in regard to the woman lying at his feet. I was tempted for a moment to embarrass him by saying that I had suddenly remembered it would cost only three napoleons to extract one from the sea, or that it would cost ten.

But at that very moment my line suddenly gave a terrific jerk. I gave another jerk, and screamed. In one bound Guido was at my side and took the line from my hand. I gladly yielded it to him. He began drawing it in, first a small bit at a time, then, as the resistance diminished, in great handfuls. We could see the silver body of a huge fish gleaming in the dark water. It resisted no longer, but ran swiftly to meet its pain. At last I felt I understood the dumb creature's suffering; that swift flight toward death seemed like a cry. Soon it lay gasping at my feet. Luciano had pulled it out of the water with his net, and seizing it roughly in one hand pulled out the hook with the other.

He prodded the great fish all over:

"A John Dory, and it weighs about seven pounds!"

He was quite overwhelmed by its size, and named the price they would have asked for it in the fish-market. Then Guido remarked that the tide was on the turn, and that we were not likely to catch any more fish. He said fishermen believe the fish won't bite when it is slack water, and that therefore they cannot be caught. He moralized on the dangers an animal was led into by its appetite. Then he began laughing and said, quite unaware that he was compromising himself:

"You are the only one here this evening who knows how to fish."

My victim was still flapping about in the bottom of the boat, when Carmen gave a scream. Without moving, and with suppressed laughter in his voice, Guido asked:

"Another John Dory?"

Carmen replied in confusion:

"I thought it was, but it has let go of the hook!"

I am convinced that Guido, unable any longer to contain himself, had squeezed Carmen in the dark.

I was beginning to feel ill at ease in that boat. I no longer cared about catching anything, and kept moving my line to and fro so that the poor creatures should not bite. I said I was sleepy, and asked Guido to put me on shore at Sant' Andrea. Then I tried to remove any suspicion that I might be going because I was shocked by what Carmen's sudden cry had betrayed, and told them about my baby's screaming fit, saying that I should like to get back and make sure it was not ill.

Guido, obliging as usual, brought the boat to shore. He offered me the fish I had caught, but I refused. I proposed to throw it into the sea again and set it free, at which Luciano set up a howl of protest and Guido good-naturedly observed:

"If I thought I could give it life and health again I gladly would. But the poor creature is no good for anything now except to be served up on a dish."

I followed them with my eyes, and noticed that they did not take advantage of the space left free by me. They were still sitting as close as possible to each other, and the boat put off again, with its prow rather far out of the water, because of the extra weight astern.

I regarded it as a punishment from heaven when I found that my baby had an attack of fever. Hadn't I caused it to fall ill, by pretending to Guido to be anxious about its health when I was not really so in the least? Augusta was still up, but Dr. Paoli had just been and had reassured her by saying that so sudden and violent a fever could not mean the beginning of a serious illness. We stood for some time watching Antonia, who was lying huddled up in her little cot, with dry lips and feverish cheeks, her brown curls all in disorder. She did not cry at all, but moaned quietly from time to time, then fell back at once into a state of torpor. My God! How dear she seemed to me now that she was ill. I would willingly have given years of my own life if only it would make her breathe more easily. How could I ever forgive myself for thinking for a moment that I was not very fond of her, and for having spent all the time while she was suffering away from her, and in such company!

"She is so like Ada," Augusta said with a sob. It was true! We noticed the likeness now for the first time, and it became more and more striking, the bigger Antonia grew, so that I sometimes trembled to think her fate might be like that of the poor creature she resembled.

We went to bed at last, after putting the baby's bed beside Augusta's. But I was unable to sleep. I felt a weight on my mind, just as I used on those nights when my sins of the preceding day were mirrored in images of pain and remorse. My baby's illness weighed on me as if it had been my doing. I rebelled at last against my own sense of guilt, for I was innocent and had nothing to hide. I could tell Augusta everything. So I told her about my meeting with Carmen, of the position she had occupied in the boat, and of her scream, which I attributed to some violent caress on Guido's part, though I could not be certain. But Augusta was quite certain, for otherwise why should Guido's voice have betrayed so much amusement? I tried to make her take a less serious view of it, but she insisted on my going into every detail. I made a confession on my own account, describing the feeling of exasperation which had driven me out of the house and my remorse at not

having loved Antonia more. I at once felt much better and
fell sound asleep.

Next morning Antonia was better; she had almost lost
her fever. She was lying there quite quietly, and her
breathing was regular, but she was pale and exhausted, as
though she had spent all the strength of her little body
in the short battle for life from which she had come out
victorious. In the midst of my sense of relief I remembered
with regret that I had compromised Guido horribly, and
tried to make Augusta promise not to tell anyone of my
suspicions. She protested that it was not a question of
suspicions, but definite evidence; and I could not convince her to the contrary. However she promised whatever
I wanted and I went off quietly to the office.

Guido had not yet come, and Carmen told me they
had had very good luck after I left them. They had caught
two more John Dory, not so big as mine, but weighing
quite a lot. I did not believe her, and thought it was very
unlikely they should have employed themselves otherwise
after my departure than before. Had there been no slack
water then? And how many hours had they stayed out at
sea?

In order to convince me Carmen called on Luciano to
confirm her statement that they had really caught two
John Dory, and from that moment I believed Luciano
capable of any baseness in order to ingratiate himself with
Guido.

During the idyllic calm that preceded the sulphate of
copper deal, something rather odd took place in the office,
which I have never forgotten, partly because it throws
light on Guido's extraordinary conceit, partly because it
reveals an aspect of myself which I find it a little difficult
to recognize.

One day we were all four in the office together, but
as usual the only one who talked about business at all was
Luciano. Something he said sounded to Guido like a reproach, which he found it hard to endure with Carmen
there. But it was not easy for him to defend himself, for
Luciano could prove that some deal he had advised Guido
to go in for months ago, and which he refused to touch,
had turned out very well for the person who had interested
himself in it. At last Guido said that he despised business,
and that if fortune did not favor him in this direction he

could find plenty of ways, much more intelligent, of earning money. The violin, for example. Everybody agreed with him, but I made a certain reservation:

"You will have to work hard at it," I said.

He was annoyed by my qualified agreement, and hastened to say that if it was a question of working he could have done a lot of other things too, literature for example. Again everybody agreed with him, but I showed a little hesitation. I could not remember very clearly what any of the great writers looked like, and I tried to recall their faces, hoping to find one who resembled Guido. He positively shouted at me:

"Would you like to hear some good fables? I can invent them quite as well as Æsop."

We all laughed except him. He had the typewriter brought, and wrote off his first fable rapidly just as if he were writing under dictation, with sweeping movements hardly suited to the ordinary operation of typing. He handed the sheet to Luciano, but thought better of it, and took it back and fixed it in the machine again. His second fable however gave him more trouble than the first, so that he forgot to make his inspired gestures, and was obliged, on the contrary, to correct what he had written several times. It is my opinion that the first fable was not his at all, and that the second only was of his own invention; it was indeed just what I should have expected from him. The first fable was about a bird who suddenly noticed that the door of its cage was open. At first it thought it would take advantage of this to fly away, but on second thoughts decided not to do so, feeling that if the door got shut during its absence it would lose its liberty. The second was about an elephant, and really was elephantine. The huge beast, feeling weak in the legs, went to consult a famous doctor, who when he saw his enormous limbs exclaimed: "I never saw such strong legs!"

Luciano was not to be taken in by such fables, partly because he did not understand them. He laughed a great deal, but obviously because he thought it comic that a thing like that should appear to anyone to be salable. He laughed out of politeness when it was explained to him that the bird was afraid of being deprived of the liberty to return to its cage, and that the man admired the strength of the elephant's legs, however feeble they might

be from an elephant's point of view. Then he said:
"What would you get for two fables like that?"
Guido replied condescendingly:
"The pleasure of writing them is sufficient reward,
but if one went on writing them one would make a great
deal of money."

Carmen, however, was in a great state of excitement.
She asked for permission to copy the two fables, and was
profuse in her thanks when Guido offered to give her the
sheet they were written on, signed with his own hand.

What had all this to do with me? There was no need
for me to compete for Carmen's praise, seeing that, as I
have already said, she did not interest me at all; but when
I remember how I behaved I am obliged to conclude that
we can be armed for the fight even by a woman we do
not desire. And after all did not the medieval heroes fight
for ladies they had never seen? It happened that my
bodily pains suddenly became acute at that moment, and
I felt that the only way to relieve them was to meet Guido
in the lists by writing fables like him.

I asked for the typewriter, and I really did invent
mine. It is true that the first fable I wrote had been in
my mind for some days, but I improvised the title on the
spot: "Hymn to Life." Then, after a moment's reflection,
I wrote underneath it "A Dialogue." I thought it would
be easier to make animals talk than to describe them. My
fable sprang from the following very brief dialogue:

THE CRAB (*impaled on a hook, reflectively*): *Life is
sweet, but one must watch where one sits down.*
THE JOHN DORY (*just off to the dentist*): *Life is sweet,
but one must rid it of those treacherous monsters
who hide steel fangs in tasty flesh.*

Now came the second fable, but my supply of animals ran out. I looked at the dog lying in his corner, and
he looked back at me. His gentle eyes reminded me that
a few days ago Guido had come back from hunting covered with fleas, and had gone to clean himself in the
lumber-room. I at once found the fable I wanted and
wrote it down easily:

*There was once a prince who was bitten by a great
many fleas. He prayed to the gods to grant him one flea*

*to himself (as large as they liked, but only one), and to
distribute the others among the rest of mankind. But not
one of those fleas would consent to stay alone with that
fool of a prince, and he was obliged to keep them all.*

At the moment I wrote them my fables seemed to me
excellent. The things that issue from our own brain have
a peculiarly charming air, especially when they are newly
born. To tell the truth I still like my dialogue, even now
that I have had so much practice in composition. "The
Hymn to Life" sung by a dying creature cannot fail to
arouse the sympathy of those who have to watch it die. It
often really happens that the dying spend their last breath
in describing the cause to which they think they owe their
death, thus raising a hymn of praise to the life of all who
succeed in avoiding that accident. As to the second fable I
have nothing to say about it. It was acutely interpreted by
Guido himself, who laughingly exclaimed:

"It is not a fable, it is only an excuse for calling me
a fool."

I laughed too, and the pain that had inspired me to
write it at once vanished. Luciano laughed when I explained what I meant by it and decided that no one would
pay anything either for mine or Guido's fables. But Carmen was not at all pleased. She gave me a penetrating
look, which was something quite new in her eyes, and
which I understood as readily as if she had said in so many
words:

"You don't like Guido!"

I was quite startled, for at the moment she was right.
I thought it was foolish of me to behave as if I did not
like Guido, just when I was working so disinterestedly for
him. I must be more careful how I behaved in future.

I said gently to Guido:

"I readily agree that your fables are better than mine.
But you must remember they are the first ones I have
ever written in my life."

He would not give way.

"Perhaps you think that I have written some before?"

Carmen's look had already become kinder, and to
make it kinder still I said to Guido:

"You certainly have a particular gift for fables."

This compliment made them both laugh and myself

too; all of us quite good-naturedly, for it was obvious that
I had spoken without malicious intention.

The sulphate of copper business brought a much
more serious atmosphere into our office. We had no time
now for fables. We accepted almost everything that offered. We occasionally made a profit, but when we did
it was a small one, whereas our losses were always considerable. Guido, who was so generous at other times, was
curiously mean in business. When something turned out
well he immediately made haste to liquidate it, for he
was always in a hurry to pocket his small gains. But when
he got involved in an unprofitable transaction he could not
make up his mind to get out of it; for he always wanted
to put off the moment when he would have to pay out
of his own pocket. I think that is why his losses were always considerable and his gains so small. A business man's
qualities are simply the sum of all that is contained in him
from the crown of his head to the soles of his feet. The
Greek phrase "Wise fool" would be very appropriate to
Guido. He was often very astute, but he was often very
stupid. He was full of ideas, but did nothing with them
except to grease the steep incline on which he kept slipping lower and lower.

The twins descended on him at the same time as
the sulphate of copper. His first impression was one of
unpleasant surprise, but directly after he had announced
their arrival to me he made a joke that I thought so funny
that I burst out laughing; and he was so gratified by his
success that he could not help laughing with me. Speaking
of his two children as if they were on a par with sixty
tons of sulphate he said:

"I am condemned to work wholesale, I am!"

To comfort him I reminded him that Augusta was
again in her seventh month, and that I would soon have
reached his tonnage in the matter of babies. He replied
smartly:

"To me, as an experienced bookkeeper, the two things
don't seem to be the same."

After a few days he had grown very fond of the two
infants, and for a short time remained much attached to
them. Augusta, who spent part of each day with her sister,
told me that he devoted several hours to each of them
every day. He nursed them and sang lullabies to them, and

Ada was so grateful to him that a new love seemed to spring up between husband and wife. He paid a pretty large premium to an insurance society to guarantee a small sum to his children when they came of age. I remember this because I had to enter the sum on the debit side of the account.

I was invited to come and see the twins. Augusta told me that Ada would like me to go in and see her too. She was still obliged to stay in bed, though it was ten days since the children's birth.

The babies were in two cradles in a dressing-room adjoining the parents' bedroom. Ada called to me from the bed:

"Are they pretty, Zeno?"

I was startled by the sound of her voice. It seemed to me softer; even though she had put a certain amount of effort into it to make it carry, it was all the same softer than it used to be. No doubt it was motherhood that gave it that softer character, but I was moved by it because I noticed it particularly when she addressed herself to me. That new quality in it made me feel as if instead of calling me by my Christian name, Ada had added some other affectionate title like "dear" or "brother." I was truly grateful to her and felt very gentle and affectionate. I replied gaily:

"They are darlings, and so exactly alike! I really don't know which I like best!"

I thought them two horrid little monsters really. They were both crying at once, in different keys.

Guido very soon returned to his former way of life. After the sulphate business he came to the office more regularly, but on Saturday he always went off shooting and only returned late on Monday morning, just in time to look in at the office before lunch. In the evenings he went fishing, and often stayed out at sea all night. Augusta told me how unhappy Ada was, partly because she was terribly jealous, and partly because he left her alone for a great part of the day. Augusta tried to calm her by reminding her that there were no women when he went hunting and fishing. But Ada had been told—Augusta did not know by whom—that Carmen sometimes accompanied Guido when he went out fishing. Guido had admitted it himself when she confronted him with it, but said there was no harm in his being nice to a member of his staff, especially as she was so useful to him. Besides, had not Luciano always been there too? In the end he promised not to invite her again, if Ada did not like it. He said he could not give up shooting or fishing, though it was true the former cost him a good deal. He was working hard, he said (there certainly was plenty to do just then in the office), and he thought he deserved a little recreation. Ada did not agree with him; she thought the best recreation he could have was with his family, and to this theory Augusta gave her unconditional support, though I ventured to suggest that it might be rather a noisy recreation.

Augusta exclaimed:

"But don't you come home every day at the times you should?"

This was true, and I was obliged to confess that there was a great difference between Guido and me, though I did not feel much inclined to boast about it. I kissed Augusta and said:

"You deserve all the praise for having employed such drastic methods of education."

Meanwhile poor Guido's affairs went from bad to worse. At first they had only one nurse for the two children, for it was hoped that Ada would be able to feed one of them herself. She was however not strong enough to do so, and they had to take another nurse. When Guido wanted to make me laugh he would walk up and down the office, beating time to the words: "One wife . . . two infants . . . two nurses . . . !"

There was one thing that Ada specially hated: Guido's violin. She could stand the children's crying, but the sound of the violin was intolerable to her. She said once to Augusta:

"I feel as if I should like to howl like a dog when I hear him playing."

It was very odd, for Augusta loved to hear the unmusical strains of my violin proceeding from the study when she passed by.

"But surely Ada was in love with him when she married him," I exclaimed in surprise. "And isn't his violin the best part of Guido?"

All this gossip was forgotten the first time I saw Ada about again. It was I who first realized that she was

ill. One day early in November, a cold, damp, sunless
day, I left the office earlier than usual, at three in the afternoon, and hurried home, thinking how nice it would be
to rest and dream for several hours in my warm little study.
I had to go down a long passage to reach it, and when I
got to Augusta's work-room I stood still because I heard
Ada's voice inside. It was very soft or uncertain (which
was perhaps the same thing), just as it had been the day
she had spoken to me. I opened the door and went in,
curious to see how Ada, who was usually so calm and self-
contained, came to have a voice like that; it rather reminded me of an actress who is trying to move other
people to tears without being able to weep herself. The
voice was somehow artificial, or seemed so to me because,
without being able to see the person to whom it belonged,
I was hearing it again for the second time after so long,
and detected in it the same emotional quality. I thought
they must be talking about Guido, for what other subject
could move Ada in that way?

As a matter of fact the two women were only discussing domestic details, over a cup of tea; the washing, servants, etc. But directly I saw Ada I realized that her voice
was not put on. I was the first to notice a change in her
face, and was greatly moved by it; and her voice, even
though it did not correspond to any feeling in particular,
mirrored her whole personality so faithfully that I at once
felt it to be genuine. I am not a doctor, so the possibility
of her being ill did not occur to me; I was inclined to attribute the change in her appearance to the effects of her
convalescence after childbirth. But how was it that Guido
had not noticed the great change that had come over his
wife? I who knew her eyes by heart, and used to fear them
so much because I had at once realized how coldly they
took stock of things and persons, whether to accept or
reject them, now saw at once how changed they were.
They seemed to have grown bigger, to have grown almost
out of their sockets in their effort to see more clearly.
Those great eyes made a painful impression in her pale
and shrunken face. She clasped me warmly by the hand.

"You are so good," she said. "I know you never miss
an opportunity of coming home to see your wife and
child."

Her hand was damp with perspiration, and I know

that to be a sign of weakness. But I thought that as she grew stronger Ada would recover her original color and the firm sculptural lines of her cheeks and brow.

I felt sure her words were meant as a reproof to Guido, and replied good-naturedly that Guido, as the head of the business, had more responsibilities than I had, and was more tied to the office.

She gave me a searching look, as though to discover whether I was speaking seriously.

"All the same," she said, "I should have thought he might have found a little time for his wife and children," and her voice sounded quite tearful. She recovered herself however, and added with an appealing smile:

"Then there is his shooting and fishing, as well as business; and that takes up a great deal of time."

With an eloquence that surprised me she proceeded to enumerate the delicious viands that appeared on their table in consequence of Guido's sporting expeditions.

"I would willingly go without it all," she added with a sigh. But she did not complain of being unhappy. On the contrary, she said she could not imagine now being without the twins, whom she adored. She added with a touch of humor that she loved them even more now that each of them had its own nurse. She did not get much sleep, but at least when she had once fallen asleep there was no one to disturb her. When I asked her if she really slept so little, she became grave at once and said pathetically that that was her chief trouble. Then she added more lightly:

"But I am better now."

She left soon after, and gave as a reason for leaving that she must go round and see her mother before it got dark, and that she could not stand the temperature of our rooms, which were heated by two great stoves. To me they seemed only pleasantly warm, and I thought it a sign of hardiness on her part to find them too hot.

"You don't seem so delicate after all," I said, smiling. "You will see how different you feel when you have reached my age."

She was flattered to hear herself spoken of as being too young. Augusta and I accompanied her to the gate. She seemed to feel a great need of our affection, for during those few steps she walked between us, taking first Au-

gusta's arm and then mine. I at once stiffened mine, for
fear of giving way to my old habit of squeezing the arm of
every woman who came my way. At the gate she went on
talking for some time, and at the mention of her father
the tears stood in her eyes, for the third time within a
quarter of an hour. When she had gone I remarked to
Augusta that she was not a woman, but a fountain. Although I realized that Ada was ill I did not attach much
importance to it. Her eyes had become larger, her face
thinner; her voice had changed and her whole character
seemed to have become more affectionate and clinging
than was her wont, but I attributed all this to weakness
after giving birth to twins. In fact I proved myself a magnificent observer in that nothing escaped me, but a perfect
ignoramus because I did not utter the one important word:
Disease.

Next day the obstetrician who was treating Ada had a
consultation with Dr. Paoli, who at once spoke the word
that I had failed to say: *Morbus Basedowii.* Guido told
me all about it and described the symptoms very learnedly,
expressing much sympathy for Ada, who suffered a great
deal. Without wishing to be unkind I think that neither
his sympathy nor his knowledge was very great. He assumed a melancholy air when he mentioned his wife, but
while dictating letters to Carmen he manifested a great
joie de vivre and delight in giving instructions. He always
believed that the Basedow who had given his name to the
disease had been Goethe's friend, though when I looked
it up in an encyclopedia I saw at once that he was quite a
different person.

Basedow's disease is undoubtedly a very remarkable
one. It was most important for me to have found out
about it. I read various monographs on the subject and
felt as if the secret of our physical existence had only just
been revealed to me. I think there must be a good many
people like me who go through periods in which certain
ideas usurp their mind to the exclusion of every other.
But the same thing happens in the community; now it
will be Darwin who reigns supreme, whereas before it
was Robespierre or Napoleon. At one time it will be
Liebig or even Leopardi; at another, Bismarck fills the
whole horizon.

But I alone lived by Basedow! He seemed to me to

have penetrated to the roots of life, and shown it to be as
follows: all living beings are ranged along a certain line,
at one end of which is Basedow's disease. All who are
suffering from this disease use up their vital force reck-
lessly in a mad vertiginous rhythm, the heart beating without control. At the other end of the line are those wretched
beings, shriveled up by native avarice, and doomed to die
from a disease that looks like exhaustion but is really
cowardice. The happy mean between these two maladies
is to be found in the middle of the line, and is called
health, though it is really only a suspension of movement.
Between the center and Basedow's end are to be found
all those whose life is consumed in desire, ambition, pleasure, or even work; toward the opposite end those who
merely sprinkle crumbs on the plate of life and eke out
a long, miserable existence that can only be a burden to
society. But even this burden seems to be a necessary part
of life. Society goes forward because Basedowians urge it
on, and does not fall into the abyss only because the
others hold it back. I am convinced that if one were to
constitute a society one might do it more simply, but it
is actually made like this, with a goiter at one end and a
dropsy at the other; and nothing can be done about it.
Those at the center have the beginnings of either goiter or
dropsy, and all along the line throughout the whole of
humanity there is no such thing as perfect health.

According to Augusta, Ada had not actually a goiter,
but she had all the other symptoms of the disease. Poor
Ada! She had seemed to me the embodiment of health
and perfect balance, so that for a long time I imagined
her to have chosen her husband in the same cool, calculating spirit in which her father selected his merchandise.
And now she had been attacked by a disease that drove
her in quite a contrary direction, into psychological perversity. I too suffered from a very slight form of her disease,
and it took me some while to get rid of it; for a long time
I thought too much about Basedow. I still believe that
at whatsoever particular spot of the universe one settles
down one ends by becoming poisoned; it is essential to
keep moving. Life has its poisons, but counter-poisons too
which balance them. It is only by moving about that one
can avoid the first and profit by the second.

My disease became an obsession, a dream, almost a

nightmare to me. It must have originated in a certain
line of reasoning; by perversion we mean a deviation from
health, the kind of health which was ours during part of
our life. Now I knew what Ada had been like when in
good health. Might not her perversity lead her to love me
whom she had spurned when she was well?

I don't know how this fear—or hope—first took root
in my mind.

Perhaps it was because Ada's soft and husky voice
seemed to express love when she was speaking to me. Poor
Ada had grown very ugly, and I no longer found her desirable; but when I came to look back over our past relationship I could not help feeling that if she had really
suddenly fallen in love with me I should be almost in the
same unfortunate situation as Guido with regard to the
Englishman who had sold him sixty tons of sulphate of
copper. It was a precisely similar case! Several years ago I
had proposed to Ada, and had never revoked my proposal
except in so far as I had married her sister instead. There
was no law to protect her but the laws of chivalry. I felt
myself so deeply pledged to her that if, after the lapse of
many, many years she had come to me with Basedow's
goiter and all complete, I should have felt obliged to
honor my signature.

But the prospect, I remember, made me feel more
tenderly toward Ada. Up to that time, when I was told of
the suffering Guido caused Ada, I had not of course been
glad, but at the same time I could not help thinking with
a certain satisfaction of my home, which Ada had refused
to share, and where people did not suffer. Now the tables
were turned; the Ada who had rejected me with disdain
no longer existed, unless my medical authorities erred.

Ada was seriously ill. A few days after this Dr. Paoli
recommended her being sent away from her family to a
nursing-home at Bologna. I heard this from Guido, but
Augusta also told me that even at such a moment he had not
spared poor Ada's feelings. He had the impudence to suggest putting Carmen in charge of the house during her
absence. Ada had not the courage to say openly what she
thought of such a proposal, but she did say that she would
not stir from home unless she was allowed to entrust the
management of everything to her Aunt Maria. Guido
agreed at once, but continued to toy with the idea of hav-

ing Carmen at his disposal, in Ada's place. One day he
said to Carmen that if she had not been so busy at the
office he would have asked her to look after his house for
him. Luciano and I looked at each other, and could neither
of us hide an expression of malicious mirth. Carmen
blushed and murmured that she could never really have
accepted.

"Yes," said Guido angrily. "It is those idiotic con-
ventions that prevent one doing what one wants, however
convenient it may be."

He said no more however, and it is surprising that he
should have cut short such an interesting sermon.

The whole family went to the station to see Ada off.
Augusta asked me to bring some flowers for her sister.
I arrived a little late with a lovely bunch of orchids, which
I handed to Augusta. Ada stood watching us, and when
Augusta gave her the flowers she said:

"I thank you both with, all my heart."

She meant that she looked on the flowers as coming
from me too. I regarded this as an expression of sisterly
affection, sweet to receive, though rather chilly. Basedow
certainly had nothing to do with it.

Poor Ada looked like a bride, with her great eyes apparently wide with happiness. Her disease was able to
simulate every emotion.

Guido went with her to settle her in, and was to
return in a few days' time. We stood on the platform waiting for the train to start. Ada remained at the window and
went on waving her handkerchief till we were out of sight.

Then we went home with Signora Malfenti, who was
quite overcome. When she parted from us she kissed Augusta and then gave me a kiss too.

"Forgive me," she said, laughing through her tears.
"I did it without thinking, but if you will let me I should
like to give you another kiss."

Even little Anna, who was not twelve years old,
wanted to give me a kiss. Alberta who was about to give
up her project of a national theater in order to become
engaged, and who was generally rather cold to me, shook
me warmly by the hand on this occasion. They all felt
very kindly toward me because my wife was in blooming
health, and at the same time they were able to manifest
their dislike for Guido, who had let his wife get ill.

But it was just about now that I showed signs of being not quite such a perfect husband. I was the innocent cause of a good deal of pain to my wife on account of a dream, which I told her about without thinking.

This was my dream: Augusta, Ada, and I were all three looking out of a window together, the smallest window that was to be found in either of our three houses, Ada's, mine, and my mother-in-law's. We were at the kitchen window at my mother-in-law's house, which in reality opens on to a little courtyard, though in my dream it opened straight on to the Corso. The window-frame was so narrow that Ada, who was in the middle and had hold of both our arms, was actually leaning against me. I looked at her and found that her eyes had become quite cold and definite again, and that the outline of her face had recovered its former purity; I could see her neck covered with the light curls I had known so well when she used to turn her back on me. In spite of her appearance of coldness, which I regarded as a sign of recovered health, she clung to me as closely as I thought she was doing during the table-turning on the evening of our engagement. I said joyfully to Augusta, making an effort to interest myself in her too: "Look! She has completely recovered. But where is Basedow?" I asked a second time; and then I saw him. It was he whom the crowd was following. He was an old beggar man, dressed in a stiff brocade cloak that was all in rags: a mane of untidy white hair, blown about by the wind, covered his massive head, and his eyes were starting from their sockets with fear, a look I had seen in wild beasts at bay, a menacing, fearful look. And the crowd shouted after him: "Kill him, the charlatan!" Then came an interval of empty darkness. Immediately after this I found myself alone with Ada on the steepest stairs in any of our three houses, the stairs that lead up to the roof of my house. She was standing a few steps above me, but she was facing me, and seemed as if she wanted to come down the stairs while I was going up. I put my arms round her legs and she bent over toward me, either from weakness or because she wished to be closer to me. For a moment I seemed to see her disfigured by her illness, but looking at her anxiously I succeeded in seeing her again as I had seen her in the window, in all her health and beauty. She said to me in her usual hard voice: "Go

on in front, I will follow you directly." I turned eagerly
to go down, but had just time to see the trap-door in the
roof open very gradually and Basedow's head peer through,
with its white mane and half-fearful, half-threatening face.
I saw his feeble legs too and his poor thin body, which was
only half hidden by the cloak. I managed to run away, but
I cannot remember whether I was only going in front of
Ada or trying to escape from her.

I apparently woke up exhausted in the middle of the
night, and in my state of semi-consciousness told the whole
or part of the dream to Augusta, before falling into a
deep, restful sleep. I think in that semi-conscious state I
must have blindly followed my old desire to confess my
sins.

Augusta's face next morning had the waxen pallor it
always wore on state occasions. I remembered my dream
perfectly, but could not remember quite how much of it
I had told her. She said with an air of tragic resignation:

"You are unhappy because she is ill and has gone
away, and now you are dreaming about her."

I protested, laughing, and teased her a little. Ada
was not the significant figure in my dream, but Basedow,
and I told her about my studies and their practical application. But I don't know whether I succeeded in convincing
her. It is difficult to defend yourself when you are taken
unawares in a dream. It is quite a different matter to return to your wife fresh from having betrayed her, and in
full consciousness of so doing. But such manifestations of
jealousy on Augusta's part could not really do me any
harm, for she loved Ada too much to let it cast a shadow
between them, and she was more tender than ever toward
me, and more grateful for the smallest sign of affection.

Guido returned from Bologna a few days later, with
the best possible news. The head of the nursing-home
guaranteed a perfect cure provided that, when she returned home, Ada lived a very quiet life, and was spared
any kind of worry. Guido naïvely told us the diagnosis,
quite unconscious that it confirmed a good many suspicions that the Malfenti family had entertained about him.
I said to Augusta:

"I am threatened with more kisses from your mother."

Guido was apparently not very comfortable at home
under Aunt Maria's management. He would walk up and

down the office muttering:

"Two children . . . three nurses . . . no wife!"

He did not come very often to the office either, for he went out more and more often fishing and shooting, and worked off his ill humor on his prey. But when, toward the end of the year, the news reached us that Ada was supposed to be cured and was about to come home again, he did not seem wild with joy. Had he got used to Aunt Maria, or did he see her so seldom that he found her very easy to put up with? Naturally the only sign he gave me of not being better pleased was that he expressed a doubt as to whether Ada was not leaving the clinic rather too soon, and before they could be certain that she might not have another relapse. And when after a comparatively short time, in fact in the course of the winter, she was obliged to return to Bologna, he said to me triumphantly:

"Didn't I tell you so?"

But I think the only joy he felt was the triumphant sense of having been able to foresee something. He did not wish any harm to Ada, but he would gladly have kept her at Bologna for some time yet.

When Ada returned, Augusta had just given birth to Alfio, and was still in bed. She showed a touching solicitude for Ada. She asked me to meet her at the station with some flowers, and to tell her that she wanted to see her that same day if possible. And if Ada could not come straight from the station she begged me to come back at once so as to tell her all about her, and whether she had entirely recovered her beauty, of which the family was so proud.

Guido, Alberta, and I were the only ones at the station to meet her, because Signora Malfenti spent a great part of her time with Augusta. On the platform Guido tried to convince us how pleased he was to see Ada again; but Alberta pretended to be very absent-minded, in order, as she told me afterwards, not to have to reply to his remarks. For my part I no longer found any difficulty in pretending with Guido. I had got quite used to pretending not to notice his partiality for Carmen, and I had never dared to allude to the way he treated his wife. So I had no trouble in appearing to lend him my best attention when he dilated on his joy at his dear wife's return.

When the train came in punctually at twelve o'clock,

he hurried forward to meet his wife, who was just getting out. He took her in his arms and kissed her affectionately. When I saw him stooping down to kiss her, I said to myself: "What a good actor!" Then he took Ada by the hand and led her up to us, saying: "She has come back to us at last, beautiful as ever!" In this he showed himself for what he was, a sham and a humbug, for if he had really looked the poor woman in the face he would have seen that she had nothing left of the beauty we had known. Ada's face had lost all its shape; though she had got fatter, her cheeks seemed to have grown in the wrong place, as though the flesh had forgotten where it belonged and had become attached too far down. So that they looked more like swellings than cheeks. Her eyes had returned to their sockets, but it had been impossible to repair the ravages they had caused during the time they were displaced. The clear and characteristic lines of her face had become blurred and distorted. When I took leave of her outside the station, I saw by the brilliant rays of the winter sun that the whole coloring of her face, which I once loved so much, had become changed. She had grown paler, and there were little red patches here and there on her cheeks. It seemed as if health had departed from her face and only a feeble imitation had taken its place.

I told Augusta that Ada had completely recovered her girlish beauty, and she was delighted. What surprised me was that, after she had seen her several times, she entirely confirmed my false report. She said:

"Yes, she is as lovely now as when she was a girl, and my child will be just like her."

Evidently a sister's eye is not very discriminating. It was some time before I saw Ada again. She had too many children to look after, and so had we. Ada and Augusta used to arrange to meet several times a week, but always at times when I was out.

The time for making up our balance-sheet was approaching, and I had a great deal to do. I have never worked so hard as during this period of my life. Some days I would remain at my desk till ten o'clock at night. Guido offered to get me an accountant, but I would not hear of it. I had accepted the job and I meant to see it through. I wanted to make up to Guido for the fatal month when I had been away from the office, and I was glad that Carmen should see how industrious I was, for she would know it could only have been inspired by my love of Guido.

But as I proceeded in making out the accounts, I gradually began to discover the heavy losses we had incurred during our first year of business. I was worried by it and said something to Guido about it privately, but he was just going out shooting and would not wait to hear what I had to say.

"You will see that it is not as serious as you think, and besides the year is not over yet."

There was exactly a week before the New Year. Then I took Augusta into my confidence. At first she could only think of it as a possible loss to me. Women are always like that, and Augusta was unusually excited, even for a woman, at the thought of my personal losses.

Should not I, she said, be held partly responsible for Guido's losses? She wanted me at once to consult a solicitor. I must meanwhile break off all connection with Guido, and stop going to the office.

It was not easy to make her see that I could not be held responsible for anything, as I was only one of Guido's employees. She maintained that as I had no regular salary I could not be considered as an employee, but was more like a partner. Even after I had succeeded in convincing her, she remained of the same opinion still, because she then discovered that I should lose nothing if I stopped going to the office, where I should certainly end by ruining my business reputation. Good Lord! My business reputation! But I agreed with her that it was important for me to preserve it, and though her arguments were all wrong it was decided that I should do as she wished. She agreed to my finishing the balance-sheet as I had begun it, but said I must then arrange to return to my own little study, where it was true that I made no money, but where I also could not lose any.

Then I made a curious discovery about myself. However much I wished to do so I could not give up my work. I was astonished! To explain how this could be I must here have recourse to an analogy. I remembered it was the custom in England in the olden days to punish criminals condemned to hard labor by binding them on a wheel worked by water-power; thus compelling the victim to move his legs to a certain rhythm, as otherwise they would be broken. All work strikes one as having this compulsory character. The position remains the same whether one works or not; and I may say that Olivi and I were both equally bound to the wheel, the only difference being that I did not have to move my legs. Of course the result was different, but I now know for a certainty that it deserved neither praise nor blame. The point really is whether one is bound to a wheel that is moving or standing still. The difficulty of freeing oneself is the same in either case.

I went on going to the office for several days after I had finished my balance-sheet, although I had made up my mind not to go again. When I left the house I was still uncertain; I walked uncertainly in a direction which was almost always that of the office, and, as I went on, the direction became more and more definite till I found myself sitting on my usual chair opposite Guido. Fortunately he begged me at this moment on no account to desert my post, and I at once agreed to remain, since I had meanwhile discovered that I was chained to it.

I closed my balance-sheet on the fifteenth of January. It was a calamitous one! We closed with a loss of half our capital. Guido did not want to show it to young Olivi, fearing that he might give us away; but I insisted, hoping that with his great experience he might discover some error in it which would change the whole position. Some entry, I thought, might have got shifted from credit to debit by mistake, which would make a very considerable difference. Olivi smilingly promised Guido to behave with the utmost discretion, and spent a whole day going through the accounts with me. Unfortunately he found nothing wrong with them. I confess I learned a great deal from that revision, and should feel quite ready now to draw up much more formidable balance-sheets.

"And what do you propose to do now?" inquired the spectacled youth as he went away. I knew very well what he wanted to suggest. My father, who had talked to me about business from my childhood up, had already taught me what ought to be done. Granted that we had lost half our capital, the laws of sound finance decreed that we ought to liquidate the business, and possibly start it again on a fresh basis. I allowed him to repeat the advice. He added:

"It is a mere formality." Then he said smiling: "If

you don't, it may cost you dear!"

That evening Guido glanced at the balance-sheet,
which he had not yet had time to take in. He did it without any method, verifying this or that entry at random. I
wanted to put a stop to his futile labor, and told him what
Olivi had said: that we ought to go through the little
formality of liquidating the business.

Up to then Guido's face had been contorted by the
effort to find a mistake in the accounts which would explain everything. He frowned and contracted his brow like
someone who has a bad taste in his mouth. But when I
told him what Olivi had said his face suddenly cleared,
and he was all attention. He could not understand at first,
but when he did he burst out laughing. I interpreted his
expression thus: face to face with those immutable figures
he remained hard and bitter, but he recovered his gaiety
and self-confidence directly the painful problem was put
into the shade by a proposal that demanded a rapid and
final decision.

He refused to understand. The advice seemed to him
to have been given by an enemy. I explained that its chief
value was in regard to the obvious danger of our losing
more money and becoming bankrupt. It would be a criminal offense to go bankrupt after a balance-sheet like the
one we had now registered in our books, unless we had
taken some such step as that advised by Olivi. And I
added:

"The punishment ordained by our law for criminal
bankruptcy is prison."

Guido's face became so crimson that I feared for a
moment he was going to have a stroke. He shouted:

"In that case I don't need any advice from Olivi! I
can deal with it perfectly well myself if that happens."

I was impressed by his air of determination, and felt
as if I had to deal with someone who was perfectly conscious of his own responsibility. I lowered my voice. I
quite went over to his side and, forgetting that I had just
put forward Olivi's advice as worthy of consideration, I
said:

"That is just what I said to Olivi. It is your responsibility, and it does not concern us, whatever you may
choose to decide about a business that belongs only to

you and your father."

As a matter of fact it was to my wife and not to Olivi I had said this, but it was true that I had said it to somebody. After listening to Guido's manly speech I should have felt quite equal to saying it to Olivi, for I have always found decision and courage irresistible. I cannot help loving recklessness too, though it is not always the result of those two qualities, but often of very inferior ones.

As I wanted to repeat everything he said to Augusta, in order to set her mind at rest, I still insisted:

"You know they say, and probably with truth, that I have no gift whatever for business. I can carry out what you tell me to do, but I can't assume any responsibility for what you do."

He assented eagerly. The role I had sketched out for him gave him so much satisfaction that he quite forgot his annoyance over the unfavorable balance-sheet. He said emphatically:

"I alone am responsible. Everything is in my name and I absolutely refuse to allow anyone else to share the responsibility with me."

This was all excellent for repeating to Augusta; in fact it was a great deal more than I had asked for. And you should have seen the air with which he said it; he looked more like an apostle than someone on the brink of bankruptcy! Supporting himself comfortably on the unresisting balance-sheet he played to perfection the part of lord and master. On this occasion, as so often in the course of our life together, my sudden impulse of affection was quenched by his expression of ridiculous and exaggerated self-esteem. Yes, there was no getting out of it; that great musician played out of tune! I said sharply:

"Do you wish me to make a copy of the balance-sheet tomorrow, to send to your father?"

I was on the point of saying something more drastic still, namely that directly I had closed the accounts I intended to leave the office and not come back again. The only reason I did not do so was that I could not imagine how I should fill up my spare time. But my question was an admirable substitute for the statement I had refrained from making. I had incidentally reminded him that he was not the only master in that office.

He showed some surprise at my question; it did not seem to him quite in keeping with what had been said before, to which I had evidently agreed; and he replied in his former tone:

"I will instruct you how to make the copy."

I loudly protested. I have never in all my life shouted so much as I did at Guido; sometimes he really seemed to be deaf. I said that the law regarded the accountant as responsible for the accounts, and I made it clear that I was not going to provide him with purely imaginary columns of figures.

He turned pale and admitted that I was right, but that it was in his power to forbid me to make extracts from his books. I was obliged to agree, whereupon he declared that he would write to his father himself. It seemed as if he were going to sit down at once and do so, but he changed his mind and proposed that we should go and get a breath of fresh air. I had nothing against it; I imagined that he had not yet digested the balance-sheet, and wanted to take a little exercise in order to do so.

Our walk reminded me of the night I got engaged. We could not see the moon, because there was a good deal of mist high up; but lower down the air was quite clear, and we could walk along without thinking. Guido remembered that evening too, and said:

"This is the first time we have been out together after dark since that evening. Do you remember? You were explaining to me that kissing went on in the moon as well as here. But that kiss in the moon is for eternity; I am sure of it although we can't see the moon tonight. But here on earth. . . ."

Was he going to begin talking about Ada again, his poor sick wife? I interrupted him, but quite gently, almost as if I agreed with him (had I not come with him in order to help him to forget?).

"Of course one can't always be kissing here below. Besides, it is only the image of a kiss they have up there. Kissing is, above all, movement."

I tried to avoid anything that bore on his affairs, Ada and the balance-sheet, but I was only just in time to stop myself saying something that was on the tip of my tongue, namely that up there in the moon a kiss did not produce twins. But he could find no better way to escape that

balance-sheet than by complaining of his other misfortunes. And, as I had foreseen, he began talking against Ada.
He thought her illness made her irritable, jealous, and at
the same time lacking in affection. He ended by exclaiming
mournfully:

"Life is hard and unjust."

I felt it was impossible for me to say a single word
that implied any criticism of him or Ada. But I felt I must
say something. He had ended by discussing life and had
found two epithets for it which certainly did not err on
the side of originality. If I succeeded in finding something
better it was because I was able to start by criticizing what
he had said. One is often led to say things because of some
chance association in the sound of the words; and directly
one has spoken one begins to wonder if what one has
said was worth the breath spent on it, and occasionally
discovers that one has started a new idea. I said:

"Life is neither good nor bad; it is original."

When I thought it over I felt as if I had said something rather important. Looking at it like that I felt as if
I were seeing life for the first time, with all its gaseous,
liquid, and solid bodies. If I had talked about it to someone who was strange to it, and therefore deprived of an
ordinary common sense, he would have remained gasping
at the thought of the huge, purposeless structure. He
would have asked: "But how could you endure it?" And
if he had inquired about everything in detail, from the
heavenly bodies hung up in the sky which can be seen but
not touched, to the mystery that surrounds death, he
would certainly have exclaimed: "Very original!"

"So life is original, is it?" said Guido, laughing.
"Where did you read that?"

I did not bother to assure him I had not read it anywhere, for in that case he would have attached much less
importance to my words. But the more I thought of it
the more original life seemed to me. And one did not need
to get outside it in order to realize how fantastically it
was put together. One need only remind oneself of all that
we men expect from life to see how very strange it is, and
to arrive at the conclusion that man has found his way into
it by mistake and does not really belong there.

Though we had not agreed beforehand in which
direction we should go, we found ourselves, like last time,

on the ascent to Via Belvedere. When we reached the
parapet on which he had lain last time, Guido climbed up
on it and lay down just as before. He was humming to
himself, probably still oppressed by his thoughts, and no
doubt going over and over again the inexorable figures in
his account-book. I was thinking that it was on that very
spot I had wanted to kill him, and when I compared my
feelings then with my feelings today I could not help
wondering afresh at the incomparable originality of life.
But I suddenly remembered that a very little while ago I
had been angry with poor Guido for having wounded my
vanity, and that on one of the worst days of his life. I
tried to analyze my feelings. The tortures that Guido had
suffered from the balance-sheet I had drawn up had
caused me no particular pain, and I began to entertain a
doubt regarding myself, and at the same time remembered
a curious passage of my childhood. The doubt was this:
"Am I good or bad?" The memory was inspired suddenly
by this doubt, which I had evidently entertained before,
for I saw myself as a tiny child, still dressed, I am almost
certain, in petticoats, and lifting up my face to ask my
mother, who was smiling down at me: "Am I good or
naughty?" The doubt must have been put into the child's
head by having heard itself called good by so many people
and naughty, in fun, by so many others. It is not surprising that the child became confused by the dilemma. Was
ever anything so original as life? It is extraordinary that the
doubt which it had imposed on the child in so puerile a
form should still remain unsolved by the grown-up person,
even after he had lived half his life.

Once more by night, and on the very spot where I had
once been tempted to commit a murder, I fell a prey to that
doubt in a most acute form. The child whose head had
only just emerged from its baby cap could not have suffered much when that doubt began to stir in its mind, for
children are taught that even if you are naughty you can
become good again. In order to escape from my agony of
mind I tried to believe the same, and I succeeded. Otherwise I should have had to mourn over myself and Guido
and our melancholy lot. But the resolution I took at that
moment renewed the illusion! I resolved to stand by
Guido, and collaborate with him in developing his business, on which depended his own life and that of his

family; and I resolved to do it without any hope of personal gain. I saw myself traveling, negotiating, and intriguing, all in his interests, and even entertained the possibility of becoming, in order to help him, a really remarkable and enterprising business man. Such were the thoughts that went through my mind on one dark night of this very original life!

But Guido had already stopped thinking about the balance-sheet. He left his post on the mall and seemed to have recovered his serenity. As if he had just drawn a conclusion from some line of reasoning of which I knew nothing, he told me that he had decided to say nothing to his father, lest the poor old man should undertake the huge journey from his summer sunshine into our wintry fog. He went on to say that the losses seemed enormous at first sight, but that they were not really so bad if one did not have to bear them all alone. He would ask Ada to make herself responsible for half the sum and in return would give her part of the next year's profits. He himself would bear the other half of the losses.

I said nothing. I felt that it was impossible for me to offer my advice, as I should be drawn into doing exactly what I did not want to do, and setting myself up as an arbiter between husband and wife. Besides, at that moment I was so full of good resolutions that I thought it would be really quite a good thing for Ada to become a partner in a business run by us.

I accompanied Guido to the door of his house, and gave him a long handshake, silently to renew my vow of good will toward him. Then I tried to find something nice to say to him, and at last invented the following:

"I hope the twins will have a good night, and allow you to get some sleep; you must be in need of rest."

As I went away I bit my lips with vexation at having found nothing better to say. As if I did not know that now the twins had a nurse each they slept about a quarter of a mile away from his room and could not possibly have disturbed his slumber! But in any case he must have understood that my intentions were good, for he accepted my good wishes gratefully. When I got home I found that Augusta had gone to her bedroom with the children. Alfio was at her breast and Antonia was asleep in her cot, with the back of her curly head turned toward us. I had

to explain why I was late, so I told her of the method
Guido had evolved for getting out of his difficulties.
Augusta thought Guido's suggestion shameful:

"I would refuse if I were Ada," she exclaimed vehemently, though in a low voice so as not to disturb the
children.

I began to argue with her, still under the influence of
my virtuous resolution:

"So if I were to get into the same difficulties as Guido
you would not help me?" I said.

"It is an entirely different thing," she said, laughing.
"We should always want to do what was best for them!"
and she pointed to the two children. Then, after a
moment's reflection, she added: "And if we advise Ada
to put her money into a business that you are just about to
have nothing more to do with, shan't we feel obliged
to pay her back supposing she loses it?"

It was an absurd idea, but in my new role of altruist
I exclaimed:

"And why not?"

"But can't you see that it is our first duty to think of
the dear children?"

Of course I saw! It was only a rhetorical question
without any meaning.

"Haven't they got two children as well?" I asked triumphantly.

She burst out laughing at this and made so much
noise that she frightened Alfio, who stopped feeding and
began to cry. She busied herself about him, still laughing,
and I accepted her laughter as a tribute to my wit, though
at the moment I asked the question I had felt a sudden
wave of affection for everyone who had children, and for
all the children of those parents. Her laughter, however,
quite drove the feeling away.

My dismay at finding that I was not really good was
becoming less acute. I felt as if I had solved that distressing
problem. One is neither good nor bad, just as one is not
so many other things besides. Goodness is the light that
in brief flashes illuminates the darkness of the human
soul. A burning torch is needed to light the way (there had
been moments in my life when such a torch shone on my
path and it certainly would again), and the human intelligence must choose by its light the way it will have to

take afterwards in the dark. So that one could continue
to do good always, and that was the important thing.
When the light returned to guide one it would neither surprise nor dazzle. Perhaps I should even blow it out straight
away, as I should have no need of it; for I should have
learnt how to keep my resolution, how not to lose my way.

The resolution to be good is a peaceable and practical
one, and I had now become calm and cool. It was curious
that this access of virtue had enormously increased my
self-esteem and belief in my own powers. What could I do
for Guido? In his office, it is true, I was as superior to all
the others as old Olivi was to me in my own. But that
did not prove much. To get to business: What advice
should I give to Guido the next day? Should I rely on my
inspiration? But even at the gaming-table one cannot always rely on one's inspiration when one is playing with
other people's money. To keep a house of business going
one must find some work for it every day, and that can
only be done by devoting hours on end to organizing it.
I was not the person for a job like that, nor did I see why,
just for the sake of being good to Guido, I must be condemned to a life of continual boredom.

All the same I could not help regarding my sudden
virtuous impulse as a responsibility that I had assumed
toward Guido, and I could not get to sleep. I sighed deeply
several times and even groaned once, no doubt at the
moment when I was feeling that I ought to bind myself to
Guido's office as Olivi was bound to mine.

Augusta murmured, only half awake:

"What is the matter? Have you quarrelled with
Olivi again?"

That gave me a brilliant idea! I would advise Guido
to take young Olivi as his business manager. He was such
a serious, hard-working young man; yet it was distasteful to
me to have him in my own business for I always felt he
was only waiting to succeed his father as director and oust
me altogether. It was obviously to everyone's advantage
that he should be in Guido's office instead. If he were to
give him a good position in his business, Guido would be
saved and young Olivi would be much more useful in
that office than in mine.

I was so excited by the idea that I woke Augusta to
tell her about it. She was so enthusiastic that she became

quite wide awake. She thought it would be the easiest way
for me to get free from the dangerous muddle of Guido's
business. I fell asleep again with a quiet conscience; I had
found a way of saving Guido without condemning myself to perpetual bondage; in fact I was now completely
free.

Nothing is more disagreeable than to have one's
advice rejected when one has even sacrificed several hours
of sleep to thinking it out. I was obliged to sacrifice an illusion too; the idea that I might be of some use in arranging
Guido's affairs for him. I had really made a superhuman
effort. First I had fought my way through to real goodness, then to absolute objectivity, and all they did was to
send me to hell!

Guido treated my advice with utter contempt. He
did not believe that young Olivi was capable of doing it;
he disliked his prematurely old appearance and particularly
loathed his spectacles, which shone so horribly on that
pale face. The reasons he gave were such as to make me
feel that the only thing he really wanted was to annoy
me. He finally said that he would be quite glad to appoint
old Olivi instead, at the head of his office. But I did not
see any way of inducing the old man to go in with him;
besides, I did not feel equal to undertaking the management of my own affairs at a moment's notice. I was foolish enough to discuss it with him, and to say that old Olivi
was not good for much. I told him how much money he
had made me lose, all because of his obstinacy in refusing
to buy dried raisins at the right moment.

"Well!" exclaimed Guido. "If the old man is as bad
as that, what chance is there of his son being any better?
He is simply his pupil."

This was the first good argument he had produced,
and it was all the more irritating to me because my foolish
gossip had supplied him with it.

A few days later Augusta told me Guido had suggested to Ada that she should indemnify him for half his
losses. She refused, and said to Augusta:

"First he is unfaithful to me and then asks for my
money!"

Augusta had lacked courage to advise her to give
him any money, but assured me she had done her best
to make Ada reconsider her verdict on her husband's in-

fidelity. Ada's reply suggested that she knew a good deal
more about it than we realized. And Augusta argued with
me as follows:

"I know one ought to be prepared to sacrifice everything for one's husband, but do you really think that it
applies to Guido too?"

During the next few days Guido's behavior was really
extraordinary. He would come to the office from time to
time, but never stay there for more than a quarter of an
hour; he dashed out again as if he had left his handkerchief at home. I heard later that he always went to Ada
with fresh arguments—always decisive—to induce her to do
what he wanted. He looked like someone who has been
crying or shouting too much, or has just been in a fight,
and even when he was with us he could not repress his
emotion; it choked him and brought tears to his eyes. I
asked him what was the matter. He replied with a sad but
friendly smile, as much as to say that he had no quarrel
with me. Then he tried to control himself enough to be
able to talk to me without getting too excited. At last he
brought out these few words: Ada was making him suffer
by her jealousy.

He then went on to tell me that they spent their
time in discussing their personal affairs, whereas I knew
that there was also that question of "debit and credit"
between them.

But it appeared that the latter was of no importance;
so he said, and so Ada said to Augusta, to whom she never
talked of anything but her jealousy. And the violent nature
of those discussions, which left such deep traces on Guido's
face, made it possible that they were speaking the truth.

But afterwards it appeared that nothing was talked of
by the two but this money question. Ada was entirely
absorbed in her emotional grievances, but she was too
proud ever to mention them to Guido, and he, perhaps
partly because he was conscious of his guilt, and also because he was afraid of encountering Ada's jealous anger,
went on discussing business as if nothing else existed in
the world. He ran after money with untiring perseverance,
while she, who was not in the least interested in business,
countered his proposal with one unvarying argument: she
must keep her money for her children. And when he tried
other arguments, his peace of mind, the advantages the

children themselves would derive from his work, the sense of security he would have if he could only put himself right with the law, she always dismissed him with a hard "No," which exasperated him, and made him, like a child, only the more determined to get what he wanted. Yet both of them, when talking about it to anyone else, thought they were perfectly accurate in saying that the only difference between them was jealousy and wounded love.

A sort of misunderstanding prevented me from interfering at the right moment to put an end to this dreadful money question. I could easily have proved to Guido that it really had very little bearing on his affairs. I am rather slow at figures and can only understand things when I have them all set out in black and white in a book, but I think I arrived fairly soon at the conclusion that the sum Guido demanded from Ada would not have made very much difference. What was the point, really, in her making over her money to him? It could not diminish his losses unless she consented to throw her money directly into the balance-sheet, a thing that Guido had never asked of her. The criminal court would not have been much impressed to discover that after such heavy losses he was prepared to risk a little more by attracting more money into the business.

One morning Guido did not put in an appearance at the office, which surprised us as we knew that he had not gone out shooting the evening before. At luncheon Augusta told me, in a state of great agitation, that he had made an attempt on his life the evening before. He was out of danger now. I must confess that this news, which Augusta took so tragically, only made me angry.

He had adopted that drastic method to break down his wife's resistance. I soon discovered that he had omitted no precaution, for before taking morphia he had been careful to be seen with the uncorked bottle in his hands. So directly he fell into a coma Ada sent for a doctor and he was very soon out of danger. Ada had passed an awful night, because the doctor had thought it his duty to make certain reservations about the effects of the poison, and her agitation was increased by Guido himself, who, when he came to, and even before he recovered consciousness completely, overwhelmed her with reproaches, calling her his enemy, his persecutor, the one person who prevented him from doing the good work he wanted to do.

Ada immediately gave him the loan he asked for, but at last, in an endeavor to defend herself, she spoke openly to him, and poured out all the grievances she had smothered for so long. They finally came to an understanding, for Augusta thought he had succeeded in dissipating all Ada's suspicions as to his fidelity. He had emphatically protested his innocence, and when she mentioned Carmen he had explained:

"Are you jealous of her? Well, if you like, I will send her away this very day."

Ada had made no reply, meaning that she accepted his proposal, and assuming that he would feel bound by it.

I was astonished that Guido was able to behave thus while still under the effect of morphia, and was tempted to believe he had not even swallowed the small dose he said he had. I thought that one of the effects of the clouding of one's brain by sleep was to soften the hard kernel of the mind and induce the most naïve confessions. Had not that very thing happened to me recently? This only tended to increase my distaste and contempt for Guido.

Augusta wept as she told me of the state in which she had found Ada. Her eyes were wide with terror, she had lost every trace of her former beauty.

My wife and I had a long discussion as to whether it would be better for me to call on Guido and Ada at once, or to pretend to know nothing about it and wait till Guido came to the office. The thought of that visit filled me with horror. How could I see him without telling him what I thought of him? I said to myself: "It is a cowardly thing to have done! I have no desire to commit suicide, but if I decided to do so I should certainly do it thoroughly!"

That was how I looked at it, and I wanted to say so to Augusta. But I thought I should be doing Guido too much honor by comparing him to myself, so I said:

"One doesn't need to be a chemist to destroy the very delicate organism of the body. Not a week passes in our town but some little seamstress swallows a solution of phosphorus which she has prepared all by herself in her attic; there is no antidote to this primitive poison.

She is carried off to die, her young face distorted by moral and physical pain. What agonizing moments her innocent little soul has had to endure!"

Augusta refused to admit that the soul of the seamstress was so very innocent, but after a brief protest she renewed her attempt to make me call on Guido and Ada. She said I need not be afraid of feeling embarrassed. She had talked to Guido, who had treated the matter very calmly and as if he had only behaved in the most ordinary way.

I left the house without giving Augusta the satisfaction of seeing that I was convinced of her arguments. After hesitating a moment I decided to do what she wanted. During the short walk between our houses the mere rhythm of walking made me take a milder view of Guido's action. I remembered the direction in which the light had pointed, that a few days ago had illumined my mind. Guido was a mere child, a child to whom I had promised to be indulgent. If he did not succeed in killing himself first, even he would arrive at maturity.

The servant showed me into a room that I took to be Ada's boudoir. It was a gloomy day, and it was dark inside that little room, with its single window covered by a dark curtain. On the walls hung portraits of Ada's and Guido's parents. I was only there a few minutes before the servant came to call me and took me into the bedroom. It was large and bright even on a day like that; for it was lit by two high windows and had a light wallpaper and furniture. Guido was lying in bed with a bandage round his head, and Ada was sitting beside him.

Guido received me without any embarrassment; on the contrary, he was most grateful to me for coming. He seemed half asleep, but he woke up to greet me and was soon wide enough awake to give me his orders for the office. Then he sank back again on the pillow and closed his eyes. I wondered if he had remembered that he ought to give the impression of being still under the effects of morphia. In any case it was impossible to be angry with him; all my fondness for him returned and I felt very sympathetic. It was a moment or two before I could trust myself to look at Ada; but when I did look I was agreeably surprised, for I expected something much worse. Her eyes were larger than usual, it is true, in fact disproportionately so, but her cheeks had lost their swollen appearance, and she seemed to me to look more like herself. She had on a full red dress that buttoned up to the neck, and her slender body seemed quite lost in it. There was something very virginal about her appearance, and her large eyes gave her an air of great severity. I could not have explained exactly what I thought about her, but I had the impression of standing before a woman who resembled the Ada I had known.

Suddenly Guido opened his eyes wide, took from under his pillow a check on which I saw Ada's signature, and gave it to me, asking me to pay it in and credit it to an account that I was to open in Ada's name.

"In the name of Ada Malfenti or Ada Speier?" I asked Ada playfully.

She shrugged her shoulders and said:

"You two will know which will be best."

"I will tell you later how to make the other entries," said Guido, with a sharpness in his tone which I found offensive.

I felt inclined to interrupt the somnolence into which he had once more sunk back, by telling him that if he wanted entries made he had better make them himself.

Meanwhile a large cup of black coffee was brought in, which Ada handed to him. He brought out his arms from under the sheets and raised the cup to his lips with both hands. He looked exactly like a child, with his nose buried in the cup.

When I said good-by he promised to come to the office the next day. I had already said good-by to Ada, so I was rather surprised when she joined me again at the front door. She brought out with difficulty:

"Zeno! Please come here a moment. There is something I want to say to you."

I followed her into the little room I had waited in before; from it I could hear the crying of one of the twins.

We remained standing, facing one another. She was still breathing heavily, and this made me think for a moment that she had called me into that dark little room to beg me for the love I had once offered her in vain.

Her great eyes were terrible in the darkness. I felt quite frightened, and wondered what I ought to do.

Wasn't it my duty to take her in my arms, and spare her the shame of having to ask anything of me? A host of resolutions sprang up in my mind at the same moment! One of the great difficulties of life is guessing what a woman wants. Listening to what she says is no help, for a whole speech may be wiped out by a single look, and even that is no guide if one is alone with her, by her own invitation, in a cozy, dark little room.

As I could not guess what it was she wanted I tried instead to understand myself. What did I want? Did I want to kiss those eyes and that skeleton body? I could not give a decisive answer because only a short time ago I had seen her looking so severely virginal, and as desirable as when I had loved her as a girl.

Her agitation had now given way to tears, and I was still in the dark as to what she wanted, and what my feelings were toward her. At last in a broken voice she told me again how much she loved Guido; so I had no right to her, then, no duties toward her. She stammered out:

"Augusta told me that you wanted to leave Guido, and not take part in his affairs any more. I must beg you to go on helping him. I don't think he is capable of carrying them on alone."

She asked me if I would go on doing what I had been doing before. It was really very little and I thought I might offer to do a little more. I said:

"Since you wish it, I will go on helping Guido. I will do my best to help him more effectually than I have done hitherto."

There I was exaggerating again! I realized it the very moment I had committed myself, but it was too late then to turn back. I wanted to tell Ada, falsely perhaps, that she meant a great deal to me. She did not want my love, only my support, but I spoke in such a way that she might think I was ready to grant her both.

She suddenly seized me by the hand. A thrill went through me. A woman who offers you her hand offers you a great deal. I have always felt this; and when I take a woman's hand I feel as if I were taking her altogether. I was conscious of Ada's body close to mine and as we stood thus locked together I felt as if we were embracing each other. It was certainly an act of intimacy.

She added:

"I must return to Bologna at once to the sanatorium, and it will be a great comfort to me to know that you are with him."

"I will stay with him," I said resignedly. Ada must have thought my air of resignation referred to the sacrifice I was making for her. But I was really resigning myself to returning to my very ordinary everyday life, since she had no thought of joining me in the very exceptional life I had dreamed of.

I made an effort to come down to earth again, and immediately found myself confronted with a problem of bookkeeping which was not easy to solve. I had got to credit Ada's newly opened account with the amount that was written on the check. That was clear; but it was not at all clear what bearing this could possibly have on Guido's debit and credit account. I said nothing about it to Ada, for perhaps she was ignorant that such a thing existed in the world as a day-book in which such very diverse accounts were entered.

But I did not want to leave that room without saying something more. Instead of talking about bookkeeping I carelessly threw out a remark, just for the sake of saying something, which I soon felt to be very significant for Ada, Guido, and me, but above all for me, because I was compromising myself again. The remark seemed to me to be so important that I remembered for years afterwards how lightly I had opened my lips to utter it in that dark room, with the four portraits of their ancestors, wedded there on the wall, looking down at us. I said:

"You ended by marrying a queerer man even than me, Ada!"

It is strange how a word can bridge time! It is itself an event that is linked to other events. And those words of mine became a tragic event because they were addressed to Ada. I should never have been able by thinking about it to evoke so vividly the hour in which Ada had chosen between Guido and me in that sunny street where, after days of waiting, I had at last succeeded in meeting her; and how I had walked beside her trying to force a smile from her which I then hailed as a promise! And I remembered too, how the difficulty I experienced in controlling the muscles of my legs made me feel inferior to Guido, who moved with even more ease than Ada herself, and whose only mark of inferiority was the extraordinary stick that he insisted on carrying.

She said in a low voice:

"Yes, that is true!"

Then, smiling fondly at me she said·

"But I am so happy for Augusta's sake that you have proved yourself a much better man than I ever imagined."

She sighed and went on:

"So glad, that it comforts me a little for finding Guido quite different from what I expected."

I said nothing; I still did not know what to make of it. I felt as if she had said that I was now what she had hoped Guido would become. Was she in love with me then? She went on:

"You are the best man of our family, all our hope and trust is in you." She seized me by the hand again, and perhaps I pressed hers too hard, for she withdrew it so quickly as to leave me no further doubts. It again became quite clear how I was expected to behave in that little boudoir. Perhaps it was to mitigate the sudden withdrawal of her hand that she threw me another caress. "Now that I know what you are really like, I hate to think of having made you suffer. Did you really suffer so much?"

I gazed back into my dark past in search of that suffering and murmured:

"Yes!"

Little by little the memory of Guido's violin came back to me, and then how they would have turned me out of their drawing-room if I had not clung to Augusta; and then again the drawing-room in the Malfentis' house where one couple made love at a Louis Quatorze table, while the other couple watched them from another table. And I suddenly remembered Carla; for she had seen Ada too. I heard her voice again quite distinctly, telling me I belonged to my wife—meaning Ada. The tears rose to my eyes and I repeated:

"Yes. A great deal! A great deal!"

Ada actually sobbed as she said: "I am so very, very sorry."

She pulled herself together and said:

"But now you love Augusta!"

A sob interrupted her for an instant, and I trembled,

not knowing whether she had stopped short to see if I should confess or deny my love. Fortunately she did not give me time to speak, but continued:

"Now we are really able to feel to each other like brother and sister. I need you; I have got to be a mother to that great child of mine, I have got to protect him. Will you help me in my difficult task?"

Her emotion made her almost lean against me, as in my dream. But I forced myself to concentrate on what she was saying. She was asking me to love her like a brother; the bond of love which I thought bound me to her was thus transformed into a fresh right claimed by her from me. I promised at once to help Guido, to help her, to do everything she wanted. If I had been calmer I should have told her how unequal I felt myself to the task she had allotted me, but this would have destroyed the never-to-be-forgotten emotion of that moment. And I was so moved that I was incapable of feeling my insufficiency. At that moment I could not believe in anyone's insufficiency. Even Guido's only needed a light breath of enthusiasm to blow it away.

Ada accompanied me to the landing and stood leaning on the banister to watch me go down. That was what Carla used to do, but it was curious that Ada, who loved Guido, should do it too, and I felt so grateful to her that before I went down the second flight I looked up and waved to her again. Lovers always did that, but clearly friends might do so too.

I went away with a light heart. She had come with me to the top of the stairs, but no farther. There was no room for doubt. Our position was now this: I had loved her and now I loved Augusta, but my former love gave her a claim on my devotion. She went on loving "that man of hers," but reserved for me a strong sisterly affection, not only because I had married her sister, but to make up to me for everything she had made me suffer, which now constituted a secret bond between us. This relationship of ours was very sweet, and of a fragrance rare in this life. Ought not such sweetness to have brought me health? And in fact I did walk that day without difficulty or pain; I felt magnanimous and strong, and was conscious of a new sense of security in my heart. I forgot that I had ever been unfaithful to my wife (and that in a very discreditable manner), or, if I remembered it, I resolved never to do anything of the sort again; and I really felt myself to be what Ada said I was, the best man of the family.

When this heroic mood slowly faded away I should have liked to revive it, but Ada had meanwhile left for Bologna, and I could not succeed in squeezing a fresh stimulus out of what she had said to me. I would do what I could for Guido, but a resolution like that could neither increase the air in my lungs nor the flow of blood in my veins. I still entertained a very tender feeling for Ada in my heart, which was renewed each time she sent me an affectionate message in her letters to Augusta. I heartily reciprocated her affection and watched the course of her treatment with eager solicitude. Perhaps even yet she might recover all her former health and beauty!

The day after my conversation with Ada, Guido came to the office and began discussing the entries he wanted to make. He said:

"Let us put half our debit and credit account down under Ada's name."

So that had been all the time what he wanted to do, and it was really quite useless. If I had still been his mere unreflecting agent, as I had been up to a few days ago, I should have made those entries without thinking any more about it. But now I felt it my duty to tell him everything. I thought it would stimulate him to work if he knew that he could not so easily cancel the losses he had incurred.

I explained to him that, so far as I knew, Ada had given him the money to put down to her credit on her own account, and that it would not be at all the same thing if we put half his losses down in the opposite column. Further, that part of his losses which he intended to bear himself ought to go down to his account. But then the whole of his losses ought to go down to his account as well, and instead of cancelling them that would only make them more evident. I had thought about the matter so much that I had no difficulty in explaining it to him. I concluded:

"Supposing we found ourselves in the position Olivi foretold—which God forbid—a practiced eye would at once discover from the books exactly what your losses were."

He gazed at me in astonishment. He knew enough about bookkeeping to understand me, and if he could not do so it was because his wishes prevented him from accepting the evidence. Then I added, so that there should be no fear of his misunderstanding:

"Don't you see that there was no point in Ada making this payment?"

When at last he understood he grew very pale and began to bite his nails nervously. He stood there rapt in thought, but made an effort to control himself, and with his comic, magisterial air insisted that all the entries must be made as he had prescribed, adding:

"In order to relieve you of all responsibility I am ready to make the entries myself and sign them with my own name."

I saw quite clearly that he wanted to go on dreaming, but there is no room for dreams in double entries!

I remembered all I had undertaken on the heights of Via Belvedere, then I remembered Ada in her dark little boudoir, and I said magnanimously:

"I will make the entries you wish. I don't think they need the authorization of your signature. I am here to help you, not to put obstacles in your way."

He shook me warmly by the hand.

"Life is difficult," he said, "and it is a great comfort to me to have a friend like you near me."

We looked feelingly into each other's eyes. His were shining.

To avoid giving way to a like emotion, I said smiling:

"Life is not difficult, but very original."

He laughed heartily at this sally.

Then he stood over me to see how I proposed to settle that profit and loss account. It was all done in a few minutes. The account ceased to exist, but not without dragging Ada's account with it into the abyss. We credited her nevertheless with the amount in a small separate note-book, in case a sudden catastrophe should destroy all other evidence of the loan, and as proof that we had paid her the interest. The remainder of the profit and loss account went to swell Guido's already very considerable debit account.

Accountants are by nature a race of animals much inclined to irony. While making those entries I thought to myself:

"One account, that known as profit and loss account, died a violent death; the other—Ada's—died a natural death, because it was impossible to keep it alive. Only Guido's we could not succeed in killing; its eternal debit is an open grave that sooner or later will swallow up all our undertaking."

Bookkeeping remained a subject for discussion in the office for a long time. Guido racked his brain to discover another method of protecting himself against the wiles of the law, as it pleased him to call them. I think he must have consulted an accountant too, for one day he came into the office and proposed destroying all the old books, and opening new ones in which we were to put down a sham sale in some name or other—Ada's money figuring as payment of the same. It was painful to have to undeceive him, for he had hurried to the office full of such lively hopes. But the fraud he now proposed to perpetrate was quite revolting to me. Hitherto we had only played at shifting real transactions about from one column to another; only somebody who had implicitly given his consent to the procedure could possibly suffer from it. But now he was proposing actually to invent business transactions that had really never existed. I too saw that it was the only possible way of covering up every trace of our losses. But what a price to pay for it! We should be obliged to invent the name of a buyer, or to ask somebody's permission to write him down as such in our books. I had no objection to seeing the old books destroyed, though I had written them with so much care, but it would be a nuisance to have to make new ones. I made various legal objections that in the end convinced Guido. It was not so easy to forge a whole business transaction; we should have to forge as well all the documents proving the existence of the wares in question and of our right of possession.

He gave up that plan, but the following day he arrived in the office with a fresh one, which also involved destroying all the old books. I was tired of seeing all the work of the office held by discussions of this sort, and protested:

"To see all the time you spend thinking about it, one would suppose you were actually proposing to become bankrupt! Otherwise what difference can such a small reduction of your income make to you? No one has been justified hitherto in asking to see our books. What we have got to do is to work, and not waste our time in thinking about such follies."

He admitted that the thought had become a positive obsession with him. How could he help it? He only needed a short run of ill-luck to plunge straight into an encounter with the criminal law and finish up in jail!

I knew from my study of law that Olivi's statement of what is incumbent on a business man who shows a balance-sheet like Guido's could not be improved on, but I advised him, in order to escape from his obsession, to consult a solicitor friend of his own.

He replied that he had already done so, or rather that he had not been to him for that express purpose, because he did not wish to confide his secret to a solicitor, but that he had contrived to turn the conversation on to the subject while out shooting with his friend. So that he knew, alas, that there had been no mistake and no exaggeration in what Olivi had said!

Realizing what an inane occupation it was, he ceased exercising his ingenuity on fresh schemes for falsifying the accounts, but did not thereby recover his peace of mind. Whenever he came to the office he stood with lowering brow, gazing at his account-book. One day he confessed to me that as he came into our room he suddenly thought he was standing in the entrance of the prison, and wanted to run away.

One day he said:

"Does Augusta know all about our balance-sheet?"

I blushed because I thought the question implied a reproach. But it was clear that if Ada knew about it Augusta might do so too. This did not occur to me at once; instead I thought that I deserved any reproach he might address to me. I murmured however:

"She may have heard of it from Ada or perhaps from Alberta, to whom Ada may have said something about it."

I thought I had taken into account all the possible ways by which Augusta might have heard about it, without however denying that she had had it direct from the

fountain head; that is to say, from me. I anyway implied
that it would have been useless for me to keep silence.
It would have been much better, and I should have felt
much more loyal and upright, if I had said straight out
that I had no secrets from Augusta. The simple fact of
pretending not to have done some perfectly innocent thing
that it would have been much better to own up to, is quite
enough to endanger a really genuine friendship.

I will set down here, though it has no bearing on
Guido nor on my story, that a few days later that cackling
broker, with whom we had had some dealings over the
sulphate of copper, stopped me in the street and gazing
up at me—a procedure to which his insignificant stature
obliged him—said ironically:

"They tell me you have been doing some big business
lately, like your sulphate of copper deal!"

When he saw me turn pale he shook me by the
hand and added:

"For my part I wish you every success. I hope you
don't doubt my word!"

Thereupon he left me. He had probably had news
of us from his little daughter, who was in the same class
as Anna at school. I did not mention the encounter to
Guido. My chief duty was to save him from unnecessary
worries.

I was surprised that Guido took no steps to get rid
of Carmen, for I knew he had definitely promised his
wife to do so. I expected Ada to return home after several
months' absence, as she had done last time. But instead
of returning to Trieste she went to stay in a villa on Lake
Maggiore where, shortly afterwards, Guido joined her
with the children.

On his return, either because he remembered his
promise or because Ada had reminded him of it, he asked
me if I did not think it would be possible to employ Carmen in my office—that is to say, in Olivi's. I knew there
was no post vacant in that office, but as Guido was so
insistent I consented to go and talk to my chief about it.
By a fortunate chance one of Olivi's staff was leaving just
then, but his salary was lower than Guido had been giving
Carmen during the last few months; for, as far as I could
see, it was his custom to charge his donations to his
women friends to the general expenses account. Old Olivi

asked me about Carmen's qualifications and offered to take
her on the same terms as the employee who was leaving,
though I gave her a brilliant testimonial. I told Guido,
who scratched his head in his embarrassment and annoyance.

"What does he mean by offering her a lower salary
than what she has been receiving? Couldn't you persuade
Olivi to give her the same for the present?"

I knew it was out of the question and, moreover,
that Olivi was not in the habit, like us, of regarding a
woman employee as his wife! If he had thought that
Carmen deserved a krone less wages than he had offered
her he would have cut them down pitilessly. The end
of it was that Olivi did not get her, and did not even
ask for a definite answer; while Carmen continued to roll
her lovely eyes in our office.

Between Ada and me there was a secret, which remained important just because it was a secret. She wrote
regularly to Augusta, but never told her of the discussions
she had had with me, nor that she had confided Guido to
my care. I said nothing about it either. One day Augusta
showed me a letter from Ada which concerned me. She
began by asking for news of me, and ended by appealing
to my goodness of heart, and begging me to tell her
something of how Guido's affairs were going. My heart
beat at the thought of her appealing to me, but grew
calm again when I saw that she had, as usual, only applied to me for news of Guido. Once more I had no excuse for taking any liberties.

I said nothing about it to Guido, but agreed with
Augusta that I had better write to Ada. I sat down, fully
intending to write to her only about business, and said
that I was very pleased at the way Guido was conducting
his business now; he was so industrious and alert.

This was true, or at least I was satisfied with him on
that particular day, because he had succeeded in making
some money by the sale of goods that he had had stored
in the town for some months past. It was true that he
did seem rather more industrious, though he still went out
fishing and shooting every week. I rather exaggerated my
praise of him because I hoped it might hasten Ada's recovery. I reread the letter, but was not satisfied with it.
Something was lacking. Ada had addressed herself to me,

and certainly wanted to have news of me as well, so that
I should be lacking in courtesy if I failed to give her any.
And by degrees—I remember it as distinctly as if it had
just happened—I felt as embarrassed, sitting at that table,
as if I had been face to face again with Ada in her dark
little boudoir. Ought I to press the hand she had held out
to me?

I wrote on, but was then obliged to rewrite my letter
because I had used some compromising expressions; I
was longing to see her again, I wrote, and I hoped she
would soon have recovered all her former health and
beauty. But this seemed to suggest that I wanted to hold
for life a woman who had only offered me her hand. My
duty was only to press her hand, to hold it long and
tenderly in my own, so that she might understand that I
meant a great deal more than I could ever say.

I won't repeat here all the phrases I passed in review,
trying to find something which might take the place of
that long, tender, eloquent handshake—but only the
phrases I actually wrote. I said a good deal about my approaching old age. I could not stand still a moment without growing old. Each time the blood circulated in my
veins something crept into my flesh and bones which be-
tokened old age. Every morning when I woke the world
took on a grayer hue; I only did not notice it because
everything was of the same dull hue. There was not one
touch of the coloring of the day before; otherwise I should
have detected it and my regret would have driven me to
despair.

I remember very well the complete satisfaction with
which I posted that letter. There was nothing compromising in the words themselves, but if Ada were feeling like
me she would understand perfectly that affectionate handshake. It did not require much penetration to guess that
my long disquisition on old age meant no more than that
I feared love could no longer catch me up in my rapid
flight through time. I seemed to be crying out to love:
"Come to me, come!" But I am not at all sure that I
really wanted this love and, if I feel any doubt about it,
it is simply because I know that I really did write something of the sort.

I made a copy of the letter for Augusta, leaving out
my disquisition on old age. She would not have under-

stood it, but it is better to be on the safe side. I might
have blushed to feel her eye on me, while I was holding
her sister's hand in mine. Yes! I was still capable of blushing. And I really did blush when I received a note of
thanks from Ada which made no mention at all of my
discourse on old age. I felt that she had compromised herself much more by this than I had ever done. She had
not withdrawn her hand from my pressure. She had left
it lying passively in mine, and for a woman to remain
passive is a form of giving consent.

A few days after I had written the letter I discovered
that Guido had been gambling on the Bourse. I learnt it
through an indiscretion of the broker Nilini.

I had known him for years, for we had been at school
together; he had been obliged to leave suddenly to go
into his uncle's office. We had met again occasionally,
and the difference in our fortunes had given me a certain
ascendancy over him. He would be the first to salute,
and he made various attempts to get into closer touch
with me. This seemed to me quite natural, and I was the
more surprised that at a certain moment—I don't remember exactly when—he took up a very haughty attitude
toward me. He no longer took any notice of me when I
met him, and made hardly any response to my greeting. I
was a little worried by this, for I am very thin-skinned
and easily hurt. But what could I do about it? Perhaps
he had discovered I was in Guido's office, and despised
me because he thought I held a subordinate position in
it or, what is equally probable, his uncle being now dead
and he on his own as a stock-broker, he had become rather
pleased with himself. In narrow circles like ours this sort
of thing often happens. Without there being any open
enmity, two people suddenly begin to look at each other
with dislike and contempt.

So I was surprised to see him come into the office
one day when I was alone there, and ask for Guido. He
took off his hat and held out his hand. Then he immediately sank into one of our great armchairs. I watched
him with interest. It was years since I had been at such
close quarters with him, and the dislike he had shown me
made me observe him with the closest attention.

He was about forty at that time, very ugly and almost entirely bald, except for an oasis of thick black hair

at the back of his neck and another on his temples; he had a thick nose and a yellow, hairy face. He was short and thin, and had to stretch up so much when he talked to me that I used to feel a sympathetic pain in my own neck, the only feeling of sympathy he aroused in me. On that particular occasion he seemed to be trying to restrain himself from laughing, and his face was contracted by a sarcastic or contemptuous smile that I could not regard as personally offensive, seeing that he had greeted me in such a friendly way. I discovered later that nature, in a whimsical mood, had stamped that expression on his face. His jaws did not close properly, and on one side of his mouth there always remained a gap, which compelled him to wear habitually an ironical expression. It was perhaps in order to adapt his character to a mask, which he only succeeded in casting off when he yawned, that he took such apparent pleasure in teasing people. He was no fool, and there was often a poisoned head to his arrows, though he preferred to shoot them at the absent.

He talked a great deal and rather fancifully, especially when discussing the Bourse. He spoke of the Bourse as if it were an individual, and would describe it as a terrible being, breathing out threats; or as sleepy and inert, with a face susceptible to tears or laughter. He saw it dancing up the steps of a rising value or tearing down again at breakneck speed; he saw it caressing one stock and throttling another, or again, giving people lessons in industry and temperance. Only crafty and capable people could hope to do business with such a being. There was plenty of money lying scattered about on the floor of the Bourse, but it was not so easy to stoop down and pick it up.

I offered him a cigarette and kept him waiting while I dealt with some correspondence. He grew tired of waiting after a while, and said he could not stay any longer. He had only come to tell Guido that some shares, which bore the strange name of Rio Tinto and which he had advised Guido to buy the day before, had already gone up about ten per cent in value. He laughed heartily.

"While we sit talking here the closing prices will have done the rest. If Signor Speier wanted to buy those shares now, I don't know what he might not have to pay for them. I saw at once in which direction they were going."

He went on boasting of the insight which his long familiarity with the Bourse had given him. He broke off to ask me:

"At which school do you think one learns most: the University or the Bourse?"

His lower jaw fell a little more and emphasized his expression of sarcasm.

"The Bourse of course!" I replied emphatically.

This won me an affectionate handshake when he at last took his leave.

So Guido was gambling on the Bourse! If I had been more on the spot I might have guessed it before, for when I had shown him an exact list of the quite considerable profits our last undertakings had brought in, he had read it through smiling, but with a touch of scorn. He thought we had had to work too hard to win that small amount of money. Yet, with about a dozen such transactions we should have covered our losses of the year before! What ought I to do now, I who only a few days before had been singing his praises?

Guido came into the office soon after, and I told him exactly what Niliri had said. He stood listening so intently that he did not even notice I had found out about his gambling; then he rushed away again.

I told Augusta about it that evening, and she thought it advisable to leave Ada in peace, but to warn Signora Malfenti of the danger Guido was running. She begged me to do what I could to prevent him committing any further follies.

I thought carefully over what I ought to say to him. Here was an opportunity of putting my good resolutions into practice, and redeeming the promise I had made to Ada. I knew how I ought to approach Guido in order to ensure his listening to me. I ought to explain to him that it is always very foolish to gamble on the Bourse, but especially for a business man with a balance-sheet like Guido's behind him.

Next day I began brilliantly.

"So you have started gambling on the Bourse? Do you want to end in prison?" I said severely. I was prepared for a scene, and was holding in reserve the threat that since he was acting in such a way as to compromise the firm I proposed to leave his office on the spot.

But Guido disarmed me at once. He had kept the secret so far, but now with engaging boyish frankness he went into every detail of what he had been doing. He was dealing in mineral shares of some country or other, and had already made enough almost to cover our last year's losses. The danger was over now, and he could tell me all about it. If he were so unlucky as to lose what he had gained he would simply give up gambling. If, however, fortune continued to favor him, he would at once put all his books in order, for they still continued to cause him considerable anxiety.

I saw there was nothing to be angry about; that on the contrary one ought to feel rather pleased with him. As for the bookkeeping, I told him he could set his mind at rest about that, because directly one had money in hand it was the easiest thing in the world to settle the most tiresome account. Directly Ada's account had been restored to its proper place in our books, and that bottomless pit which was Guido's account had to some extent been filled up, our bookkeeping would be able to put a smiling face on things.

Then I proposed that we should begin to carry out the reforms at once, and put down his speculations on the account. Fortunately he refused to do this, otherwise I should have become a gambler's accountant and should thus have taken on a still greater responsibility. As it was, things took their course as if I had never existed. He rejected my proposition for reasons that seemed to me good. He said it was a bad omen to pay one's debts too quickly, and it is indeed a widespread superstition at all gaming-tables that other people's money brings one good fortune. I don't really believe this, but when I play I omit no precaution.

For a while I reproached myself for having accepted all Guido's statements without protest. But when I saw that Signora Malfenti took the same view, and told me of the large sums her husband had made by gambling on the Bourse, and when I found that even Ada looked upon gambling just as if it were any other kind of business, I realized that no one could possibly blame me for anything that might happen on that score. My protests would never have sufficed to stop Guido on the downward slope, unless they had been supported by all the other members of his family.

And so it came about that Guido continued gambling, and all his family with him. I was of their train too in the sense that I entered on a rather curious relationship with Nilini. I could not really endure him, because I knew him to be ignorant and conceited, but apparently I was so successful in hiding my real feelings (which I did for Guido's sake because he hoped for good tips from him), that he came to look on me as a devoted friend. I don't deny that it was partly my desire to avoid the uneasy sensation his dislike had produced in me, which made me nicer to him; a sensation that was increased by the sarcastic expression on his ugly face. But I did not carry my friendliness further than to shake hands with him and greet him when he came in or went out. He, on the other hand, was extremely friendly to me, and I could not help accepting his proffered courtesies gratefully; perhaps that is after all the greatest proof of politeness one can give in this world. He procured contraband cigarettes for me and only made me pay what they cost him, which was next to nothing. If he had been more sympathetic to me I might have been persuaded to use him as my intermediary for gambling on the Bourse, which I never did because I could not face having to see him often.

I saw him too much as it was! He spent hours at our office in spite of the obvious fact that he was not in love with Carmen. He actually came to keep me company. He had apparently taken it into his head to instruct me about politics, into which he had some insight owing to his activities on the Bourse. He represented the Great Powers to me as shaking each other cordially by the hand one day and boxing each other's ears the next. I don't know if he foretold what was coming, for I disliked him so much that I could never listen patiently to him. I kept a silly, fixed smile on my face all the time, which he misunderstood, and interpreted as a smile of admiration; but that was not my fault.

I only know that he repeated the same things every day. It was easy to see that he was not whole-heartedly Italian, from the fact that he thought Trieste had better

remain Austrian. He adored Germany, and above all
the German trains, which arrived with such marvelous
punctuality. He was in his way a Socialist, and would
have liked it to be illegal for any single individual to possess
more than a hundred thousand kronen. I did not smile
one day when, in conversation with Guido, he acknowledged that he possessed exactly one hundred thousand
kronen, and not a penny more. I did not smile, nor
even ask him whether he would have modified his theory
supposing he had made a great deal of money. Ours
was a very curious relationship. I could not bear to laugh
either with him or at him.

When he had fired off one of his theories he would
raise himself in his armchair so that his eyes were gazing
at the ceiling, while that strange gap between his two
jaws was aimed straight at me. I am sure he could see
with that gap! If ever I tried to take advantage of the
position he had got into in order to think of something
else, he would call me to attention by saying suddenly:
"Are you listening to what I am saying?"

After that effusion of Guido's which I found so
sympathetic it was a long time before he talked to me
again about his affairs. Nilini said something to me about
them first, but he also had become more reserved on the
subject. I heard from Ada that Guido was still making
money.

When she returned to Trieste I noticed that her looks
had gone off again very much. She had not exactly got
fatter, but her face had become puffy. Her cheeks, which
had filled out, seemed to have grown in the wrong place
again, and made her face look almost square. Her eyes
were bursting out of their sockets. I was very much
surprised, because Guido and several other people who
had been to see her said that she was getting stronger
and handsomer every day. But health in a woman is
surely above all her beauty.

Ada had other surprises in store for me. She greeted
me affectionately, but only in exactly the same way as
she had greeted Augusta. There was clearly no secret
between us any longer, and she had evidently forgotten
that she had ever wept at the thought of having caused
me to suffer. So much the better! She would have forgotten too that she had any claim on me! I was her

good brother-in-law, and she loved me solely because of
the terms of perfect affection I was on with my wife,
which always aroused the admiration of the Malfenti
household.

One day I made a discovery that suprised me extremely. Ada still believed herself to be beautiful! Away
there on the lake they had been paying court to her and
she was evidently proud of her successes. She probably
exaggerated them, for it seemed rather excessive to pretend that she had been obliged to leave her summer
retreat in order to escape the persecutions of a lover.
There may have been a grain of truth in it, I admit; for
she probably did not appear so ugly to anyone who had
not known her before. But there was not much in it,
surely, with those eyes and that complexion, and a face
that shape! She seemed, of course, uglier to us because
we remembered what she had been and could realize
what ravages her disease had made.

One evening we invited her and Guido to spend the
evening with us. It was a pleasant family gathering, a
kind of sequel to our twofold engagement. But the luster
was gone from Ada's hair.

When they got up to go, I was left a moment alone
with Ada, helping her into her coat. I at once had the
sense of a slight change in our relationship. We were
left alone and perhaps we should be able to say something to one another which the presence of the others
made impossible. While I helped her on with her coat
I was thinking it over, and finally made up my mind
what it was I wanted to say:

"You know that he has taken to gambling," I said
gravely. I sometimes wonder whether I did not hope by
these words to evoke the memory of our last meeting,
which I could not allow to be so lightly forgotten.

"Yes," she said smiling, "and he is quite right. He
is doing very well now, from all they tell me."

I smiled with her, whole-heartedly. I felt relieved of
all responsibility. As she left me, she murmured:

"Is that Carmen still in the office?"

She was gone before I had time to answer. Our past
no longer existed between us. But there was still her
jealousy, as lively as at our last meeting.

When I look back over it, I feel as if I ought to

have realized some time before I was actually told, that
Guido had begun losing on the Bourse. The triumphant
air disappeared from his face and it wore again that look
of anxiety which had appeared on it at the time of the
balance-sheet.

"Why do you worry about it?" I asked him innocently, "when you have already got all you need in
your pocket for covering those false entries. You need
never go to prison with all that money about you." At
that moment, as I discovered later, he had not a penny
in his pocket.

I believed so firmly in the fortune he was supposed
to have made that I paid no attention to all the indica-
tions that ought to have put me on the right track.

One evening in August he carried me off fishing
with him again. It was very unlikely that we should
succeed in catching anything, with a dazzling moon like
that. But he insisted on going, for he said we should
find it a little cooler out at sea. And that was in fact
all we found. After one attempt we did not even bait
our hooks again, but let our lines hang down from the
boat, while Luciano rowed it out to sea. The moon's
rays must have penetrated to the bottom of the sea,
lighting up all the wiles of the fisherman for the fishes
big and small, so that they only nibbled at the bait but
never let the hook come near them. Our bait only gave
them a little extra meal.

Guido was lying in the stern of the boat; I was in
the bow. After a while he murmured:

"How melancholy all this light is!"

He probably said so because the light prevented him
from sleeping, and I agreed, just to please him, and also
because I did not want to disturb the solemn peace of
that scene by any stupid argument. But Luciano protested, saying that he loved the bright light. As Guido did
not answer I tried to reduce him to silence by saying that
the light was certainly sad because it lit up this sad world
and also because it prevented us fishing. Luciano laughed
and said no more.

We were all silent for some time. I yawned in the
moon's face several times. I regretted having let myself
be persuaded to come out in the boat.

Suddenly Guido said:

"You're a chemist. You will be able to tell me which is the most efficacious—pure veronal, or veronal and sodium."

I did not even know there was such a thing as veronal and sodium. A chemist cannot be expected to know the whole world by heart. I know enough of chemistry to be able to look up anything in my books and even to discuss—as you will see in this case—things of which I know nothing.

Veronal and sodium? But everyone knows that compounds of sodium are the most easily assimilated of any. I remembered, and was able to reproduce more or less accurately, a hymn in praise of sodium which had been sung by one of my professors at the only one of his lectures I ever attended. Sodium was the vehicle on which all the other elements rode when they wanted to move more rapidly. The professor had shown how chlorate of sodium passed from body to body till it sank, by law of gravity, into the deepest hole in the world, namely the bottom of the sea. I don't know if I succeeded in reproducing exactly what the professor had said, but at that moment, with the spectacle of that immense quantity of chlorate of sodium in my mind's eyes, I spoke of sodium with infinite respect.

After a moment's hesitation, Guido said again:

"If one wanted to die, ought one to take veronal and sodium?"

"Yes," I replied.

Then, remembering that there are cases where one may want to simulate a suicide, and not at once realizing that I was reminding Guido of an unpleasant episode in his own life, I added:

"And if one doesn't want to die, one must take pure veronal."

Guido's exhaustive inquiries about veronal ought to have opened my eyes. But I at once became so interested myself in the possible uses of sodium that I did not notice anything odd. In the course of the next few days I was able to demonstrate to Guido by various new experiments that sodium really possessed the qualities I had attributed to it. You added sodium to mercury in order to facilitate the amalgamation of two bodies, this amalgamation being no other than a close embrace or union of bodies. Sodium, I showed, was the assimilating medium between gold and mercury. But Guido had already lost all interest in sodium, probably because his prospects on the Bourse were better at the moment.

Ada came three times to the office in the course of a single week. It was only after her second visit that it occurred to me she might have something to say to me.

The first time she came, she ran into Nilini, who had planted himself there in order to continue my political education. She waited a whole hour, expecting him to go; but she made the mistake of entering into conversation with him, so that he thought it his duty to stay on. After I had introduced them to each other I breathed a sigh of relief to see the gap between Nilini's jaws no longer turned toward me. I took no part in their conversation.

Nilini was quite witty, and astonished Ada by saying that there was just as much malicious gossip to be heard at the Tergesteo as in a fashionable drawing-room. With this difference, according to him, that they were better informed at the Bourse than elsewhere, on this as everything else. Ada thought he was being unfair to women, and said she had never heard any malicious gossip and did not know what he meant by it. At this point I intervened, and said that during all the years I had known her I had never heard a single unkind word come from her lips about anyone. I smiled as I said this, for I really intended it is a reproach. She did not talk against other people, for the simple reason that she took no interest whatever in anyone else's affairs. When she was well she had only thought about her own affairs, and when she became ill the very small corner she had kept for other things was entirely filled by her jealousy. She was an out and out egoist, but she accepted my words gratefully, as if they were really a tribute.

Nilini pretended not to believe either her or me. He said he had known me for many years and thought me a very naïve character. This amused both Ada and me. But I was very much irritated when, for the first time before a third party, he announced that I was one of his dearest friends and that therefore he must know me thoroughly. I did not dare to protest, but I felt my modesty as much offended by his impudent assertion as a girl who has been accused in public of having given herself to a man.

I was so naïve, declared Nilini, that Ada might easily, with a woman's well-known subtlety, have been as malicious as she liked in my presence without my being aware of it. I thought Ada was amused by his compliments, which seemed to me in very doubtful taste, but afterwards discovered that she had let him run on in the hope that he would exhaust his stock of eloquence and go away. She would have had to wait a long time for that!

The second time Ada came she found me with Guido. It was then that I noticed an expression of impatience on her face, and realized that it was really to me she wanted to talk. Till she returned the third time I indulged in my usual dreams. At bottom, it was not love she asked of me, but she too often wanted to be alone with me. It is difficult for men to know exactly what it is that women do want, for they often do not know themselves.

Her words excited no new feeling in me. Directly she had an opportunity of speaking to me her voice became strangled with emotion, but not because it was I to whom she was talking. She wanted to know why Carmen had not been sent away. I told her all I knew about it, including the effort we had made to find her a post in Olivi's office.

She at once grew calmer, for what I was saying corresponded exactly to what Guido had told her. I heard later that her fits of jealousy came on at regular intervals. They began without any apparent reason, and a reassuring word would be sufficient to dispel them again.

She asked me two more questions: Was it really so difficult to find a post for an employee like Carmen, and was her family obliged to depend entirely on her earnings?

I explained to her that it was in fact very difficult in Trieste just then to find jobs for women in offices. As for her second question, I was unable to answer it as I knew no other member of Carmen's family.

"And Guido knows the whole family," she muttered angrily, while the tears again streamed down her cheeks.

When she was going, she shook hands with me and thanked me. Smiling through her tears she said she knew

she could count on me. Her smile gave me pleasure,
because it was certainly not addressed to a brother-in-law,
but to someone who was bound to her by secret ties. I
tried to prove that I deserved such a smile and murmured:

"It is not so much Carmen I am afraid of for Guido,
it is his speculations on the Bourse."

She shrugged her shoulders:

"Oh, you need not worry about that. I talked to
Mamma about it. Papa used to speculate there too, and
made heaps and heaps of money."

I was rather taken aback by her reply, and insisted:

"I don't like that Nilini. It is not at all true that he is
a friend of mine."

She looked at me in surprise:

"He seems to be a gentleman. And Guido likes him
very much too. Besides, I think that Guido is very
careful in business now."

I had made up my mind never to say anything
against Guido, so I was silent. When I was alone again,
it was not of Guido I thought, but of myself. Perhaps it
was a good thing that Ada had at last come to seem
to me like a sister, and nothing else. She neither promised nor threatened me with anything in the nature of
love. For the next few days, however, I walked about the
streets in a very unsettled state of mind. Something
seemed to have upset my balance. I could not understand myself. Why did I feel exactly as if Carla had just
given me up? Nothing fresh had happened to me. I
honestly believe that I have always needed to be in the
middle of an adventure, or of some complication that
gives the illusion of one. Yet there was nothing in the
least complicated now in my relations with Ada.

One day Nilini was preaching louder than ever from
his armchair; there was a cloud upon the horizon; money
was growing dearer. The market had suddenly become
saturated and could not absorb any more.

"Let us throw in some sodium," I said flippantly.

He was not at all pleased at my interruption, but
pretended he had not heard, so as not to be obliged to
get angry and interrupt his sermon. He said there was
suddenly a shortage of money everywhere, so it had gone
up in price. He was only surprised at it happening just
now, whereas he had prophesied it for a month later.

"They must have packed all the money off to the moon!" I said.

Nilini did not deign to look at me, but went on staring at the ceiling.

"This is no laughing matter," he said. "It is extremely serious. Now we shall be able to see who is the real fighter, and who is going to give in at the first blow."

Just as I was quite unable to understand how there could possibly be a shortage of money in the world, so I never guessed that Nilini was numbering Guido among the fighting men who were to prove their valor. I was so accustomed to defend myself from his sermons by paying no attention to them, that even this one, which I actually listened to, passed over my head without making the smallest impression on me.

A few days later, however, Nilini began to sing to quite a different tune. He had made a discovery. He had found out that Guido was doing business with another broker. Nilini began protesting in an injured tone of voice that he had never failed Guido in anything, and that he had behaved with the utmost discretion. Could not I bear him out in this? Had he not always made a secret of Guido's affairs even to me whom he regarded as his dearest friend? But now he was going to throw all reserve to the winds and shout into my ears that Guido had lost everything and was up to his neck in debt. As far as the business was concerned which had been done through him, he asserted that it would recover with the smallest improvement in the situation, and they could afford to wait for better times. It was monstrous that the first time things went wrong Guido should have treated him like this.

Nilini's jealousy was far worse than Ada's. Nothing could appease him. I tried to get some definite facts out of him, but he only became more and more furious, and went on talking of the wrong that had been done him, so that, contrary to his own intentions and to my hopes, he remained perfectly discreet and gave nothing away.

That afternoon I found Guido in the office. He was lying at full length on the divan in a curious state between sleep and desperation. I said:

"Is it true that you are ruined up to the ears?"

He did not answer at once. He only raised his arm and covered his face with it. Then he said:

"Was there ever anyone more wretched than me?"

He lowered his arm and changed his position, turning over on his back. He shut his eyes again and seemed to have completely forgotten my presence.

I had no consolation to offer him. It made me quite angry that he should think himself the unhappiest man in the world; it was not even an exaggeration, it was a lie pure and simple. I would have helped him if I could, but to comfort him was out of the question. In my opinion, not even people who are more innocent and more unhappy than Guido deserve pity, otherwise there would be no room for anything but that feeling, which would be very tedious. The law of nature does not confer the right to be happy, on the contrary it condemns us to pain and suffering. Wherever the feast is spread parasites will flock to it from all parts, and if there are not enough of them they hasten to breed more. Soon there is only sufficient for the barest need, and very soon all is devoured, for nature does not calculate, she only makes experiments. When there is no more left the number of consumers must dwindle, by a process of pain and death, and thus the balance is restored for a moment. What is the use of complaining? Yet all do complain. Those who have had no share at all of the prey die arraigning the injustice of nature; those who have had their share feel that it ought to have been bigger still. Why don't they live and die in silence? On the other hand it is pleasant to see the joy of someone who had succeeded in securing a good share of the booty, and flaunts himself in the sun, amidst the plaudits of the crowd. The only cry I should allow is the cry of triumph.

But Guido! He not only lacked the power to conquer, but even to hold the riches he had got. He would come from the gaming-table and weep over his losses. He could not even behave like a gentleman; he sickened me. That was why, at the moment when he probably most stood in need of my sympathy, I had none to give him. Not all my many good resolutions could move me so far.

Meanwhile Guido's breathing was becoming gradually louder and more regular. He had fallen asleep! What an unmanly way to meet misfortune! They had stolen his booty and he quietly closed his eyes and dreamed, perhaps, that it was still in his possession, instead of opening them wide and trying to snatch back a small part of it.

I was curious to know whether Ada had been told of the calamity that had befallen him, and asked him in a loud voice. He started, and it was a few moments before he could accustom himself to his misfortune, which suddenly rose again before him to its full stature.

"No!" he murmured, and again closed his eyes.

I believe it is a fact that all who have received a violent blow have a tendency to sleep. Sleep restores one's strength. I stood a few moments irresolute, looking at Guido. If he insisted on sleeping how was one to help him? It was not the moment for sleep. I took hold of him roughly by the shoulder and shook him:

"Guido!" I said.

He had really been fast asleep. He looked at me doubtfully, his eyes still heavy with sleep, and asked:

"What is it?" Suddenly he got angry, and shouted out again: "What is it you want?"

I wanted to help him, otherwise I should have had no right to wake him up. I got angry too and shouted that this was not the moment for going to sleep; that we must get to work quickly and save what we could. We must decide what was to be done, and discuss it with all the members of our family here and in Buenos Aires.

Guido sat up at last. He was still rather disconcerted by my rough method of waking him. He said bitterly:

"It would have been much better if you had let me go on sleeping. Who do you imagine can help me now? Don't you remember what means I had to adopt last time in order to get the little I then needed to save me? But now it is a matter of very large sums of money. Who do you propose I should turn to now?"

I felt quite unsympathetic, even angry, at the thought that I should have to rob myself and my own family in order to help him.

"Aren't I still here?" I said. My avarice, however, at once stepped in to modify my first generous impulse:

"Isn't Ada still there? And your mother-in-law. Can't we all combine to save you?"

He rose and came toward me, evidently intending to embrace me. But I was determined to avoid that at all costs. Now that I had offered to help him I had a perfect

right to take him to task, and I made the utmost use of
it. I upbraided him for his weakness and for his conceit,
which had really been the cause of his ruin, and which he
was even yet not free from. He had acted just as he
thought fit, without consulting anybody. How often I had
tried to find out what he was engaged on, so that I might
restrain him if necessary, and save him from the very
danger into which he had fallen; and he had always refused
to tell me anything, and had persisted in confiding only in
Nilini.

At this Guido smiled; he actually smiled, poor man!
He said that for the last fortnight he had had nothing to
do with Nilini; he thought his ugly mug would bring him
ill-luck.

How characteristic of him that smile was, and that
falling asleep; he could ruin everyone belonging to him
and still go on smiling. I put on a very severe judicial air;
if I was going to save Guido I should have to educate
him first. I wanted to know how much he had lost, and
flew into a rage when he said he could not tell exactly. I
was still more furious when he named a relatively low
figure, which turned out to be the sum that must be paid
at the fortnightly settlement, which was only five days
ahead. Guido asserted that the end of the month was still
a long way off and things might easily change before
then. The shortage on the money market could hardly last
for ever.

I shouted:

"I suppose if there's a money shortage on the earth
you'll get some down from the moon!" I said he must not
go on gambling for a single day longer. His losses were
already huge and we must not take the risk of increasing
them. I said that his losses would have to be divided into
four parts, and borne by me, by him (that is to say his
father), Signora Malfenti, and Ada; that we must return
at once to sound, unspeculative business methods, and that
I refused ever to see Nilini or any other broker in our
office again.

He very gently asked me not to shout so much, because the neighbors might hear us.

I made a great effort to calm myself, and succeeded in
so far as only to go on abusing him under my breath. I
said it was positively criminal to lose as much as he had

done, and in such a way: one must be an absolute idiot
and worse, to get into such an impasse. I was determined
that not a word of my lecture should be lost on him.

But here Guido made a mild protest. Was there
anyone who had not at some time or other speculated on
the Bourse? Our father-in-law, for instance, who was such
a respectable business man, had not let a day pass without
some speculation. And then, Guido was sure, I had
speculated myself.

I protested that there was gambling and gambling. He
had staked the whole of his patrimony on the Bourse;
I had only staked a month's income.

Guido's childish attempts to shift his responsibilities
on to someone else made a melancholy impression on me.
He asserted that Nilini had induced him to play for much
higher stakes than he had ever meant to, by holding out
to him the hope of winning a great fortune.

I laughed and made fun of him. It was no use to
blame Nilini; he was only looking after his own interests.
Besides, after he had left Nilini, hadn't he plunged head-
long into still further losses through the medium of another broker? It would have been time enough to boast
of his new business connection if, unknown to Nilini, he
had begun speculating à la baisse. What was the use of
changing his broker only to pursue the same ill-fated policy
as before? Guido begged me at last to leave him in peace,
and with a sob in his throat acknowledged his error.

I left off attacking him. I was genuinely sorry for him
now, and would gladly have embraced him, if he had
allowed me. I said I would at once see about providing
my share of the money and that I would also undertake
to speak to our mother-in-law. He, for his part, was to tell
Ada all about it.

My pity for him increased when he confessed to me
that he would not mind speaking to his mother-in-law instead of me, but that he was tortured by the thought of
having to speak to Ada.

"You know what women are! They don't understand
business, or at least only when it turns out well." He said
he would prefer not to speak to Ada, but could ask her
mother to tell her what had happened instead.

This decision removed a great weight off his mind,
and we went out together. When I saw him walking

along beside me with his head drooping, I repented of
having been so cruel to him. But if one was fond of him,
what else could one do? He really must be brought to his
senses, or he would be totally ruined. What sort of terms
must he be on with his wife, if he was so afraid of speaking to her?

But he almost immediately contrived to enrage me
again. As we walked along he was engaged in perfecting
the plan he had thought so brilliant. Not only was there
no need for him to speak to his wife, but he would not
see her at all that evening, for he would go straight out
shooting. Having made this proposal he cast all care aside.
The mere thought of getting out into the open air and
leaving all his troubles behind was enough to restore him
completely, and drive every cloud from his brow. I was
furious with him! He might easily go back to the Bourse
with the same regardless air and play away the whole
remaining capital of his family and mine.

He said:

"I am going to allow myself this one last pleasure,
and I invite you to come too, on condition that you undertake not to say a single word that would remind me of
what has happened today."

Up to this point he had been talking gaily. But when
he saw my serious face, he became more serious too. He
added:

"You must agree that I need a little rest after such a
shock as this has been. It will be easier for me afterwards
to take my place again in the fight."

His voice trembled with emotion; I could not doubt
his sincerity, so that I succeeded in controlling my irritation, or only showed it in so far as to refuse his invitation,
saying that I must remain in town to see about collecting
the necessary funds. This was surely a reproof in itself! I,
the innocent one, must remain at my post, while he, the
culprit, could go off and amuse himself as he pleased.

We had already reached Signora Malfenti's front
door. His face had not resumed the joyous expression it
had worn before at the thought of the pleasant hours that
awaited him; so long as he was with me he kept on his face
the fixed expression of conventional grief which I had
called back to it. But before leaving me he gave vent to

his feelings by a display of independence which I felt was partly inspired by resentment.

He said he was surprised to find what a good friend he had in me. He hesitated to accept the sacrifice I had offered to make for him. He wished me definitely to understand that he did not consider me bound in any way whatever, and that I was free to give or not exactly as I thought fit.

I feel certain that I blushed. To escape from my embarrassment I said:

"Why should you imagine I want to withdraw, when only a few minutes ago I offered to help you, without your having asked anything of me?"

He looked at me rather doubtfully and said:

"Since you wish it I accept without more ado. Thank you. But we must make a fresh contract, and each of us must receive the share he deserves. So that from henceforth, if business comes our way and you are willing to go on dealing with it, you must have a proper salary. Yes, we must put the company on a totally different basis. Then there can be no danger of any trouble accruing to us from our suppression of last year's losses. It will only have been a lesson to us."

"It's no use your thinking any more about those losses; we have finished with that. What you have to do now is to try and win over your mother-in-law. That is all that matters."

And so we parted. I have no doubt I smiled at the naïveté with which Guido had betrayed to me his inmost feelings. He had made all that long speech solely in order that he might accept my gift, without having to show me too much gratitude. But I did not demand it of him. It was quite enough for me to know that he really owed it.

For my part, as soon as I had parted from him I felt a sense of relief as well, as if I too had just escaped into the open air. I felt I had regained the freedom I had lost when I set about trying to educate Guido and put him on the right path. The teacher is really much more chained than the pupil. I had fully made up my mind to get the money for him. It is difficult for me to say whether I was really doing it out of affection for him or for Ada, or perhaps also because I felt that a certain responsibility might attach to me for having worked in his office. In any case I resolved to sacrifice part of my own fortune, and even today I look back on that moment in my life with great satisfaction. The money would save Guido and procure me a quiet conscience.

I walked about till dark in this exalted frame of mind, and then found it was too late to catch Olivi at the Bourse. I was obliged to apply to him in order to get a large sum of money. Then I decided that it was not really so urgent. I had a certain amount of money at my disposal which would be enough to cover the fortnightly settlement. There was plenty of time for me to take all the necessary steps before the end of the month.

I put Guido out of my mind for the whole evening. Later on, after the children had been put to bed, I several times made up my mind to tell Augusta about Guido's financial collapse and how it was going to affect me, but I hated the thought of discussing it, and decided it would be better to wait for Augusta to give her consent when everything had been arranged, and the settlement of Guido's affairs was in full swing. Besides, I did not see why I should have all this tiresome business just when Guido was out amusing himself.

I slept perfectly and went to the office next morning with rather a light purse. I still had in my pocket the old envelope that Carla had returned to me and which I was saving up religiously for her or for one of her children, and I had drawn a little money from the bank. I spent the morning reading the papers, while Carmen sat sewing and Luciano employed himself in various feats of multiplication and addition.

When I went home to lunch I found Augusta quite bewildered and cast down. She was very pale, as she always was on occasions when I had made her suffer. She said to me gently:

"I hear that you have decided to sacrifice part of your fortune to save Guido! I know I had no right to have been told."

She was so doubtful about her right that she hesitated. Then she began to reproach me for not having told her.

"But I am not like Ada. I have never opposed your will in any way."

It was some time before I discovered what had happened. Augusta had arrived at Ada's house just when she was in the middle of discussing Guido with her mother. When she saw her, Ada had burst out crying and told her of my generous offer, which she absolutely refused to accept. She had begged Augusta to ask me not to persist in it.

I saw at once that Augusta was suffering from her old malady, jealousy of her sister; but I took no notice of it. Ada's attitude surprised me.

"Do you think she was offended?" I asked, pretending to look very surprised.

"No! no! Not offended!" cried the straightforward Augusta. "She hugged and kissed me . . . perhaps it was really meant for you!"

That seemed an odd enough way of expressing herself. She kept her eyes fixed on me suspiciously, as if she were trying to read my thoughts.

I protested.

"Do you really believe Ada is in love with me? What can have put that into your head?"

But I could not succeed in pacifying Augusta, whose jealousy I found terribly tiresome. It was true that Guido had stopped enjoying himself by then, and was no doubt having a horrible time between his wife and his mother-in-law; but I was having a sufficiently bad time myself, and I could not help feeling my sufferings were disproportionately great, seeing that I was entirely innocent.

I tried to calm Augusta by caressing her. But she drew her face away, so that she could look at me better, and uttered a gentle reproof, which moved me deeply.

"I know you love me too," she said.

It was clearly not Ada's state of mind, but mine, that she was troubled about. I suddenly had an inspiration that I thought must prove my innocence.

"So Ada is in love with me?" I said laughing. Then, drawing away a little from Augusta so that she could see me better, I puffed out my cheeks and opened my eyes very wide so as to make myself look like Ada. Augusta gazed at me in astonishment for a moment, but soon guessed what I was doing. She burst out laughing, but at once felt ashamed of herself.

"No!" she said; "please don't laugh at her."

Then she admitted, still laughing, that I had succeeded in imitating exactly the bulges that gave Ada's face
such an odd appearance. And I knew that I had, for while
I was imitating her I had actually felt as if I were kissing
Ada. And when I was by myself I repeated the process with
a mingled feeling of desire and disgust.

In the afternoon I went to the office hoping to find
Guido there. I waited for some time, then decided to go
and look for him at his house. It was necessary that I
should know whether or not I was to ask Olivi for the
money. I must fulfill my duty, painful though the prospect
was of seeing Ada's face still more distorted in her efforts
to express her gratitude. Who knows what surprises that
woman still had in store for me!

On the steps leading up to Guido's house I ran into
Signora Malfenti who was ponderously ascending. She
told me at great length everything that had been decided
about Guido's affairs up to then. When they separated
the evening before they had almost agreed that it was
essential to do all they could to save that unfortunate man
from the ruin that threatened him. It was not till the next
morning that Ada discovered I was proposing to collaborate in covering Guido's losses, and then she absolutely
refused to accept. Signora Malfenti tried to make excuses
for her.

"What are you going to do about it? She cannot
reconcile it with her conscience to rob her favorite sister."

At the top of the first flight of steps the Signora
stopped to get breath, to enable her to go on talking. She
said with a smile that everything would turn out well for
everybody concerned. Before lunch she and Ada and Guido
had gone to consult a solicitor, an old friend of the family
who was now little Anna's guardian. The solicitor had said
there was no need to pay; gambling-debts did not come
under the law. Guido had taken the opposite point of
view, and talked about honor and duty, but she was sure
that if everyone, including Ada, decided not to pay, he
could very soon fall into line.

"But will his business be declared bankrupt on the
Bourse?" I asked in bewilderment.

"Probably it will!" replied Signora Malfenti, with a
sigh, before climbing the last flight.

Guido was in the habit of lying down after lunch, so

that we were received by Ada in the little boudoir I knew
so well. When she saw me she betrayed a moment's uneasiness; only a moment, but enough for me to notice
and remember, for it was as clear as if she had confessed
it to me herself. Then she made an effort to control herself, and offered me her hand with a decided, almost virile
movement, which seemed meant to contradict the feminine hesitation that had preceded it.

She said:

"Augusta will have told you how grateful I am to you.
I feel too bewildered at the moment to express to you
what I really feel. I am ill too. Yes, I am very ill! I ought
really to go into the nursing-home again at Bologna."

A sob interrupted her. Then she went on:

"I want to ask you one favor. Please tell Guido that
you find you can't let him have any money. It will make
it much easier for us to persuade him to do what ought to
be done."

She had sobbed before, thinking of her own illness;
she sobbed again now, before going on to talk about her
husband:

"He is only a child, and must be treated as such. If
he knows that you are ready to let him have that money,
he will cling all the more obstinately to his idea of throwing away the rest, quite uselessly, for now we know for a
certainty that a bankruptcy on the Bourse is not illegal.
The solicitor told us so."

She gave me the opinion of a high financial authority
without ever asking for mine. As an old *habitué* of the
Bourse I thought that my opinion might have had some
weight alongside that of the solicitor, but I quite forgot
what my opinion was, even if I had ever had one. It was
obvious to me, however, that I was put in an awkward
position. I could not back out of the promise I had made
Guido; it was in return for that promise that I had thought
myself authorized to shout so many insults in his ear,
pocketing thereby a sort of interest on the capital that it
was thus impossible for me to refuse him.

"Ada!" I said hesitatingly, "I don't think I can go
back on my word like this, from one day to another.
Wouldn't it be better if you tried to persuade Guido to
do things as you want them done?"

Signora Malfenti, with the peculiar sympathy she

always showed me, said that she understood perfectly well the situation in which I found myself, but that she thought when Guido discovered he could only obtain a quarter of the money he needed he would be obliged to submit with a good grace to their will.

But Ada had not yet exhausted her supply of tears. With her face hidden in her handkerchief, she said between her sobs:

"You did very, very wrong to make him such an extraordinary offer. Now one sees what a great mistake you made!"

She seemed to me to waver between gratitude and resentment. Then she said she did not want my offer ever to be mentioned again, and begged me not to procure the money for him, for if I did she would not let me give it him, or would forbid Guido to accept it.

I felt so embarrassed that I ended by telling a lie. I told her that I had already procured the money, and pointed to my breast pocket where that very light envelope was lying. Ada looked at me now with an expression of genuine admiration which might have given me pleasure if I had not known how little I deserved it. In any case it was that lie, for which I can give no other explanation than my strange tendency to try and appear to Ada better than I really was, that prevented my waiting for Guido and made me get out of the house as quickly as possible. It might easily have happened that, contrary to all expectation, I should have been asked to hand over the money I said I actually had with me, and what sort of a figure should I have cut then? I explained that I had urgent business at the office, and hurried out of the house.

Ada accompanied me to the door and assured me that she would persuade Guido to come to me himself and thank me for my kindness, refusing at the same time to accept it. She made this statement with so much determination that I was quite startled. I could not help feeling that so definite a resolution was aimed in part also at me. No! at that moment she certainly did not love me. My generosity had been too great. It threatened to overwhelm those whom it was supposed to benefit, and it was no wonder if they rose up and protested. On my way to the office I tried to shake off the unpleasant impression that Ada's behavior had made on me, by reminding myself that the sacrifice I proposed to make concerned Guido and no one else. What had Ada to do with it? I promised myself to make Ada see this at the earliest opportunity.

I went to the office simply in order to avoid having another lie on my conscience. A fine rain had been falling since the early morning, which had made the air very chilly; spring was slow in coming. A few steps would have taken me home, whereas to reach the office I had to walk down a much longer street, which in itself was sufficiently annoying. But I thought I had a duty to fulfill.

Guido joined me shortly afterwards. He sent Luciano away, so as to remain alone with me. He had on that agonized air which was such a help to him in his disputes with his wife, and which I knew only too well. He had evidently been crying, and shouting too.

He asked me what I thought about his wife and mother-in-law's plan, which he knew I had already been told of. I was not very ready with my reply. I did not want to tell him my opinion, which was contrary to that of the two women, and at the same time I knew that if I were to agree with them I should only provoke fresh scenes with Guido. I hated to seem to grudge him my assistance, and agreed on the whole with Ada that the decision ought to come from Guido and not from me. I said that we must make some calculations and work things out and hear what other people had to say about it. I was not a good enough business man to be able to pronounce an opinion on such an important matter. To gain time, I asked him if he would like me to consult Olivi.

This was enough to make him scream:

"That idiot! I beg you to leave him out of the question!"

I did not feel in the least inclined to work myself up in defense of Olivi, but my calmness had no effect on Guido. We were in a precisely similar situation to that of the day before, only now it was his turn to scream and mine to be silent. It is a matter of temperament; I felt so very awkward that all my limbs were absolutely paralyzed.

But he insisted on my saying exactly what I thought about it. So I began to speak and, by an almost divine inspiration, spoke very well; so well that if he had paid the smallest attention to what I said the subsequent catastrophe would never have happened. I said that I was inclined for the moment to consider the two questions separately, that of the fortnightly and that of the monthly settlement. Not such a very large sum was required for the former and one must induce the two women to consent to that relatively light loss. Then we should still have plenty of time before us to make wise provision for the other settlement.

Guido interrupted me to say:

"Ada told me that you have got the money all ready in your pocket. Have you got it with you now?"

I blushed. But I speedily found another lie which saved me:

"As they would not accept the money when I was at your house, I deposited it at the bank. But we can draw it out again as soon as we like; early tomorrow morning, if necessary."

He reproached me for having changed my mind. And only the day before I had declared that everything could be put in order at once, and that there was no need to wait for the second settlement! Here he was overtaken by a violent fit of rage and finally sank helpless on to the sofa. He would chuck Nilini out of the office, and all those other brokers who had encouraged him to speculate. Oh! when he had begun speculating he had foreseen, of course, that he might be ruined, but not that he would come under the thumb of women who understood nothing, less than nothing about it!

I went up and shook him by the hand. If he had let me, I would have embraced him. All that I had ever wanted was that he should make up his mind, as he had done now, to give up gambling and settle down to regular work. Then our future would be secure, and he would regain his independence. He would have a short, difficult time to go through first, but after that everything would be quite simple and straightforward.

He left me soon afterwards still depressed, but calmer. Weak though he was, he seemed to have come to a definite decision.

"I am going back to Ada," he murmured, with a bitter but confident smile.

I accompanied him to the door, and would have gone all the way home with him, but his carriage was waiting for him outside.

Nemesis seemed to pursue Guido. Half an hour after he had left me I thought it would be wise if I were to go to his house and see if there was anything I could do for him. Not that I thought he was in any particular danger, but I was now entirely on his side, and might have helped to persuade Ada and Signora Malfenti to help him. A bankruptcy on the Bourse was not at all to my taste, and all things considered, though his losses were by no means insignificant even if divided between four of us, they were not enough to ruin any of us.

Then I reflected that my chief duty at the moment was not so much to assist Guido by my presence as to have ready the sum I had promised him for the following day. I at once went in search of Olivi, and prepared myself for a fresh struggle. I had thought out a system of paying back the large sum to my firm, over a period of several years, though I should be obliged during the next few months to spend whatever remained over of the money I had inherited from my mother. I hoped Olivi would not make any difficulties, for up to that time I had never asked for anything but my share of the profits and the interest due to me, and I could undertake not to worry him again with similar requests. It was clear that I might hope to recover from Guido at least a part of the sum.

I was unable to find Olivi that evening. He had only just left the office when I got there. They thought he had probably gone to the Bourse. But I could not find him there, so went on to his house, where I heard that he was at a meeting of the Economic Association, in which he occupied an honorary post. I might have gone on to look for him there, but by now it was getting late, and the rain was falling heavily and uninterruptedly, turning the roads into streams of water.

The deluge continued all night, and was remembered for many years as a record. The rain went on falling steadily, without a moment's cessation; pouring, pouring down in sheets. The mud was washed down from the hills that surround the city on all sides, and combined with the refuse of the streets to block up the few canals. I decided at last to go home, after waiting vainly under shelter for the rain to stop, and finally making up my mind that it was useless to hope for a change in the weather; but even where the pavement was highest I had to wade through water. I hurried home as fast as I could, soaked to the skin and cursing the weather. I was cursing partly at having spent all that long time in hunting for Olivi. I can well believe that my time is not so very precious, but I know I suffer horribly when I have to waste it in some useless occupation. As I hurried along, I thought to myself: "I will leave everything till tomorrow, when it will have cleared and be fine and dry again. Tomorrow I will go to Olivi, tomorrow I will go and see Guido. I will get up as early as you please, if only the weather is dry and fine." I was so convinced of the reasonableness of this view that I told Augusta we had all agreed to wait till the next day before making any decision. I changed into dry clothes and nice, warm, comfortable slippers, and after supper went early to bed and slept soundly and dreamlessly till morning, while the heavy rain whipped the window panes without ceasing.

So that it was getting late before I heard what had happened during the night. First we were told that the rain had caused floods in various parts of the town, and then that Guido was dead.

It was not till much later in the day that I heard what had really happened. At about eleven o'clock, when Signora Malfenti had left them, Guido told his wife that he had swallowed an enormous quantity of veronal. He tried to convince her that all was over with him. He kissed her again and again, and implored her to forgive him for having made her suffer. Then, before his speech became incoherent and almost inaudible, he assured her that she had been the only love of his life. She did not believe this assurance, any more than she believed he had really taken enough veronal to kill him. Nor did she believe he had really become unconscious; she imagined he was only pretending, so as to get more money out of her.

But after an hour, when she saw him sink deeper and deeper into sleep, a kind of terror seized her, and she wrote a note to a doctor who lived not far from their house. In the note she said that her husband was in need of immediate help, as he had swallowed a large quantity of veronal.

Up to then there had been nothing to warn the servant that anything was wrong; she was an old woman

who had only been with them a short time, and she had
no idea of the nature of her mission.

The rain was responsible for the rest. The servant was
almost up to her knees in water, and lost the note. She
only discovered this when she was actually shown in to
the doctor. But she succeeded in persuading him that it
was urgent, and induced him to go back with her.

Dr. Mali was a man of about fifty-five, not the least
clever, but a practical doctor who had always done his
duty as well as he could. His regular practice was not very
large, but he had a great deal of work to do for a society
that had a very large membership, and for which his fees
were very small indeed. He had not been home long, and
had just succeeded in drying and warming himself by the
fire. One can imagine how reluctant he was to tear himself away from his warm, snug corner. When I was trying
to unravel the causes of my poor friend's death I made a
point of getting to know Dr. Mali. All I could gather from
him was this: that when he got outside the door and
felt the rain soaking him actually through his umbrella,
he repented having studied medicine instead of agricul-
ture, for the peasant, he said to himself, stops at home
when it rains.

When he reached Guido's bedside, he found Ada
much relieved. Now that she had the doctor there it was
easier for her to remember what a trick Guido had played
on her a few months ago, when he pretended to commit
suicide. She was able now to shift all responsibility on to
the doctor, to whom she gave a full account of what had
happened, and of the reasons that led her to think this
might also be a false alarm. The doctor took it all in with
one ear, and listened with the other to the torrents of rain
pouring down the street. As he had not been warned that
it was a case of poisoning, he had brought with him none
of the instruments necessary for treating the case. He
stammered a few words of excuse which Ada could not
hear. The worst of it was that he could not send anyone
else to fetch the stomach pump he needed; he would have
had to wade twice through that flood himself. He felt
Guido's pulse and found it excellent. He asked Ada
whether Guido was accustomed always to sleep very
soundly. She said yes, but not as soundly as that. The

doctor then examined Guido's eyes; they at once reacted
to the light. He finally left, after having recommended
her to give him a spoonful of very strong coffee from time
to time.

I heard also that when he had got down to the street
and was setting off home again, he muttered furiously:

"It ought to be illegal to pretend one has committed
suicide in weather like this!"

When I heard all this from the doctor I did not dare
to reproach him openly for his carelessness; but he guessed
what I was thinking, and began defending himself. He
said he was so astonished when he heard next morning
that Guido was dead, that he thought at first he must have
come to, and taken another dose of veronal. It was impossible, he said, for a layman to realize how used the doctor
becomes to protecting himself against his patients, who
are continually making attempts on his life, in their selfish
insistence on saving their own.

After about an hour, Ada got tired of trying to force
the spoonful of coffee between Guido's teeth, and noticing that he absorbed less and less of it, and that most of
it went onto the pillow, she took fright again and begged
the servant to go for Dr. Paoli. This time the servant managed not to lose the note. But she took more than an hour
getting to the doctor's house. When it is raining like that
one naturally feels one must stop from time to time and
take shelter under a porch. Rain like that does not only
soak, it positively scourges one.

Dr. Paoli was not at home. He had been called out by
a patient a little while before, and had gone off saying
he hoped to be back before long. But it looked as if he
had chosen to wait at the patient's house for the rain to
stop. His housekeeper, who was a kind elderly person, insisted on Ada's servant sitting down by the fire and getting
thoroughly warm. The doctor had not left his patient's address, so the two women spent several hours sitting by the
fire together. The doctor did not come back till the rain
had stopped, and day was breaking when he at last got to
Ada, armed with the necessary instruments. But only one
task remained for him now; to hide from Ada that Guido
was already dead, and to get Signora Malfenti to come,
without Ada realizing it, so that she might help her in her
first access of grief.

And so it happened that the news reached us rather late and without many details.

As I got out of bed, anger surged up in me for the last time against poor Guido: how he complicated every misfortune by playing the fool like that! I left the house alone, for Augusta could not leave the baby to its own devices. When I got outside, I hesitated for a moment. Hadn't I better wait till the bank opened and Olivi would be in his office, so as to be able to appear before Guido armed with the money I had promised? So little did I believe really that things were as bad with Guido as they were reported to be.

I heard the full truth from Dr. Paoli, whom I met as I went upstairs. I was so startled that I almost fell down the stairs backwards. Ever since we had spent so much of our time together Guido had been a very important person to me. So long as he was alive I saw him in a peculiar light, and in that light part of my days was passed. When he died the light was suddenly refracted as though it had passed through a prism. It was that which dazzled me so much at first. He had had many faults, but I saw at once that now he was dead nothing remained of them. In my opinion the wit who, in a cemetery full of laudatory epitaphs, asked where the sinners were buried, was a fool. The dead never have been sinners. Guido was pure now. Death had purified him.

The doctor was deeply moved by Ada's sorrow. He told me something of the horrible night she had lived through. They had succeeded at last in making her believe that the amount of poison which Guido had swallowed must have been fatal; that nothing could have saved him. She must on no account discover the real truth.

"The truth is," the doctor, shaking his head, "that if I had arrived a few hours sooner I could have saved him. I found the bottles still full of poison."

I examined them. It was certainly a strong dose, but not much stornger than the first time. He showed me several little bottles, all labeled: "Veronal." Not veronal and sodium then. I could appreciate the significance of this better than anyone. I knew now that Guido had not intended to kill himself. But I have never said a word to anyone.

Paoli left soon after, warning me not to try and see

Ada for the moment. He had prescribed a strong sleeping-draught and did not doubt that it would soon take effect.

As I stood in the passage I heard a subdued lamentation coming from the little room where Ada had twice received me. From time to time I heard a few unintelligible, grief-stricken words. The word "he" was repeated several times, and I tried to picture what she might be saying. She was trying to set up a new relationship between herself and the dead man. It would have to be very different from the one she had had with the living. It was clear to me that she had sinned against her husband while he was alive. He had died for a sin that they had all committed, for he had gambled on the Bourse with the approval of them all. It was only when it came to paying up that they had left him alone. And he had made haste to pay. I had had nothing to do with it, yet I alone of all his relations had felt it was my duty to help him.

Poor Guido was lying all alone in their bedroom, covered by the sheet. The *rigor mortis* was already far advanced. There was no sense of strength in that rigidity, only an immense surprise at being dead without having wished to die. His dark, handsome face seemed to wear a reproachful expression; but the reproach could not be intended for me.

I went back to Augusta, to urge her to go and be with her sister. I was deeply moved and Augusta burst into tears and embraced me.

"You have been a brother to him," she murmured. "I quite agree with you now, and am ready to sacrifice part of our fortune to keep his memory pure."

I took pains that every honor should be paid to my poor friend. First of all I put up a notice on the office door, announcing that the office was closed on account of the death of the chief. I myself composed the obituary notice. The arrangements for the funeral were not made till the following day, and Ada herself took part in them. Then I was told that she had decided to follow his coffin to the grave. She wanted to give him every possible proof of her affection. Poor thing! I knew only too well what terrible pangs of remorse one may suffer beside a grave. I had suffered enough myself at the death of my father.

I spent the afternoon shut up in the office with Nilini. We were engaged in drawing up a provisional balance-sheet. The situation was really terrible! Not only was the entire capital of the firm lost, but Guido owed as much again, if his debts were to be paid in full.

I ought to have put all my energies into working for my poor dead friend, but I found I could do nothing but dream. My first thought had been to give up my whole life to working in that office for the sake of Ada and her children. But should I really be able to carry it through?

Nilini, as usual, went on chattering, while I was looking far ahead into the future. He too felt the need now of a fundamental change in his relations with Guido. He understood it all now! When he treated him so unfairly poor Guido was already stricken by the disease that was to lead him to commit suicide. Everything was forgiven and forgotten!

"I am made like that," he said. "I can't bear ill-will against anyone. I was always fond of Guido, and I still am."

Nilini's dreams ended by mingling with mine and imposing themselves upon me. There was no hope of repairing a catastrophe like this by slow business methods; the only hope was in fresh speculations on the Bourse. Nilini went on to tell me about a friend of his who had saved himself at the very last moment by doubling his stakes.

We spent several hours in conversation, but Nilini's proposal to carry on Guido's gamble was made shortly before midday, and I at once agreed to it. My joy in accepting it was almost as great as if I had succeeded in bringing my friend to life again. I ended by buying, in poor Guido's name, a number of new shares with such odd titles as Rio Tinto, Southern France, etc.

This was the beginning of forty-eight hours of the hardest work I have ever done in my life. I stayed at the office till evening, pacing up and down with great strides, waiting to hear if my orders had been carried out. I was afraid the news of Guido's suicide might already have reached the Bourse, and that they might refuse to do any more business in his name. But, as it turned out, they did not put his death down to suicide till several days later.

When Nilini finally told me that all my orders had been carried out there began for me a time of terrible anxiety, increased by the fact that at the very moment of receiving the purchase papers I was told that I had already

lost quite a lot on what I had bought. When I look back
on it, the very anxiety I felt produces on me the impression
of actual work. I have the curious sensation of having sat
for forty-eight hours on end at the gaming-table trying to
exercise a magnetic influence on the cards. I noted every
fluctuation in the prices, I brooded over it and, if I must
tell the truth, willed it up or down according as it best
suited me, or rather my poor friend. I got no sleep at
all.

Fearing lest some member of the family might step
in and interfere with the work of salvation I had taken
upon myself, I spoke to no one about the fortnightly settlement, when it came. I paid it all myself, for everyone
else had forgotten about it, busy as they were in preparing
the corpse for burial. As a matter of fact I had less to
pay than had been supposed in Guido's lifetime. The tide
had suddenly begun to turn in my favor. My grief at
Guido's death had been so great that I thought I might mitigate it somewhat by taking every possible risk both with the
money of my firm and my own personal money. I was
sustained by that vision of benevolence which had inspired me long ago at Guido's side. But I suffered so intensely from the state of agitation I lived in at this time,
that I have never again gambled on my own account.

In consequence of poring over the money market,
my only occupation during those few days, I was actually
not present at Guido's funeral. This was how it happened.
The shares we were interested in took an upward leap
that very day. Nilini and I spent all our time in working
out how much of our losses we had won back. Old
Speier's fortune was now only reduced by half, a magnificent result that filled me with pride! Exactly what
Nilini had predicted had now taken place. It was true that
his original prophecy had been made in a very doubtful
tone, but now this naturally vanished and he repeated it
with the utmost confidence. I remembered that he had
foreseen what actually happened, but also the exact opposite, so that it was impossible for him to be in the wrong;
but I did not say so to him, for it was essential to me that
he should work at the business with the whole energy of
his ambition. I hoped that his will might influence the
prices too.

We left the office at three, and set off at a run, for

we had just remembered that the funeral was to take place at a quarter past three.

When we got to the top of the Volti di Chiozza, I saw the procession in the distance, and even thought I recognized a carriage that a friend had put at Ada's disposal for the funeral. Nilini and I leapt into a cab and told the driver to follow in the procession. We went on talking about our speculations all the way. Our thoughts were so far from our dead friend that we even complained because the carriage went so slow. Who knows what might be happening on the Bourse, now that we were no longer there to keep an eye on it? Suddenly Nilini looked me straight in the face, an unusual thing for him, and asked me why I did not gamble at all on my own account. I blushed, I don't quite know why.

"For the moment," I said, "I am only working for my friend."

Then, after pausing a moment, I added:

"I will think of myself later." I wanted to encourage him in the hope that he might be able to induce me to gamble, simply because I was bent on keeping him friendly for the moment. But meanwhile I was saying to myself what I did not dare say to him: "I will never put myself in your hands!" He went on with his sermon:

"Who knows if you will ever have such an opportunity again," he said. He forgot that he himself had taught me there were fresh opportunities on the Bourse every hour.

When we reached the place where the carriages generally stop, Nilini put his head out of the window and gave a cry of surprise. Our cab was still following the procession, which seemed to be going on to the Greek cemetery.

"Was Guido a Greek Catholic?" he asked in surprise. And the procession was, in fact, passing the Catholic cemetery and proceeding toward one of the others, Jewish, Greek, Protestant, or Serbian.

"Can he have been a Protestant!" I wondered. But I at once remembered having gone to his marriage in the Catholic Church.

"It must be a mistake!" I exclaimed, thinking for a moment that they were going to bury Guido in the wrong place.

Nilini suddenly burst out laughing, and laughed so unrestrainedly that he fell back helpless on the back of the seat, with his huge mouth wide open, seeming to fill the whole of his little face.

"We have made a mistake," he said. When he at last succeeded in bridling his mirth, he overwhelmed me with reproaches. I ought to have noticed where we were going. Surely I must have known what time it was to be, and might have been expected to recognize the people. It was someone else's funeral!

I was in a great state of irritation. I had not shared his mirth, and found his reproaches hard to bear. Why hadn't he kept a better lookout himself? I suppressed my vexation simply because the Bourse was of more importance to me than the funeral. We got out of the carriage to see where we were, and made our way toward the entrance into the Catholic cemetery. Our carriage followed us. I noticed that the survivors of the other dead person looked at us with surprise, unable to explain to themselves why, after having accompanied him so far, we abandoned him at the very last moment.

Nilini went on ahead impatiently. He said to the porter, after a moment's hesitation:

"Has Signor Guido Speier's funeral procession arrived yet?"

The porter did not seem surprised by the question, though I thought it rather comic. He replied that he could not say. He only knew there had been two funerals in the cemetery during the last half-hour.

We took counsel together in our perplexity. There was evidently no means of discovering whether the funeral was already inside the cemetery or not. Then I made up my mind. It was obviously impossible for me to burst into the middle of the service, which perhaps had already begun, and interrupt it. So I decided I would not enter the cemetery at all. On the other hand I could not risk meeting the procession on my way back. So I gave up all thought of taking part in the burial and decided to go back to the town, making a long detour beyond Servola. I left the carriage to Nilini, who wanted at least to put in an appearance, because he knew Ada.

I walked fast so as to avoid meeting anyone, and joined the country road leading to the village. I no longer minded having made a mistake about the funeral, and not having paid the final honors to poor Guido. I had no time to waste in religious practices. I had another duty to perform: I must save the honor of my friend and defend his inheritance for the sake of his widow and children. When I told Ada that I had succeeded in retrieving three-quarters of his losses (I ran through the whole account again in my mind: Guido had lost his father's fortune twice over and now, after my intervention, that fortune was only reduced by half; so I really had recovered three-quarters of his losses), she would certainly forgive me for not being present at his funeral.

The weather had become glorious again. The air was soft and delicious, and the countryside, still wet from the recent rain, was bathed in brilliant sunshine. After being confined to the office for so many days, my lungs expanded and I found it delightful to exercise my limbs. I was full of health and strength. Health is all a matter of comparison. I compared myself with poor Guido, and rose victorious from the same battle in which he lay vanquished. Everything around me seemed to breathe out health and energy. Everywhere the young, green grass was springing; the catastrophic floods of a few days ago had sunk into the frozen earth, which now drank rapturously the sun-rays it had waited for so long. Yet if that blue sky were to remain long without a cloud, it too would become hateful. It is only now as I write that I make this observation drawn from everyday experience; it did not strike me then. At that moment my soul was filled with joy: joy in my own well-being and in the perennial well-being of nature.

I quickened my steps. I rejoiced to feel myself so light and free. As I came down the hill into Servola I almost broke into a run. When I reached the promenade of Sant' Andrea I slackened my pace again, but I still had a marvelous sense of ease. The air seemed to bear me along.

I had completely forgotten that I was coming from the funeral of my dearest friend. My whole being breathed victory. But my elation was a homage to my poor friend's memory; it was for his sake that I had entered the lists.

I went to the office to look at the closing prices. They were a little slacker, but not enough to damp my as-

surance. I was determined to go on speculating, and did
not doubt of attaining my end.

I was compelled at last to go to Ada's house. Augusta came to open the door to me. She said at once:

"Whatever can have possessed you not to come to
the funeral? and you, the only man in the family!"

I put down my hat and umbrella, and said, in some
perplexity, that I should like to speak to Ada and her together, so as not to have to repeat myself. But meanwhile
I could assure her that I had a very good reason for missing the funeral. I no longer felt quite so confident as
before, and suddenly my side began to pain me again,
perhaps because I was tired. It must have been that Augusta's remark made me doubt the possibility of explaining my absence, which was naturally regarded as scandalous; in my mind's eye I could see before me all who
had taken part in that gloomy function distracted for a
moment from their grief by the speculation as to where
I could possibly be.

Ada never came. I heard later that she had not even
been told I was waiting to see her. I was received by Signora Malfenti, who began speaking to me in a severe
tone such as I had never known her to use before. I
muttered some excuses, but I was very far from feeling
as sure of myself as I had been during my rapid flight
from the cemetery to the town. I stammered as I began
to tell her a few half truths about what I had been doing
in my attempt to rehabilitate Guido, and said that quite
a short while before the hour of the funeral I had been
obliged to wire some instructions to Paris, and had not
felt I could leave the office till I received an answer. It
was true that Nilini and I had been obliged to telegraph
to Paris, but it had been two days ago, and we had also
received the reply two days ago. But I realized that the
truth was not a sufficient excuse, perhaps because it was
impossible for me to tell it all, or to talk about what I
regarded as my most important operation: my attempt
to influence the world exchanges by will-power. But Signora Malfenti forgave me when she heard the amount by
which I had already reduced Guido's losses. She thanked
me with tears in her eyes. I again became not only the
one man in the family, but the best one. She asked me

to come with Augusta in the evening to see Ada. She would meanwhile tell her all about it. For the moment she was not in a condition to receive anyone. I went off only too gladly with my wife. She did not feel it necessary either, to say good-by to Ada before leaving. The poor creature alternated between desperate floods of tears and such prostration that she was even unaware who was in the room.

A faint hope remained to me:

"So it was not Ada, then, who noticed my absence?"

Augusta confessed that she would rather have said nothing about it, for Ada's anger at my failure to be at the funeral had passed all bounds. She had insisted on an explanation, and when Augusta was obliged to say she knew nothing about it, not having seen me herself, she gave way again to her despair, crying out that of course one must expect Guido to be treated like that when he was dead, because all the family hated him.

I did think Augusta might have spoken up for me, and reminded Ada that I was the only person who had offered to help Guido in the way he wanted. If they had listened to me he would have had no need to commit suicide, or even to pretend to.

But Augusta had said nothing. She had been so much moved by Ada's despair that she feared it might seem an outrage to her grief to enter on a discussion. But she was sure that Signora Malfenti's explanations would convince Ada how unjust she had been to me. I must say I thought so too, and looked forward in perfect confidence to witnessing her surprise and expressions of gratitude. Everything about her was excessive on account of Basedow's disease.

I went back to the office, where I learned that there was again a slight upward movement, very slight as yet, but enough to warrant the hope that the shares would be up next day as high as they had been that morning.

After dinner I was obliged to go and see Ada alone; Augusta could not come with me because the baby was ill. Signora Malfenti received me, and said she was obliged to attend to something in the kitchen and must therefore leave me alone with Ada. She added that Ada had begged to be left alone with me, because she had something to

say to me which no one else must hear. She led me into
the little boudoir where I had twice before seen Ada alone,
and before taking leave of me said laughing:

"You know she is not quite ready to forgive you yet
for not being at Guido's funeral, but—almost!"

My heart always beat faster in that little room. But
this time it was not for fear of finding myself loved by
someone I did not love. During the last few moments, and
solely in consequence of what Signora Malfenti had said,
I was conscious of having committed a serious breach of
friendship toward poor Guido. I sat down and began
studying the portraits of Guido's parents. The old Señor
wore a satisfied air, which I felt he owed entirely to my
intervention, while Guido's mother, a thin woman in a
dress with full sleeves, and a huge hat balanced precari-
ously on mountains of hair, was very severe-looking. But
then everyone puts on an unnatural face in front of the
camera, and I looked away, feeling almost ashamed of
myself for trying to read their character in those faces.
The mother could certainly never have forseen that I
should not have attended her son's funeral.

But the way in which Ada spoke to me came as an
unpleasant surprise. She must have spent some time in
preparing what she wanted to say, and she paid not the
smallest heed to my explanations, protests, or corrections,
which she could not have foreseen. She galloped along
like a frightened horse to the bitter end.

She was dressed very simply in a black boudoir gown.
Her hair was in great disorder, as if she were continually
running her fingers through it, in a kind of desperate
need to find something for them to do. She came up to
the table at which I was sitting, and rested her hands on
it so as to see me better. Her face was quite thin again
and had shed once more that uncanny fullness which grew
all in the wrong place. She was no longer beautiful, as
she had been when Guido won her for himself, but no
one looking at her would have remembered her illness.
There was no trace of that now, only a great sorrow,
which entirely transformed her. I could understand her immense grief so well that I was unable to speak. All the
time I was looking at her I kept wondering what words
I could think of to say to her, which should be equivalent
to taking her in my arms and comforting her as a brother:

then perhaps she might weep and ease her overburdened heart. When she began to attack me I wanted to defend myself, but I did it too feebly, and she did not hear.

She went on talking, talking, talking: I cannot remember all she said. Unless I am mistaken she began by thanking me gravely but quite coldly for all I had done for her and her children. Then she suddenly began to reproach me:

"And yet you drove him to his death for something that was not worth the trouble!"

She lowered her voice as if she wanted to keep secret what she was saying to me, and there was more warmth in her tone of voice, due no doubt to her love for Guido, and perhaps also—or did I merely fancy it?—for me:

"I forgive you for not having come to his funeral. You were unable to do so, and I forgive you. He would have forgiven you too if he were alive. What good would you have done beside his grave? You, who never loved him! Kind as you are, you might have shed tears for me, you might have wept to see my tears, but you would have shed none for him. You hated him! Poor Zeno! My poor brother!"

It was monstrous that she should say a thing like that, which was such a parody of the truth. I protested, but she would not listen to me. I believe I must have screamed; anyway I had the sensation of doing so, in my throat:

"But it is all a mistake, a lie, a calumny. How can you possibly believe such a thing?"

She went on, still in a low voice:

"But I did not really love him either. I was never unfaithful to him, even in thought, but I felt for him so little that I had not even the strength to protect him. I watched your relationship with your wife, and I envied you both. I thought what you gave her was better than what he offered me. I am grateful to you for not having come to the funeral, for otherwise I might not even yet have understood anything. But now I see it all; I understand it all. No, I did not love him either; if I had, how could I have hated even his violin, which was the most perfect expression of his great soul?"

When she said this I rested my head on my hands and hid my face. The charges she brought against me were

so unjust that it was impossible to discuss them; and their
unreasonableness was so mitigated by the gentle, almost
affectionate tone of her voice that I had not the heart
to refute them sternly, as I must have done if I was to
issue victorious from this duel. And then Augusta had
set me an example of consideration, by keeping silence
in the presence of such bitter grief. But when I closed
my eyes I saw in the darkness that her words had created
a new world, like all words which are not true. I seemed
to see myself as having always hated Guido, as having
stood by his side ever on the watch for an opportunity to
strike him down. And then she had spoken of Guido and
his violin together. If I had not known that she was almost beside herself from grief and remorse, I might have
thought she had set up his violin as a part of Guido, in
order to bring home to me my hatred of him.

Then in the darkness I saw again Guido's dead body,
still wearing that expression of astonishment on his face
at finding himself lying there lifeless. I raised my head
in horror. It was better to face Ada's accusations, unjust
as they were, than to go on looking into the dark.

But she still continued talking about Guido and me:

"Poor Zeno, you went on living with him without
realizing that you hated him. It was impossible! It had
to end like this! There was a time when I was foolish
enough to think I might use the love I knew you felt for
me, to build up a defense for him who so much needed
it. But he could only have been protected by someone who
loved him and, between ourselves, he was loved by no
one."

"What more could I have done for him?" I asked.
Hot tears fell from my eyes, to persuade her of my innocence, and to persuade myself. Tears sometimes take
the place of loud argument. I was not even sure if I ought
to speak at all; still less could I cry out and dispute loudly
with her. But I had somehow to crush her assertions—so I
wept.

"You might have saved him, dear brother. Between us
we ought to have saved him, you and I. But I, though I
was at his side, could not save him because I did not
really love him; and you were never there; you were absent,
always absent till he was actually in his grave. Then you

appeared armed with a great love for him. Till then you gave no thought to him at all. Yet he was with you up to that last evening. And you might have guessed, if you had paid any attention to him at all, that something serious was going to happen."

Tears prevented me from speaking, but I stammered out something to the effect that the night before he had spent amusing himself out shooting in the marshes, so that no one could possibly have foreseen in what way he would spend the following night.

"He had to have shooting, he had to have it!" She rebuked me in a loud voice. Then, as if all her strength had been spent in the effort of that one cry, she suddenly collapsed and fell in a faint on the floor.

For an instant I remembered that I hesitated to summon Signora Malfenti. I thought her fainting might reveal the meaning of what she had been saying to me. The next moment I called for help.

Signora Malfenti and Alberta came hurrying in. Her mother bent over her, and said to me as she lifted her up:

"Has she been talking to you about those hateful speculations?" Then: "This is the second time she has fainted today."

She asked me to go away for a moment, and I went out into the passage and waited there till I heard whether I was to go in again or go away. I prepared myself for further explanations with Ada. She was forgetting that if only they had done what I had suggested, the catastrophe would never have happened. It ought to be enough to remind her of this, in order to convince her of the wrong she was doing me.

Soon after Signora Malfenti joined me, and said that Ada had recovered and would like to say good-by to me. She was lying on the sofa, where I had been sitting up to a few minutes ago. When she saw me she began to cry, and those were the first tears I saw her shed. She held out her hand to me, damp with perspiration, and said:

"Good-by, Zeno dear! Please remember! I want you always to remember! Don't ever forget!"

Signora Malfenti broke in to ask what it was I was always to remember, and I told her that Ada was anxious for an immediate settlement of Guido's affairs on the

Bourse. I blushed as I uttered this lie, and was afraid
lest Ada might contradict me. But instead of that she
burst out:

"Yes! yes! everything must be settled at once! I don't
ever want to hear that horrible place spoken of again!"

She had become very pale again, and to quiet her
Signora Malfenti said that everything should be done at
once as she wanted.

Then Signora Malfenti accompanied me to the door
and begged me not to be over-hasty. I was to do whatever
I thought best in Guido's interests. But I answered that
I had lost confidence in myself. The risks were enormous,
and I could no longer venture to play with other people's money in that way. I didn't really believe in gambling on the Bourse, and I no longer believed in my power
to influence the rise or fall of stocks. So I should make
an immediate settlement, and be thankful that things had
gone as well as they had.

I did not repeat to Augusta what Ada had said. Why
should I distress her? But just because I told them to no
one, those words continued to beat on my ears like a
drum, and went on echoing for many years. Even today I
often find myself brooding over them. I can hardly say
that I loved Guido, but only because he was such a strange
man. And I stood by him as if he had been my brother,
and helped him in every way I could. No, I don't deserve
Ada's reproof.

I was never alone with her again. She did not feel
the need to say anything more to me, and I never demanded an explanation, perhaps because I did not want
to intensify her grief.

On the Bourse things turned out as I had foreseen,
and Guido's father, after hearing in one cable that he had
lost the whole of his fortune, was naturally pleased to
find that half of it still remained intact. Unfortunately
I did not get the pleasure I expected from my handiwork.

Ada behaved affectionately to me up to the time
when she set off to Buenos Aires with her children to
join her husband's family. She always liked to see Augusta
and me. I sometimes tried to believe that her speech had
been due to a sudden mad outburst of grief and that she
did not even remember it. But once when she talked of

Guido before us she repeated and confirmed in two words everything she had said that day:

"No one loved him, poor darling!"

Just as she went on board the boat she kissed me. (She was carrying one of the children, who was not very well.) Then, at a moment when no one was by, she said to me:

"Good-by, Zeno, my brother. I shall always remember that I did not love him enough. I want you to know this. I leave my country gladly, for I feel as if I were leaving my pangs of conscience behind."

I reproached her for tormenting herself like that, saying she had been a good wife, and that I knew all about it and could bear witness to it. I don't know if I succeeded in convincing her. She said no more, her sobs overcame her. But long afterwards it seemed to me that in taking leave of me like that she had wanted to renew her attack on me. But I know that she judged me unfairly. I certainly have no need to reproach myself with not having loved Guido.

It was a gloomy, miserable day. One innocent-looking cloud seemed to be spreading over and darkening the whole sky. A great cargo boat, with its sails hanging inert from the masts, was being rowed out of the harbor. Only two men were at the oars, and row as they might they scarcely succeeded in stirring the great ship. Perhaps out at sea they would find a slight breeze to help them.

From the deck of her steamer Ada waved good-by to us with her handkerchief. Then she turned away. Her last look must be for Saint Anna, where Guido was buried. Her slender little figure took on a fresh grace as she was carried away from us. The tears blinded my eyes. She was leaving us forever. Never again should I be able to prove to her that I was innocent.

Psychoanalysis

I

May 3, 1915.

HAVE finished with psychoanalysis. After practicing it assiduously for six whole months I find I am worse than before. I have not yet told the doctor, but nothing will make me change my mind. Yesterday I sent to say that I was prevented from coming, and I shall let him expect me for a few days. If I could be sure of laughing at him without getting into a rage, I should not mind seeing him again. But I am afraid I should end by assaulting him.

Since war broke out, this town has become more tedious than usual, and to fill up the time that I used to give to my treatment, I have returned to my beloved notebooks. I had not written a word for a year, obeying the doctor in this as in everything else; for he asserted that during the cure I must not examine myself except in his presence, as any self-examination that was not controlled by him would only strengthen my resistances, and prevent my being able to give myself up completely. But now I am more unbalanced and in worse health than ever, and I think that writing may help to work off the mischief that the treatment has done me. Anyway I am certain that this is the only way to give prominence to a past that it is no longer painful for me to dwell on, and to banish the hateful present as quickly as possible.

I had abandoned myself to the doctor with such

entire confidence that when he told me I was cured I believed him absolutely, and gave no credence to the pains which still continued to torment me. I said to them: "You are not really there!" But now I can doubt no longer. They really are there. The bones in my legs have turned into sharp fish-bones that wound my muscles and my flesh.

But I should not mind that so much: that is not the reason I am giving up the cure. If, during the hours of self-examination which I spent with the doctor, I had continued to make new discoveries and to experience fresh sensations, I would never have given it up, or at least I would have waited till the end of the war, which puts a stop to all my other activities. But now that I have seen through it, and know that it is nothing but a stupid illusion, a foolish trick that might take in an hysterical old woman, how can I any longer endure to be in the company of that ridiculous man, with his would-be penetrating eye, and the intolerable conceit that allows him to group all the phenomena in the world round his grand new theory? I am going to employ my free time in writing as I please. And, to begin with, I shall write the story of my cure. All sincerity had disappeared between me and the doctor; now I breathe again. I am no longer under constraint. I have no longer got to try to believe, nor to pretend to believe if I don't. I forced myself to be cringingly subservient to him just in order to hide what I was really thinking, and that encouraged him to invent some fresh monstrosity every day. I ought to be cured, for they have found out what was the matter with me. The diagnosis is exactly the same as the one that Sophocles drew up long ago for poor Œdipus: I was in love with my mother and wanted to murder my father.

I did not even get angry. I listened enraptured. It was a disease that exalted me to a place among the great ones of the earth; a disease so dignified that it could trace back its pedigree even to the mythological age! And I don't feel angry, even now that I sit here alone, pen in hand. I can laugh at it whole-heartedly. The surest proof that I never had the disease is that I have not been cured of it. This proof should surely convince the doctor himself. He need not worry; his words have not been able to spoil the memories of my youth. I have but to close my

eyes and immediately there rises up before me my love for
my mother, and the great respect and affection I felt for
my father.

And then the doctor attaches too much importance
to those confessions of mine, which he refuses to give
back so that I may look at them again. My God! He has
only studied medicine, and so he has no idea what writing
in Italian means to us who talk dialect but cannot express
ourselves in writing. A written confession is always mendacious. We lie with every word we speak in the Tuscan
tongue! If only he knew how we tend to talk about things
for which we have the words all ready, and how we avoid
subjects that would oblige us to look up words in the
dictionary! That is the principle that guided me when it
came to putting down certain episodes in my life. Naturally it would take on quite a different aspect if I told it
in our own dialect.

The doctor confessed to me that during the whole of
his long practice he had never met with such violent emotion as I displayed before the images that he believed himself to have suggested to me. That was why he was in
such a hurry to say I was cured.

And I did not simulate that emotion; it was really
one of the strongest I have ever felt in my life. I was
bathed in perspiration while creating the images, and in
tears when I recognized them. The idea of being able to
live again one day of innocence and inexperience gave me
inexpressible delight. It supported me and gave me courage
for months and months beforehand. Was it not like the
miracle of plucking in October the roses of May? The
doctor himself assured me that the image in my memory
would be clear and complete, so that it would be another
day added to my life. The roses would have all their fragrance, even perhaps their thorns.

And by dint of pursuing these memory-pictures, I at
last really overtook them. I know now that I invented
them. But invention is a creative act, not merely a lie.
My inventions were like the fantasies of fever, which walk
about the room so that one can survey them from all sides
and even touch them. They had the solidity, the color,
and the movement of living things. My desire created
these images. They existed only in my brain and in the
space into which I projected them; I felt the air, I saw

the light that was in this space, and even its hard corners, just as in any other space that I have ever walked through.

When I fell into that dream-state which was to aid in creating the illusion, and which was probably only a mingling of great energy with extreme inertia, I thought my dream-pictures really were an actual reproduction of the past. I might have suspected at once that they were not, because directly they had vanished my memory of them was free from any excitement or agitation. I remembered them as one remembers an event one has been told by somebody who was not present at it. If they had been actual reproductions, they would have continued to move my tears or laughter as they had done when I first saw them. The doctor noted everything down. He said:

"We have had this, we have had that," though we had really had nothing but graphic signs, mere skeletons of images.

I was persuaded into the belief that it was really my childhood I was evoking, because the first picture placed me in a relatively recent epoch, of which I still retained a pale memory that the image seemed to confirm. There was one year in my life during which I was already going to school, while my brother had not yet begun; and the hour I evoked seemed to belong to that year. I saw myself coming out of the house one sunny morning in spring, and walking through the garden on the way down to the town, on and on, with my hand in that of our old servant Catina. My brother did not appear at all in this dream-scene, but he was the hero of it. I thought of him so happy and free at home, while I had to go to school. I went there with a dragging step, and with anger in my heart, and felt as if I wanted to cry. I only saw one of those walks to school, but the bitterness in my heart told me that I should have to go to school every day, and that every day my brother would stay at home—for ever and ever. Whereas actually I believe that my brother, who was only a year younger than me, soon after went to school too. But at that moment the truth of my dream seemed to me indisputable. I was condemned eternally to go to school, while my brother was allowed to stay at home. As I trotted along beside Catina I counted up how long my torture would last: Till midday! While *he* is at home! And I remembered that on other days, whenever I had

been scolded at school, or threatened with punishment, I
had always thought: "They can't touch him." It was an
extraordinarily realistic vision. Catina, whom I knew to
have been short, seemed to me tall on that occasion, because I was so little. She had always seemed immensely
old; but then children always think grown-up people are
old. On the way to school I also saw in my dream the curious little columns that used, at that time, to border the
pavements in our town. I was born early enough to have
seen those little columns even when I was quite grown up,
in the center of the town, before they were removed. But
in the street I walked along that day with Catina there
were none left almost before I had outgrown my childhood.

My faith in the authenticity of these images was not
shattered even when, stimulated by the dream, my sober
memory began to evoke other details of that period; of
which the chief was that my brother envied me too, because I went to school. I was sure that I had been conscious of this, but it was not at first enough to throw
suspicion on the truth of my dream. Later on it deprived
it of every vestige of truth; there certainly had been jealousy, but in my dream it had got attached to the wrong
person.

My second vision carried me back also to a comparatively recent date, though earlier than the first. I saw a
room in our house, but I don't know which, for it was
larger than any that is there in reality. The curious thing
is that I saw myself shut up in that room, and was at
once aware of a fact that the vision alone could not have
revealed to me: the room was a long way off from another
room in which my mother and Catina used to sit. Also I
had not yet begun going to school.

The room was quite white, indeed I had never seen
such a white room, nor one so entirely flooded with sunlight. Could it be that the sun was really shining through
the walls? It must have been high in the sky, but I was
still in bed with a cup in my hand from which I had drunk
up all the *caffelatte;* and I was going round and round
the empty cup with my spoon, trying to get out the sugar.
There came a point when I could not get any more out
with the spoon, and then I tried to reach the bottom of
the cup with my tongue. But I was unsuccessful. I ended

by sitting with the cup in one hand and the spoon in the other, watching my brother, who was in a bed next to mine, still busy drinking his *caffelatte*, with his nose buried in the cup. When he at last raised his head I saw his face all wrinkled up in the sun, which shone full on it, while mine, for some reason or other, was in the shade. His face was pale and slightly disfigured by a protruding jaw. He said:

"Will you lend me your spoon?"

Then I noticed for the first time that Catina had forgotten to give him a spoon. I replied without the slightest hesitation:

"Yes, if you will give me a piece of your sugar in return."

I held my spoon up, to enhance its value. But at once I heard Catina's voice in the room, saying:

"For shame! You little Jew!"

Fright and shame brought me back with a start to the present. I should have liked to argue with Catina, but she, my brother, and I—that tiny, innocent little Jew—plunged together into the abyss and disappeared.

I was sorry to have felt so much ashamed as to have destroyed the image I had built up so laboriously. It would have been much better if I had quietly given my brother the spoon gratis, and not tried to discuss that bad action, which was probably the first I had ever committed. Perhaps Catina would have called in my mother to punish me, and so I should have seen her again at last.

I did see her a few days later, or imagined that I did. I ought to have realized at once that it was an allusion, for the image of my mother, as I evoked it, bore too much resemblance to the portrait I have over my bed. But I must confess that in that vision of her my mother behaved like a living person.

The sun! the sun! dazzling sunlight! From the picture of what I thought to be my youth, so much sun streamed out that it was hard for me not to believe in it. Our dining-room in the afternoon. My father has come home and is sitting on the sofa beside my mother, who is printing initials in indelible ink on a lot of white linen scattered all over the table at which she is sitting.

I am under the table playing with some marbles. I move nearer and nearer to Mamma. I probably want her

to join in my game. Suddenly I seize hold of the linen
that is hanging down from the table, in order to pull myself up by it; and now a disaster happens. The bottle of
ink falls on my head, soaking my face and my clothes and
Mamma's skirt and leaving a slight stain on Papa's trou-
sers. My father lifts his leg to give me a kick. . . .

But I got back in time from my long voyage and
found myself safely here, grown-up and old. I must confess that the threatened punishment positively hurt me,
and immediately afterwards I felt sorry to think that I
had not been there to see Mamma's protecting gesture,
which I know must have followed. But who can stop
those pictures, once they have taken flight through time,
which never before had seemed so much like space? At
least I thought so while I still believed in the authenticity
of the pictures. Now alas, to my sorrow I believe in them
no longer, and know that it was not the pictures that fled,
but my eyes from which a veil was lifted, so that they
looked out again on real space, where there is no room
for spirits.

I will describe some visions that came to me another
day, and which the doctor regarded as so important that
he declared I was cured.

In the state between sleep and waking into which I
had sunk I had a dream that was fixed and unmoving as a
nightmare. I dreamt of myself as a tiny child, only to see
what a baby's dreams are like. As it lay there, its whole
small being was filled with joy. Yet it was lying there
quite alone. But it could see and feel with a clearness with
which in dreams one sometimes perceives quite distant
objects. The baby, who was lying in a room in my house,
saw, God knows how, that on the roof there was a cage,
built on solid foundations, without doors or windows, but
filled with a gentle light, and pure, perfumed air. And
the child knew that he alone could reach that cage, and
that he need not move to get there, for the cage would
come to him. In it was only one piece of furniture, an
armchair on which was seated a beautiful woman, perfect
in shape and dressed in black. She had fair hair, great blue
eyes, and exquisitely white hands; she wore patent-leather
shoes on her feet, which shed a faint reflection from under
her skirt. She seemed to me to be one indivisible whole in
her black dress and patent-leather shoes. It was all part of

her. And the child dreamed of possessing that woman, but
in the strangest manner; he was convinced that he would
be able to eat little bits off her at the top and the bottom!

Looking back on it now I am surprised that the doctor, who professed to have read my manuscript so attentively, was not reminded of another dream I had had before going to see Carla for the first time. When I thought
of it some time later, the dream I have described seemed
to me exactly the same, with slight variations that made
it more childish.

But the doctor took everything carefully down, and
then said with a rather sly air:

"Was your mother fair and good-looking?"

This question surprised me, and I replied that so
was my grandmother too. But from his point of view I
was completely cured. I opened my mouth wide to rejoice
in his rejoicings, and listened meekly to his prescription:
no more self-examination, no more analysis, no more meditation on the past, but a thorough and gradual re-education.

From thence onward those sittings became a torture
to me, and I went on with them only because I have always found it as difficult to stop once I am in motion, as
to start when I am at rest. Occasionally, when he said
something altogether too wide of the mark, I ventured
mildly to object. It was by no means true, as he assumed,
that every word and every thought of mine were criminal.
That made him stare. I was cured, and I refused to admit
it. It was sheer blindness! He had shown me that I had
wanted to carry off my father's wife—my mother!—and I
would not allow that I was cured. It was unheard-of obstinacy. However the doctor admitted that I should be
more completely cured when I had finished my re-education, and had accustomed myself to look on such things
as the desire to kill my father and possess my mother as
the most innocent things in the world, for which one
need feel no remorse, since they often cropped up in the
best families. After all, what harm could it do me? One
day he told me I was like someone recovering from an
illness who has not yet got accustomed to doing without
fever. Only have patience! I should get used to it in time.

He felt that he had not won me completely, and besides re-educating me he went back to the cure from time

to time. He tried me with dreams again, but I had no
more authentic ones. Tired at last of waiting, I ended
by inventing one. I should never have done it if I could
have foreseen the difficulties attending my invention. It
is not easy to stammer a few words as if one were half-
asleep, to be covered with perspiration or grow pale, without betraying oneself; to go crimson from the effort one
has made, and not to blush! I talked as if I were seeing
the woman in the cage again, and as if I had persuaded
her to put one of her feet through a hole that had suddenly appeared in the wall of her cell, so that I might
suck it and eat it. "The left one, the left one!" I murmured, adding a singular detail that should make it more
like the dreams that had gone before. I thereby showed
that I had grasped perfectly the disease that the doctor
insisted on my having. The infant Œdipus was just like
that; he sucked his mother's left foot, leaving the right
one to the father! In the imaginative effort I made to
deceive the doctor I almost succeeded (and this is no contradiction) in deceiving myself too, so that I could actually taste that foot. It made me feel quite sick.

The doctor could not have been more eager than
I was myself, that I should continue to see those pictures
of my childhood, whether genuine or not, which had come
to me spontaneously, without my needing to invent them.
As they would no longer come when I was with the doctor, I tried to evoke them away from him. There was a
danger of my forgetting them, as I was by myself, but
then I was not hoping to be cured by them! I wanted to
see once more in December the roses of May. I had seen
them once; why should they not come again?

I found solitude sufficiently boring, but at last something came which for a while took the place of my visions.
I thought I had made an important scientific discovery.
I suddenly felt called to complete the physiological theory
of color. My predecessors, Goethe and Schopenhauer, had
never dreamed how far one might go simply by a skillful
arrangement of the complementary colors.

I must tell you that I spent my time in my study,
lying on a sofa facing the window, from which I could see
a stretch of the sea, and the horizon. One evening, when
the sun was setting and the sky was broken by clouds, I
lay there a long while watching a white cloud take on a

marvelous shade of pure tender green. The clouds in the west were fringed with red, but a pale red, bleached by the white rays of the sun shining directly upon it. The light dazzled me, and after a while I closed my eyes. Then it was clear to me that all my attention and love had been given to that shade of green, for its complementary color was produced on my retina, a brilliant red that had nothing to do with the luminous, but pale red of the sky. I gazed in enchantment at the color that I had myself brought into being. My great surprise came when I opened my eyes again, for then I saw that flaming red spread over the whole sky and cover up my emerald green, so that for some time I was unable to see it. So I had actually found a way of painting nature! I naturally repeated the experiment several times. The strange part was that I had actually endowed the colors with movement. When I opened my eyes again, the sky would not at once take on the color from my retina. There was a moment's hesitation during which I could just detect the emerald green from which the red had sprung, and which seemed to have been destroyed by it. It emerged now from within and spread in all directions like a giant conflagration.

When I had convinced myself of the accuracy of my observations, I carried them to the doctor, hoping to animate our tiresome sittings a little. The doctor polished me off by saying that my retina had become ultrasensitive from so much nicotine. It was on the tip of my tongue to reply that in that case the visions that we had regarded as a reproduction of events of my childhood might also have been due to the same poison. But that would have betrayed the fact that I was not yet cured, and he would have tried to induce me to begin again from the beginning.

But the idiot did not always treat me as if I was poisoned. That is evident from the method of re-education adopted by him to cure me from what he called my smoking-disease. This is what he said: smoking did not hurt me at all, and if I only could persuade myself that it was harmless it would really become so. Then he went on to say that now that my relations with my father had been brought to light and judged by my adult consciousness, I should be able to see that I had adopted that vice merely in order to compete with my father, and had attributed a poisonous effect to tobacco because of my secret conviction that he would punish me for attempting to compete with him.

I left the doctor's house that day smoking like a Turk. He wanted to make an experiment, and I lent myself to it with enthusiasm. I smoked without ceasing, all day long. This was followed by a sleepless night. My chronic bronchitis had broken out again, of that there could be no doubt; the spittoon bore witness.

Next day I told the doctor I had smoked a great deal and that it no longer did me any harm. He regarded me with a complacent smile and I could guess from his expression how proud he felt of himself. He proceeded with my re-education in quiet confidence, and the certainty that every sod he stepped on would eventually bear fruit.

I remember very little of that re-education. I submitted to it, and every time I left his room, shook myself like a dog coming out of the water. Like the dog I remained wet, but was never drenched.

But I remember my indignation on hearing my tutor state that Dr. Coprosich was right in addressing to me the words that had so roused my indignation. Was it true then that I deserved the blow which my father aimed at me just before he died? I don't know if that was one of the things he said, but I distinctly remember him saying that I hated old Malfenti, whom I had substituted for my father. There are so many people who think it impossible to live in the world without a certain amount of affection; but I, according to him, was quite lost without a modicum of hatred. I wanted to marry one or other of his daughters, it did not matter which, because all I needed was to see their father in a position where I could reach him with my hatred. I did my best to dishonor the family I had married into, so far as it lay in my power; I was unfaithful to my wife, and, if I had been able, it was clear that I would have seduced Ada and Alberta. Of course I am not attempting to deny this, and it even made me laugh when the doctor, in saying it, put on an air of Christopher Columbus discovering America. All the same I think he must be the only person in the world who, hearing that I wanted to go to bed with two lovely women, must rack his brain to try and find a reason for it!

I found it still more difficult to bear what he felt it necessary to say about my relations with Guido. He had

heard from my own account how much I disliked Guido
on first making his acquaintance. According to him I
never ceased to do so, and Ada was quite right in regarding my absence from his funeral as a final manifestation
of my dislike. He quite forgot that I was at that very moment engaged in my labor of love to save Ada's fortune,
and I did not deign to remind him of it.

Apparently the doctor had made some inquiries about
Guido on his own account. He insisted that as Ada had
chosen him it was impossible he should have been what I
had described. He discovered that an enormous timber-
yard, quite close to the house where he practiced his psychoanalysis, had belonged to the firm of Guido Speier &
Co. Why had I never mentioned it?

If I had mentioned it, it would have added a fresh
complication to my already very difficult statement. The
fact that I omitted it is only another proof that no confession made by me in Italian could ever be complete
or sincere. There are a vast number of different kinds of
wood, which in Trieste we call by various barbaric names,
taken from our own dialect, from Croatian, from German,
and sometimes even from French (*zapin*, for instance,
which does not with us only mean *sapin*). Who would
have provided me with the necessary vocabulary? Was I,
at my age, to enter the employ of a Tuscan timber-mer-
chant? Besides, that timber-yard belonging to the firm of
Guido Speier & Co. showed no profits whatever. And then
there was nothing for me to say about it, because it was
always in a stagnant condition, except when thieves came
and made the wood with barbaric names fly through the
air as if it was destined to be made into tables for experiments in psychic research.

I suggested to the doctor that he might get some information about Guido from my wife, from Carmen, and
also from Luciano, who has now become a respected merchant. I know for a fact that he did not apply to any of
them, and can only suppose that he abstained from fear
that his whole edifice of false charges and suspicions
would crumble, when confronted with the facts. I wonder
why he took such a violent dislike to me. He is probably
also a hysteric, who avenges himself for having lusted after
his mother, by tormenting innocent people.

In the end I felt quite worn out by this incessant

duel with the doctor whom I was paying. I don't think those dreams were very good for me, and the freedom to smoke when I liked gave me my final *coup de grâce*. I had a happy idea: I paid a visit to Dr. Paoli.

I had not seen him for a good many years. He had grown rather gray, but his spare figure was as upright as ever, and he had not put on any fat. He still looked at things with a caressing air. I suddenly realized why he always makes that impression. I think it is that he enjoys observing things, and he observes the beautiful and the ugly with the same satisfaction with which he might caress someone he loved.

I went to him with the intention of asking him whether he thought I ought to go on with psychoanalysis. But when I found his cold, penetrating gaze fixed on me, my courage failed. Perhaps he would think I was merely making a fool of myself, at my age, to be taken in by such quackery. I hated keeping silent about it; it is true that it would have simplified my position very much if Dr. Paoli had forbidden me to go on with psychoanalysis, but I could not long have endured being caressed by those great eyes of his.

I told him of my insomnia, my chronic bronchitis, the eruptions on my face which were tormenting me just then; of the sharp stabbing pains in my legs, and finally of my inexplicable lapses of memory.

Paoli analyzed my urine in my presence. The mixture turned black and Paoli looked grave. At last I was going to have a true analysis after all this psychoanalysis. I felt quite touched as I remembered the time, now long past, when I was myself a chemist and made true analyses; I thought fondly of retorts and reagents. The element that is being analyzed sleeps till it is summoned imperiously to life by the reagent. There is no resistance in the retort, at least it yields to the smallest rise in temperature, and shamming is out of the question. Nothing took place in that retort to remind me of my behavior with Dr. S., when, to please him, I invented fresh details of my childhood in order to conform to Sophocles' diagnosis. Here was only the truth. The thing that had to be analyzed was imprisoned in the phial and, incapable of being false to itself, awaited the reagent. When that came it always responded in the same way. In psychoanalysis, on the other hand, neither the same images nor the same words ever repeat themselves. It ought to be called by another name: psychical adventure, perhaps. Yes, that is just what it is. When one starts such an analysis, it is like entering a wood, not knowing whether one is going to meet a brigand or a friend. Nor is one quite sure which it has been, after the adventure is over. In this respect psychoanalysis resembles spiritualism.

But Paoli did not think that sugar was the trouble. He wanted to see me again next day, after he had polarized the liquid.

I meanwhile went off triumphant, sure that I had got diabetes. I was tempted to go at once to Dr. S. and ask him how he would propose to analyze the psychical causes of that disease in order to cure it. But I had had enough of that individual and felt I could not bear to see him again, even to poke fun at him.

I must confess that the thought of diabetes was very sweet to me. I spoke of it to Augusta, who listened to me with tears in her eyes.

"You have talked so much about diseases all your life," she said, "that you were bound to end by having one." Then she tried to console me.

But I loved my disease. I thought with sympathy of poor Copler, who preferred real diseases to imaginary ones. I agreed with him now. A real disease was so simple; you had only to let it work its will. And, in fact, when I looked up the description of my sweet sickness in a medical prescriber, I found a whole program of life (not of death!) drawn up for the various stages of the disease. Farewell resolutions! Henceforth I should be free of them. Everything would pursue its own course now, without any intervention.

I further discovered that my disease was always, or almost always, very agreeable. The invalid eats and drinks a great deal, and suffers very little so long as he is careful to avoid getting abscesses. Then he sinks into a delightful state of coma and dies.

It was not long before I was called to the telephone by Paoli. He said he could find no trace of sugar. I went to see him next day, and he ordered me a diet, which I only kept to for a few days, and a medicine illegibly scribbled on a prescription, which did me good for a whole month.

"That diabetes gave you a fright, I know!" he said smiling.

I denied this, but did not tell him that I felt very lonely now that I was deserted by my diabetes. He would never have believed me.

It was about this time that Dr. Beard's famous work on neurasthenia fell into my hands. I followed his advice and changed my medicine every week, according to the prescriptions, which I copied clearly out of his book. For a few months I thought the treatment was doing me good. Not even Copler, in the whole course of his life, could have had such consolation from drugs as I had then. My faith in them evaporated by degrees, but I had had a certain respite from psychoanalysis, and kept putting off my return from day to day.

One day I met Dr. S. by chance. He asked if I had decided to give up treatment. He was most polite, much more so than when he had had me in his clutches. He was evidently anxious to get hold of me again. I told him I had a great deal of business to attend to, family affairs, which took up all my time and attention, but that directly I had settled them and had some time to myself again, I should return to him. I wanted to ask him to give me back my manuscript, but I did not dare; it would have been as good as confessing that I wanted to have nothing more to do with his treatment. I decided to put off asking him till another time, when he should have realized that I had given up all idea of returning to him, and become reconciled to it.

Before we parted, he said a few words with the obvious intention of drawing me again into his net.

"If you examine your state of mind," he said, "you will find a great change in it. You'll see that you will want to come back to me of yourself, when you realize how much good I did you in a comparatively short space of time."

What I really think is that, with his help and by dint of studying my psyche, I only infected myself with new diseases.

My one thought now is how to recover from his treatment. I avoid dreams and memories, which produced such a state of confusion in my poor head that it is hardly sure yet whether or not it is firmly fixed between my shoulders. I am terribly absent-minded. While I am talking to someone I am all the time trying to remember what it was I said or did a little while ago, and have quite forgotten. Or it may be a thought I am trying to recapture, which I feel to be of enormous importance, as much importance as those thoughts my father had a short while before he died, and which he likewise failed to remember.

I must put a stop to all this folly, unless I want to end in a lunatic asylum.

May 15, 1915.

We have been spending the two feast-days in our villa at Lucinico. My son Alfio is recovering from influenza, and is to stay on for several weeks with his sister. We shall come back here for Whitsun.

I have succeeded at last in getting back again to my former good resolutions, and I have given up smoking. I feel much better already, since renouncing the liberty which that fool of a doctor forced on me. Today we have reached the middle of the month, and I am struck by the obstacles that our calendar places in the way of carrying out a straightforward, well-ordered resolution. All the months are a different length. In order to demonstrate my resolution properly I ought to stop smoking at the same time that something else comes to an end—the month, for instance. But except for July and August, December and January, there are no two successive months that have an equal number of days. Time is really very ill-ordered!

In order to be able to concentrate better, I spent the afternoon of the second day alone, on the banks of the Isonzo. Nothing helps one to concentrate so well as gazing for a long time at running water. One remains perfectly still oneself and all the necessary diversion is provided by the water, which is never the same for a single instant, either in color or design.

It was a wonderful day. A strong wind must have been blowing in the upper air, for the clouds were continually changing shape, but down below there was no movement in the atmosphere. From time to time the sun, which already gave some warmth, found a gap in the swiftly moving clouds and streamed through, flooding with light some expanse of upland or some mountain peak, and lifting the tender May green out of the shadow that covered all the landscape. The air was warm, and there was something spring-like even in that flight of clouds across the sky. There could be no doubt the weather too was convalescent!

In my contemplative mood I enjoyed one of those moments that niggard life so rarely grants, when one ceases to feel oneself a victim, and can take a large, impersonal view of things. In the midst of all that green, so exquisitely radiant under the fitful sun-rays, I was able to smile at life and at my malady. Women played a great part in both. Even the details of a woman's body—her feet, her waist, her mouth—were enough to fill my days. And as I looked back over my life and my malady, I felt that I loved and understood them both. How much better my life had been than that of the so-called normal healthy man who, except at certain moments, beats or would like to beat his mistress every day. But I had always been accompanied by love. Even when I was not thinking of my mistress, I still thought of her in the sense that I craved her forgiveness for thinking of other women as well. Other men leave this mistress disillusioned and despairing of life. I have never known life without desire, and illusions sprang up afresh for me after every shipwreck of my hopes, for I was always dreaming of limbs, of gestures, of a voice more perfect still.

I remembered that among the many lies I had imposed on that profound observer, Dr. S., one was that I had never betrayed my wife after Ada went away. He built up a whole theory on that lie. But on the river-bank I suddenly realized with horror that for some days past, perhaps since I had given up treatment, I had not run after any woman except my wife. Was I really cured then, as Dr. S. pretended? I am getting old and it is some time now since women ceased to take any interest in me. If I were to lose interest in them, there would be an end to all relationship between us.

If such a doubt had assailed me in Trieste I should at once have known how to solve it. Here it was a little more difficult.

A few days before I had had in my hands the memoirs

f Da Ponte, an adventurer who was contemporary with Casanova. He too must certainly have passed through Lucinico, and I dreamed of meeting one of his powdered ladies, with her limbs hidden by a crinoline. Good Lord! How did those women manage to give themselves so quickly and so often, cased as they were in all those clothes?

I found the thought of a crinoline sufficiently exciting, in spite of my cure. But it was rather an artificial desire that it aroused, and it did not suffice to reassure me.

The proof I was in search of came to me soon after, and certainly reassured me, though I paid dearly for it. In order to obtain it I spoilt and destroyed the purest relationship I have ever had in my life.

I happened to meet Teresina, the eldest daughter of a peasant who had settled on a plot of ground near to my villa. Her mother had died two years before, and the large family of small brothers and sisters had found a second mother in Teresina, a robust girl who rose early to begin work, and went to bed directly the day's work was over, to rest before beginning again. That day she was leading the donkey, which was generally entrusted to her young brother, and she was walking beside the cart laden with new hay, because so small a beast would not have been able to carry the girl's weight as well, going up the hill.

A year ago Teresina had seemed to me quite a child, and I had felt nothing but a fatherly affection for her. Only the day before, when I had seen her again for the first time, although I noticed that she had grown, that her sunburnt face had become more serious, and her slender shoulders had widened out above the swelling curve of her breasts, her undeveloped, hard-worked little body made me look on her still as a mere child, in whom I could only admire her extraordinary activity and the maternal instinct that she lavished on her little brothers and sisters. If it had not been for that odious cure, and the necessity of verifying on the spot exactly what stage my malady had reached, I should have left Lucinico this time too, without troubling her perfect innocence.

She wore no crinoline, and her round, smiling little face was innocent of powder. She was barefooted and I could see halfway up her naked leg. Neither her face, feet, nor legs sufficed to kindle my desire. Her face and such

limbs as I could see were all the same color; they belonged
to the open air, and there was no harm in their being
abandoned thus to the air. Perhaps that was why they
failed to excite me. But I was shocked to find myself so
cold. Could it be that after my cure I needed a crinoline
to stimulate my imagination?

I began by stroking the donkey, which was thus
obliged to take a few minutes' rest. Then I turned my attention to Teresina, and put in her hand no less than ten
kronen. It was my first attempt on her virtue! Last year I
had given her and her brothers *centesimi* only, as an expression of my fatherly affection for them. But everyone
knows that fatherly affection is quite a different thing.
Teresina was dumfounded by such a magnificent gift. She
carefully lifted her skirt to put the precious piece of paper
away in her pocket, and as she did so I caught a glimpse
of her leg above the knee, but that was just as sunburnt
and chaste.

I returned to the donkey and kissed it on the head.
My display of affection aroused its own. It stretched out
its neck and emitted that impressive cry of love which I
have always listened to with respect. How far-reaching it
is, and how significant, with that first cry which it utters
again and again like an invocation, growing feebler and
feebler till it ends in a despairing sob. But to listen to it
at such close quarters was positively painful.

Teresina laughed, and her laughter encouraged me.
I turned again to her and seized her suddenly by the forearm, moving slowly up it with my hand toward the shoulder, and studying my sensations the while. Thank Heaven
I was not cured yet! I had stopped the treatment just in
time.

But Teresina urged on the donkey with a stick. She
evidently intended to go on and leave me behind.

I could not help laughing heartily; I felt very happy,
even if the peasant girl would have none of me. I said:

"Have you a lover? You ought to have. It would be
a pity if you hadn't got one yet."

She answered, as she continued to move away from
me:

"When I take one, he will certainly be younger than
you!"

Even this could not obscure my happiness. I should

have liked to read Teresina a little lesson, and turned over in my mind that episode in Boccaccio—"Maestro Alberto of Bologna virtuously shames a lady who would have shamed him for falling in love with her." But Maestro Alberto's reasoning took no effect, for Madonna Malgherida de' Ghisolieri said to him: "Your love is precious to me, as that of a wise and valiant man must always be, and therefore, *saving my honor,* impose your will on me, as on all things that are yours."

I tried to improve on this:

"When will you begin to look at old men, Teresina?" I shouted, so that she might hear me—for she was already some way off.

"When I am old too," she shouted back without even stopping, and bursting out laughing.

"But the old men won't look at you then. You mark my words! I know them!"

I shouted at the top of my voice, enjoying a joke that was directly inspired by my sex.

At that moment the clouds opened at various points in the sky and let some sun-rays through, which fell straight on Teresina, who was now about fifty yards away and more than thirty feet above me. She was dark and small, but shining!

The sun did not shine on me! When you are old, you have to stay in the shade, however witty you may be.

The war has reached me at last! I used to listen to stories of the war as if it were a war in times gone by, which it was amusing to talk about, but about which it would be foolish to excite oneself; when, to my astonishment, I found myself right in the middle of it, and was surprised then to think I had not realized that I must sooner or later become involved. I had lived quite peacefully in a building of which the ground-floor had caught fire, and it had never occurred to me that sooner or later the whole building, with me in it, would go up in flames.

The war took hold of me, shook me out like a rag, and robbed me at one blow of all my family, including my steward. From one day to the next I became a completely new man or, to be more exact, every one of my twenty-four hours was different. Since yesterday I have felt a little calmer, for after waiting a whole month I have at last had news of my family. They are safe and sound at Turin, while I had already lost all hope of ever seeing them again.

I have to spend the whole day in my office. There is nothing for me to do there, but the Olivis, who are Italian citizens, have had to go, and all the best of my employees have gone off to fight in one place or another; so I must stick to my post and superintend it all. I go home in the evening laden with the huge warehouse keys. Today, when I felt so much calmer, I took this manuscript with me to the office, thinking it might help to pass the time. And it did in fact procure me a wonderful quarter of an hour, which reminded me that there was once a time in the world's history when one could allow oneself the luxury of sitting down in peace and quietness to enjoy such trifles as this.

It would be nice if someone were to invite me seriously to fall into a state of half-consciousness in which I might live again even one hour of my former life. I should laugh in his face. How could one give up a present like this to pursue such frivolous trifles? It is only now that I feel myself definitely detached from my preoccupation with health and disease. As I walk through the streets of our unfortunate city I am conscious of being a privileged person who does not have to go and fight and who daily has what he needs to eat. In comparison with all the rest I feel so happy (especially since I had news of my family) that I should be afraid of provoking the wrath of the gods if everything were absolutely well with me.

My first encounter with the war was a violent one, of which I can now see the comic side.

Augusta and I had returned to Lucinico to spend Whitsun there with the children. On May 23rd I got up early, for I had to take some Carlsbad salts and go for a walk before my morning coffee. It was during this cure at Lucinico that I realized that the heart carries on its restorative work much better on an empty stomach, and spreads a sense of well-being through the whole body. My theory was to find remarkable confirmation that very day, when I was compelled to practice a long and salutary fast.

Augusta raised her white head from the pillow to wish me good morning, and reminded me that I had promised to get my daughter some roses. Our only rose-tree had finished flowering, so I was obliged to get them from elsewhere. My daughter has grown into a fine girl, and is very like Ada. I had suddenly forgotten to behave toward her as a stern mentor, and had assumed the role of a cavalier who respects femininity even in his own daughter. She at once realized her power and abused it, to Augusta's and my great amusement. She had expressed a wish for some roses, so I must procure some for her.

I proposed to walk for about two hours. The sun was shining brightly, and as I intended to walk all the time and not to stop till I got back home, I did not even take a coat or hat with me. I fortunately remembered that I should have to pay for the roses, so I did not leave my pocket-book at home as well as my coat.

I went first of all into the neighboring property, belonging to Teresina's father, to ask him to cut some roses, which I would call for on my way back. I entered the great courtyard surrounded by a partially ruined wall, but found no one there. I shouted Teresina's name. The youngest of the children, aged about six, came out of the house. I put a few coppers into his hand, and he told me the whole family had gone off early to the other side of the Isonzo for a day's work on a field of potatoes which needed earthing up.

This was quite welcome news to me, for I knew the field, and it would take me about an hour to reach it. As I had decided to go for a two hours' walk I was glad to be provided with a definite goal. There was no danger now of my interrupting it by a sudden attack of laziness. I set off across the plain, which lies higher than the road so that I could only see from it the tops of a few flowering trees which grew along the sides. I was in a cheerful mood; I felt so light and airy in my shirt-sleeves and without a hat. I breathed the pure air with delight, and as I walked along did some of Niemeyer's lung gymnastics, which I had been practicing now for some time past. A German friend had taught me the exercises, and they cannot be too highly recommended to anyone living a sedentary life.

When I got to the field I saw Teresina working on the side nearest the road. I went toward her, and then caught sight of her father and little brothers at work a little farther on. I should think they must have been between ten and fourteen years old. Though one feels exhausted after any unusual effort when one is old, one nevertheless feels younger than when doing nothing, because of the accompanying sense of excitement. I went to Teresina and said gaily:

"There is still time, Teresina. Don't be too long."

She did not understand, and I did not think it necessary to explain. Since she had forgotten, I could go back to my old relations with her. I had already repeated the experiment, and the result had again been favorable. In addressing those few words to her I had caressed her, and not with my looks alone.

I soon came to an agreement with her father. He would let me cut as many roses as I liked, and we should certainly not quarrel about the price. He was going to return to his work at once, while I had begun to set off homeward, when he changed his mind and ran after me. When he caught me up, he asked in a low voice:

"Haven't you heard anything? They say war has broken out."

"Well yes, we all know that! It has been going on for nearly a year," I replied.

"I don't mean that," he exclaimed impatiently. "I mean the other with . . ." and he made a gesture in the direction of the Italian frontier. "Haven't you heard anything about it?" He waited anxiously for my reply.

"You can rest assured," I said with complete confidence, "that if I have heard nothing about it, it means that there is nothing to hear. I have just come from Trieste, and the very last thing I heard was that they will have nothing to do with the war. In Rome they have turned out the Government that wanted war, and have put in Giolitti."

He was reassured at once.

"Then all these potatoes that we are just covering up, and which promise so well, will be ours after all. There are so many of those scaremongers about." He wiped away the sweat that was pouring from his brow with his shirt-sleeve.

Seeing that I had made him happy, I tried to make him happier still. I do so like to see people enjoying themselves. So I said a number of things which I hardly like to remember. I asserted that even if war had broken out it would not be fought anywhere near there. First of all

here was the sea, which it was time they began fighting
n, and then in Europe there were battlefields enough and
o spare. There was the whole of Flanders and several
departments in France. I had heard say—I could not remember by whom—that there was such a shortage of
potatoes in the world that they even cultivated them with
great care on the field of battle. I talked a great deal, keep-
ng my eyes fixed the while on the slender little form of
Teresina, who was crouching down to feel the earth with
her hand before she began digging.

The peasant went back to his work, with his mind set
completely at rest. But I who had given him part of my
own tranquillity had so much less left for myself. It was
clear we were too near the frontier at Lucinico. I would
speak to Augusta about it. Perhaps we should do well to
return to Trieste, or anyway to move farther from the
frontier, in whichever direction. It was true that Giolitti
was now in power, but one could not tell whether, once
he had arrived there, he would continue to see things in
the same light as when someone else was in power.

My uneasiness was increased by a chance meeting
with a troop of soldiers who were marching toward Lucinico. They were none of them young, and they were
shabbily dressed and ill-equipped. They were carrying what
we used to call a "*darlindana*" in Trieste, a kind of old-
fashioned long bayonet, which in the summer of 1915 the
Austrians had had to fetch out of their old stores.

I continued to walk behind them for some time,
eager to be at home again. But the unpleasant odor that
emanated from them at last forced me to slacken my pace.
My anxiety and my haste were equally foolish. It was
ridiculous to be alarmed just because I had been talking
to a timid peasant. I could see my villa in the distance
now, and there was no sign of the soldiers on the road.
I began walking faster so as to get the sooner to my
caffelatte.

It was at this point that my adventure began. At a
bend of the road I was suddenly stopped by a sentinel,
who shouted:

"*Zurück,*" at the same time pointing his gun at me.
I was going to talk German to him because he had given
his command in German, but that was the only word he
knew and he repeated it threateningly several times.

There was nothing for it but to go *zurück* and I did so rather hurriedly, looking behind me constantly to make sure that he was not going to enforce his words by firing; and even when he was lost to view I did not slacken my pace.

But I had not yet given up the idea of reaching my villa as quickly as possible. I thought that by climbing the hill on my right I should come out a good way behind the threatening sentinel.

It was not a difficult climb, especially as the tall grass had been trodden down by many footsteps. It seemed as if a whole crowd had come that way before me, driven to do so, no doubt, by the impossibility of going along the road. As I walked I recovered my assurance, and decided that directly I reached Lucinico I would protest to the mayor against the treatment I had received. If he allowed people who had country houses to be treated like that, very soon everyone would give up coming to Lucinico.

But when I reached the top of the hill I was unpleasantly surprised to find it already occupied by the regiment of soldiers who smelt like venison. A number of soldiers were lying in the shade of a cottage belonging to some peasants I had known for a long time; at that hour there would be no one in it. Three of them seemed to be sentinels, but they were not facing the direction I had come from; others were standing in a semicircle in front of an officer, who was giving them orders, which he illustrated by pointing to a map he was holding in his hand.

I had not even a hat that I could take off in greeting him. I bowed several times, and putting on my best smile advanced toward the officer who, when he saw me, stopped talking to the soldiers and stared at me. The five Czech soldiers who were gathered round him also gave me their best attention. Under the fire of all those eyes, and on the uneven ground, I found it a very difficult matter to move at all.

The officer shouted:

"*Was will der dumme Kerl hier?*" (What does the fool want here?)

Amazed at being insulted like this without the slightest provocation, I should have liked to make a dignified and manly protest, but thinking discretion to be the better part of valor I left the path and was going toward

the hill beyond which lay Lucinico. The officer began
shouting at me that if I took another step he would order
his men to fire. I at once became very polite, and from
that day to this I have always been most polite. It was
monstrous that I should be obliged to treat with an uncivil
lout like that, but there was at least this advantage, that
he talked German fluently. It was such an advantage, that
the more I thought of it the easier it became for me to
talk gently to him. Supposing the horrible creature had
not even understood German! I should have been lost.

It was a pity I could not talk the language very
fluently myself; otherwise I should have had no difficulty
in making his Highness laugh. I told him my *caffelatte*
was waiting for me at Lucinico, and that I was only
parted from it by his division.

He did laugh, on my honor he laughed. He laughed
and swore at the same time, and had not the patience to
hear me out. He said that other people would drink up my
coffee for me at Lucinico, and when he heard my wife
was waiting for me there, as well as the *caffelatte*, he
shouted:

"*Auch Ihre Frau wird von anderen gegessen werden.*"
(And other people will eat up your wife as well.)

By this time he was in a better temper than I was. I
think he was sorry to have said something that the loud
laughter of his five soldiers might have made to seem
offensive; he became serious, and explained to me that I
must not hope to see Lucinico again for some days, and
he advised me as a friend not to ask any questions, because
this in itself would be enough to compromise me!

"*Haben Sie verstanden?*" (Do you understand?)

I did understand, but could not so easily resign myself to giving up my *caffelatte*, which was less than half a
mile away. So I hesitated to turn back; for it was clear
that if I went down the hill again I should certainly never
reach my villa that day at all. To gain time I said politely
to the officer:

"But to whom must I apply for permission to return
to Lucinico and fetch at least my hat and coat?"

I ought to have realized that the officer was in a
hurry to be left alone with his map and his men, but I
never expected to arouse his fury to the extent I did.

In a voice that seemed as if it would burst the drum

of my ear he shouted that he had already told me not to
ask any more questions. Then he bade me go where the
devil took me ("*wo der Teufel Sie tragen will*"). The
idea of being taken anywhere was not displeasing to me
for I was extremely tired; but I still hesitated. The officer
meanwhile, by dint of shouting at me, had become more
and more enraged, and in threatening tones called to his
side one of the men who were gathered round him, and
calling him *Signor Caporale* ordered him to take me
down the hill and not to lose sight of me till I was well
on the road leading to Gorizia. If I hesitated to obey him
for a moment he was to fire.

On hearing these instructions I was almost glad to
be on my way down again.

"*Danke schön*," I said, without the least touch of
irony. The corporal was a Slav who spoke Italian fairly
well. He thought it best to seem brutal in the officer's
presence, and shouted: "*Marsch!*" to me, to indicate that I
was to go ahead. But when we had gone a short distance
he became quite gentle and friendly. He asked if I
had any fresh news of the war and if it was really true
that Italy was coming in. He awaited my reply anxiously.

So not even they knew whether they were at war or
not! I wanted to cheer him as much as possible, so I gave
him the same news that I had already imparted to
Teresina's father. This weighed on my conscience afterwards. In the awful storm that burst soon after, all the
people I tried to reassure probably perished. What a horrified expression of surprise death must have graven on
their faces. My optimism was invincible. Surely I must
have felt that the officer's words meant war, still more the
tone in which he spoke them!

The corporal was much relieved, and showed his
gratitude by advising me to make no further attempt to
reach Lucinico. After hearing my news he felt sure that
the order forbidding me to go home would be withdrawn
on the following day. In the meantime he advised me to
go to Trieste to the *Platz Kommando* who would perhaps
grant me a special permit.

"To Trieste?" I exclaimed, horrified. To Trieste without a coat or hat, and without my *caffelatte*?

According to the corporal a close cordon of infantry
was being drawn across the road into Italy at this very

moment, forming a new and insuperable frontier. He said with a condescending smile that in his opinion the shortest way to Lucinico was via Trieste.

I had now heard this so often that I was getting resigned to it, and set off for Gorizia, intending to catch the midday train to Trieste. I was excited, but I must say that I felt very well. I was more light-hearted than I had been for a long time. I was not at all sorry to be obliged to go on walking. My legs were rather tired, but I thought I could hold out as far as Gorizia, my breathing was so free and deep. Once my legs had warmed up to walking at a good rate, I got along without any difficulty at all. I went at an unusually quick pace, beating time as I walked, and with my physical well-being my optimism returned. They were threatening here and threatening there, but they wouldn't really fight. And that is why when I reached Gorizia I hesitated as to whether I had not better reserve a room in the hotel to spend the night, and go back to Lucinico next day to make my complaint to the mayor.

I hurried to the post-office to telephone to Augusta. But they could get no answer from my villa.

The only thing I remember about the clerk at the post-office is that he was a little man with a scanty beard whose small stature and stiff movements gave him a rather absurd and pompous air. When he heard me swearing furiously at the dumb telephone he came up to me and said:

"This is the fourth time today that we have had no reply from Lucinico."

When I turned toward him his eyes shone with a malicious joy (I was mistaken in saying I remembered nothing else!) and he gave me a piercing look as if to see whether I was really as surprised and angry as I seemed. It was a good ten minutes before I really understood. Then I had no further doubts. Lucinico was already in the line of fire, or would be in a few minutes' time. It was not till I was on my way to the café to drink the cup of coffee I had been waiting for since the early morning, that I realized the full significance of that eloquent glance. I at once changed my direction and went to the station instead. I wanted to be nearer to my family and, in accordance with the direction of my friend the corporal, I took a ticket for Trieste

It was during my brief train journey that war broke out.

Thinking that I should soon be at Trieste, I did not even drink the cup of coffee I had been panting for so long, though I should have had plenty of time for it. When I was alone in my compartment my thoughts turned at once to my family, from whom I had been separated in so strange a manner. Nothing unusual happened to the train till beyond Monfalcone.

Apparently the war had not yet got as far as this. I recovered my peace of mind by reflecting that at Lucinico things would by now have reverted to what they were on this side of the frontier. Augusta and my children would probably already be in the train on their way into Italy. The peace of mind which this thought gave me combined with the vast and astounding calm produced by hunger to send me into a sound sleep.

It was probably hunger also that woke me. My train had come to a standstill in the middle of the great stony plain known as the Sassonia di Trieste. The sea was not visible, though we must have been very near to it, for a light mist prevented me from seeing far. The Carso has a great charm in May, only to be appreciated by one who has not been spoilt by the brilliant colors and exuberance of spring in other places. The stone that everywhere emerges from the soil is encircled by a tender green, which soon becomes the predominant note of the landscape.

At another time I should have been in a terribly bad temper at not being able to eat when I was so hungry. But the tremendous nature of the historic event I had witnessed this day impressed me so much that I resigned myself to the inevitable. The guard to whom I gave a good cigarette could not even procure me a bit of bread. I told no one about my experiences that morning. I thought I would wait till I got to Trieste and found a friend. No sound of fighting reached my ears from the frontier toward which I was going. We had stopped there in order to let eight or nine trains go winding down the long serpentine curves toward Italy. The open wound, as they soon began to call the Italian front, in Austria, had broken out again and needed more matter to feed it. And the poor men advanced toward it shouting and

singing. From every train that I passed issued the same
sounds of joy and intoxication.

When I reached Trieste night had already descended
on the city.

The darkness was lit by the glow of many incendiary
fires, and a friend who saw me going toward my house in
my shirt-sleeves called out to me:

"Have you been taking part in the sack too?"

At last I was able to get something to eat, and I went
to bed at once, overcome by an immense fatigue, which
was caused, no doubt, by the hopes and fears that chased
each other perpetually through my mind. I was still feeling very well, and during the short time before I fell
asleep, when I had become accustomed by psychoanalysis
to retain the images that came to me, I remember I had
one last childish idea with which to end my day: No one
had been killed yet at the frontier, so it was still possible
for peace to be patched up again.

Now that I know my family to be safe and sound I
don't dislike the life I lead. There is not much for me to
do, but I cannot say I am altogether idle. One is not
allowed to buy or sell. Trade will begin again when peace
has come. Olivi sends me good advice from Switzerland.
If only he knew how inappropriate it is to these surroundings, where everything is entirely changed! At the moment
I am doing nothing.

March 24, 1916.

I have not touched this notebook since May of last
year. And now suddenly Dr. S. has written from Switzerland asking me to send him as much as I had written up
to now. It is an odd request, but I have no objection to
sending him these notes as well; they will show him pretty
clearly what I think of him and his treatment. He already
has all my confessions; let him keep these few pages too,
as well as a few more, which I shall willingly add for his
edification. I have very little time, as business takes up
my whole day. But I shall let Dr. S. have it, and not
spare him. I have thought about it so much that my
ideas on the subject are quite clear.

He is no doubt expecting to receive more confessions
of weakness and ill-health, and will receive instead an

account of my perfect health; as perfect, that is, as my rather advanced age permits. I am cured! I not only have no desire to practice psychoanalysis, but no need to do so. And my good health is not merely the result of feeling myself to be a privileged person among so many martyrs. It is not only by comparison with others that I feel myself to be well: I really am well, absolutely well. For some time past I have realized that being well is a matter of conviction, and that it is a mere day-dreamer's fantasy to try and get cured otherwise than by self-persuasion. Of course I have pains from time to time, but what do they matter when my health is perfect? I may have to put on a poultice now and then for some local ailment, but otherwise I force my limbs to keep in healthy motion and never allow them to sink into inertia. Pain and love—the whole of life, in short—cannot be looked on as a disease just because they make us suffer.

I admit that my fate had to change, and my body to be warmed up by fighting and above all by victory, before I arrived at the conviction that I was well. It was my business that cured me, and I should like Dr. S. to know it.

Up to the end of August in last year I watched the convulsions of the world in a state of horrified inaction. Then I suddenly began to *buy*. I underline this word because it has a greater significance than it had before the war. At that time, when a business man used it, he meant that he was ready to purchase a particular article. But when I used it I meant that I was ready to become a buyer of any goods that offered themselves. Like all strong characters I had only one idea in my head, and on this I lived, and made my fortune by it. Olivi was not at Trieste; if he had been he would never have allowed me to take such a risk; he would rather have left the profits to others. But for me there was no risk at all. I was absolutely convinced of the success of my venture. First of all, in accordance with a time-honored custom in time of war, I proceeded to convert my whole fortune into gold; but there was a certain difficulty about buying and selling gold. Ready money, as being more easy to handle, was my merchandise, and I laid in a large stock. I sold from time to time, but my sales were far smaller than my purchases. Because I had begun at the right moment, I was so lucky

in my buying and selling that I soon acquired the means
of realizing more ambitious schemes.

I remember with pride that my first purchase was
apparently sheer lunacy, and I only made it in order to
put my new idea into practice as soon as possible. It consisted of a stock of incense. The seller boasted of the possibility of using incense as a substitute for resin, which was
already beginning to run short. As a chemist, I knew for
an absolute certainty that incense could never take the
place of resin, from which it differs *toto genere,* but I
thought the world would soon reach such a pitch of misery
that it would be *obliged* to accept incense as a substitute
for resin. So I bought! A few days ago I sold quite a small
portion of it, and received as much for it as I had originally
paid for the whole amount. When I pocketed the money
my breast swelled at the thought of my strength and
abounding health.

When the doctor gets the last part of my manuscript,
he will have to give me back the whole. I should be able to
write it all over again with absolute certainty now; how
was it possible for me to understand my life when I did
not know what this last part was going to be? Perhaps I
only lived all those years in order to prepare for it!

I am not so naïve as to blame the doctor for regarding life itself as a manifestation of disease. Life is a little
like disease, with its crises and periods of quiescence, its
daily improvements and setbacks. But unlike other diseases
life is always mortal. It admits of no cure. It would be like
trying to stop up the holes in our body, thinking them to
be wounds. We should die of suffocation almost before we
were cured.

Our life today is poisoned to the root. Man has ousted
the beasts and trees, has poisoned the air and filled up the
open spaces. Worse things may happen. That melancholy
and industrious animal—man—may discover new forces
and harness them to his chariot. Some such danger is in
the air. The result will be a great abundance—of human
beings! Every square yard will be occupied by a man. Who
will be able then to cure us of the lack of air and space?
The mere thought of it suffocates me.

But it is not only that, not only that. Every effort to
procure health is in vain. Health can only belong to the
beasts, whose sole idea of progress lies in their own bodies.

When the swallow realized that emigration was the only possible life for her, she enlarged the muscles that worked her wings, and which became by degrees the most important part of her body. The mole went underground, and its whole body adapted itself to the task. The horse grew bigger and changed the shape of his foot. We know nothing about the development of certain animals, but it must have existed, and can never have injured their health.

But spectacled man invents implements outside his body, and if there was any health or nobility in the inventor there is none in the user. Implements are bought or sold or stolen, and man goes on getting weaker and more cunning. It is natural that his cunning should increase in proportion to his weakness. The earliest implements only added to the length of his arm, and could not be employed except by the exercise of his own strength. But a machine bears no relation to the body. The machine creates disease because it denies what has been the law of creation throughout the ages. The law of the strongest disappeared, and we have abandoned natural selection. We need something more than psychoanalysis to help us.

Under the law of the greatest number of machines, disease will prosper and the diseased will grow ever more numerous.

Perhaps some incredible disaster produced by machines will lead us back to health.

When all the poison gases are exhausted, a man, made like all other men of flesh and blood, will in the quiet of his room invent an explosive of such potency that all the explosives in existence will seem like harmless toys beside it. And another man, made in his image and in the image of all the rest, but a little weaker than them, will steal that explosive and crawl to the center of the earth with it, and place it just where he calculates it would have the maximum effect. There will be a tremendous explosion, but no one will hear it and the earth will return to its nebulous state and go wandering through the sky, free at last from parasites and disease.

ITALO SVEVO, *whose real name was Ettore Schmitz, was born in Trieste in 1861. He was educated in Trieste and in a commercial school in Germany, whence he returned to his birthplace to begin a business career that he pursued successfully until his death. Svevo's first two novels,* Una Vita *(1893) and* Senilità *(1898; English translation:* As a Man Grows Older*), were not welcomed by critics and readers. In 1912 Svevo met James Joyce, who called attention to him and encouraged him to continue writing.* La Coscienza di Zeno *was published in 1923, and Svevo's rank as a major writer was already established when he died in an accident in 1928.*

VINTAGE BIOGRAPHY AND AUTOBIOGRAPHY

V-2024 **CARO, ROBERT A.** / The Power Broker: Robert Moses and the Fall of New York

V-608 **CARR, JOHN DICKSON** / The Life of Sir Arthur Conan Doyle

V-888 **CLARKE, JOHN HENRIK (ed.)** / Marcus Garvey and the Vision of Africa

V-261 **COHEN, STEPHEN F.** / Bukharin and the Bolshevik Revolution: A Political Biography

V-746 **DEUTSCHER, ISAAC** / The Prophet Armed

V-747 **DEUTSCHER, ISAAC** / The Prophet Unarmed

V-748 **DEUTSCHER, ISAAC** / The Prophet Outcast

V-617 **DEVLIN, BERNADETTE** / The Price of My Soul

V-2023 **FEST, JOACHIM C.** / Hitler

V-225 **FISCHER, LOUIS (ed.)** / The Essential Gandhi

V-132 **FREUD, SIGMUND** / Leonardo Da Vinci

V-969 **GENDZIER, IRENE L.** / Franz Fanon

V-979 **HERZEN, ALEXANDER** / My Past and Thoughts (Abridged by Dwight Macdonald)

V-268 **JUNG, C. G.** / Memories, Dreams, Reflections

V-728 **KLYUCHEVSKY, V.** / Peter the Great

V-280 **LEWIS, OSCAR** / Children of Sanchez

V-634 **LEWIS, OSCAR** / A Death in the Sanchez Family

V-92 **MATTINGLY, GARRETT** / Catherine of Aragon

V-151 **MOFFAT, MARY JANE AND CHARLOTTE PAINTER (eds.)** / Revelations: Diaries of Women

V-151 **PAINTER, CHARLOTTE AND MARY JANE MOFFAT (eds)** / Revelations: Diaries of Women

V-677 **RODINSON, MAXINE** / Mohammed

V-847 **SNOW, EDGAR** / Journey to the Beginning

V-411 **SPENCE, JOHNATHAN** / Emperor of China: Self-Portrait of K'ang-hsi

V-133 **STEIN, GERTRUDE** / The Autobiography of Alice B. Toklas

V-826 **STEIN, GERTRUDE** / Everybody's Autobiography

V-100 **SULLIVAN, J. W. N.** / Beethoven: His Spiritual Development

V-287 **TAYLOR, A. J. P.** / Bismarck: The Man and the Statesman

V-275 **TOKLAS, ALICE B. AND EDWARD BURNS (ed.)** / Staying on Alone: Letters of Alice B. Toklas

V-951 **WATTS, ALAN** / In My Own Way: An Autobiography

V-327 **WINSTON, RICHARD AND CLARA** / Letters of Thomas Mann 1899-1955

VINTAGE BELLES—LETTRES